D0752713

ATTENTION: ORGANIZATIONS AND CORPORATIONS
Most HarperTorch paperbacks are available at special quantity discounts for bulk purchases for sales promotions, premiums, or fund-raising. For information, please call or write:

Special Markets Department, HarperCollins Publishers, Inc., 10 East 53rd Street, New York, N.Y. 10022–5299. Telephone: (212) 207–7528. Fax: (212) 207-7222.

EDITH LAYTON

THE CONQUEST

HarperTorch
An Imprint of HarperCollinsPublishers

This is a work of fiction. Names, characters, places, and incidents are products of the author's imagination or are used fictitiously and are not to be construed as real. Any resemblance to actual events, locales, organizations, or persons, living or dead, is entirely coincidental.

HARPERTORCH
An Imprint of HarperCollins*Publishers*
10 East 53rd Street
New York, New York 10022-5299

Copyright © 2001 by Edith Felber
ISBN: 0-380-81863-9

First HarperTorch paperback printing: August 2001

HarperCollins ®, HarperTorch™, and ❦™ are trademarks of Harper-Collins Publishers Inc.

Printed in the United States of America

Visit HarperTorch on the World Wide Web at www.harpercollins.com

10 9 8 7 6 5 4 3 2 1

For Barbara Metzger,
fine writer, sagacious reader, and friend.
With thanks

One

*H*E REGAINED CONSCIOUSNESS TO FIND HIMSELF sprawled on the ground, dizzy and confused. He tried to sit up and a wave of pain washed over him, so profound it made him feel sick. He couldn't move anyway. Some enormous thing was pinning him to the ground. That thing was screaming. He didn't believe it. This was impossible; it couldn't be happening.

His head was a jar of thunder, but he concentrated, trying to block pain and force awareness. The last thing he could remember was riding along the road, thinking about what his father had said. There was much to think about. For once the usual litany of complaints and demands made sense. He hadn't been paying attention to the road, but then he never expected to be pitched off his horse. He was an excellent rider, it was a simple country road, and the weather was fine too. In fact, he had left the highway to enjoy the day and relax from the hard riding he'd done all morning.

He found the perfect place: a quiet lane surrounded

by fields of vivid yellow blooming rapeseed. Scarlet cups of poppies bobbed above green grasses in the meadows as his horse ambled along peacefully. He half listened to birdsong, feeling the newly warm sun on his upturned face.

He remembered the horse stumbling, and his surprise. Then the way he'd gripped the reins, trying to hold up the horse by sheer force. He had heard the crack of gunfire too.

Gunfire? He blinked, scowled, his thoughts reeling. The war was over, this was England, he was safe, he was home. But he'd heard gunfire—afterward, as he felt himself being borne down to the ground. And then crushed into it.

The light seemed to be draining away now; he could hardly see, much less think. He ran a hand over his eyes, and recoiled. He stared at his hand. It was dripping red. He'd spread blood all over his face, into his eyes. His last thought was that he really should get up and help his horse. Except his horse was lying on him and that made it difficult. He smiled at the absurdity, and welcomed the darkness.

Alexandria was washing the dishes after luncheon when she heard a babble of excited voices at the front door. She couldn't hear what they were saying, but there was too much commotion for her to ignore. She knew her brothers well. She quickly laid down the dish and ran into the front hall. When she got there she found the boys taking the front door off its hinges.

"Have you lost your *minds*?" she demanded.

Rob swiped a lock of hair back from his eyes and she saw how they sparkled. He hopped from foot to foot in a fever of excitement. "No, Ally, but we have to carry him on something, don't we? We can't just drag him. And where are we going to get a hurdle? The door's fastest. It's famous! The most exciting thing!" he said as he avidly watched Vincent and Kit trying to unscrew the hinges. "We thought he was dead. I was sure he was. But Vin here put his hand on his throat and he was alive! Since we're the closest house, we're bringing him here."

"*We* are?" Vin muttered as he kept trying to unscrew a hinge off the door. "I asked the little villain to stay with him to keep ants or animals or such away, but he insisted on helping us. Can't blame him for not staying on alone, though. It's a bad sight."

Alexandria sighed. Another wounded creature for her to tend to when the boys got tired of it. "Leave the door alone," she commanded. "Go back and treat it where you found it. If it's that big, you can't have it."

All three boys gaped at her.

"Where are you going to put it?" she asked in exasperation. "The barn? There's scarcely room for poor old Thunder. And how do you know the thing isn't diseased? We can't have Thunder catching anything. Tend to it in the wood, and then let nature take its course."

"It's a *man*," Rob said, his eyes wide. "And he's half dead."

"There's a horse, too," Vin said, bending to his task again, "but I think he's all right. He's trembling and covered with blood, but it's only a graze because you can see a furrow where the wound is. And he's sprained a hock, we think. But the man looks almost gone. He must have hit his head or something. We can't tell how much of the blood is his and how much the horse's."

"Lud!" Alexandria gasped, untying her apron. "Why didn't you say so? You boys get the door. I'll get towels, water, some salts . . . Did any of you think to fetch the doctor?" She saw their expressions. "I didn't think so. Rob, stop standing and gaping. Be useful. Saddle Thunder and go fetch the doctor." She cast a critical eye on the door. "I'll get some lard. Those old bolts will take you a year if you don't grease them. Now, where is he?"

It was only half a mile, and Alexandria ran all the way, but when she got there she thought she might be too late anyway. The man lay at the side of the road at the foot of the hedgerows. She stopped in her tracks, breathing hard, a hand on her heart. He was a tall man, well dressed, but he was tumbled in a graceless heap, like a child's cast-off rag doll. The dark head was flung far back, the long face was gray. One of his legs was bent at an impossible angle, and his neck didn't look much better. Her breath caught. She looked closer. It wasn't his neck but his neckcloth that was awry, unraveled and splattered with crimson.

Vincent saw the direction of her horrified gaze. "I had to unwind his cravat to see if there was a wound," he explained. "There wasn't. At least I couldn't find it. Just blood, as you see. It may be from his horse," he said, gesturing to the horse that stood head down and trembling, nearby. The animal had an oozing wound on its flank. Vin knelt beside the man and looked up at Alexandria with worry in his eyes. "I felt his neck for signs of life," he said. "There were some—when we left him."

Alexandria bent and put a trembling hand to the

man's neck. She breathed a sigh of relief to feel a faint but steady throb beneath the clammy, cold skin.

She rose, swallowed hard, and nodded. "Well," she said with more courage than she felt, "we'd better get him on the door, hadn't we? Don't jostle him," she added, though she didn't know how they could help it.

Vincent was sixteen, Kit fifteen. Though they were of average size for their age, neither was big enough to take a grown man's weight, and this fellow was very tall, if lean—and a dead weight, Alexandria discovered. She knelt by his head and put her hands under his shoulders to support that vulnerable neck. The boys positioned themselves at either side of him. They awaited her signal. She nodded. They lifted.

Not much moved but their own muscles.

"Put him down," Alexandria said, though he hadn't been moved more than an inch. "Put the door right next to him, at his side. Now, if we don't try to lift high, just inch by inch, we can do it."

They tried again, desperation adding energy. Alexandria looked down as she strained, terrified that motion might cause some unseen wound to bleed anew. None did.

Working together, scarcely breathing for fear of dropping their burden, they edged the man onto the door, pulling and tugging him the rest of the way. Alexandria was shaking with exhaustion and fear when they were done.

"Well," she said again with bravado, "let's get the door up and get back to the house."

"We'll never," Vin said, shaking his head. "We need Thunder and some rope so we can pull it, like a sledge. But we'll never carry him all the way."

"And you told Rob to take Thunder," Kit said sadly.

Alexandria looked around. "We'll use his horse," she said.

"It's hurt!" Vin said.

"It lives," she said. "It walks, doesn't it?" she asked angrily. She was angry at circumstance as well as herself. She loved animals as much as the boys did. But as always, reason had to be stronger than her own weak will. "We have to get him home," she went on. "The horse should be there too. If it can walk, it can pull. At least better than we can, right?"

They looked at the horse. The blood crusted on its side was terrible to see on its otherwise glossy roan coat.

"We could go to town, and see if we can get help," Vin said.

"And leave this man here in the dirt to bleed to death?" she demanded, her voice shaking. "Who knows where the doctor is and what he's doing, or if he can come at once?"

Kit went sprinting back for a rope. Then they fastened it around the door, tied that to the horse, and with many apologies and promises of treats, patting and whistling, they got the animal headed toward their cottage. Still, by the time they reached the front yard they were all sweating as hard as the horse was, and holding back tears. The horse's wound had opened again. The man was grayer in the face.

Vin took the horse to the barn. Alexandria crouched down by the wounded man. She bathed his cold face and stroked the lank black hair from his forehead as Kit went to fetch a blanket to keep him warm. She still couldn't see a wound and decided they should strip him here in the yard to find if there was one. There was no way to get him in the house. That made her fight back angry tears, because it was a hard thing for a man to die in a yard like a stray dog, when there was a bed nearby. She put a hand over his heart to reassure herself that he still lived, then began to undo his jacket. Her hands shook as she struggled to peel it away.

The boys helped her get the tight-fitting jacket off. They gasped and cringed every time they had to shift the poor fellow. But he didn't stir on his own. The shirt came off next, and they sighed to discover no great mortal gaping wound beneath. Still, by the time the doctor arrived, Alexandria wondered if he should have saved himself the trouble of hurrying.

Alexandria watched in anxious silence until the doctor straightened from his examination of his patient. The man now lay on the bed, where the doctor had helped to carry him.

"Well, one thing is certain, he's a gentleman," Dr. Pace finally pronounced. "That's clear. Or at least he's a wealthy man brought up as a gentleman, because he's clean, barbered, and his nails and teeth are taken care of. His horse, his clothes, even his underlinen are of the finest. We should open the bag you found on his saddle and go through it to find out more, his name and whereabouts. In case he doesn't waken," he added.

Alexandria looked up sharply.

The doctor avoided her eyes as he closed his case. "It's a possibility," he said defensively.

Her brothers always said her accusing gaze could make a saint stammer. She let it speak for her.

"I've taken care of what I can see," the doctor

protested. "The leg's fractured. In two places. I've set it. Lucky he was out for that, it would have been a brute of a thing to do with him awake. There are cuts and bruises. I dressed them. I think most of the blood came from the horse, though. The lads said its side was grazed. Those shallow wounds bleed like the devil. Young Vin tells me he's got it stopped now. I'll see for myself before I leave. But as for this poor fellow? I can't see any such wound on him. Still, he isn't stirring."

He saw Alexandria's alarm and answered her unspoken question. "Why doesn't he wake?" He sighed. "It could be temporary. It could be worse. Who knows what's been damaged inside the head? I can't see through bone so I can't know the extent of it. And the horse may have rolled over on him. It may be that he bleeds internally. I don't know. When—if—he wakes, he can tell me where it hurts."

"And if he doesn't wake?" she asked tersely.

He shrugged. "Then we must find his relatives and let them see to him."

"I don't like going through a man's personal items," Alexandria said uneasily. "It is an invasion of his privacy."

"So is death," the doctor said gruffly. "If he doesn't regain his wits, he'll die, whatever else his injuries." He frowned at her expression. "An unconscious man can't drink or eat, can he?" he asked rhetorically. "It would be a pity for a man to die among strangers."

They both stared at the tall stranger lying in her bed. Silent and ashen, he lay back, his long nose pointed at the ceiling. He looked as though he were already dead, though more careful scrutiny showed his chest still rising and falling.

Alexandria nodded, and swallowed hard. "Help me look through his belongings, please."

The boys had brought in the leather bag they'd found strapped to the unknown man's saddle. Alexandria picked it up with unsteady hands, put it on a table by the window and stood back to watch the doctor unfasten it. He whistled in surprise as he peered inside.

"As I said, a wealthy gentleman, to be sure." The doctor removed linens, handkerchiefs, two fine white neckcloths, and a pair of neatly folded clean shirts of the best design, and carefully laid them aside. He picked up a fat leather purse, drew open the strings, and his eyes widened. "Only a fool carries this much money with him," he said with a scowl as he laid aside the purse. "A fool, or a deadly shot," he added, as he gingerly slid a long pistol out from under a pair of hose.

"Or a criminal," Alexandria said, shaking her head. "He also had a knife in his jacket."

"*And* that small pistol inside the boot I had to slice off," the doctor said thoughtfully. "And no name anywhere," he said, shaking the last items out of the satchel. A set of silver razors, a small bottle of scent, a hairbrush, toothbrush, and a folding metal cup tumbled out onto the bed. There was an enameled snuffbox that contained some fine white powder. The doctor took a pinch and brought it to his nose. "For the headache, nothing more," he said, pouring it back.

He scooped up the contents of the case and started putting them back where he'd found them.

"Nothing more than an initial on any of it. *D.* The same as on that fine ring he wears," the doctor said, eyeing the bedside table and the ring they'd pried off the stranger's hand. "A sapphire, unless I miss my guess, set in onyx. Must have cost a pretty penny. Interesting design. Might tell us something, if he hasn't stolen it. Might tell us something that way even so. I'll take it with me and ask Vicar to have a look. The man's a fiend for knowing rank and precedence," he remarked absently, as he closed the case. "Always preaching the renunciation of worldly aims and goods, but he's got a library of books on stately homes and such."

He dropped the heavy ring into his pocket. "The saddlebag had a looking glass, a map, and another pistol," he said thoughtfully. "That's a lot of artillery for an amble in the countryside. Why? What was he doing here? *Is* he a thief? Some sort of spy? Or a man on some other sort of deadly business? I'm not at all sure you ought to keep him here."

As the doctor put what he'd discovered back in the saddlebag, Alexandria glanced over at the man who owned the things. He seemed even more vulnerable now as they picked over his worldly goods. "Whatever he is, he can hardly hurt us now," she said. "Besides, moving him now might kill him, or do him more injury."

"Aye, so it might, but it wasn't him I was thinking of." The doctor's brows came down. He fixed Alexandria with a troubled look. "Look, my girl, there was interference here. I doubt he shot his own horse while riding it. Whoever put him in this situation may want to be sure he doesn't recover. I'm not at all sure I shouldn't carry him back to town, no matter the risk to him. The risk to you may be greater."

Alexandria's head shot up. "Who's to know he

didn't die when he was set upon? No one, unless we tell them, and I certainly won't. Furthermore, if I see any strangers, I'll be sure to send word to you. I think he should stay here. I don't want his death on my hands."

"You may have it at your doorstep anyway," the doctor said heavily. "Every hour he sleeps is another off his chances. If he doesn't wake by morning, I doubt he will."

"What can I do?" she asked.

"You have the will to keep a battalion alive, my child. But it's not in your hands now. Or mine. I suggest prayer."

"Aside from prayer," Alexandria said through gritted teeth.

"Cold compresses on his brow. He might run a fever—if he lives. The fever could burn out the infection, which would be better than him just getting colder and stiffer. But it's dangerous too. For him and for you." She didn't flinch. The doctor sighed, picked up his bag, and went to the door. He looked back at her. "Watch him like a hawk. Have one of the lads sit up with you too. We don't want him thrashing. We don't want him waking to fever dreams either, thinking you're an enemy. Keep him warm. Keep him still. If he wakes, make him drink. Send for me if there's any change at all."

There was no change during the long hours Alexandria sat by the downed man's bedside. The boys came in and out of the room all day to look at their uninvited guest with worried and fearful expressions. Their mood darkened as the fine afternoon turned to a hazy evening and faint shadows crept into the room. Alexandria called Vin in to take her place while she made sure the boys had their dinner. It was a hasty affair, more of a picnic lunch than a dinner, bread and cheese, cold meat pie, apples and nuts. Aware of the silent struggle going on upstairs, there was none of their usual gaiety as they choked it down.

She hurried back from the kitchen and sent Vin down to get his own dinner. It wasn't full dark yet, but she lit a lamp so she could see her patient better, and she settled herself in a chair close by the bedside again. She looked closely for any sign of change.

There was none. It was as if a stone man lay in her bed. She shivered. What if he did die? Would she ever rest easy in her bed again, knowing a soul had departed this earth in it? She frowned at the selfish thought. He was a poor lost soul; he deserved better.

But what could she do for him? Nothing. What would they do if he never woke? Poor fellow. To die alone among strangers who wouldn't even mourn for him, but only remember that he'd brought darkness and death to their house. What a terrible legacy. He must have had a life that meant more. Or did he?

Alexandria wondered if anyone would miss him. She studied that long, angular, gray face, trying to guess the secrets his possessions hadn't revealed. He wasn't that old. Perhaps somewhere above thirty? Certainly of an age to have a wife and children, in any event. Or perhaps he didn't have a family. He'd been alone, after all. He wore no wedding ring. And he wasn't a handsome man. *Poor fellow*, she mused, staring at him sadly. He was actually homely, with that long nose, that bony face, those high cheekbones over gaunt cheeks.

She turned away, feeling as helpless as she did when the boys brought her some wild thing she knew couldn't be saved—a baby bird or rabbit, a defenseless creature wrenched from its nest too soon. In those cases, in order to placate the boys even though she knew better, she'd put the sufferer in a box lined with cotton, set out water, then leave it alone and wait until morning to learn its fate. It hurt and angered her to think she couldn't do much more for this man now.

She turned, dipped the washcloth in the basin, and wrung it out. His straight black hair had flopped back over his high forehead again. She gently pushed it back and took the cloth . . . and looked down into a pair of open eyes.

She drew a surprised breath. Those eyes were fine and clear and azure blue. Blue as a jay's wing, blue as speedwell in the spring. They held a world of intelligence, humor, and tenderness. They lent humanity, animation, and personality to that long, bony face. How could she have thought he was homely? she wondered as she stared, transfixed, at the beauty she saw in those azurine depths. He was remarkably attractive, he was . . .

Alive.

"Lord," he said in a soft slurred voice, "an angel. But since I doubt I'm bound for heaven, I must be alive. Hello, angel. Am I too late to ask your hand for this next dance?"

And clearly not in his right mind.

Two

*H*ER UNINVITED GUEST WASN'T OUT OF HIS SENSES for long, but Alexandria soon wished he was. The man was obviously in exquisite pain and yet his first words to her had been a gallant attempt at flirtation. His color remained ashen, his lips were thinned, and he was white around the mouth.

"I am Drum," his next words came with effort. "And you, my dear hostess, are . . . ?"

"Alexandria Gascoyne," she said quickly. "Please, where does it hurt?"

"Everywhere," he said simply. He frowned. "Gascoyne? Do I know you?"

"I shouldn't think so," she said. "We found you by the road and brought you here."

"Still, I think I do," he said, and winced. "But it's hard to think at all. So. Mistress Gascoyne. I am alive, and I am in . . . ?"

"My bed," she said in a rush, and was startled to see him attempt a wan smile. "You needed tending to quickly, and our house was closest to your accident. We didn't dare move you further. In fact, the doctor wondered if you'd regain consciousness. I'll bet you wish you hadn't," she added ruefully. "I've some powders he left with me to ease your pain a bit. I'll get a glass and we can see if they work. First I'll send one of the boys to fetch him. He said he needed to speak to you so he could find out the extent of your injuries. All he could discover were some cuts and bruises, and your leg, of course."

"Of course?" he said, puzzled. He frowned, then stifled a groan as he tried to move. "Of course," he said with difficulty. "It doesn't obey me anymore. Broken, is it?"

"In two places. It's in a splint," she said when she saw his confusion. She hesitated. "Can you move the other?"

His lucent eyes flew open wide. He shifted, trying to struggle to a sitting position. She quickly placed two hands on his shoulders, but she didn't have to restrain him. He wasn't thrashing from fever.

"It works," he said, sinking back to his pillow. "Everything else seems to work as well—though I wish I hadn't asked them to. My head hurts more than anything else. It feels wrecked." He saw her alarm and his eyes widened again. He raised a hand to his cheek. "Is it? I mean to say—do I still have a face?"

"Oh yes, of course you do," she said quickly, removing her hands from his shoulders. "I was just worried about your poor head. Where does it hurt?"

He smiled and tilted back his head. He might have been about to say everywhere again. His expression said it for him. Before he fainted.

Alexandria gasped and quickly felt for his pulse. Once reassured that he still lived, she shouted for Vincent. The cottage was small enough that he was by her side in moments, a piece of bread still in his hand, his brothers two steps behind him.

"He woke up!" Alexandria said excitedly. "Saddle Thunder and get the doctor."

"He looks dead," Rob commented, looking at their visitor.

"Well, he fainted," she said, "but he woke! And said his name was Drum."

"What sort of name is that?" Rob asked.

"None at all, likely," Kit said. "He could have meant his head felt like a drum, he might have been saying anything. He's raving from the fever just the way the doctor said he would."

"Feverish? Need me to hold him down?" Rob asked excitedly.

"No," Alexandria said. "You can see he's not moving. He was in terrible pain, though, and may wake again at any time. So, go!" she told Vincent.

"No," he said, "I'll stay here. It makes sense. I'm biggest, and can handle the fellow if we have to do it. Kit should stay too. Rob's the lightest and won't weigh Thunder down much, so they can fly. It's not that dark yet. Rob, ride like the wind, no loitering. Go."

Rob nodded and ran from the room.

Their visitor, "Drum," was still senseless when Rob returned, alone, and looking very nervous about it. He stared at the man on the bed as he gave his report. Alexandria sat by the beside, Kit roamed the room, and Vin stood by a window.

"Doctor says that there's nothing to do while he's

unconscious," Rob said unhappily. "He says as to how it was a good sign that the fellow woke up and tried to give his name. But since he's out again, he could sleep through the night or wake and go out again. Anyway, the doctor says there's nothing to do now but wait, and he'd rather come for that in the morning, when he's more awake himself. He said it was a long day for him. And that if the man wakes we should give the powders for the headache, and watch for a fever. He said I should sit up with you too. Said you'd need all of us because madmen have the strength of ten men."

"Well, he's not mad," Alexandria said to chase the fear and excitement rising in their eyes. "He's just a man in pain. So. We'll wait." She settled herself back in the chair. "Bring me my sewing. You'll have to do the dishes, tend to Thunder and this man's horse, and do your lessons too. No excuses. Now, shoo! And come in to say good-night before bedtime."

She raised a finger before they could protest. "If he so much as stirs a toe I'll call you. But there are chores to be done, and you need your sleep. There's no sense in all of us sitting up tonight."

"I'll nap and then come in at midnight," Vin said firmly. "That way you can get some sleep too. I'll stay with him until four, when Kit can take over. It's not that much earlier than his usual time for getting up. There's no sense in *you* sitting up all night either. We're not children anymore, Ally," he said more gently. "If there's any problem, we'll wake you, don't worry."

"And what about me!" Rob asked angrily, before she could answer.

"You, little bantam, can play rooster for a day," Vin

told him with a grin. "You can get up with the sun and wait outside the doctor's house to be sure he gets here first thing."

"Capital!" Rob said.

Alexandria felt easy tears come to her eyes.

"What's the matter, Ally?" Rob asked.

"My boys are acting like men," she said simply.

"Well, we are—almost," Kit said. "And it's time you saw it."

"Time you let us help you," Vin said more gently.

She wiped her eyes. "Now then. Go about your business. I'll read in here until you come in at midnight."

"Is it all right if we come in here when we're done?" Rob asked. "You were reading us *The Odyssey*, remember? So, if he's still sleeping, can you keep reading it, low?"

They all waited for her answer.

Alexandria smiled with relief. They might be assuming responsibility, but she still had her job. "That's a good idea. If all this scurrying to and fro hasn't awakened him, nothing will." She cast a worried look at the still figure on the bed. "I've heard that even sleeping people can hear voices. If so, it may comfort him to know he's still in the world. Yes, come in later, we'll go on as usual until . . ." She hesitated. ". . . things change."

The man lay still while all around him monsters clashed, ogres thundered, heroes fought storms and sorcerers, and sirens wove spells thick as smoke in the beams of the ceiling above him. Alexandria read on in a low, thrilling voice as the boys sat and stared into the air, seeing the words come to life in their minds. The man on the bed didn't stir. But once, when a log in the hearth cracked in two from the heat of the fire, a faint frown appeared on his face. It might have been because he was in pain. It could have been because he was swimming up to consciousness, trying to understand what he heard. It might have been because he was heating up, growing even warmer than the little room.

No one in the room noticed. They were too enthralled by the story.

Drum heard a voice. It woke him from an uneasy sleep. He gathered his muscles to sit up and see what he heard, but recoiled in pain at the effort. He stopped and lay still, perspiring from the effort. *Just as well. Moving might be dangerous. Who knew who was watching?* But he remembered that he was safe. No more gunfire, no more danger. His leg was hurting because it was broken. He ached because he'd fallen from his horse. His head was splitting because it *had* almost split when he'd fallen.

He opened his eyes carefully and stared up at leaping shadows on a tilted ceiling. He saw darkened beams, rough white plaster work. A peasant cottage, surely. It was obviously night, firelight and lamplight the only illumination. He felt weighed down, blankets were piled over him, he wished he could throw them off because he was too warm. But that was too hard to do. The voice that he heard thrumming through his aching head in his sleep was still speaking. It was a woman's voice, comforting, soft. But she was speaking in a foreign tongue.

He frowned. France? Spain? Italy? Perhaps. He'd been abroad on dangerous missions before. But no. He remembered. That was years ago. Before the little Emperor was sent to Elba. . . . Elba! Was he there? No. He hadn't been there since Napoleon had broken parole and marched on Europe. Then Napoleon had been sent to St. Helena. Drum had seen it for himself, he'd been there too. And he knew he wasn't there now. He was remembering.

The voice spoke *Greek?* Was he in Greece then? No, that couldn't be. He hadn't been there since his Grand Tour. He remembered more. The year, the season, the month, and date. Yes, a year had passed since he'd been on St. Helena. He was certainly in England. He'd been shot from his horse. He felt sick, his leg blazed, he was in an agony of pain from head to toe, especially head. It started to throb in time to the soft cadences of the speaking voice that had called him from sleep.

He turned his head with effort. There were four people in the room with him. Two were young lads, one was a boy. They all had light hair, and sat listening as though mesmerized to a woman reading to them from a book in her lap. He remembered her. She'd spoken to him once. He'd thought he remembered her name. But it was only a vague memory and surely he'd never have forgotten her.

Was it a death watch? Was he dying? His heart raced until he saw they were paying no attention to him. They were wholly attentive to the book the woman was reading. She sat close to the fire, holding her book, speaking those ancient words he'd learned in school. *The Odyssey*. He was inordinately proud of himself for remembering that. It meant he was beginning to function again. He watched her for a while, trying to collect his thoughts, feeling them spinning away again and shattering into impressions until he reined them back.

The boys were towheads and she had auburn hair, but that wasn't the only reason he didn't think she was their mama. She didn't seem old enough. But she might have been any age, she had that kind of ageless appeal. Still, he couldn't see her closely and knew he wasn't thinking very well. He was seeing well enough though, to feel the pull of a powerful attraction to her. Who would not?

She sat bathed in a rosy-gold glow from the reflected firelight. She wasn't beautiful. There was too much strength in that face, too much character for beauty. She had a light complexion, expressive eyes under winged brows, a straight nose, and even features. Her mouth was perfect, full and soft—and warm. How did he know that? Did he know that?

What he could see showed a high bosom on a sturdy frame. The curve of her neck, the slope of her shoulders, even her arms were well shaped. Smooth, shining hair was pulled back in an unfashionable style that nevertheless fit her. She could have been the model for the eternal woman, a medieval madonna, a woman in a painting he'd seen in Rome, a Bottecelli Summer, a Titian Venus. Too robust for fashion, and not beautiful, no. Lovely.

He smiled. Not so bad to die in the bed of a lovely woman. He wondered if he'd done that once before too—in a smaller sense. What had his father said?

"Too many women, Drum. It was, perhaps, understandable, if not satisfactory to me, when you were younger. But think of the birthday you have coming! For two years you've done little but go to your friends' weddings. Have you one friend left who is unwed?"

Drum remembered how he'd paused to think about it. "One," he'd finally said, because it was true. He seldom lied to his father. He wasn't a saint, a man had to prevaricate now and then. But he liked his father. More, he loved and respected him.

"So. A great many weddings, you'll agree, Drum," his father said. "When will you attend to your own?"

"I'd thought to do that when I found a woman I could love as you loved my mama," he'd answered honestly.

He was ashamed now, remembering. His father's high cheekbones turned ruddy and he'd turned away. Drum felt terrible—then, and now. He hadn't meant to bring his father pain.

"You loved Mama and I'd have no less a marriage for myself," he said to cover the shame he'd felt at causing his father distress. But he was only human, and so had added, before he could be nagged again, "But when she was gone you didn't join a monastery, sir. You have not lacked for companionship. Speaking of which, how is dear Mrs. Dane?"

His father looked down at his fingertips. "The lady and I have parted ways, Drum. It was no disaster for either of us, not even after all these years," he added in response to Drum's jolt of surprise. "Because it was, as you say, a matter of companionship, and not of the heart. And one of a few other such, as you correctly noted. But there's no comparison between our cases. I'm five and fifty, my dear boy. And I have an heir— you. I continued our line. You have not. Our family is documented back to the year 1033, we were champions of King Cnut. Now, after all our travails, our triumphs, all our history—are you going to let our line come to an end?"

Drum remembered his smile fading.

His father had looked at him with unspeakable sorrow. It was worse than rage. "You're intensely eligible, Drum," he'd said. "And lamentably single. I wish that to change. It's time!"

Time. It was time, and no denying it anymore. That had preoccupied Drum this morning as he rode back down to London again. That made him unaware of his surroundings, unprepared, for the first time since he could remember, for any ambush. Why should he worry about ambush here in England? Because a man who had worked for the government just years before should always be alert.

He'd been vexed with his problem then—as now. He groaned, thinking about it again. How could he offer for any woman if his heart wasn't involved? And why hadn't it been?

One by one his boon companions had fallen in love. It was very like falling, or so it seemed to him. Each of them had been like a man out for a stroll, falling down into a hole and landing in a world he'd never known. One day a friend would be laughing, no more on his mind than the joke he was hearing. The next, he'd be confounded, awash in emotions, ready to change his life forever because of some female he'd met. And each of his friends *had* changed his life. Each had become one of a pair. Not just a matched pair, like two horses pulling in tandem. More than that. They'd each become like one arm of a scissors, purposeless without the other they were matched with.

Drum felt loneliness. He knew restlessness. He wished for a soulmate too. What was the secret? How was it done? Why couldn't he fall in love? There were females he delighted talking to, others he delighted in dallying with. But none he wanted to devote his life to, and he knew no other way of treating a wife.

He liked women. There was little as delicious as a woman's companionship, nothing as exciting as her full body and full-bodied laughter. He liked a woman's point of view, he enjoyed the way she had of civilizing things, and he relished the way she could make a man feel wild too. He had female friends as well as lovers, but the damnable part of it was that they were seldom the same people. He'd actually proposed marriage to one woman, but she hadn't accepted the impulsive offer he'd made, half in pity, half in desire, all in the spur of the moment. She'd married someone who offered her his soul. *I would too,* Drum thought in anguish, *in a breath, in a heartbeat! If I could only know how one goes about falling in love!*

He felt physical pain now too. His leg, his head. The heat made it worse. He was suffocating, stifling. He tried to turn to cast off the bedcovers. He strained. But twist and turn as he might, he couldn't move.

"There, there," a soft voice said, "It's all right. Be still. We're here to help."

He opened his eyes. The woman leaned over him. So did the three lads. They were as close as his eyelashes, holding him so tightly he hurt even more. Her eyes were intent, filled with almost as much pain as his own must be. Brown, lovely brown. The boys stared at him from blue eyes, green eyes, black eyes. He must still be dreaming. He shut his own eyes, gritted his teeth.

"I'd be still," he said, "*if* I weren't being baked."

They exchanged frightened looks and gripped him harder.

"It's damn . . . deuced hot in here," he managed to say. "Could I prevail upon you to remove some blankets before I'm completely cooked?"

"Oh!" the woman said.

"Told you," one of the boys said to her.

"Got him swaddled," another said. "How many blankets are there on him?"

"Five," she said, then added defensively, "We're supposed to keep him warm."

Their silence was eloquent. But they loosened their grips on him. She lifted off a blanket, then another, and another. "There," she asked him. "Is that better?"

He nodded and grimaced as he did because it sent his head spinning. He felt his vision waver. He fought back. "Thank you," he said, but it was definitely growing darker in the room.

He felt an arm around his shoulders and smelled her perfume. *Honeysuckle,* he thought, taking a deep breath of it, as comforted as he was aroused by it, remembering high summer and all its sweetness.

"Drink this, please," she said softly, in his ear. "It will help the pain."

He doubted her. Nothing could ease this pain. It had teeth. He felt an arm behind his head, and a cup at his lips. The stuff tasted bitter enough to be medicine, so he drank it all and lay back, exhausted, on his pillow.

He was sliding away again when he heard her voice at his ear, low, urgent.

"Please, tell me your name again."

"Drum," he said, "My name's Drum . . . Drum . . .

Gads, but my head is splitting. Are you sure that was medicine?"

She left him alone for a minute, a year, he couldn't tell. The others were talking to her, telling her he was hearing drumming in his ears. He nodded, he was.

"Is there anyone we should send for?" she asked at last. "Anyone waiting for you?" she asked a little more desperately.

It took him a while to answer, because the thinking took that long. This potion she'd given him had begun to blunt his wits. He was pleased with himself when he came up with an answer. He thought of his father, of course. But then he thought about the fact that he might very well die before he could oblige his father by fulfilling his dearest desire. It made him very sad. It was such a soft, easy sorrow that he found himself drifting off into it.

"Is there anyone who'll be worried at not hearing from you?" she persisted.

He frowned. He knew what she meant; there was no need for her to talk to him as though he were a child.

"Is there anyone who'll miss you if you don't return?" she asked again.

He sighed. "Yes, and no. That's the problem, you see."

And then it got too dark for him to hear what she answered.

Three

"**N**O," HE SAID, PUTTING A HAND OVER THE CUP. "No more medicine, please."

Alexandria looked down at her patient in surprise. He hadn't spoken in two days.

"I woke early this morning," he said, "before dawn. While you were still sleeping." He smiled, wearily.

She clutched her wrapper around her neck. She had made sure someone was always by him, even being certain someone slept at the side of his bed, since the doctor advised he never be left alone. She had come straight from her own bed to relieve Kit when the first faint stains of dawn touched the sky outside the window. When Kit left, shaking his head to let her know their patient hadn't stirred, she'd settled in a chair and must have fallen asleep again. She woke, surprised at her lapse. But then, she'd had little sleep since he'd arrived. She went right to the bedside to see if her guest still breathed.

But he did more, he spoke.

"I had time to think," he went on. "I realized every time I opened my mouth you put a sleeping draught in it. I'd rather be awake now."

He still looked pale and ill, of course. But she had to admit he didn't look as though he were dying anymore. He'd obviously been in excellent condition before his accident. Slender as he was, he projected a sense of strength. The doctor and the boys had gotten him into one of their father's old nightshirts. His shoulders stretched the shirt tight and the sleeves ended high above his wrists. Alexandria could only blush to think how short the garment probably was elsewhere on this tall gentleman.

He'd been carefully groomed before his accident. Now his beard had begun to grow in, shadowing his face. His straight, jet-black hair flopped every which way around that long face because he'd been tossing and turning. But his eyes, those astonishing bright azure eyes, were clear and sane as he gazed at her. There was entreaty in them too.

"The doctor said—" Alexandria began, but he cut her off.

"Yes," he said with a faint smile, "he said I must wake in order to drink soup and take my medicine, and sleep in order to heal. I heard him," he said, noting her surprise. His lips twisted. "Sometimes. Between the drinking and the healing. I promise to be good, not thrash or run to delirium as the boys seem to fear I will do. Will you take me at my word? I'd rather not be drugged into submission anymore."

His smile was so winsome and wan, filled with humor and understanding, that she'd have allowed him anything in that moment.

He saw it in her expression. "Good," he sighed. "Now, if I may wash? Brush my teeth? And perhaps shave? It's trivial, and the least of my woes, I know. But being unkempt makes me feel less like myself. I kept feeling this Methuselah's beard of mine this morning. I was afraid I'd wake you the way my hand scraped over it." He ran a hand over his chin again. "I could use a shears now, I think. I'm amazed how fast it's grown. Or has it? How long have I been here?"

"Two days—three now," she corrected herself. "But of course. I'll just go get you some water and shaving soap," she said, glad of an excuse to leave the room, dress properly, and set herself to rights before she saw him again. She could feel her hair had come down, and she still wore her night robe and a wrapper.

"I have razors in my kit," he said quickly, "so you needn't trouble your husband, or father, or brothers for theirs."

"I have no husband or father, and my brothers don't shave yet," she said. "But they will. This very morning. Because I'm not at all sure your hand's steady enough to do the job yourself."

He smiled. "Don't worry. I've done it under poorer conditions—in the dark, without water or soap, and aboard rocking ships. The worst I can do is lop off a bit of nose, and that might be an improvement."

It *was* a very long nose, with a high arch. But she thought it was impressive rather than ugly, and it suited him. "You'd look foolish with a button of a nose," she said impulsively. Then, realizing how rude it was to make such a personal remark to a stranger, she quickly asked, "How do you feel, aside from untidy? And please," she added, "What is your name, sir? We asked, but all you kept saying was that your head was drumming."

Now he laughed. And winced a second later. "Ouch. I still have a broken head, don't I? If I'd said 'trumpets,' you'd have reason to call the doctor double quick. As it is, I was only telling the truth. The name's Drummond, but everyone calls me Drum."

"Well then, welcome, Drum," she said with relief, "We'll find out more about you later, I'm sure. Speaking of that, is there anyone you'd like us to send for? Your wife, your family?"

"I've no wife, and no desire to alarm my family. But if you bring me a pen and some paper, there are some people I'd like to write to, if I may."

"If you can, you may, or else I'll do it for you," she said. "I'm sorry you come to us under such circumstances, but we'll try to make you as comfortable as possible. I'll send the boys in."

She left quickly, glad it was a Sunday, so the boys weren't at school. She was brave, resourceful, and competent. She ran the house and took care of three children. But she'd never shaved a man, and certainly never gone so near to a strange one. Shaving him would be an unsettling, intimate act. She didn't know if her hands would have been any steadier than her patient's. At least, not with those wise and knowing eyes of his on her every movement.

She hurried down the narrow stair, and ducked her head into the kitchen. The boys were having their breakfast and looked up at her in alarm. "He's awake and in his right mind!" she said, smiling. "But he needs some help. Kit and Vin, go up, please. He's asked for his shaving tools. So bring him a basin, some warm water, and soap, and make sure he doesn't cut his throat trying to make himself presentable. And Rob? When you're done eating, go tell the doctor. I'll get dressed, then see what else we can do."

The house felt different, Alexandria thought, as she went up the narrow stair again. And not just because she then had to go up the next short flight of steps to the little room in the attic she'd taken since the injured man had been brought to her bed. The cottage was small. Suddenly, it felt smaller. His waking presence made him a true guest. They'd never had a guest before. How long would he stay with them? Their budget was carefully reckoned, but adequate. Still, a guest for weeks would surely call for new economies.

She dismissed her worries as foolishness. He'd want to be gone as soon as he was able; he'd already asked to write to his friends. He seemed to be a gentleman. Why would he want to stay a second longer than necessary in a tiny cottage in the middle of nowhere? But first, he had to be well enough to leave. Alexandria was wildly curious to know exactly who he was and how he'd met his accident, but just as eager to get him on his way.

She dressed quickly. It wasn't easy. The room was tucked under a corner of the thatched roof, and she had to bend double to stand. But there was no sense in making Rob share his tiny room with his brothers. They'd offered, but she told them flatly that the attic room was big enough for her. So it was. Barely. She shared the space with a dress form, trunks, boxes, and a cot, but counted herself lucky it wasn't yet summer. She'd have roasted up there if it was.

When she was done she pulled a comb through her

hair, then drew it back and tied it with her best blue ribbon to match her best gown. He said he didn't feel right when he wasn't well groomed. She felt capable of handling anything when she knew she was dressed well. Anything, up to and including a fascinating strange gentleman.

She had put on her finest clothes. But it *was* Sunday, she reassured herself, and so it wasn't just because of her interesting patient, it only made sense to dress well today. She bent to look at the result of her preparations in a tiny clouded glass. The gown, which she had made herself, was high necked and tied under the waist like the fashion plate she'd modeled it after. Her hair glowed like polished mahogany even in the dim light of the lone half-moon window. Her face was clean. She looked neat and proper. She smiled at her image. A gentleman was probably used to ladies that looked much more than that. *But it doesn't matter what he's used to*, she told herself, and hurried out.

She heard arguing as she went down the stairs. She hadn't realized how young the boys sounded until she head the new voice, deep, smooth, and very resolute, as it vied with them. As she entered the room the boys were grouped around the gentleman's bed, looking harassed. Their guest was white-faced and grim around the mouth. They froze, as though in tableau.

Drum was half sitting up, but Vin and Kit had their hands on his shoulders, obviously holding him back. Alexandria's gaze traveled to where Drum's good leg extended from under the covers. One high-arched foot was almost on the floor. She noted a light covering of dark hair on that long and muscular limb. When he saw the direction of her gaze, he hastily drew back his leg and thrust it under the bedcovers again.

"There's no need to bring your sister into this," Drum told the boys angrily.

"There's no way to keep her out," Vin said. "He wants to get up!" he told Alexandria.

"No," she said, "he can't. The doctor said you were not to stir," she told Drum.

He corrected her. "He told you to hold me still if I thrashed around. I'm not thrashing. I merely want to get out of bed."

"Your leg is broken," she said.

"My other leg is not," he replied through clenched teeth.

"You propose to hop?"

"I propose to move slowly and carefully, while holding on to something," he answered.

"Then you obviously didn't hear everything," she said. She clasped her hands together. He was an imposing man. Even in his current state he had an air of command. And he was of a class of men she'd seldom met but had been taught to respect. She was no one, and moreover, she'd been trained to obey. Still, she knew what she had to do.

"He also said you'd injured your head and maybe your brain and moving would only jostle it more," she said. "I hate to think what walking—or hopping— would do to it. Please stay in bed. We've sent for him. When he gets here maybe he'll change his mind. But I don't want the responsibility of something happening to you."

"It will be my responsibility," Drum said. "It's my

head, after all. I think I can walk, and I want to, and I will, you know."

"It's my bed and my house," she said firmly, the way she spoke to the boys when she refused to hear any more nonsense. "When you're in your home, you can turn cartwheels if you wish. *Not here.*"

He stared at her. Then he lay his head back on the pillow and chuckled. "Oh, lord," he said. "It hurts but it's worth it. No one's spoken to me like that since I was ten! No, I lie. They didn't dare when I was ten. Eight, then. No. I lie again. My father spoke that way just the other day," he said ruefully.

"I'm sorry if I seem rude," she said, because she realized she had been, "but it's for your own good."

"Yes, Mama," he said meekly.

The boys grinned and, with obvious relief, took their hands from his shoulders.

Alexandria smiled. "We're your hosts, not your jailers. Anything you need you have only to ask—we'll bring it to you."

Now he looked hunted. "I can't," he said. "What I wanted to do . . . the short of it is . . ."

"He wanted to go to the Jericho by himself," Rob reported. "Vin promised to bring him a thunder mug, but that only made him try to get up faster."

"*Rob!*" Alexandria cried. "That's not a subject to bring up in polite company!" But it was one they had to talk about. "We do have such," she told Drum, trying to sound matter-of-fact. In truth, she was trying just as hard not to blush. She'd wanted to show him they were not country bumpkins, and here she was discussing chamber pots with him! It was outrageous!

But what did it matter? Where was her head? Who

cared what he thought of her? She was in charge of the house and family, she reminded herself, and had done everything as she should. She could certainly handle this. She took a deep breath. The best way was to behave as though this wasn't embarrassing her to bits— to speak as though it were flower pots, not chamber pots, she was discussing.

"We don't have anything so grand as a close stool, but there's no reason to be shy," Alexandria said, avoiding his eyes. "This is the countryside. The necessary is far from the house, so the boys use such things all the time when they're sick. There's one in every bedchamber; in fact, there's one in that table, by the window. The boys can get it for you. Everyone can leave the room if you like, but I really do think Vincent should help you so you don't fall on your nose."

"I'm *not* shy," Drum said with an excess of patience. "We use them in the city too. We seldom discuss them, though. We don't have to." He appealed to her. "The thing is that I've had worse injuries, I feel better every minute, and I don't believe in coddling myself. I hate to feel like an invalid."

Alexandria stayed silent.

"But I suppose I must," Drum said on a resigned sigh. "Fine. Thank you. And certainly," he added, sliding her an interested glance, "I'd prefer if you left—unless of course . . . ?"

She was out the door before he could finish the sentence.

Now that Drum could see him clearly, he watched the doctor with interest. The man was thin, white-haired, and stooped, an old man saved from being considered ancient by the brightness of his eyes and the power of his voice. He shooed Alexandria and the boys from the room.

"So, young fellow," he said jovially, as soon as he was alone with his new patient, "I'm Dr. Pace. And whom do I have the pleasure of addressing?"

"The name is Drummond," Drum said, "Derek DeMacy, Earl of Drummond, but friends call me Drum. I suppose, strictly speaking, I should ask the lads here to call me Drummond, but circumstance prevented strict speaking when I came here."

The doctor's eyebrows went up. "I've heard of you. Quite the ornament of the ton. What are you doing here, my lord?"

"I was visiting my father. His seat's to the north. I was halfway home to London, it was a glorious day, I wandered off the road. And into ambush."

"Be that as it may," the doctor said, "your mind's working. Now let's have a look at your body. Unbutton your shirt, if you please, my lord."

Once he'd surveyed Drum's bruises, he drew the covers back to look at his splinted leg. He prodded and poked, asked questions, and then stepped back from the bed. "You're sound," he said. "At least, mostly, excepting your leg and head. Still, don't put on your walking shoes, and don't call for crutches. I don't know what's going on in that head."

"I assure you I've returned to my senses," Drum said. "I doubt I've rattled my brains. I've a hard head."

The doctor waved him to silence. "Aye, hard as stone, but even stone can be cracked. And your leg's broken in two places. It was a blessing you were out when I came to call. Setting it would have been a hard thing to do with you awake. *I'm* not made of stone. As it is, because I had time to linger without guilt, I did the job extra fine. I expect it will heal straight—in six weeks, at the least. With no jostling about."

"A bit of jostling can't be avoided," Drum said. "Obviously I can't ride, but I can send for my carriage. I must leave."

"Must?" the doctor asked. "You're a stoic, my lord, but you're in considerable pain even now, unless I miss my guess."

"It doesn't signify," Drum lied.

"Indeed." The doctor nodded. "Maybe not. But your life *is* my concern. In sum, my lord, a carriage ride such as you suggest would unhinge more than your leg. I deem it a matter of life and limb—literally. And since as I understand it you're halfway betwixt your ancestral seat and your London home, and both are equally far from here, there's nothing for it but for you to stay on here until you're more on the mend."

"Yes," Drum said wryly, "of course. There's plenty of room for me here, why not? Doctor, the poor lady of the house is sleeping in the eaves, or so the lads tell me. There's scarcely room to turn around in this place as it is. I haven't seen more than this room, true. But this is a cottage, and I have seen others. A family of wrens would be crowded in here. I need to send for my valet so I'm no longer a burden on the boys. Where is he going to sleep? In the stable? I understand it's filled to capacity with my horse and theirs."

The doctor shook his head. "Arrangements can be made. Alexandria is willing to make them. I caution you, my lord. Remove yourself at your own risk." His brows lowered. "And since you met with an accident on your way here, I don't suggest going out to look for more now. What was that about, eh? Someone taking shots at you? Had they any cause?"

Drum concentrated on the buttons he was doing up. "Oh, good cause, I'm sure," he murmured. The doctor eyed him sharply. Drum shrugged. "At least, there may still be some who think so. I worked with the War Office until the peace—and after, for a while."

The doctor relaxed. "I doubt it would be anyone from here. The war's been over for years, and it never affected us much. Little Combe is a sleepy village, my lord, known more for its spring brew than its politics. Mark my words, it was probably some lad trying his hand with his father's gun that he took on the sly. The lads here think that's it. They have their eyes on a sneaky fellow they despise, and they're likely right."

"I'll have to talk to them," Drum said with a frown. "It may be so. Still, hasty conclusions can be lethal."

"So you're staying?"

Drum gave a deep sigh. "If you won't let me go today, then only long enough to send a message and get my valet here to help me dress and go."

"Only a valet? Not family or friends?" the doctor asked, his eyebrows going up.

Drum lay back on his pillows. "I've both, but I won't summon either. Oh, my father's fond. Too fond," he muttered almost to himself. "He worries about me too much. I can hardly add to those worries with this, can I? There's no need, anyway. I'll survive. As to friends"—he gave a crooked smile—"I've many. But like any sane man, only a few I really care for. By some strange stroke of fortune, most of them are either family men now, with babes on their knees or on the way, or else they're newly wedded. I won't sound the alarm and have them drop everything to come pelting here. Trust me, doctor, they'd come running if they thought I was in trouble."

"So if you've no one waiting for you, why not stay on until you heal?"

"Apart from inconveniencing my hostess?" Drum asked. He turned a mild but searching gaze on the doctor. "By the way, how well do you know her?"

"Alexandria?" The doctor raised his eyebrows again. "I've known her since she was a child. A delightful girl. Pretty as she can stare, as you can see."

"No," Drum said thoughtfully, "not pretty. She's lovely."

"Aye," the doctor agreed readily. "You're right. Clever, capable, and charming. And loyal. Took care of her brothers like a mother hen when she wasn't much older than them. Been taking care of them single-handed since Gascoyne died three years back, too."

"I see," Drum mused. "A young woman of sterling reputation too, of course?"

The doctor looked puzzled. "Of course. Well, there was talk when she left for a few weeks a few years ago, but when Gascoyne died, she came rocketing back. But you know small town gossip."

"Indeed," Drum said, his smile freezing, "I do. And so do you." His voice grew silky. "And so perhaps you've thought she's also lonely here in this little village famous only for its spring brew? Perhaps in need of a husband too?"

"Why, yes," the doctor said, "she was so busy with the lads, she never gave courtship a thought."

"Doctor," Drum said, "I thank you for your care, but

I refuse to pay such an exorbitant fee for your services."

"But that's nonsense,' the doctor said, flustered. "My fee is very reasonable."

"You know what I mean," Drum said sternly. "I'll pay in gold, sir. Not in blood."

The doctor frowned and put out a hand to feel Drum's forehead.

Drum turned his head away. "I'm alarmed, not feverish," he snapped. "My dear sir, I know you're well meaning. But charming as she may be, I've no desire to marry Miss Gascoyne. Actually, I've a friend who found his wife through just such a circumstance. That worked out well, as it happened. It wouldn't in this case, not for me. My father's a proud man. I've promised him a daughter-in-law of equal rank, name, and fortune to ours. Miss Gascoyne is lovely. And accomplished, I'm sure. But as she doesn't meet those requirements, she's not a candidate for my hand, I'm afraid."

They both heard the gasp before they saw Alexandria standing in the doorway, her expression an illustration of outrage.

"I took you in!" she said, rounding on Drum. She came to the side of his bed and shook a trembling finger at him. "I nearly ruptured myself dragging you here! I gave you my bed, I sat up all night so you wouldn't die, I *worried* about you. I'd have done the same for a b-badger!" She stumbled over her words in her fury. "Or an owl or a fox cub, and I *have* done. I wouldn't marry you for love nor money, you conceited, dreadful, horrible man! I asked you to stay on out of charity, not any idea of matrimony!"

"Indeed?" Drum asked calmly. "And the fact that you'd have a single gentleman staying under your roof, with no chaperone, never occurred to you? Or the consequences of such a thing? The first day or so even the strictest critic would agree was unfortunate but unavoidable. But a bachelor of some note, staying here alone with an unchaperoned female of any reputation, for longer than that? You'd be compromised. I'd be in a pretty predicament. You didn't know that? Really?" He laughed, not nicely. "This may be a remote place, my dear. But I had no idea it was on the moon."

Alexandria's flushed face turned white. She turned to the doctor, who stared back at her with matching surprise and dismay.

"Oh, my!" she said, sinking to a chair. "I never, ever . . . Doctor," she cried, looking at him with horror, "help me get this fellow out of here right now!"

Four

HE PAIN IN HIS LEG WAS SICKENING, BUT HE RE-
fused to take the doctor's powders until his fate
was resolved. So Drum was pleased by the distraction,
even if it caused some discomfort too.

His bedchamber was on the second floor of the little
cottage, but he'd already worked out the fact that it was
right above the kitchen, and its chimney—which acted
like a speaking tube through the hearth to the one in his
room. He could hear all the voices below, where everyone in the cottage had congregated. He lay back, exhausted by pain, his nerves jangling with frustration at
his impotent state, listening to his hostess argue with
the doctor about his immediate fate. It made him feel
like a child again—but not a loved and cosseted one.

"I will *not* leave this house, it's where I *live*, and you
know what trouble the boys can get into," his hostess
cried in vexation.

"I'll keep them in line," Drum heard one of the older
lads say.

"And cook for them?" she shot back. "And see that they wash and do their studies, and take care of their chores too? As well as taking care of that—that—*ingrate* upstairs? No, this house and everything in it *is* my responsibility, Vincent. I don't see why we can't just put him on a hurdle or rip the dratted door from the hinges again and drag him to your place, doctor!"

Drum could picture her waving her arms and pacing. She obviously paused for breath and control, and then went on in pleading tones, "He must go! He may be an insufferably proud and conceited oaf. But he also may be right—at least in the eyes of the world. So take him away, there's the solution."

"We'll help," Drum heard one boyish voice volunteer.

"You can leave his horse here," another lad said. "We'll take care of it, it will be no extra trouble."

Drum grimaced. Hard to think his horse was more welcome that he was. He supposed he had sounded unbearably pompous. But *oaf*? He'd been called many things in his time, but never that. Still, there was no help for it. He might have sounded like an arrogant ass and a boor, but he had spoken only truth. There was no conceit in it.

It had nothing to do with personal appeal. He *was* a prime target for marriage-minded females. The sad truth was that single men of his class were hunted by women. Men of his class, title, and money were positively stalked. A popular joke was that the London Season was aptly named, since it meant it was open season on bachelors. If a fellow couldn't be caught by flirtation or got by hard bargaining with the lady's father, he was too often trapped into marriage by fair means or

foul. An unwary fellow could be caught by a kiss or a
cuddle—if there was someone else watching. And
there usually was someone else watching.

There were so many ploys. Get the gent drunk,
arrange a private meeting, turn an ankle so that he had
to help. The point was to get him close, then close in
on him—in a private encounter that could be made
public. It was cold, it was crass, it was undoubtedly
cruel. But it usually worked. A gentleman's name was
all important, a young woman's reputation even more
so. Both could be ruined if marriage didn't follow
folly.

Usually such marriages were cursed from the start.
Invented by desperate females, they boded nothing but
lifelong ill will for all concerned. Such was not for
him.

It was also true that his good friend Rafe had been
compromised by chance. But the marriage he'd had to
make had been the making of him. That was rare.
Maybe it was because the woman his friend had married was extraordinary. Maybe because Rafe had been
ripe for wedlock himself. He'd been at loose ends,
heartsick about losing the woman he'd thought had
been the love of his life, willing to throw his bachelorhood away because he simply didn't care anymore.

But Drum cared—a lot. He'd been a bachelor too
long to marry simply for the sake of propriety now. If
he couldn't wed for love—and it seemed he could
not—he'd marry for advantage, and he could see no
better one than pleasing his father. And so a poor unknown from the middle of nowhere was simply not acceptable as a wife for him, no matter how lovely or
charming she might be.

And, as lovely as his reluctant hostess was, Drum had known more beautiful women, much wealthier ones, and many more with better breeding and station. He hadn't succumbed to any of them. But even if Alexandria Gascoyne were leagues above them in everything, it wouldn't matter. He'd be damned if he'd be finessed into matrimony just because he was flat on his back, helpless, and in mortal pain.

He was willing to grant she might not be angling for his name. But he couldn't take any chances. Let them drag him off on a hurdle. Let them strap him to his horse, smack it on the rump, and send it home. He'd be willing to let them put him on that damned door and strap it on the roof of the Royal Mail coach, for that matter. Whatever it took. He couldn't stay here any longer under these conditions. He wouldn't. He'd escaped before from enemies when he'd been wounded. He'd do it again, even if it turned out to be an enemy of a different sort that had him now.

"Move him? Fine. And so maybe kill him," he heard the doctor say. The other voices downstairs stilled. "Who knows if his skull hasn't been as damaged as his leg?" the doctor went on. "I've seen such cases. The patient feels and looks sound, rises from bed, and keels over dead. Bleeding, swelling, shards of bone in the brain—there are too many variables, and the slightest movement might shake something loose. He won't be out of danger for a month. As it is? Every time I leave him I wonder if I'll see him alive again."

Drum's eyes opened wide. He felt a cold chill slide down his back and lodge in his stomach. He shivered. It was an exaggeration, surely. Calculated to get them to agree to keep him here. But why should the doctor care about that? His head still hurt like blazes, true. His vision was still a bit blurred. . . .

Drum stared up at the ceiling, trying to tamp down terror, cast out fear. He'd done it before. He'd do it again. If a fellow was afraid of death he couldn't go on living at all. Death could come to any man at any time. There was nothing he could do if it were true. He refused to fret about it.

"Let him send for his valet, as he wishes," the doctor went on. "The fellow can stay here, or with me and ride over every day to care for him. As for you, Ally, we can have some respectable female stay on here with you till he leaves."

"Some respectable *miniature* female," his hostess said bitterly.

Drum chuckled. It was just what he was thinking.

"Where would she stay?" Alexandria asked angrily. "There's hardly room for an extra hen in the coop . . . What am I saying? *Hen?* With us and the valet and his puffed-up nincompoop of a master living here, there'll hardly be room for a pot of chicken soup! And what sort of woman would be willing to come live so close to complete strangers?"

"Mrs. Tooke, from over Appleton way," the doctor said promptly. "A nice woman, a widow, very respectable. She lives with her daughter and *her* three daughters. She'd be happy to come here, even if it means she had to sleep on the roost with the chickens. She'll say it's for charity's sake, but the poor creature will be glad of a rest. They run her off her feet there."

"Doctor," Alexandria wailed, "if I have to put another cot in this house, there'll be no floor for her feet to walk on!"

"You'll like living with her," the doctor said with decision. "You'll like it even more if you consider the consequences of turning the earl out. For God's sake, woman! He might not live to get as far as the garden gate!"

There was a moment of shock, followed by a long, thoughtful silence in the kitchen—and in the upstairs bedchamber.

"Here it is," Alexandria said, stepping aside and pressing back against the doorjamb so her visitor could look into the tiny attic room. "Rob's with his brothers. I'll be in his room. The doctor is persuasive, but you can change your mind, you know. This room is scarcely big enough to turn around in."

Mrs. Tooke was of middle years, neat and trim, if a bit weary looking. Her brown hair was spiced by silver, bringing light to a gentle, pleasant face. She peered beyond Alexandria's shoulder and looked around the room with pleasure.

"My dear," Mrs. Tooke said softly, "this room will be mine, alone." She sighed. "I haven't had my own room for many years. I shared one with my sister until I met my dear Leon. Then I shared one with him, and now I share with my granddaughters. It will be an adventure to be by myself. I know the house is crowded to the roof. But believe me, I haven't had such solitude for years. Now, tell me, how may I best help you?"

"You're doing it right now. The fact is that you're a device." Alexandria grinned at Mrs. Tooke's expression. "You are to be an ornament, Mrs. Tooke. You see, since my guest reminded us that convention says a single young woman shouldn't stay in a house with an eligible bachelor, we must have a respectable woman with us. Now, forget I'd rather take up with a snake than the eligible bachelor who's here. And that I'd never, ever even think of marriage with him. But remember that he thinks I would!"

"Is he so repugnant to you?" Mrs. Tooke asked, alarmed.

"I can't say, I don't know him. But he is that arrogant. So all you have to do is be here. Relax and enjoy yourself however you can. You're doing me a great service. Because now that you're here, I can stay on in my own house without fear of being considered a fortune hunter." She smiled to take the tinge of bitterness from her voice. "So thank you, but your presence is your only job."

"Well, but I like being of use. I know how to deal with invalids. I also can cook, and do enjoy it," Mrs. Tooke said. "I can feed chickens, garden, sew, and clean, and I don't mind doing that either." Now she smiled at Alexandria's expression. "I love my grandchildren, but they arrived one, two, three, and are all under the age of five. Just having so little to do would be a real vacation, believe me."

"I'd never ask you to work for me," Alexandria protested.

"No work at all would be too dull," Mrs. Tooke said. She shook her head. "You should know that after all these years, my dear. We've often wondered how you got on here by yourself. It's a pity the cottage is so far from town, or we'd have lent a hand. In our defense, Mr. Gascoyne wasn't the friendliest of men, was he? At least not to us womenfolk. He had his cronies, all bachelors, schoolmasters like himself. And it seemed he had little use for our husbands as well. He acted as though everyone in the village was beneath him, and I suppose we were, in scholarship. And so, though we worried about you after he died, we thought his friends would provide."

She seemed embarrassed. Alexandria was too, because one look around the cottage showed how little any of those friends had helped. "And you seemed so self-sufficient we didn't dare impose on you either," Mrs. Tooke added. "For that, I'm sorry, because you were only a girl, weren't you? It was wrong of us."

"Don't be sorry," Alexandria said. "You did offer to help, I remember." She remembered more. How shocked and distraught she'd been. How anxious to keep the family together. How frightened and suspicious of everyone else. With good cause. Hadn't they been raised that way? "I suppose I had too much pride to accept," she said briskly. "At any rate, I'm grateful you're here now. So settle in, and do as you wish. I have to see what my reluctant patient is up to now. Come down later if you want, I'll introduce you. The boys say he's in his right head today. I think he'd rather he wasn't. Between his leg and his head and his pride, it's hard to say which pains him worse. I'd almost pity him—if he were at all pitiable."

She laughed, and stepped down the stair. But she paused to straighten her gown and smooth her hair back before she entered the earl's room. *My room,* she reminded herself. It had taken her years to establish the place as her own after Mr. Gascoyne had gone.

She'd painted the walls and put pretty samplers on them, brought in a rag rug, stripped the great bed, sewn new sheets and fashioned a flowery comforter for it.

She'd dragged out the heavy chair and desk, and used her entire legacy to buy the spindly chair and delicate table that were there now to replace them. She'd hung lace curtains, and scented the air with her own dearly bought and carefully hoarded honeysuckle soap. Finally, she felt the room was hers, and hers alone.

The earl dominated it now. She could hardly believe how easily he'd done it. He had few possessions, but he filled the room with his personality.

She stepped into the room. It was the first time she'd done so since she'd begged the doctor to throw him out. He looked up. It was not a pretty sight. One side of his angular face was scraped and had turned an ugly shade of purple and yellow. If he were handsome it would have ruined his looks and would have seemed a pity. As it was, his battered face did nothing to destroy his dignity. Pity was out of the question. He was still regal, distant, and full of banked power. He sat up against his pillows and watched her warily with those unnaturally lovely, uncomfortably acute azure eyes of his. She felt like bowing, but refused to scrape.

"Good morning," she said stiffly. "Are you ready for luncheon?" She carefully avoided addressing him as "my lord," as the doctor delighted in doing. It was her room. She was fighting for her rights as mistress of it and her house.

"Why, thank you, yes, I am," he said. "The doctor said I can have more than gruel and I confess I'm looking forward to it. If you can restrain yourself from adding rat poison. Look, Miss Gascoyne, I didn't mean to sound like an . . . the way I did. I only spoke truth. If I could, I'd leave on the instant. But I can't. Believe me, you also can't know how sorry I am to impose on you like this."

"It's nothing," she lied. "Now Mrs. Tooke's here, we can both relax. I'll introduce her to you soon." She forced herself to meet those knowing eyes. "She's very respectable. In fact, she comes from a fine family. You should have much in common, actually. She's only in this little village because she married beneath herself, they say. Doubtless you can commiserate about having to tolerate lesser beings. Now. Some soup and a wing of chicken?"

"Touché," he said, wincing. "I deserve it, I suppose. And though I don't deserve such a fine luncheon, I'd very much appreciate whatever you bring me."

She turned. "I'll just get your tray."

"A moment, please," he said. "There's something else I'd like to say. Please listen. It may be *oafish* of me to remind you, but after all, we don't know if I'll still be here to say it by the time you get back, do we?"

Alexandria's head shot up. She stared at him, and a slow blush warmed her cheeks. "Oh, lord!" she said. "I forgot. You heard every word we said downstairs, didn't you? I should have thought . . ."

"You were otherwise occupied," he said with a small smile. "Look, Miss Gascoyne, I want you to know that *I* wouldn't want me as a guest. At least, not in this condition. It was kind and generous of you to take in a wounded stranger, and being repaid by suspicion can't have been pleasant. My suspicions were as crude as they were rude. I apologize. All I wanted to ask is if you could get me paper and a pen so I can write some letters to cancel some appointments, and most important, let my household know where I am and what I need. I'd like to get things moving so that I can unburden you as soon as possible."

She paused. It was nicely said, there was no denying it. She might as well be gracious too. "I will," she said, "but it might be better if you dictated your letters. Otherwise we'd have to bring in a lap desk, and the way your leg feels right now I doubt it would be practical. I'll be glad to write them out for you—if they're not too personal, that is?"

"No, I'll save my love letters until I can remember more poetry," he said wryly. "All that springs to mind at the moment is Richard's lament for a horse, and various funeral odes."

" 'How are the mighty fallen,' " she quoted, low. But not so low that she didn't win a sudden amused smile from him. It felt so good to have someone understand her so readily that she changed the subject. "Well then, I'll be happy to write any letters for you. Is there anything else I can get you?" she asked.

"Don't forgive me *that* quickly," he said, grinning. "I deserve a week of cold shoulders and cutting looks, at least. As for what you can get me? Do you think you could manage a new leg? I suppose not. Ah, well, I'd be delighted by luncheon and a letter or two, then some of the doctor's delicious poppy extract. That's exhilaration enough for now. I'll try to sleep the rest of the day away."

"You don't have to drug yourself into submission on my account," she said quickly.

"I assure you, it's on mine," he said. "The poppy leads to strange dreams, but they're better than the reality of my condition just now. Strange indeed . . ." he mused. "Do you know, when I first found myself here, and you were all here in the room with me, talking, I thought I was abroad because I couldn't understand a word I overheard. It was all Greek to me. Literally."

She hesitated, then smiled. "Oh, that. That was reality. I was reading *The Odyssey* to the boys. For their lessons."

"In the *original?*" he asked, astonished.

"Yes, their father was a schoolmaster." she said coolly. "He insisted the boys be educated. I'm a mere female, but they were at it so much I couldn't help learning some of it. At least so I was told, and so I was allowed to learn more."

"Forgive me," he said. "I put my foot wrong again, didn't I? Maybe because the other one hurts so much. The damn . . . deuced thing hurts like blazes. I can bear that. But the doctor said I have to lie still to help it mend. That's hard for me. So I'll take the medicine until I can stump around and shake off the fidgets. I'm not a convenient patient, but I'll try to be an obedient one. The less I do, the faster I'll heal. And I will, I promise. I'm not ready to die just yet." He slanted her a conspiratorial smile. "Only the good die young, remember?"

Five

"*I* THOUGHT YOU'D BE ASLEEP!" ALEXANDRIA EX-claimed. She'd tiptoed into the earl's room, only to find him sitting up and looking decidedly . . . grumpy.

"I've had enough. My dreams were all right when they were fantastical, but now they bore me. Even if they were magical, I'm feeling so much better I don't need them anymore," he said, his eyes kindling at the sight of her—and the tray she bore. "Is that for me?"

"Well, actually it was for me," she admitted. "I was going to stay here while you slept. I'll just go get another cup, and some cakes, if you think you can eat them."

"I think I could eat them and a horse. How is mine, by the way?"

"Fine," she said, looking at him curiously. "Are you really feeling better?"

"The worst is over," he said, his eyes still on the tray. "What discomfort remains is more annoying than desperate now. I heal as quickly as I tumble into trouble in the first place. Is there enough for us both, do you think?"

"I'll be sure there is," she said with a smile, turning to go.

"No, don't leave!" he said quickly. "Please. I'll take my tea later. Talk is more important now. I'm not used to lying in bed in the daytime. And it is a glorious day, isn't it?" he added sadly, glancing out the window. "Could you open the window? I'd like to feel a breeze and breathe some fresh air."

She put down her tray, drew back the curtain and threw the shutters open all the way.

He sighed. "Now I can hear the birds, at least. Lying up here alone makes me feel like the last man on earth. It's the countryside too, so quiet. The lads are at school, right? I could hear you and Mrs. Tooke downstairs . . . Lord! I'm prattling. Please stay and talk. I can just about bear doing without the use of one leg, but getting on without my mind is rather more difficult. After all, this isn't London, you know." He grinned. "At any rate, I've slept enough."

The thought of him lying alone upstairs with no one to talk to and nothing to do had occurred to her. It would be horribly boring for her, and she was accustomed to the quiet of the countryside. *It must be hellish for him,* she thought, which was why he was trying so hard to be convivial. She wondered how much it cost him to beg a simple country woman to stay and chat a while, and decided to make it easier for him. Firmly suppressing the little surge of personal pleasure at the thought of passing the time chatting instead of simply watching over him, she prepared to do just that.

Alexandria lifted the lid off the little teapot. "You can have this cup. Don't argue, if you please," she added before he could speak. "It's no great sacrifice. I didn't want to leave you alone all afternoon so I brought my sewing, and provisions for when I felt like having some. That isn't now."

She took the tray they'd been using as his desk and table, and settled it on his lap. "I even brought some macaroons, but I'll get you some of Mrs. Tooke's scones later. She's the woman the doctor sent to make it possible for you to stay, remember?" Alexandria was pleased to see he looked guilty, and with that unspoken concession, decided to let the matter drop. "There are other benefits of having her here, it turns out. At least for me. She's a marvelous cook. She's baking today, and we have cream and berries."

"Tea and scones? And forgiveness?" Drum asked. He picked up his cup, took a sip of the amber liquid and sighed. He laid his head back. "I don't deserve such treatment, and you know it," he said with a rueful smile. "I could have been in trouble. Instead I find myself in the lap of luxury."

"In a poky little room in a cottage in the back of nowhere?" She laughed as she settled herself in the chair by the window. "There's no need for flattery, I already promised you the scones, remember?"

"It isn't the size of the room, or the location, it's the treatment and the company that I'm grateful for," he said, picking up a freshly baked macaroon.

"Yes," she said sweetly, her eyes on her sewing. "I'm sure that while we might not compare to an evening at the opera or the theater, we certainly equal a night at Brooks or Almacks, or some glittering London soiree." She looked up to see an arrested look in his eyes. "I know about those places. We get a newspaper as well as a magazine," she explained. "Mr. Gascoyne was very fond of the *Gentleman's Magazine*. They once published a letter of complaint he wrote."

A faint frown appeared to darken those cerulean eyes. "Mr. Gascoyne? You always refer to him that way?"

"Yes, he insisted. He was old-fashioned and believed familiarity bred contempt," she said simply.

"Well, I don't hold with that," Drum said. "Neither does my father, and it's been said he has the stiffest neck in the kingdom. Still, yours must have done something right. Just look at the lads. And you. You've done very well."

He paused and took a look at her. He found her as refreshing as the tea and cakes she'd brought. He enjoyed her unexpected sense of humor and appreciated the way she struggled with the difficult problem of finding herself responsible for him. But amiability was one thing. In this situation it was vital that he keep the conversation and his thoughts on an even keel. She was his nurse and comforter now, so of course he'd like her. But he hardly knew her. It was time to remedy that, at least.

"You've kept the family together, which can't have been easy," he said. "From what the doctor said, you aren't much older than your brothers, and weren't that old when your father died."

"It wasn't hard," she said, concentrating on her stitching. "It's all I know, after all."

He watched her as she stitched. She was nothing like the women he was used to, or any of the ladies of

London. They wore curls or ringlets these days. Her
gleaming hair was pulled back in a queue, as a gentleman might have worn his a generation before. Stray
gossamer filaments of it were stirred by the breeze
from the open window. It shone from cleanliness, not
pomade, he realized, and that was unusual in ladies of
the ton. Many didn't use oils to tame their hair because
their own did the trick. London put a premium on
looks, not frequent use of soap.

It was more than her hair. Drum knew fashion, and
Alexandria Gascoyne either didn't want or couldn't afford it. She wore an old gown with a vaguely pink floral pattern today, though she'd look much better in any
of the bold colors that were the current craze. Not that
she looked bad to him. She really was quite lovely, he
thought, watching her, though she didn't seem to know
it or at least refused to capitalize on it. He guessed she
was at least one and twenty but it was hard to say; she
had the bearing and demeanor of a much more mature
woman. Her manner was open, almost masculine in its
directness. Her appearance was not.

Men in London spoke about the virtues of country
women, the attractions and abilities of milkmaids with
their clear eyes and fine complexions and strong con-
stitutions. They were thought to be ignorant and
gauche, but freer, more robust, ribald, and passionate
than other women. More disease-free, too. That meant
there was considerable call for them in the brothels, so
much so that madams commonly met incoming stage-
coaches with offers of employment for girls just arriv-
ing from the country. Alexandria Gascoyne had that
kind of fresh loveliness, but Drum wasn't misled. Her
mind was anything but provincial.

Still, it was hard to appraise her mind when her body was so close. Her figure was sturdy but not overblown, she had fine, full breasts, a waist that curved to a firm, rounded bottom . . .

He looked away. She exerted a strong pull on his senses. He acknowledged it, and firmly put the knowledge aside. Sensual pleasure was vital to a man's happiness—at least, to his happiness. But if there was one thing he knew, it was propriety, and he was cursed with common sense. This wasn't the time or place, he reminded himself, and she certainly wasn't the woman to think such things about.

"The boys don't look like you," he said, trying to turn his train of thought. "Your hair for one thing, their eyes for another. In fact, they don't resemble each other that much either."

She smiled. "You're observant. There's no reason they should. We're not related, and neither are they. They're adopted."

He was surprised. He hadn't heard much, but enough to get the impression that the late Mr. Gascoyne had been a private and solitary man, not the usual sort to take in foundlings.

"Mr. Gascoyne came to a crossroads in his career some years ago," Alexandria explained, keeping her attention on her stitching, "He lost his position at Eton—"

"*That's* where I know the name from!" Drum cried, suddenly remembering a little man stalking down the corridors, his sour face wrinkled as a walnut, looking as unapproachable as everyone said he was. "I was never in his classes, but didn't he teach Latin?"

She nodded. "Ancient studies, too. But he lost that

position and had to find another. We have a school not far from here—Eaton's Academy for Young Gentlemen. E-a-t-o-n, with an *a*, that is." She smiled at his expression. "Yes, the name's *supposed* to remind people of that other school. It's not as elevated or ancient as Eton, of course, but it's not a bad place. It's for self-made men who want their sons to rise in the world. Mr. Gascoyne heard about a position opening there. Since he'd lost his job partially because of his . . . inflexibility, it was said, his friends suggested that having a son himself would go a long way to showing that he really liked and understood boys.

"It turned out to be not only wise, but economical," she went on briskly. "The foundling home pays a stipend for each child taken off their hands, you see. Mr. Gascoyne taught classics but he had a firm grasp of mathematics and realized that three can eat as cheaply as one. At least, a pot of soup goes very far, and clothes can be handed down. So he took them in size order, Vin, Kit, and Rob. And got the job." She bit off a thread. "The boys still go to Eaton's, but they live here. They hitch Thunder to a cart and ride there every day. It's cheaper and better for everyone that way."

"How did your mother cope with all those boys?" Drum asked.

"She didn't," she said abruptly. "She was long gone. I was the one who took care of them. It was no problem for me because they're good lads, and weren't infants when we met. We had a housekeeper for a little while but I soon took over her duties. As I said, Mr. Gascoyne was a frugal man."

Her sunny mood had darkened. The room seemed darker too. Drum was annoyed with himself. He was usually more facile than that. "You know about the clubs and galas in London because you read the London papers. Have you ever been there?" he asked, to nudge the conversation down a smoother track.

"Never," Alexandria said. "There was neither time nor opportunity."

"I thought not," he told her. "Don't believe everything you read. I can tell you some evenings at the best clubs are amazingly boring when none of your friends are there, or even if they are, they may get into some witless argument that lasts for hours. Some nights at Almacks it's hard to suppress your yawns. Most nights, actually. And not all soirees glitter. Some frankly fizzle, like fireworks on a damp night. Most are held in rooms that are too hot, with the company too loud and the food too scarce, stale, or paltry."

"I'm sure it must be unendurable," she said with a faint smile, her eyes on her needle.

He grinned. "Right. I manage. It's only that the city isn't always the glittering vision it seems from the countryside."

"This countryside, at least," she said with a sigh. "We don't have stately homes here, so there are no house parties or balls. The local squire lives in a farmhouse. We have a smith's shop, which the road just reaches before it goes running back to the highway. It serves three other tiny hamlets nearby, or it wouldn't have enough business to exist at all. Time stopped here once when Good Queen Bess rested for an hour at our well while on one of her processions through the countryside. Then it marched on without us."

"Did you ever visit anywhere else?" he asked curiously.

Her face grew still, her voice harsh. "Once. I went to Bath. For all of seventeen days. But then I got word that Mr. Gascoyne was sick. He was gone by the time I got back." She looked up at him. "Please don't pity me. I have more than many women do. The boys, this house, my own place in life. That's not inconsiderable."

"Any suitors?" he asked casually, popping another macaroon in his mouth.

She smiled. "Hordes," she said. "Now you know everything about me. In all fairness, may I begin my inquisition?"

He pretended to choke. "My dear!" he said, "I know nothing about you at all. You're as evasive as an eel, slippery as one too. I'm an open book! You have my name, my rank—my life, in sum."

One eyebrow lifted as she stared at him. "Yes," she said levelly, "you're a London gentleman, a nobleman of fame and fortune. That's the sum of it? Fine, then. And so I'm a country woman of no particular note, and adequate means. There we are. Shall I get your scones now?"

He crossed his arms over his chest. "I'm five and thirty," he said, "bedeviled because my father wants me to marry and I haven't found the lady of his dreams yet. I went to Eton, as I said, then Oxford. I served my country by working for the War Office, which means I've lived abroad a great deal. I have a few good friends and many more acquaintances."

She sat back, listening with rapt attention.

"I like to sing," he went on, "and am not crushed that my leg is, because I'm not that keen on dancing. I get into heated arguments about politics. I fence, box, ride, and drive, but don't consider myself a Corinthian or a dedicated sportsman of any kind. I read and go to plays, but am not an intellectual. I'm in demand at parties because I can flatter anyone for anything at any time. I'm very good at conversation, because that's what we wastrel London gentlemen excel at. I can talk for an hour on any subject, and even make sense sometimes."

Drum was very pleased with himself for making her laugh again. Too pleased, he knew. But he was careful and knew himself well. To flirt was not to fall. To charm was not the same as making a misstep. He'd pass the time pleasantly, amusing both himself and her. Why not? It was no great task. He'd think of her as a nun, a charming one, a woman who was his nurse and hostess, but one already taken by another, far more powerful than he was. Society was just that.

Alexandria Gascoyne, pretty, charming, and kind as she was, could be nothing else to him anyway. She had neither birth or wealth. Nothing but that lovely face, figure, and personality. That might be enough for her to make her way in the world, but not his world. A schoolmaster's daughter, she might be a suitable wife for some other schoolmaster, a clerk, or maybe even some member of the middle gentry. But not for him, he thought hastily. She was too far beneath him in class to be a wife, too middle class for the role of his mistress. She was respectable, after all.

But still, he thought idly, it *could* be said that she was a scholar's daughter. That was no shame. It wasn't as though she was a maidservant, a tavern wench, a seamstress, or an ignorant farm girl . . . He thought of his father's reaction and killed that train of thought. He liked Alexandria, he was definitely attracted to her, but he was, after all, not a boy, not a fool, and certainly not in love—which as dangerous as it might have been for him, was really too bad, he thought sadly.

He changed his line of thought. "With lots of cream, please," he said suddenly.

She'd been sitting, digesting what he'd said, waiting for him to go on. Now she startled and looked her question at him.

"You did say scones?" he asked. "So that must be what I smell now, right?"

"No, I don't think so," she said slowly. "It's my new perfume. You know what they say about us country girls, using vanilla for scent? I tried butter." She waited for his appreciative grin, then added, "Don't worry, I'll just go get your scones now."

"I'll try to confound the doctor and be alive by the time you get back . . . but you'd better hurry."

He lay back after she'd gone. So. He'd live. He felt better than he'd expected, much sooner too. He'd been wounded before and knew the way of it. He'd been lucky. Recuperation would be swift, and now, it seemed, amusing too. He only had to find out who had shot at him and make sure it never happened again. He'd do it, then leave as soon as reinforcements got here to make that easier. He closed his eyes, content.

He was lying absolutely still when Alexandria, bearing another laden tea tray, returned. His head was back, his elegant nose pointed at the ceiling. She couldn't see him breathing. She was so startled her hands shook. She put the tray down carefully, signaled to a startled Mrs. Tooke, and then the pair of them crept closer to his bed, not knowing they were holding their own breaths. They bent and stared. He was breathing, lightly, slowly, and evenly, sleeping soundly. Alexandria shared a relieved look with Mrs. Tooke.

"Gads," he drawled, his eyes still closed, "a fellow can't shut an eye around here without worrying about getting a lily planted on his chest. And here I was hoping for a tea tray instead."

"My lord," Mrs. Tooke said, ducking a quick curtsey, "we were just concerned."

"Well, so am I," he said with a smile, opening his eyes. "Are those wonderful scones for me?"

Alexandria was annoyed that he'd made a May game of her terror. "Mrs. Tooke, this is Lord Drummond," she said stonily. "My lord, this is Mrs. Tooke. She's the good neighbor who has come to stay with us so that *you* can stay on here without worrying that I'm going to have to bring a vicar, not just tea, when I enter your—*my* bedchamber."

"Alexandria!" Mrs. Tooke gasped.

Drum laughed. "Don't worry, my dear lady. I richly deserved that. But the more important question is if I deserve some cakes too? I've been very good, you know. Haven't stirred from this place since they laid me here. I did try, but my hostess had three strong men hold me down, she was that anxious to keep me in her bed."

Alexandria held her tongue as Mrs. Tooke handed him a napkin, poured tea for him, filled a plate with cakes and cream and placed it at his elbow. He sighed.

"A lady who knows how to treat a man," he said with pleasure. "I thank you."

Mrs. Tooke nodded. "Handsome manners," she said with approval, "just like your father. You have the look of him too."

Drum had a cake halfway to his lips. He paused and looked up at her. "You know him?"

"I knew him," she said, "once upon a time, when we were all young." She saw his surprise and added, "I grew up not far from his estate. Our fathers were friends. Mine was Lord Usborne."

Alexandria turned and stared. There was a second of silence even her glib guest couldn't fill. She'd thought Mrs. Tooke was going to say she'd been a nearby squire's daughter. She was *that* well born? Even Alexandria had heard of Lord Usborne, a political-minded fellow and a viscount! Mrs. Tooke was a local woman who, just like them, baked, mended, and tended house. She'd told Alexandria that she gardened and kept chickens too. She had fine manners, but no airs. Of course, Alexandria remembered, wasn't that supposed to be the very hallmark of a lady? But still, it was a shocking surprise.

"I knew your father too," Drum said smoothly. "And know your brother. He's made some improvements at the hall."

"Indeed?" Mrs. Tooke said, her face showing nothing but polite inquiry. "I wouldn't know. I haven't been back. The family was unhappy with my marriage, and so we haven't seen each other since. That was many years ago."

"Surely not that many?" Drum said with a show of great surprise. "Unless you married from the cradle?"

"*Very* like your father," she said, and they both laughed.

Alexandria listened as her guests chatted easily, talking about this name and that person. Mrs. Tooke had obviously made a misalliance, and her family scorned her because of it. The Earl of Drummond did not. Or, if he did, no one would ever know it. What a lady Mrs. Tooke was, Alexandria thought with growing respect. What a gentleman the earl was. It was all amusing, jolly, cordial. Alexandria was impressed.

So. He isn't such a bad fellow, after all, she thought. Only arrogant because of his life of privilege. She supposed he couldn't help it. But he was more than charming, he was thoughtful of other's feelings and had a lively sense of humor. That was lovely. He appreciated nonsense. She appreciated the way he looked at her too. It made her feel like a woman. That was rare too.

But she was too wise to put the least bit of importance to it. Mrs. Tooke's cheeks had gone rosy and her eyes sparkled as she chatted with him, so it was obvious he made her feel the same way. Alexandria lived a quiet life with few diversions and had never met an earl or a London gentleman. But even she knew men such as the Earl of Drummond were not thick on the ground anywhere.

He was all personality, grace, and style. His looks could be considered unfortunate until he opened those forget-me-not eyes and that glib mouth of his, when he became well-nigh irresistible. Urbane, witty, smooth, and clever—and about as sincere as the spring breeze that flirted in the window and toyed with the little hairs at the back of her neck.

Just so! she thought, watching him charm Mrs. Tooke to bits. Light, pleasant, and fleeting, those were bywords she'd better remember. They'd be the words she'd always remember when it came to this particular exotic wounded creature the boys had brought her. She'd care for him and enjoy his company while she did. The boys would have a good example of manhood to copy too. Six weeks could be a lifetime—a bitter one—if he'd been a boor. As it was, she looked forward to the days ahead.

In time, she'd let him go with the same mixture of emotions she always felt when she returned any healed creature to the wild. She'd feel relief, tinged with a little sorrow.

And that, she told herself, would be that. She was prudent. She had a good education and no illusions. She was ineligible for marriage, at least, ineligible as a wife to any man she might consider having for a husband. Mr. Gascoyne had been the last one to tell her so, and she'd fled all the way to Bath to prove him wrong—only to discover he'd been right. She knew a thing or two or three, she thought bitterly, and she'd be even wiser to remember them in her dealings with this charming nobleman.

She and this elegant earl were just as different from each other as the robins and rabbits she'd sheltered were from herself. Very different species. And if for a moment she regretted that, that was nothing new either.

Six

THE DAY HAD BEEN A RARE AND BALMY ONE, BUT now Alexandria, her little family, and Mrs. Tooke huddled around the kitchen hearth for warmth. It was spring, after all, and spring in England often forgot what it was. Tonight April thought it was November, and a cold wet wind cut around the edges of the little cottage and drove rain against the window-panes. Vic and Kit sat on the hearthstone, Rob on the rug in front of the fire. Mrs. Tooke had been given the rocking chair and Alexandria sat at the table, reading to them. It was a cozy scene, soon interrupted.

A sudden sound made Alexandria stop midsentence.

"Only the wind," Rob protested. "Go on! Read that bit again."

"No," Alexandria said, cocking her head to the side. "The wind doesn't shout 'Excuse me.' Rob, nip up-stairs and see what his lordship wants. I don't think he's in any distress," she told Mrs. Tooke, who'd half-risen from her chair. "We just saw him two minutes ago."

"Maybe he wants another cup of tea," Mrs. Tooke said, looking concerned.

"Any more tea and the man will wash out of his bed," Alexandria said with a frown. "I don't understand. He was a paragon of courage when he was in excruciating pain. Today the doctor said he was doing splendidly. In fact, he ate every scrap of his dinner and had an extra serving. But tonight he's had us get him a dozen things."

"It's the way men are," Mrs. Tooke said with a laugh. "They get peevish when they're on the road to recovery."

"Not us," Kit said. "Ally, do go on."

"Wait for Rob, or we'll never hear the end of it," Vic said.

Rob hurried back down the steps. "He wants to talk to you, Ally. Go on up and come down quickly."

Alexandria put down her book, and went up the stair. She went in the half open door and looked around the bedchamber. Nothing seemed wrong. Her patient lay propped on pillows on her feather tick, covered by the best quilts in the house. A good fire bloomed in the hearth, lamps adding their own mellow light. The windows were securely shuttered, the room was comfortably warm. Her guest had a table near his elbow that held a pitcher of water, medicines to take if he felt pain, and books he said would interest him.

She looked at Drum. He wore a slightly embarrassed expression. "What is it?" she asked. "Are you in any pain? Do you need anything? I thought you were settled for the night."

"So I was," he said, and let out a long breath. "I—I hear your voices," he said.

"Oh. I'm sorry. Did we disturb you? The boys get carried away sometimes, and we forget. I'll hush them so you can sleep." She turned to go, closing the door behind her.

"No!" he cried quickly.

She turned around and stared at him. "That's just it," he said, a little desperately. "I don't want to sleep. If I were home now, I'd be starting out for the night! My dear Miss Gascoyne, you've given me everything an invalid could want. The problem is that I'm not used to being an invalid. I hear your voices downstairs, and . . ." He flashed her a dizzying smile. "I'll confess. I want to be in on it. You *did* get me settled. The problem is that I think of it as being—planted. Yes. Exactly like being planted, watered, then abandoned and forgotten until summer."

She put her head to the side. "I'm only reading the boys *The Odyssey,* commenting on it now and then. It helps their studies."

"I read Greek," Drum said quickly. "I got marvelous marks in history," he added hopefully. "You were all in here doing that when you thought I was unconscious. Surely my being awake won't matter? There's room for Mrs. Tooke too, isn't there?"

She smiled. "Surely, there will be."

A few minutes later, they'd all reassembled in the invalid's room. Alexandria picked up her book, and on a sudden inspiration—and a belated fear that her Greek wasn't as perfect as she wished it to be—laid it down again. She looked at Drum. "Would you care to read?" she asked.

"I'd be happy to," he said, putting out a long slender hand. He took the book, and Alexandria leaned over his shoulder to point to where she'd left off.

Her cheek almost brushed his. He felt the warmth of her, and scented her elusive perfume, his nostrils widening.

She noticed again that his shoulders were really very broad for such a slender man. He smelled of good soap, and his ink-black hair looked so soft she had to restrain a sudden urge to rest her cheek against it.

She straightened up and quickly left his side. He forced himself not to look after her. They were both surprised by how unexpectedly intimate the moment had been, even in the midst of company.

She went to her chair and took up her sewing.

He picked up the book and began to read smoothly.

He hadn't got a whole page read when Rob muttered, "*Wine*-dark sea? I don't understand. I thought I knew that word. But how can a sea be the color of wine? A sea is blue, right?"

"It's a metaphor," Vic said. "Go on, sir, please."

"I know what a metaphor is," Rob said hotly, "and if it is one, it's a bad one, because water isn't purple, not by a long shot."

"Quiet, Rob," Kit ordered. "You've never seen the sea."

"Well, but I have seen a pond," Rob protested, "and a brook, and pictures of the sea. I read about the ocean too, and it's always blue. Or green," he added fairly, "Maybe even gray. But wine colored? I don't think so."

"It can be, at sunset," Drum said. "Or before a storm. It's a poetic metaphor, but not that far off. When the Aegean reflects the sunrise and sunset the waters can be any number of colors."

"You've been to Greece?" Rob breathed.

"Yes," Drum said, laying the book down. "In fact, I think it would be good if you asked me about it. It might help you understand the poem if you understand what the poet saw when he wrote it."

"He didn't. He was blind," Rob corrected him.

"Rob!" Vin said, as Alexandria sat up and gave Rob a hard look. A boy never corrected an elder, at least not in this house.

Rob knew it too. He turned red, looked down and mumbled, "Pardon me. Please go on, sir."

"But you're right," Drum said. "Homer was blind. That doesn't mean he didn't know what the world looked like. A blind man learns from those with sight. He couldn't describe the sea unless someone told him about it. I'm sure he knew many sailors."

"Did you, sir?" Rob asked. "I mean, when you were there?"

"Yes, of course," Drum said. "You can't see the place just by land. I sailed around a bit too. Let me tell you a little about Greece, how it looks and smells, the food, scenery, the people. Then you'll understand Ulysses' voyage better, I think. That's why my father sent me abroad, to learn more than books could tell me."

Alexandria bent her head to her mending again. Maybe it was why their fathers sent them, but she knew why young men went abroad, and it wasn't to better understand *The Odyssey*. Mr. Gascoyne had of-ten ranted about it. He'd rail about the injustice of the ruling classes having money to waste, sending their randy empty-headed sprouts off for a life of dissipation on the Continent in the guise of higher education. He'd sneer, saying it was educational, all right. Those overly privileged young men returned to England with more depravities than they could ever have imagined on their own.

She lifted her head a few minutes later. It was clear the Earl of Drummond hadn't wasted his father's money.

"The hills are stony and steep," Drum was saying in response to one of the boys' questions, "but the sea is magnificent, and you can see it from everywhere. It was a natural highway for the ancient Greeks. The world came to them, but they set out to see what the world was about too. They spread civilization as well as picking up more of it. They invented philosophy and drama, and gave the world all forms of art, but—yes, Kit?"

"Art?" Kit asked. "But that was the Romans, surely?"

"Romans perfected it, but the Greeks gave them their foundations," Drum said.

Alexandria smiled at the spirited discussion that followed. The boys had seen sketches of the famous Elgin Marbles that had been brought to London, and had been monumentally unimpressed by what they decided were dull, broken statues.

"Wonderful works of art can be seen everywhere there," Drum went on, "a lot intact. But don't be fooled. They might have been artistic, but the Greeks were merchants to the core. Islanders often are, like us. We gave the world Chaucer, Shakespeare, poets galore. But we also gave them wool and cheese, tin and

coal. That's why the Romans were so eager to conquer
us—not for our bards and poetry. The Ancient Greeks
shipped wine and olives. By the way, olive trees are
stunted, twisted things. You wonder who was brave
enough to taste the first bitter fruit, and who was clever
enough to discover that marinating made them delicious."

"Delicious?" Rob yipped in disbelief.

"Rob's right." Vic laughed. "I tried one once and it
twisted up my mouth like an olive tree!"

Alexandria looked up at Mrs. Tooke to exchange a
grin with her, but that lady was already looking at her
with troubled eyes. Maybe she felt the boys were too
forward, Alexandria thought sadly. Maybe they were.
But they never let her read any book through at one go,
always interrupting with questions. She thought it was
a good way to teach. The lofty Earl of Drummond had
quickly seen that and encouraged discussion too.
Alexandria sighed. There was nothing she could say to
placate Mrs. Tooke. Likely she was from an older
school, like Mr. Gascoyne, who had made lessons
strict and silent. But Alexandria had had her fill of that,
which was why she refused to do the same.

Alexandria saw the boys' rapt expressions as their
guest went on telling them about Greece. *Poor lads,*
she thought, *it's just as well they can travel in their
minds.* They'd never get farther from home than Bristol
if they didn't join the navy. She'd take care to see that
didn't happen, at least not until they had finished their
educations, when they'd more likely be clerks than
rovers. Which might be a pity, but she was a realist.
Since they had to make their way as best they could,
education was their only asset.

"Squid?" she heard Rob groan, clearly appalled. "They eat octopus and *squids*?"

"You eat winkles and prawns," Alexandria commented.

"But they're edible," Rob protested. "And they don't have legs."

"But cows do," Drum said.

Now Alexandria groaned. "Please don't remind me! If I'd any courage I'd only eat eggs."

"It's not a matter of courage, it's appetite," he said. "And there's nothing wrong with normal healthy appetites."

It wasn't the words or even the way he said them. It was the look she saw in his eyes when she glanced up at him. They were sparkling, brimming with mischief. Alexandria's breath caught. She quickly turned her gaze to her sewing again. *Appetites indeed,* she thought, angry with herself and him, as her pulse slowed again. She'd been thrown off balance by the wicked look that sparkled in his cobalt eyes. He was only flirting; the problem was that she didn't have the knack of it. She wasn't used to more than heavy-handed overtures from men in the village, or oily propositions couched as paternal advice offered by Mr. Gascoyne's old friends.

But flirting was obviously second nature to the earl. The blasted man had flirted when he'd been in terrible pain, she thought irritably. He'd probably flirt on his way to the graveyard.

She couldn't let it pass, and she couldn't hide like a mouse. She had to live with the man—and herself—a few weeks more. She lifted her head and met his azure gaze directly, though she didn't focus her own eyes.

She was brave, not stupid. If she was going to keep her composure she had to avoid seeing more than the intense color of those eyes. "I fail to see how an appetite can stay healthy on a diet of octopuses," she said loftily.

"Octopi," he corrected her gently. "It's only a matter of taste. And they vary the leggy things with fish and vegetables. Nothing as healthy as our good reliable fry-ups, of course, but they do keep their teeth and complexions longer than most Englishmen do."

"Then I suppose you'd rather have a squid than bacon tomorrow morning?" she asked sweetly.

"Oh, but I'm not one to complain about appetites!" he said quickly, grinning at her. He opened the book again. "Shall I go on?" he asked.

"Please do," she said, trying to restrain her delight. It could be a game, after all, so long as she remembered it could only be that. If she did, she had a month of laughter ahead. She expected no more, and whatever went on in the secret places of her heart, wanted no more. Or at least, so she had to keep reminding herself more and more. Not only was it unlikely there could be more for her in this friendship with the earl, but if ever she lost her head or her heart it would be immensely painful.

She knew she interested him. It wasn't vanity, it was simple arithmetic. He was bored and there were no other women around. She wasn't a Venus, but though she lived in the country she didn't live in a clamshell either. She'd interested other men in her time, many of them married or otherwise impossible. He was impossible. She accepted that and knew he did too. He was, after all, a gentleman.

She relaxed, the excitement of the flirtation fading. She sat back and listened to her guest read a story about another lost wayfarer trying to find his way home again.

The cottage was no longer empty during the afternoons; in fact, it was never empty now. Alexandria found that aside from enjoying her exotic guest's company, she was getting used to the sound of frequent laughter. She'd never realized how lonely her afternoons had been until they weren't anymore. The boys' frowzy old mongrel had died the month before and she hadn't the heart or chance to get a new puppy yet, but old Sport was all the company she had expected during the long afternoons. The earl's arrival had changed everything.

Mrs. Tooke was no bother. In fact, she was a great help. Having people around all the time again was a welcome novelty for Alexandria. She found herself taking extra care with her appearance every morning, and going to sleep with a smile on her lips every night. She'd given up her bedchamber but had gotten a whole new world in exchange.

Her work load was greater, but being busy made her happier than she could remember being in years. Her life actually seemed more important somehow. The Earl of Drummond never left the bedchamber, but she felt his presence everywhere in the house. She found herself wondering what he'd like for dinner, what he'd say about the news in the paper, what he'd think if she wore a rose-colored ribbon in her hair. He never complained, though his inactivity clearly galled him. He might be a high-born lord, but there were times—too many to suit Alexandria's sense of what was right—when she forgot his rank and only thought of his charm and appeal. So she made sure she was never alone with him. It turned out she never had a chance to be.

She and Mrs. Tooke regularly shared merry breakfasts and luncheons with him. The boys entertained him when they got home. The doctor visited frequently. The earl had been with them less than a week, and he'd completely changed the pattern of their lives.

He was as rare, fascinating, and impermanent as a swiftly falling comet that suddenly streaked across their sky. And so she shouldn't have been surprised that everything around them kept changing, just as it had since the day they'd found him.

The boys woke at dawn, as usual. They ate, hitched Thunder to the cart, and rode off to school. Alexandria and Mrs. Tooke prepared a tray and brought it up to their guest.

"Ah, the second wave. Good morning," he said happily when he saw them. The boys saw to his personal needs before they left, and it was the women's task to feed him. He hated being so dependent and they all knew it, but he tried to make a pleasantry of it and so did they.

They'd brought the paper for him to read when they had to leave to do their chores, and he read bits of it aloud now, commenting as he did. The man may have been half dead only days before, Alexandria thought, eyeing him closely, but now his color was good, his eyes clear, and his bruises fading. If it weren't for the splint on his leg, no one would guess he'd ever been in danger at all.

They were chatting about the news from London when a sudden clatter and clamor outside made Alexandria's head snap up. She stared out the window. A coach was pulling up the drive—no, two! With two liveried outriders on fine horses beside them. There hadn't been so much commotion out there since Mr. Gascoyne had died. There had never been such elegant traffic.

"What is it?" Drum asked, pausing mid-jest.

"Company," she breathed in wonder, leaning on her elbows to see out the window. One of the coaches had a crest, the other was travel stained, but still polished so brightly the sun's reflection on its glossy surface brought tears to her eyes. That glossy coach held so many cases and boxes on its top it looked like moving day. "For you."

Alexandria and Mrs. Tooke hurried down to the drive. A neatly dressed wiry man stepped out of one of the carriages. He bowed as they came near.

"Good afternoon," he said carefully. "I'm Austin Grimes, the Earl of Drummond's valet. He sent for me. I believe he's here?" But the look in his colorless eyes as he glanced around showed he could hardly believe it.

He addressed Mrs. Tooke. She gestured to Alexandria. "I'm only a visitor myself. Here is Miss Gascoyne, his hostess."

"Yes, he's here," Alexandria said. "But before you go up to see him, there are some things it would be better we settled right now."

Grimes was grave as she told him about his master's medical condition, and all the doctor's warnings. Then she told him where he could go.

"You've packed enough for a family of eight, and I'm sure the earl appreciates it, but that's all he can do from here. There's not an inch more room in my house, as you can see," she said, waving her hand in the direction of her cottage. "Even the stables are stuffed. But the doctor said you could stay on with him at his home. It's a nice house, but not on a grand scale. Nothing here is. Even he hasn't got room for five more people, so I'd suggest your . . . companions return to London—with most of that baggage."

She waited for his reaction. She got the feeling she could have waited another year.

"I'm sorry," she said, a little desperately. "It must have been a long, hard journey. But your master's doing well. It's just that there's not a speck more room here, you see."

He waited to see if she'd add more. When she didn't, he thanked her, and went up to his master's bedchamber. She was left to look at the other servants. The coachman stayed atop their carriages, looking down at her warily. The two outriders dismounted and stood by their horses, dust covered and obviously weary. "There's just room in the kitchen for the two at a time," she told them, "but you can come in that way, in turn. We've cider, tea and cakes."

Now they looked uneasy as well.

Mrs. Tooke folded her hands in her apron. "You may leave the coaches where they are for the time being," she told them, her voice firm and clear. "Tether all the horses near the stable or let them graze in the field nearby. There is hay and water, but no room for them inside. Then you may use the pump to wash up, and I'll bring out some refreshments for you."

"Yes ma'am!" They nodded in unison, looking relieved, and went to do as she said.

"They're servants to a nobleman," Mrs. Tooke explained to Alexandria as they went back into the house. "They like to be told what to do, and don't want to put a foot wrong. We'll ask his lordship what's to be done with them, but until then they need direction, you see."

"Well, now I do," Alexandria said, abashed. "There are some things books can't tell you. Mr. Gascoyne knew everything about etiquette, but he never dealt with this class of people."

"He did deal with them," Mrs. Tooke said. "And with their sons, just not well. He knew a great deal, I'm sure. Forgive me for saying so, but he was never very good with people of any class, high or low. That's why he had to come here, wasn't it?"

Alexandria nodded, looking wistful. "That's true. He was never happy with the nobility. He said blood was no indication of character, though the nobility believed it was. He wasn't happy with the middle class either. He said 'Money doesn't make the man, though the man usually thinks it does.' That was one of his favorite jokes." It was easy for her to remember that. He hadn't had many jests. "The other thing he always said was that peasants were peasants, and there was no help for it, or them," she added, looking so unhappy Mrs. Tooke frowned.

"And so he approved of . . . ?"

"Himself. And his friends—I think," Alexandria said. "But he was a charitable man for all that. Don't think I'm complaining. I'd be an ingrate if I did." She looked pensive. "I think he was one of those men who say one thing and do another. Like Mr. Bailey at the store in town. He says he has no use for children, but when the boys fetch the groceries for me they always find extra sweets in the parcel when they get home."

"Mr. Bailey does detest children. Those sweets are to win your approval," Mrs. Tooke said.

"No," Alexandria scoffed. "Why, he's almost as old as Mr. Gascoyne was."

"Yes," Mrs. Tooke said, "the age when a man hopes free sweets win smiles, especially if he has those and nothing else."

Alexandria turned wide eyes on her guest. "Never say! But he's never said a thing to make me think otherwise!"

"Yes he has, but you wisely haven't heard them. Just as well," Mrs. Tooke said. "He's much too old for you."

Now Alexandria scoffed. But she did it silently as she went to help Mrs. Tooke get refreshments for all their unexpected guests.

Seven

"NO," ALEXANDRIA SAID AS CALMLY AS SHE could, though she was ridiculously close to tears, "no, thank you. It's not necessary. No. It's preposterous!"

The boys looked disappointed. Mrs. Tooke looked thoughtful. The doctor scowled.

Drum looked at Alexandria with compassion.

"Please understand," he said. "I don't mean to insult you. But I'm a lazy, self-indulgent creature. All I'm asking, and I know it's presumptuous, is if you could see your way clear to allowing me to do this? It would make my life so much more pleasant," he added piteously. "I've had such pain and suffering, it would be pleasant to have something go right for a change."

She gritted her teeth. He wasn't the sort of man to feel sorry for himself. He was amusing himself at her expense.

"If it helps you in the process, then good," he went on. "I don't see how it can do any harm."

"It's absurd," she said. "You'll have your valet. There's no need for you to have two more of your servants staying on here. Servants in a *cottage?*" Her voice went up. She heard the shrillness in it, and took a deep breath.

"No," he said smoothly. "Servants in a barn."

"In a barn, then," she said, trying for patience. "It's just as silly, and don't say they're needed to take care of all the horses," she added hotly, "because there wouldn't be so many horses here if it weren't for them." She took another breath. "Listen, my lord. You're sending your coaches back to London, and I suggest you do the same with your grooms."

"They'll act as footmen," he said.

"Grooms, footmen, it makes no difference!" she burst out. "That's two more men and two more horses. Three servants for one man? There's no room for any more cattle *or* people here, and it's the height of absurdity *and* arrogance for you to suggest your men build on to the barn to make room for themselves!" She heard someone in the room gasp, and tensed even more.

"Height of imposition, perhaps," he said smoothly. "But arrogance? I certainly didn't intend that. I have to stay on here for weeks more. Surely adding on to your barn can't be a wicked thing? I'm not asking to add on to your house, which is charming as it is. Besides," he added, "all that hammering would give me a headache and I'm sure the doctor wouldn't approve.

"But making your barn bigger?" he asked. "Those men were once my companions in arms. We've pitched camp in other circumstances where I needed them with me, but tents would look awkward here. They're also resourceful and handy. They took measurements. We drew up plans. All they need is materials. I'll provide them. Then they can extend the barn, double it in a matter of days. Another day and they'll have sturdy sleeping lofts constructed. That way there would be a place for them to sleep as well as room for Mr. Grimes to stay on in.

"It would mean we wouldn't have to impose on the doctor," he explained. "It would mean you wouldn't have to fetch and carry for me anymore, and I can get on with my affairs while I'm here. And when I leave I'd be able to leave more than dirty sheets behind me. Where's the harm in that?"

The boys looked at her with hope. The barn was tiny, in need of repair. An addition to it would mean more room for their animals, even for them to play.

But it was wrong. Alexandria knew it in her heart, and sought words to explain why. It was impossible, because the truth was the harm would only be to her pride and happiness. Because while she was taking care of him she felt like an equal, not a servant. If he threw his largesse around, she'd feel like a paid nurse. That was what she would be.

She'd taken him in out of pity. She was *not* a beggar. She had worked hard and now was rightful mistress of this place, with enough to sustain herself and the boys. It wasn't a castle and she wasn't wealthy, but now that she was answerable to no one but herself she'd again never allow herself to feel like a supplicant in her own house.

She'd already compromised her principles. They'd just finished quarreling about another touchy point, and he'd won that one. He'd insisted on paying for their food, arguing she had more mouths to feed now. It was true, she didn't have enough money to feed them all—at least, not well—so she'd had to give in to that. Now he was asking to improve her home in ways she could not.

She knew it would as easy for him as buying a new jacket, and that it would be impossible for her to afford. It would also be like getting something for nothing, perilously close to charity. She'd had enough of that. She didn't have much, but her pride was her armor against a world that knew her circumstances. She could never tell him so, but it gave her an idea of what to say.

"And what will the rest of the world think?" she asked haughtily.

She saw his confusion, and felt much better. "My dear sir," she said, "when you do leave here, what do you think people will say about the fact that I entertained a nobleman for weeks at my home and after he was gone he left me with an entirely new structure?"

She had the pleasure of seeing him lose his cool composure. Only it wasn't the way she'd wanted him to.

Drum threw back his head and roared with laughter. Mrs. Tooke hid a smile and the doctor grinned. The boys looked as confused as Alexandria did.

"Oh, my dear Miss Gascoyne," Drum finally said, wiping his eyes. "A *structure*, is it? Where does that weigh on the scale of respectability, do you think? From your reaction one might think a gentleman leaving a lady with a 'structure' is almost as bad as him leaving her with a babe. I don't think you mean that. A barn won't adorn you, though perhaps it's a more intimate gift than a box of candy, I agree. Still, I don't know many ladies who get barns from their"—he glanced at the boys and added innocently—"gentleman guests. So I can't say."

The boys snickered. Alexandria, red-faced, shot them a quelling look.

"I can't say," Drum repeated, "but I can guess. I imagine people will think the Earl of Drummond is as bad as any other idle aristocrat, always altering the world to suit his own needs. Confined to bed for only a month, and building a *whole barn* for his convenience? They'll be shocked and appalled. I'll look like a spoiled, jaded eccentric. It will add to my reputation enormously, and not touch yours at all. Given my arrogance, along with a superior knowledge of this cruel old world, permit me to say I think most people will wish I'd broken my leg on *their* front doorstep."

Everyone in the room laughed. Except Alexandria. He'd made her look silly. And why not? she thought with resignation. He mightn't really be a spoiled eccentric, but he was a man with a title, money, and power. Her pride couldn't compete with that. Who cared about her pride but her anyway? She'd been a fool to think she could deny him anything he wanted. But she could at least stop playing the fool.

"Fine," she said, lowering her head. "Do it then. I see my objections were unreasonable."

She turned on her heel and left the room, and so didn't see his frown as he looked after her.

Alexandria was taking out her frustrations on the weeds in her kitchen garden when the boys came to tell her there was a surprise waiting for her upstairs. She left the garden and went up the stairs with dread and anticipation. She couldn't imagine what it was, and certainly didn't want another present from her imperious guest.

She had avoided him since their confrontation the night before, her excuse being she was too busy. She'd seen to it that she was. But he'd been busier, his servants going up and down the stairs all evening, until she shooed them out of the house for the night. They'd rolled themselves up in blankets and camped on her doorstep, or as near to it as not. They'd slept in the barn. She'd kept looking out the window, worried about the dampness and inconvenience they must be suffering, but they didn't seem a whit the worse for wear this morning.

They'd been at work since sunup, making marks, hammering in posts, stringing twine grids, laying the groundwork for when the lumber arrived. Even now she could see that the barn would be bigger than the cottage when it was done. Although she tried to quash the thoughts because it made her original protests seem foolish even to herself, she couldn't help getting excited thinking about the chickens she could have now, the extra storage space. Maybe a room for the boys to play or study in if the finished structure were snug and sound enough . . .

She paused at the doorstep to her bedchamber, her eyes widening. A tall, dark, elegant gentleman was sitting in a chair by the window. She was so startled it took her a second to realize he wasn't a stranger. It was only when she noticed the man was wearing a long colorful dressing robe over his shirt that she saw who it was. That, and the fact that he had one long leg propped on a stool—one long splinted leg.

"I didn't see you at breakfast," Drum said, smiling, gesturing for her to come in. "Are you ever going to forgive me?"

He looked very different from the bedridden invalid she'd known. There wasn't a particle of vulnerability left to him. Hauteur, power and elegance marked his every gesture. She restrained an impulse to curtsy. Her eyes went dark and she lowered her gaze. "I was very busy," she said, then added, "I see you're feeling better."

"I am, thank you. A man's attitude toward his sickness can go a long way to curing it. I'm shaved and dressed, after a fashion. Having my own clothes and sitting in a chair makes me feel like a healthy man again. Not that you didn't do your best for me, of course," he added quickly, "But Grimes knows my ways, and I don't hesitate to impose on him."

She only nodded, holding her hands clasped in front of her like a housekeeper waiting for her orders.

He gazed at her and felt a pang of sympathy and humor, intermixed. He knew many beautiful women, as well as homely ones, but none so dowdy as his hostess this morning. She wore a dreadful old gown. It might have had a floral pattern, once upon a time. It had traces of vague roses on it, and fit loosely, and didn't fit her inherent natural elegance at all.

She'd stopped by the window, standing with the sunlight behind her and he suddenly realized the fabric of her gown was so old and thin it was transparent. He saw the outline of the swell of her slender rib cage, the sweet arc of a breast rising above it. He looked away quickly. The pretty pink circle he saw might have been that of a faded flower but it also might have been the flowering bud of a pert and lovely breast.

He damned the sudden spontaneous rise of his own flesh in response, the flash of warmth that suffused his groin. It was instinctive and he knew it, but he couldn't afford to look further. Women of fashion wet down their thin gowns to get the same effect from a man but he knew this woman would probably rather drown herself entirely than do that. In fact, he was sure it would horrify her if she knew what he'd glimpsed. It would definitely endanger him if he kept looking. This was one woman he couldn't toy with.

He sternly repressed all traces of his physical response and discounted any mental ones as he reminded himself of facts that would still his unruly desires. Desire was not destiny. He wasn't a randy boy. Lust could be easily sated with no risk. He knew his worth. He was a nobleman of ancient lineage who needed a wife. That lady had to please his father as well as suit his own rank and station. He had enough money to buy a harem, but charming as this woman was, he simply couldn't afford her.

He looked at Alexandria's face to see if she'd noticed his unsought reaction to her body. She'd turned her head and was gazing out the window. He took the opportunity to study her, surprised to see she wasn't her usual neat self. There was a smudge of gold on one cheek. The boys said she was gardening, so it must be pollen. Some lucky bee would find her delicious, he thought. There was a streak of dirt on one white arm, leaves and twigs in her mussed hair, and she avoided his eyes.

No wonder she avoids me, he thought with guilty compassion, seeing how she glanced everywhere but at him. *It isn't my lechery. She never noticed that. It's because she tries to hide her feelings, but they're too easy to read.*

An admiring glance embarrassed her, a compliment thrilled and alarmed her, a flirtatious glance entirely disarmed and flustered her. Strange thing, he reflected, because she usually had the calm assurance of a woman up to snuff, as men described a female who knew the score and had played a game or two herself. It was clear she hadn't.

A pity he could offer her no more than flirtation, he thought, and if he was really kind he should offer considerably less. But maybe someday, somehow, he could help her. It was clear she needed some help, after all.

There was the matter of her curious isolation, for example. He'd been here for days and she'd had no company except for the doctor and Mrs. Tooke, who'd been brought by the doctor's summons. She took care of the boys like a mother, ran the house like a drill sergeant, and went over their lessons with them as well as any schoolmaster he'd ever had. Mother, soldier, and teacher, but never lover? She was a mass of contradictions. A simple country woman with more education than most men he'd met. A beautiful woman without suitors, and seemingly no desire to find any? Or at least, no resources to help her do it. He was always fascinated by a mystery, and it bothered him to see her go to waste.

"I can move around the room now too," he said, to break the sudden silence that had fallen over them.

"Well, not really. Grimes moves me. But not as much as you do. Did I really insult you?" he asked suddenly. "I never meant to alienate you. I have, haven't I? I had company all morning, but wondered where you were. Mrs. Tooke was a delightful companion at breakfast. I met with my men. Grimes was here, of course. The boys came before they went to school, but they said you were busy. Busy avoiding me. I'm sorry for that. Can we be friends again? I've missed you."

That made her look at him in surprise. "Missed me?" she asked before she could stop herself.

"I don't lie," he said seriously, looking into her eyes directly. Something in her gaze made him lower his. He brushed at an invisible spot on his silken robe. "I'll embellish the truth, of course," he added, "and avoid it sometimes too. But I never lie."

"Ah! I understand. So then I suppose you wondered why I wasn't here and felt guilty about it? Fine. *That* I can believe."

He laughed. "Yes. But I missed talking to you too," he said with complete honesty. "The doctor says I'm landed on you for at least another few weeks. He's worried about the leg, and the head. He's still not convinced that a carriage ride won't jolt something loose. In fact, I'm even forbidden to use a crutch for another week! So, if I'm to stay, and I'm afraid I must, can we declare peace? I can't help being domineering. It came with birth, you see. And I'm a natural meddler and a snoop. It helped in my work during the war, and I got used to it. I'll try to be better. But since all I can do now is talk, I require that as much as food and water. I'd like to talk with you. When you can, and when you will, of course. Will you?"

It was too nice a request to turn down. His smile was even harder to deny. It was strange how such an imperious fellow could suddenly look as innocent and eager as one of her boys, Alexandria thought. It was an enviable talent. She didn't doubt for a moment it was as practiced as his speech.

She nodded. "Yes, fine. But please, could you try to accept that I don't want anything from you? I don't want your money or any gifts. Your conversation would be nice."

"It's yours," he said. "Now sit down, please, and tell me all the gossip of the neighborhood and what you've been up to all morning."

She smiled, since even his requests sounded like orders. "No thank you. I don't want to muss your bed."

He looked confused, then chagrined. He sat in the only chair in the room. "I'll have to get another . . ." he said.

She interrupted. "No, that *I* will provide. But I don't mind standing for now, I'm too dirty to sit anyway. I've been working in the garden all morning. That's where I heard all the latest gossip too. Let me see, what's new? A new family of robins moved into the abandoned apple orchard down the road. Mmm . . . the badger was seen out late last night, and came reeling home towards dawn, and Oh! Yes. The laburnum started flowering."

He didn't laugh as she'd hoped. Instead, that long face looked very sorrowful. His eyes were gentled, blue as gentians, when he looked at her. "You've no neighbors?" he asked seriously.

"I do, of course," she said quickly. She didn't want his pity. Her chin came up. "We've nothing in common, though. Don't misunderstand, they're good people hereabouts. I'm sure they'd come in a snap if they thought I was in trouble or needed them. But we don't know them very well. The boys weren't allowed to play with the local lads when they were young. Mr. Gascoyne said he didn't want the boys associating with what he considered to be lesser minds. So we're still strangers to one another.

"Children form bonds beyond what their parents want, and childhood associations can become lifelong friendships no matter where life takes a person," she explained, as though reciting by rote, "Mr. Gascoyne knew that. He wasn't popular and didn't try to be. Now the boys are educated beyond their neighbors anyway, so they don't have much to do with each other. There's no hostility, just no friendship. It would be like asking the sheep to be friends with the cows. They live in adjoining fields, but have nothing in common." She laughed.

She didn't simper, he noticed. Her laughter wasn't a practiced trill. She had a natural, rich warm laugh that made a man want to join in. Except now.

"A rustic image from a rustic," she said derisively. "Now that will be something else to tell your London friends about your adventure in the countryside!"

"But their classmates," he asked, ignoring the way she depreciated herself, "surely they visit?"

She shook her head. "No, the boys weren't encouraged to associate with the boarders at school either. Their stations were too dissimilar and Mr. Gascoyne didn't want them lusting for things they'd never have. So their life is our home. It isn't so bad."

"And you?" he asked soberly. "Were you allowed to associate with the local children or the schoolmasters' wives or families?"

"Oh, me," she said, and turned her face toward the window again. "I was needed here. I didn't have the time to meet other girls, even if Mr. Gascoyne had allowed it."

"Damnation!" Drum said. "I don't wish to speak against your father, but what sort of a man was he, anyway?"

Her gaze swung back to him, her eyes dark. "He took in children who'd have been in the streets if he had not," she said. "Kit was small when he was young so he could've been apprenticed to a sweep and never grown taller, and gotten some deadly sickness from being sent up filthy chimneys all day. Vic was a big boy who might have gone to a mason or a hauler and been made to work his heart out before his time, like a cart horse. As it is he's a brilliant scholar. And Rob was always into mischief. He might have had an angry master, which means he mightn't be here at all today."

"And you?" Drum asked quietly, watching her expression.

She lifted one shoulder in a tiny shrug. Her lashes came down over her eyes. "Oh. Me," she said softly, with a small, sad smile. "But I was a girl. Mr. Gascoyne didn't understand them at all. He thought he was protecting me. Maybe he was. Who can say?"

He certainly couldn't, he thought with a guilty start. So instead, he told her about what he'd read in the paper that morning.

Eight

HE BARN WAS QUICKLY RENOVATED. AUSTIN GRIMES hired the men who delivered the lumber from the mill to help with it. Drum watched the new walls rise from his window, aching with impatience to see the inside. Since he wasn't permitted to go down the stairs he had to rely on everyone's reports. When it was done, they came to his room to tell him of his triumph.

"There's so much room! Room enough for *five* more horses," Vin said excitedly. "The windows are so big you can climb up to the loft and look out and see the world."

"There's light everywhere! The loft's huge," Kit said enthusiastically. "Why, a fellow could sit up there and read until nightfall without ever lighting a lantern."

"I can find no fault, my lord," Grimes said smugly.

Drum's other two servants stood in the little hall outside the bedroom because there was no room for them inside. They exchanged glances and grinned.

"The wood is superior. I've seldom seen the like," Mrs. Tooke marveled.

"Oak," Drum said, restraining an urge to bow.

"Golden oak," she went on, "smooth and shining, and requiring little upkeep, no doubt. Well done, my lord."

"The barn is altogether nicer and cleaner and bigger," Rob crowed. "We should move in there instead of the house!"

There was a sudden silence as they all looked at Alexandria. She forced a laugh. "Maybe we should. Then we'd have to put Thunder in here. Do you think he'd like this bed or yours, Rob?"

Rob's teeth worried his lip. "I suppose not, then." He looked at her imploringly. "But it's a wonderful place, Ally."

"Yes," she agreed, "and just too bad that it doesn't match this place."

Drum bit back his immediate response. Building them a matching house would have little effect on his finances, but that would be going too far. Putting an extension on a barn was one thing, buying a young woman a grand new home was another. He frowned. Alexandria had been right, in a way. There was a thin line between what the world would see as his self-indulgence and what they might think was her giving in to it—in other ways.

"But your home's historic, Rob," he said. "They're making fewer thatched cottages every year. And history has value the modern can't match."

"Yes," Alexandria agreed sweetly. "Modern folk miss all the fun we have. They don't get the chance to knock themselves silly every time they go up and down the stair if they forget to duck their heads. But the snugness is worth it. Why, we can be warm using only two sticks of wood in the hearth, so who needs room to turn around? We go outside if we want to do that. They certainly don't have the pleasure of living with nature the way our ancestors did. People in modern houses may have swallows in their eaves, but I doubt they have earwigs and mice in their roofs, or the joy of re-doing the thatch every year to keep even worse vermin out. It hardly matters, because the worse vermin enjoy living in our lovely historic walls more too."

Drum relaxed. She had a sense of humor about it. His smile slipped as she went on.

"History has value, but progress has comforts," she said reflectively. "Still . . ." She gazed out the window at the enormous new barn. "Now we have the luxury of both, don't we? We're certainly lucky. A huge addition to our barn, spanking clean and bright. To go with our tiny thatched cottage. *How* fortunate we are. Thank you, my lord," she said, curtsying to him, too low.

He looked out the window and then back at her. She was being sarcastic, but he realized she was right. The barn didn't match the house. They were horribly mis-mated. In fact, the barn didn't even match itself any-more, with the new wing so out of place and proportion. It made the cottage look paltry; the cottage made it look overdone. Altogether, it looked like some-one had run out of ideas or money. The cottage was a simple dwelling that, whatever it lacked, had pos-sessed charm. Now the whole property looked unbal-anced and unfinished. He'd done himself a favor, not her, when he'd improved her property for his own comfort.

"The barn will age in time," Drum said, wincing at how inane that sounded.

"Absolutely," Alexandria said through clenched teeth.

"I'm sorry," Drum said softly. "You must know I was only trying to repay you somehow."

She sighed. "Yes, and thank you. I'm sure in time it will look more mellow. I'll plant flowers, we'll become accustomed. But please, no more gifts. We took you in because you needed help. Anyone would have done the same. Repay us by getting well."

"And getting on my horse and riding out?" he asked with a faint smile. "I will, as soon as I can. Doctor? My head is clear and so are my eyes. Why not let me leave?"

"I told you," the doctor said. "in three more weeks, perhaps. Not a day less. Unless, of course, you want to walk with a cane the rest of your days?"

Drum didn't know who sighed harder—he, Alexandria, the boys, or Mrs. Tooke.

Only the boys and Mrs. Tooke sighed with relief.

Alexandria came to Drum's room that evening, carrying his dinner tray. She waited for him to look up before she stepped in. He was sitting in his chair again, looking gloomily out the window. He had a magazine on his lap, letters he'd written on his table. *His room? His table?* She was surprised at her own thoughts. He'd taken it over so completely she wondered if she'd ever think of it as hers again.

But he'd go one day soon, and she wondered if his presence would leave as readily. Mr. Gascoyne's occupancy had been simple to erase. He'd kept the room so spare and cold that all she had to do was bring in pretty things to expel his ghost. This man filled the place with wit and laughter. That would be harder to forget. And easier to miss.

"May I come in?" she asked when he lifted his head.

"Come in, sit, stay, talk, whatever you wish," he said. "I'm languishing from remorse and loneliness. You can cure both."

She put his tray down. "I think I'm accountable for one, and came to apologize for that. But I can't see how you can suffer from the other. I was ungracious about your gift, forgive me. But loneliness? You have your servants and my household up here so often I don't know how you have time to think, much less languish."

"There's talking and talking, my dear," he said, raising the cover on one dish and taking a sniff of the puff of steam that billowed up. "Meat pie—*bliss*," he said with satisfaction.

Then he fixed her with his knowing blue stare. "The boys amuse me, and I try to teach them things they have no way of knowing. Mrs. Tooke's a lovely woman, but I'm afraid my station makes her very aware of her own now. I think, at heart, I make her sad, and I'm sorry for it. Grimes never oversteps the line between master and servant. That's good for him, but bad for me now. Royce and Burdock, my men, can talk horses and memories of war. You're the only one that I can talk to about anything and who understands every reference I make."

"*I do?*" she asked, laughing. "Coming it too strong, my lord, as the boys would say. I like some realism in my compliments. What do I know about London? The Continent? Society and its ways?"

"Most people in London haven't read as much as you have. On balance, that makes it even. Plus, you appreciate a good jest and don't let my title get in the way of good sense. Many people take my rank very seriously, which affects me too." He grimaced. "My father, for example. Don't misunderstand. I'm an English nobleman, and I'm delighted to have had a hand in sending Napoleon on his way, because the thought of titled heads rolling in the streets of Paris or London did not thrill me. Making a man's name the most important thing about him, though, isn't good for his soul or character. So it's good to have someone stop me when I get too tyrannical. Or try to stop me," he said regretfully, glancing out the window again.

He sighed. "It's a handsome barn. For somewhere else. You were right. I was thinking we could have it thatched."

"Oh, no!" she said quickly. "Thatch is a lot of work to keep up. Age will temper it. Don't let it bother you."

"I won't if you won't," he said, looking at her steadily, his eyes filled with sincerity.

He'd be gone from here in weeks and she doubted he'd even think of her again, but he made her feel her forgiveness was the most important thing in his life. She wondered if he knew his power. Then laughed silently at herself. Of course he did. That was part of it.

"Fine," she said, and tried to think how to change the subject so he'd stop watching her. She did much better when he didn't keep looking at her. If they just talked and she could avoid the blazing azure fire of his eyes, no prickles of pleasure would ripple up and down her arms, there'd be no tingling at the back of her neck, her heart wouldn't pick up its beat. Which was better for all concerned, she told herself severely, and asked him his opinion about how long poor old mad King George would last.

They talked until she realized the lamps had to be lit and she had to go have her own dinner. After her meal, she tidied her hair, preparing herself for what was rapidly becoming one of the nicest parts of her new days. Then she and Mrs. Tooke went upstairs and crowded into Drum's bedchamber with the boys so extra lessons could begin.

Drum held his little audience captivated. They joked as much as they read now, and hung on every wonderful anecdote Drum could remember. He remembered hilarious ones tonight. Mrs. Tooke sat smiling as she knitted. Grimes stood at the edges of shadow, listening, waiting to do his master's bidding. And Alexandria beamed, watching them all.

It was a good, peaceful time. Alexandria glanced out the window and looked into the gathering night. Drum's men were in their new quarters getting ready for sleep. She could see their lantern light spilling out of the high barn windows down to the garden, casting shadows where they'd never been before. Every day her life seemed to be growing larger, and her little cottage bigger in ways the barn never could, no matter how many walls they added.

Because the cottage was being filled with conversation, laughter, and memories to treasure down through the rest of her years. She had only one worry now; she was laughing too much. She'd always been warned about that. "Too much laughter leads to tears" was what she'd always been told. Tears weren't tolerated either.

She supposed it made sense. Emotional children were harder to manage. Still, since Mr. Gascoyne had gone she'd encouraged the boys to laugh. Just the sound of it made her happy. Tonight she allowed herself to laugh like a loon and giggle until tears came to her eyes because this was a rare thing that would only happen for a little while, and for that little while, she would enjoy it.

If tomorrow brought real tears, she decided, she'd have at least earned them. It was only fair, she thought. She'd shed too many through no fault of her own.

The next day, however, brought astonishment.

Drum's friends arrived after breakfast. Alexandria saw them as she was pouring a basin of dishwater out into the front yard. They spilled out of the three coaches that had suddenly pulled up in the drive, so elegant and beautifully dressed they seemed like fairy-tale lords and ladies, come from another world.

The three gentlemen that set their polished boots down in front of her house were handsome, strong, and obviously powerful in their persons and places in life. They were examples of the highest London ton which Alexandria had only seen before in illustrations from fashion plates. Their casual clothing consisted of fitted jackets, immaculate linen and high, intricately tied neckcloths. Wrinkle-free pantaloons encased their muscular legs, their half boots were as polished as their magnificent horses' coats. One gentleman was tall, dark, and saturnine; one had dark gold hair and an extraordinary handsome face. The last was a rugged-looking fellow with military posture, attractive in spite of his outrageous red hair.

Alexandria was struck dumb by the gentlemen, but she actually gaped at the women with them. They were beautiful and graceful, and alit from their carriage like butterflies fluttering down to the ground. They were better dressed than the company Alexandria had seen at the best local weddings, although it was clear they were dressed casually for their class and kind. Their fashionable dresses were lovely hues with exquisite Madras shawls flung over their white shoulders against any chill in the morning air. Tiny tipped hats were perched on their perfectly coifed hair. Expensive as their clothing was, one look at their faces and figures showed they didn't needed further embellishment.

There was a tiny, ethereally beautiful blond woman; a raven-haired beauty; and a stunning lady with honey-brown hair, somehow made even more lovely by her one imperfection, a thin scar on her otherwise faultlessly pure cheek.

Alexandria stood dumbfounded, feeling smaller and yet in a way larger and more awkward with every second and every refined thing she noted about her guests. *His guests,* she reminded herself. She absently plucked at the skirt of her often washed gown. They might have used it as a dustcloth, she thought.

Servants stepped out of another coach. Alexandria hastily counted. The six of them, and *three servants?* Lord! Where was she going to find room to sit them all down?

As the new arrivals stared at the barn in all its obviously newly built glory, the blond woman took a swaddled infant from the arms of her maid. She anxiously studied the face of the sleeping child. "Even a cannon can't wake this one," she said with pleasure as she brushed her cheek against the baby's head. "Wasn't I absolutely right to take her along?" she asked no one in particular.

"It was absolutely the only way to save our necks," one of the men muttered.

"Huh!" she said dismissively. "Now," she said, looking around her impatiently, "where is he?"

They looked at the cottage, and finally saw Alexandria standing in the doorway. She forced herself to greet them. She clutched the basin in front of her as though for protection as she ducked her head in a bow. "I imagine you're here to see the earl?" she asked, hoping no nervousness showed in her voice.

"Indeed," the tall, dark gentleman said. "Is your mistress home?"

Alexandria's chin came up. "I am she," she said frigidly.

"Your pardon," he said, bowing. "I'm Sinclair, the earl's cousin. We got word the earl had an accident. Is he here? Is he all right?

"I'm Miss Gascoyne, my lord," Alexandria said, still with a distinct chill in her voice. "Your cousin's upstairs. He did have an accident. He's much better now, but must stay on with me until he fully recovers."

The ethereal-looking blond lady balled one gloved fist and poked the gentleman in the shoulder. "Now see what you've done," she told him crossly. "You've set her against us, and no wonder."

"Ouch!" the gentleman said, cringing, though the blow had been a mock one. "Stop, you little wasp. My dear," he told Alexandria with a quirked smile that transformed his face, making it warm and engaging, "forgive me. I was so interested in finding out Drum's whereabouts and condition, I forgot my manners. Allow me to present my company properly. I'm the Viscount Sinclair, and this is my viscountess. Here is my friend Rafe Dalton and his bride, and this little blond demon is my ward, Gilly Ryder, who belongs to poor Mr. Ryder here now, and this enchanting scrap of humanity is their infant progeny, Annalise."

"The doctor said he can't leave his room for at least another week," Alexandria said, giving each of them a slight nod to signify a bow. "I'll tell him you're here." She turned her head and looked up to see Austin Grimes at the upper window. He nodded to her, signaling they should come up.

"His valet seems to have heard all," she said, turning back to her new guests. "He must be anxious to see you, so if you'd care to come in?" She indicated the way.

The viscount frowned. "But wait, please. What are his injuries? He sent word to us, but merely that he wouldn't be able to make an engagement we'd had because he'd had an accident. That was too vague for our comfort. We really began to worry when he didn't come home and we found out he'd sent for his valet and some servants. He's done for himself in the past when he's had to and he's not a fellow who likes to admit he needs help. So when he sent for it, we came to see for ourselves. All he said was that he'd had a mishap and 'came a cropper.'"

Alexandria laughed in spite of herself. "'Came a cropper,' is it? Came down in a hurry, more like," she said more seriously. "His horse was shot. We don't know how or why yet. But it threw your cousin. The horse survived, but it fell on your cousin and broke his leg in two places, and the doctor still worries about the injuries to his head. Not that he has any symptoms now," she added quickly, because they all looked stricken at her words, "but it was . . . it seemed a near thing there for a while."

The redheaded man muttered something under his breath and then barked, "Is the doctor reputable? Why didn't you send to London for another opinion?"

Alexandria's back stiffened again. "Dr. Pace is more than reputable," she said, clutching the basin so hard her knuckles turned white. "We did the best we could as fast as we could. There was no question of sending to London when we brought your friend home on a door, or time to think of it. We were lucky enough to get any doctor so quickly, much less a good one like Dr. Pace. We had a gravely wounded man and didn't even know his name. In fact, we didn't discover it until he regained consciousness, which we wondered if he would at all. We didn't think about getting other opinions once we saw his leg, either. The important thing was to set it at once. Even so, if his problems had persisted the doctor was going to send for another consultation. As it is, Lord Drummond's healing with remarkable speed."

The redhead looked abashed. "Forgive me. It's only that he's an old friend and I very much want to see him get older. Thank you on his behalf, Miss Gascoyne."

She nodded stiffly. "Now, if you'd care to go in? It's a small cottage, so I'll stay out here while you visit. Mind your heads going in the door. His room is at the top of the stair. Please hurry, because I'm afraid he'll get so impatient he'll try to get up, and that's forbidden."

They filed toward the cottage. The viscountess paused in front of Alexandria. "Forgive us landing on you like this," she said, "but Drum's very dear to us, and when we heard he'd been hurt we had to come see him."

The fiery little blond woman paused too. "The men wanted us to stay home, but women have the same sense of loyalty as men," she told Alexandria with a smile. "How can you rest when a friend's in trouble? He'd have done the same for us. You understand."

"Yes," Alexandria said, and smiled, though she felt odd and vaguely cheated, because, for the life of her, she couldn't think of anyone but the boys who would care what happened to her.

"My brother may be along any moment," the raven-haired lady said. "Please send him up to us too."

Alexandria stood and watched them crowd into her cottage. She'd once joked about how many alien intruders the old place had sheltered under its thatch. None were as alien as these people from an altogether different world, she thought. *His people.* They'd come for him at last. He was with his kind again, and soon he'd be gone with them and she'd never see him again either.

The excitement was over, the fun was done. Life would return to normal but would never be the same. She'd be back to her routine in no time, which was as it should be, but it would be spoiled for her now. What had been commonplace would now seem like loneliness.

"Too much laughter will lead to tears," she repeated to herself. Well, she sighed, that was wrong. She didn't feel like crying. She just felt hollow.

The servants who'd come with her unexpected guests were stretching their legs, eyeing the cottage, gaping at the barn, and covertly watching her. Alexandria strolled to the garden in front of the cottage and bent her head over her newly staked sweetpeas, pretending to look at them to avoid being looked at.

Soon she was busily planning what and how to feed her guests. She had to offer tea because the nearest inn was a long way off. . . . The sound of horses in her drive made her look up.

A blazingly yellow phaeton with gilded struts and bright red wheels, pulled by cream-colored horses, came tearing down the drive, sending up a cloud of dust in its wake. The phaeton was a stunning affair, elegant and delicate as a cranefly, precariously balanced and built for speed. The two gentlemen high on the driver's seat looked like those in a sporting print Alexandria had seen. They had hard, bored faces. One was fat, one thin. Neither looked like the brother the raven-haired woman said she was expecting. One had a high beaver hat over his yellow hair; the other's dun hair was in a Brutus crop, brushed forward over his forehead.

They wore tan driving coats fastened by big mother-of-pearl buttons. The many capelets on their coats cascaded in tiers from shoulder to hip. One wore yellow trousers, the other, sky blue. Each had a bright nosegay tucked in his lapel. Members of some exclusive driving club, no doubt, Alexandria thought, as she stood staring at them. Too bad the boys weren't here to see them, they'd be in ecstasies.

The phaeton stopped and the two men stayed seated on their high perch, surveying the place as though they'd just bought it. They saw the other coaches and smiled, nodding to each other. They looked back and forth from the cottage to the barn and frowned in incomprehension at the obvious disparity of sizes and shapes.

Then they saw her. They smiled again.

"Well, well," the yellow-haired man drawled to the other. "Answers at last."

Before Alexandria could speak, he went on talking to his friend, though eyeing her. " '*Accident*,' my noble pink posterior! Drummond's found a treasure. No wonder he's rusticating. This affair has all his earmarks. Just look at the things he's imported for his comfort: servants, friends, even that new . . . edifice. He probably erected it. Looks like it was built yesterday. Speaking of comforts, it's likely not the only thing he's erected here. Just look at her. Country pleasures indeed. Here's a fine strapping wench, *now* it all comes clear."

"Not a lady," the other commented, looking her up and down.

"No, the lucky dog," the driver said. "A fellow don't need one here. And what a fellow needs, she's got. In plenty. She's comely and clean, not used town goods. God! I think it's time I went home to see what's been growing on my estate aside from turnips."

"Not on your estate," the fat man said, holding a quizzing glass up to one magnified eye. "That's the point. It's why Drum came here to the middle of nowhere. Not a whisper of scandal in his own backyard. Trust him to do it right."

Alexandria couldn't believe her ears or eyes. She didn't care who this high-born lout was related to, she wanted him gone. "*I beg your pardon?*" she asked, aping Mr. Gascoyne, the sternest schoolmaster in the nation, in his most forbidding, haughty tones.

"Darling," the driver said, his gaze sliding up and down her body, "you don't have to beg for a thing. Don't fret. We came looking for that devil Drummond, but we'll be happy to take you instead."

Alexandria wished she had a dog to set on them, or a brother or father, or a tall, broad-shouldered friend. But she did have a friend, she hoped. "He's upstairs," she said icily. "I'll just tell him you're here."

"Oh, bother that," the driver said, leaning a hand on the wheel and hopping down to her level. He put one gloved finger under her chin and forced it up so she could meet his glittering eyes. "I'm here. My pockets are as full as the fall on my trousers when I look at you, and that should be more than enough—especially for a shrewd woman of business." He lowered one eyelid in a wink.

Her eyes glittered now too, with the fervent wish to kill him. She slapped his hand away. "You're mistaken. And you aren't welcome anymore. Please leave."

"Oh, I think not," he said, clipping an arm around her waist.

"Careful!" his friend called to him.

"Of what?" he laughed.

"Drummond's a touchy fellow."

"So am I, ain't you watching?" the yellow-haired man laughed as a furious Alexandria tried to pull away. "But don't worry. Drummond's awake on all suits, and gentlemen don't duel over sluts."

Nine

"**E**WEN!" DRUM LAUGHED AS HIS COUSIN DUCKED his head under the low lintel and came into the room. "Villain! What are you doing here? I told you I was recovering."

"So you did," the viscount said calmly. "So I came."

"And you've brought your lovely lady," Drum exclaimed as the viscountess followed her husband into the bedchamber. "Ah, but why did you do that? Bridget," he asked the viscountess, "why did you follow this fellow to the ends of the earth to see me?" He struggled to stand but felt a firm but light hand on his shoulder.

"My lord, please, remember your injuries, or I shall have to do it for you," Grimes whispered from behind him.

"Yes, very well," Drum grumbled, settling down. "What's this?" he yelped as the redhead and his bride entered. "Newlyweds have better things to do than visit the decrepit—no!" he shouted, looking beyond them. "Gilly, you too?" he said to the smiling blond woman. "You wretch, come to plague me, have you? Hello, Damon, couldn't you shackle her? Can't a man die in peace anymore?"

"We thought you were," the blond woman said. "So I brought your greatest admirer to say good-bye to you," she added, smiling down at her baby.

Drum's face grew grave. "But I almost did," he said quietly.

"Just so," his cousin said, leaning at the window to make room for the others who crowded into the chamber. "Who shot at you, Drum? Have you any enemies in this part of the country?"

"I probably have them everywhere," Drum said with a shrug. "But it was more likely only some local lad taking bad aim at a passing bird. That's what the boys who live here think. I sent Grimes to make inquiries. He didn't discover a thing, and he's thorough. The locals seem innocent enough, but there's a school not far away—be damned to this blasted leg of mine!" he said in frustration. "If I could only go out and ask for myself!"

"No need. We're here," the redheaded man said simply.

"Rafe," Drum said seriously, "I thank you, but you've better things to do than investigate my problem. And I'm sure that better half of yours will agree with me," he added, smiling at the raven-haired woman.

"She doesn't," that lady said frankly. "Nothing's more important than finding out who did this to you. Don't worry about Rafe overworking. My brother's coming too and he'll be glad to lend a hand and an ear. We'll find who did this, and why."

"We heard you'd suffered terrible injuries," Gilly Ryder said anxiously, "and here you are, unable to stand."

"Vastly exaggerated," Drum said quickly. "Don't fret. I feel fine now. The leg's only broken, not falling off."

"A leg will knit," her husband, Damon, said with a frown, "but what's this we heard about your head?"

"The fall shook things loose, I think I'm a teapot now. Be serious!" Drum said in annoyance. "Nothing's wrong with it except I got a hard knock, not for the first time and probably not for the last. I tell you, I'm mending, and am sorry rumor sent you haring off to see me. Sorry," he said with a slight smile, "but flattered."

"All your friends are concerned," Gilly said. "Wycoff's at his estate with Lucy and his brand-new son, or he'd be here now—yes, it's a boy, isn't that grand?"

"I'll write to congratulate them and tell them to stay where they are," Drum said. "As soon as I'm on my feet, I'll go see them. And I promise you that *will* be soon."

"This Alexandria Gascoyne," his cousin said, looking out the window, "your hostess. Why do I know that name?"

"Because her father probably tormented you in his time. He was a schoolmaster at Eton. Latin or classical studies," Drum said. "Don't you remember? Or has this crowd in here used up so much air you can't think?"

"God!" the viscount said, his eyes widening. "*That* Gascoyne? The Little Emperor? We called him that before Napoleon had the name," he explained to his wife's bemused glance. "We thought he was a tyrant. Well, he was. Sour as a . . . Don't tell me that charming girl is his daughter? I didn't even know he was married. What woman would dare? He had the disposition of a snake and all the human kindness of a rock. He was finally dismissed for some reason or other, there were wild rumors about it. But no one cared why he left as long as he did. The whole school, teachers and students, rejoiced."

"So I'd imagine," Drum said. "He's been dead three years and his shadow still lingers here. Left her with three adopted brothers to raise. They're sound lads, but she has a hard time of it. She never complains, though—unless someone tries to do her a good turn."

"Ah, so you *are* responsible for that . . . unusual addition to the barn?" asked his cousin, still gazing at the window.

"Good turn of phrase," Gilly said with a grin.

"Wonderful euphemism," her husband agreed, as the others smiled.

Drum grimaced. "Yes, don't remind me. It looks like the barn was attacked by a sudden fall of lumber. I know. It was supposed to be useful to her. I was trying to do her a good turn because she'd done one for me. She didn't know who or what I was when the boys found me lying by the side of the road, but she took me in and nursed me back to health. I wish I knew how to repay her."

His cousin kept looking out the window, but now he was frowning. "You wrote and told us you were fine, and when we went to your town house your butler was instructed to say the same. So why on earth did you send for those fatuous lords Bryant and Tench?"

"What?" Drum exclaimed. "Those fools? I avoid them in London, why would I want them here? They're reminders of my misspent youth, mistakes I made in the past."

"So why are they here?" his cousin asked, looking down at the drive.

"Damn! They're not!" Drum said, trying to rise from his chair. "Oh, all right, don't panic," he told Grimes crossly. "I'll stay where I am, I'm not going to run down to greet them. I gave them up years ago and usually run the other way if I see them coming. You must be mistaken, Ewen. They're idlers, gossips, pleasure seekers who never grew up. Little pleasure they'd get from racketing down from London to this place. Why would they?"

"Showing off Bryant's new high-perch phaeton, probably," Gilly said, standing on tiptoe to see out the window too. "They've been bucketing all over London in it. Everyone's laying odds on when they'll tip over and break their necks."

"Laying odds, and hoping," Rafe added.

Ewen Sinclair's gaze sharpened and he frowned ferociously. "What's that damned fool doing with your hostess?" he muttered as he looked down.

Drum heaved himself up and tried to see. He got a glimpse of what was happening. It took both Grimes and Damon Ryder to hold him back as he tried to follow the others as they ran out the door and down the stairs.

Drum struggled, looking down at the scene below, his teeth clenched, hands fisted in impotent fury at what he saw. The pain in his head was nothing to the frustration he felt. It had all happened in a flash. Lord

Bryant had jumped down from the high phaeton and accosted Alexandria. He'd grabbed her and was trying to turn her head to kiss her. His friend Tench sat on the driver's seat guffawing and cheering him on. Alexandria was struggling to pull away from her attacker. That amused Bryant, he threw back his head and laughed. And then stopped—abruptly.

Because Alexandria had managed to free one hand and swing hard at his upraised chin. And she'd been clutching a enameled basin in that hand.

Drum winced. He imagined he could hear Bryant's teeth click together from the force of the blow. He grinned. A faceful of basin was not what Alexandria's admirer had been expecting from her. The smile died on Drum's lips, his eyes blazed—because Bryant brought back one fist and swung it . . . right into the basin, as Alexandria raised it as a shield and ducked. Bryant howled and hopped, holding his bruised knuckles with his other hand. Alexandria quickly stepped on his foot, gave him another clout on the side of the head with the basin, and turned to flee. Bryant followed, and ran right into Rafe's fist.

Drum finally allowed himself to be thrust back into his chair as he sighed with relief, confident that his friends could finish the defense Alexandria had started.

Lord Bryant was sure of that too.

"Get up!" Rafe roared at him.

"Not likely," Bryant cried, curling up on himself where he lay on the ground like a grub that had just been unearthed by a gardener's shovel. "You'll kill me."

"I'll try!" the redhead vowed. "But be a man and stand!"

"I'm sorry! I won't touch her again! I apologize! Just having a bit of sport," Bryant gabbled. "Didn't know she was your friend." He looked up fearfully and saw himself surrounded by a crowd of illustrious gentlefolk, all sneering down at him.

"Didn't know she was of any importance, the way she was dressed and all. Thought she was a filly, nothing more." Bryant's eyes sought Alexandria. She stood breathing hard, her eyes wide. "Pardon, beg your pardon, ma'am," he beseeched her. "Please tell them not to kill me."

"Don't kill him," Alexandria said automatically, still trying to catch her breath.

"There'd be all that trouble with an inquest, after all," the viscount said in reasonable tones.

"Well, I won't then," Rafe agreed. "You can get up and go," he told Bryant, "but don't take too long about it or I'll change my mind."

Bryant got to one knee and looked at them warily.

"Whatever possessed you to come down here to make trouble?" the viscount asked curiously.

"Wasn't thinking of making trouble," Bryant said, sniffling. "We heard you were coming here. Heard Drummond was down here too. The Season's ending, it's tedious in London, and we were looking for a bit of sport, Tench and I."

"Speak for yourself!" Tench cried from high on the driver's seat of the phaeton. He had the reins gripped hard and held high. It was obvious one move toward him would have him making off down the drive as fast as his horses could take him. "Just passing through," he assured the others, "on my way to my house."

"In Dover?" the viscount mused. "How interesting.

I wonder, did you know you're headed in exactly the wrong direction? On second thought, probably not."

Bryant lurched to his feet.

"A moment," Damon Ryder called as he came out the door. "Drum has a question. When did you hear where he was? And how?"

"Yes," Rafe said, his eyes narrowing. "A very good question."

Bryant, seeing three strong men suddenly glaring at him again, lost his courage and simply stood mute, looking at them.

Tench spoke up quickly. "Well, everyone was wondering where Drummond was. He hasn't been seen in any of his usual haunts, don't you know. We got to placing bets in the book about it. Then we heard you were all setting out of London in a scramble. Well, me and Bryant are downy ones and know Drummond is Sinclair's cousin and your friend. So we knew something was in the wind. We wanted to win the bet, have some fun too. So we asked around, especially at Sinclair's house. Not a footman in creation who won't tell something for a few coins, you know."

"I'd thought mine wouldn't," the viscount mused. "Pity, I'll have to hire on new ones."

His wife touched his sleeve. "I shouldn't. These are hard times. I never told them it was a secret, did you?"

He patted her hand. "No. You're right." He looked up. "One more thing," he asked Bryant. "When did you discover all this?"

"The morning you set out," Bryant said warily, "we followed."

The viscount looked up. Grimes stood at the high

window. He looked back into the room, and then made a gesture of dismissal.

"Then go," the viscount told Bryant. "But repeat a word of this incident to anyone and you may have to repeat the entire incident—with flourishes."

Bryant nodded, grabbed his hat from the ground and stumbled up to the high driver's seat again. A moment later, the jaunty carriage had turned and was racing back down the road.

The company stayed to tea. The men sat up in the bedroom with Drum. The women clustered in the kitchen.

The men quizzed Drum about the real state of his health and his opinion about his assailant.

"I wrote to your brother-in-law Eric, too," Drum told his friend Rafe. "Your bride said he's on his way?"

"Aye," Rafe said. "He's an old soldier, and still a bachelor, so he has all the time in the world to help you. And he can. If there's a true villain around, he'll get the scent. Wish I could stay to see the fun."

"That you do not!" Drum said, laughing, "and who can blame you? You belong with your wife and there's nowhere for her to stay unless she cares to sleep in the barn with you. This place is hardly big enough for the family that lives here, which is why I built that absurd addition to their barn. It was for my own convenience so my men could be here with me. I thought it would help them too."

Drum grimaced. "Even I can be wrong, though please don't quote me on that. Eric can stay there, there's room even for a giant like him now. He's a good man, I'll be glad of his help. So feel free to leave. I'm mending fast and will be back in London before you can miss me. Now, tell me some important things. How have you been and what have I missed?"

The men talked about horse races and wagers, boxing matches and finances.

Downstairs, the women admired Gilly's baby, gossiped about Lady Sinclair's two children, and exclaimed and applauded when they heard Brenna Dalton's shy announcement of a baby soon to come. Alexandria helped Mrs. Tooke serve tea and watched the lovely lively young women as they laughed and talked. They were so utterly unlike any women she'd ever seen up close that she felt both honored and belittled by their presence. It was an unsettling feeling, so she watched them furtively.

Which might be why she wasn't aware that they were also watching her. One particular pair of golden eyes appraised her covertly. "You were a treat with that basin, Miss Gascoyne," Gilly Ryder suddenly blurted. "You landed that rotten Bryant a facer *I'd* be proud of!"

It was an odd way for a lady to speak. Alexandria decided it must be the current fashion. She was profoundly embarrassed, aware she must have looked like a hulking farm girl to them. "I'd been emptying the basin when they drove up," she murmured. "I suppose I just hung on to it. When I realized I held it, I also realized I had a weapon." Faint color appeared high on her cheeks as she lifted her head high. "I've three younger brothers. They taught me about fighting. They said women didn't have to play by the rules. Not because they have less honor," she added quickly, "but because if someone bigger tries to take advantage of someone smaller of any gender, a different set of rules apply."

"Aye!" the petite blond lady said with satisfaction. "And wit overweighs muscle any day, if you know how to use it."

"Tell us about how you found our friend Drum," the viscountess said. "I'd wager there's a thing or two he'd never mention. Was he very sick? Have you any idea how it happened? And do you know how grateful we are that you did take him in?"

Alexandria was glad to change the subject. It was as well that she didn't know she was now the subject of discussion upstairs.

"And what about your hostess, Drum?" his cousin asked him soberly when they were through gossiping about Town. "You're a fast worker, getting on mighty intimate terms so quickly. Why, you sleep in her bed and build her a barn, and you only just met." The other men chuckled.

"I'm not just asking for the sake of a joke," the viscount went on more seriously. "You said this Mrs. Tooke is respectability itself. It's not that which worries me. It's your damnable sense of honor. I know you and your inexplicable charm too, as well as the gratitude you must feel toward her. Have you given rise to any expectations on her part, do you think?" He frowned when he saw Drum's scowl. "Come to think of it, I may be entirely out of line. Have you expectations yourself in that direction? I wouldn't blame you. She *is* lovely, well bred, and well spoken."

"Add that she has a heart of gold," Rafe said. "She took in a stranger who might have turned out to be a scoundrel. Not that you're not."

"Yes," Drum said wryly, "add that all up, because it's true. But remember that I broke my head, I didn't lose my mind. She has a heart of gold, but my father's heart is one he can document back to the Normans. Or so he keeps reminding me, and I'd certainly break it if I chose a wife he didn't approve. It's all I can do to persuade him I don't want a royal princess for my bride. So however lovely Miss Gascoyne is, and she is, I promise you I've no expectations in that direction, and thank God, neither does she. Or so she assured me when I said my staying here might compromise her and require the services of a vicar, not just a doctor. When she heard that she almost tossed my broken bones out her door."

"Then she's got good sense, too," Rafe commented.

They laughed, and changed the subject.

When the merry company left later that afternoon, they stopped to thank Alexandria for her hospitality and charity.

"We can't say how grateful we are," the viscountess told her. "We worried about what we'd do if we found Drum in any trouble here."

"We couldn't and wouldn't just leave him alone if he needed us," Damon Ryder explained.

"We were all being terribly noble," Gilly agreed, "volunteering to be the ones to stay on with him. When no one could win the title of 'noblest,' we decided we'd have to draw straws to see who got the honor, though much as we love him, we each hoped we wouldn't win."

"Speak for yourself," her husband said with mock affront, though he very obviously crossed his fingers to offset the lie.

"But now we can leave with clear consciences," the viscount said, "because it's clear he's fallen in clover and has the very best care. So again, thank you, Miss Gascoyne. We're in your debt and I don't know how we can repay you. Is there anything we can do for you?"

"Thank you, but I don't need anything," Alexandria said, straightening her spine. They stood in her dooryard, looking as out of place there as the elegant carriages that awaited them did. But it was her dooryard, and her house, and she had her pride too. They must have seen it in her altered posture, because some of them looked abashed.

"Turnabout's fair play!" Gilly Ryder said on a sudden inspiration. "You hosted Drum, we can be your hosts! We have lots of room, we all have homes in London. That would be a change of pace for you, wouldn't it? Say you'll come to visit and stay on with one of us when he's gone home again. We could show you London, have fun, and repay our debt at the same time."

"Capital idea!" Rafe agreed.

They began to argue about who would be the best host and hostess until Alexandria interrupted, silencing them. "I'm grateful," she said sincerely, "but it isn't possible. The boys need me here, and I've no time to spare. Please understand I didn't expect nor shall I accept more than your thanks. Anyone would have done the same."

They denied that heatedly, but had to accept it. Alexandria breathed a sigh of relief when they stopped trying to change her mind. For a moment the idea of going to London had been so terribly tempting she'd almost hopped in the air and cried out *yes!* as one of the boys might have done. She'd never dared think of actually visiting London, though of course she'd always dreamed of it. A moment later, she realized the enormous folly of even imagining she could go.

Stay with any of these glittering people, when she didn't have the price of fare to London, much less a hostess gift? Or the price of a new gown, much less a whole wardrobe of new clothes, which she'd need so she wouldn't look lower than their housemaids. Not to mention the need for gratuities for those servants, and extra shillings in her purse for any unexpected thing a person might need in England's greatest city. Her one trip to Bath had cost her triple what she'd expected. The extra expenses involved with staying in London couldn't even be considered. Or possibly met.

Alexandria's spirits plummeted. It was a kind invitation that hurt more than it honored her. How like the rich to forget that the poor couldn't afford to accept such a gift. Or did they expect her to stay in the scullery and go around London with their servants? Her eyes widened. Her pride wouldn't accept that. No. Better to keep dreaming of London than to actually experience it in ignominy or shame.

She waved good-bye and watched the coaches leave in fine procession, bearing Drum's visitors back to their unimaginably splendid lives. They went with merry farewells and the music of competing coaching horns. She looked up at the window, wondering what her last guest was thinking as they left. Was he feeling deserted, marooned, yearning to follow, longing to be with his own kind again?

Well, she could send one of the boys to the doctor to

beg or buy a bottle of wine for his dinner, she thought as she turned back to the house. And she could make him a raspberry tart for dessert tonight too. Spirits to restore his spirits, and something sweet to take his mind from his troubles.

Alexandria went back into the kitchen, feeling a lump in her throat and a knot in her chest, wondering why she suddenly felt worse about his yearning to go to London than for her own.

Ten

SOON AFTER DRUM'S COMPANY LEFT, THE BOYS came home from school. They did their chores, finished dinner, and now were in the barn, chatting with Drum's valet and footmen. After the dishes were done Mrs. Tooke accepted a carriage ride from the doctor and his wife and went to visit her grandchildren. The house had the eerie quiet a place holds when company has lately left, and Alexandria heard the echoes of laughter everywhere.

For the first night in months there was no need to light a fire in any hearth. Alexandria went to the door and saw the newly prolonged twilight stretching the sunset thin. She stayed a while, until the onset of growing shadows made her aware of time passing. She felt melancholy and thought her guest must be feeling the loneliness even more keenly, and so climbed the stair to see how he was doing.

He sat in the chair by the window, looking out. He didn't turn his head, but spoke the moment she entered the room. "I've stirred up your world again, haven't I? See how you're repaid for your charity. You'll think twice before you take in another vagabond, I think."

"Well, I don't know that I have a choice," she said thoughtfully. "There are so many wounded men strewn at the sides of the roads hereabouts, if I didn't take them in they'd clutter up the place."

He laughed and turned to look at her. "Seriously, Ally, I apologize for your treatment at the hands of those fools from London. And I also apologize for landing so much company on you. I've cost you a lot in time and money, haven't I? I'd like to repay you."

She blinked. He'd called her Ally, the way the boys did.

He was obviously unaware he'd spoken so familiarly and thought her surprised look was because of his offer. "I know you're proud, and I respect that. I never understood why pride was considered a deadly sin," he mused. "Surely it's merely an annoying one? Because my father's a good man and yet he has enough pride for all the British Isles. But you have to understand I have my pride too, and that means I pay my debts. Help me do that, please."

She straightened a few things on his table for something to do while she thought of an answer. Then she folded her hands and looked out the window at the empty yard. "I can't. You must understand that too. Any gift would look like more than it is. Any payment would be worse and it's not just the way society interprets such things." She shook her head. "I know that those two fops who came here to tease me are not all of society, but they're enough of it to matter, I think. Still, it isn't just that. The truth is I'd be uncomfortable with you paying me for doing what I should. Please accept that I helped someone in need. The best way to repay me is to do the same one day, remembering me."

She laughed suddenly. "No! I'm not such a saint. If you're desperate to do something, then find something charming when you get back to London and send it to the boys. I'd like that. And maybe send along a bottle of spirits for me to give to the doctor, because that was his wine you had tonight, and I pay my debts too. That would be enough."

"No, it wouldn't," he said quietly.

She couldn't disagree, but she couldn't agree either, and he knew it. So they stayed silent, knowing, not speaking. It was an intimate, companionable silence neither wanted to break.

He stole a glance at her. She'd impressed his friends even though she'd little to do it with but herself. She'd impressed them with her charm and intelligence and looks, although she'd been surprised by their company and kept so busy by them she'd had no time to change and had worn the same old gown all day.

The one she had on now was no less worn, but prettier. Whatever it had been, it had faded to a soft saffron, and she'd tied her gleaming hair with a yellow ribbon to match. It suited her. But even maidservants sported better clothes on their days off, he thought with tender pity. He'd seen them clustered like pretty pastel flowers as they strolled through the parks on their Sunday half days. If Alexandria even had a best gown, he doubted it would be half so fine. But why?

She and the boys lived simply, but had ample food. The boys were suitably dressed. Surely she had enough money to make herself a new gown? Or was every cent saved for her brothers?

Drum considered himself a scholar of his fellow man and woman. Even aborigines dressed to impress each other, if only by their tattoos. She didn't, wouldn't, or couldn't. There was always a logical reason for a person's behavior. His friend Gilly had dressed like a lad when she'd been a girl. That was shocking, but it had been a reasonable way to protect herself from attack in the vile slums from where she'd sprung. After his cousin Ewen had taken her in as his ward, she'd taken to women's clothing with her signature style and panache, and considerable delight.

If Alexandria Gascoyne wore old clothing from necessity, it was the necessity of genteel poverty and was understandable. She wasn't careless of her appearance; she was always neat and clean and presentable. But she didn't try to dress herself up in any other way. There was only one vanity he noticed she indulged herself with: She wore perfume. She always smelled of honeysuckle. It was how he had known she'd come into the room.

Why didn't she primp or preen? he wondered. Perhaps she hadn't married because the old man had been so sour he'd chased away suitors. But why didn't she have any beaux now? There had to be single men somewhere in the vicinity. Did she believe she couldn't attract a man? Or had she never learned the way of it? He suspected it was a thing she'd ruthlessly banished from her life. Drum wondered why. It wasn't because she had no interest in men. He was aware of how she looked at him sometimes. He was far from vain but knew when he interested a woman. Or was it that she ruthlessly squashed the attraction, just as he did, and for the same reasons?

Alexandria Gascoyne had many mysteries. Too bad that he loved a mystery. She enticed him—sorely—all the more as he grew to know her. He might want to know more about her, but he positively itched to know how that smooth skin would feel under his hands and if her mouth would taste like honeysuckle nectar too. Was this just an itch? Or something more? Too bad he couldn't find out.

Without question, if she were well born, he'd consider her for his wife. A man who couldn't love could do far worse than to marry someone he liked and was moreover wildly attracted to. But he couldn't marry a woman of lesser rank, and that was that. If he *loved*— Well, but that was a different story. He'd asked Gilly to marry him once, though she had no rank at all. Fortunately Gilly had known what he'd offered had come from a different sort of love, and hadn't been confused by his act of gallantry.

She stared out the window as though the familiar scene absorbed her. But he was the one who was bemused. He couldn't take this intimacy with Alexandria Gascoyne any further. She could be a friend here and now, but not later. The differences in their stations were too great. The next weeks would be difficult, being in such close proximity to her with no other women to distract him. He'd have to keep reminding himself that half of her attraction might be just that.

He was glad she chose that moment to finally speak again because his thoughts were making him grim.

"I know you must be sorry your friends left," she

said, turning and seeing his expression. "You'll be able to join them again soon."

He laughed. "You think I'm the same age as Kit or Rob? Poor little boy, is that it? Don't worry. I've been apart from my friends before. I miss them, but I promise you I miss walking more."

"You'll be thumping around on crutches soon. But not for a while," she added hastily, when she saw his azure eyes light. "You can't try until you're almost healed. That won't be for at least a few more weeks." She took pity on how disappointed he looked. "These things take time, and at that, you're lucky. Did you know Dr. Pace said that in his father's day they'd have taken your leg off because of the injuries you had? Isn't that dreadful? They didn't even try to set them back then! You're lucky you live in modern times. He feels he got the alignment just right and there should be no lasting harm—*if* you're careful."

"You *do* think I'm Rob's age." He chuckled. "I'll be good, I promise. I'm itching to walk but I'm also sorry I have to continue to be a burden to you. You haven't had a minute's rest or peace since I fell off my horse and landed myself on you and your charity."

"You're not a burden. I'm sorry you were hurt, but the truth is you've livened up our lives considerably." Her cheeks turned pink, even in the fading light.

"Well, it's true," she added defensively. "I didn't mean to say it that way, but you're right that we haven't had a moment's rest since you came. And it's been fascinating for me and the boys! Our lives just seemed to be streaming by with the seasons. We didn't know that until you arrived. So it's a fair trade, I think, because we needed to be shaken up and shown that there's a wider world out there. The boys are learning something about being gentlemen too, and in this brief time I've seen more people than I have in a long time."

"Why is that?" he asked bluntly.

Alexandria hesitated, not because he'd been so direct but because she wanted to answer him directly. It was a dangerous time of day. If she wanted safety she should light the lamps; evening was drawing in around them and secrets could be more easily spoken in the shadows. But there were times when secrets had to be spoken. She valued his opinion, respected his judgment, and thought of him as an equal though she knew very well that in the way the world judged things, he was far above her touch. But they were far from the world, after all, and he'd become a friend. She hadn't had a friend in a very long time.

He wasn't precisely a friend, either, she realized, looking at him and seeing how still he was, awaiting her answer, as though it mattered to him. She could scarcely believe it really did. That was the crux of it. She could never be completely comfortable with him because she never forgot he was a man, and a powerful nobleman at that. In fact, if he were on his feet she might have been mute with awe and uneasiness in his presence. His injury had cut him down to a size she could deal with—only just. Because of that she'd discovered he was everything her spirit yearned toward.

She gazed at him now, wondering why he affected her so profoundly. His face wasn't handsome. Better, it was unforgettable, filled with character and vivid masculine appeal. He was spare and lean, but she never doubted his power. He might never play a Romeo, but she could see him in the role of that seductive wizard,

Oberon. He was intelligent, brave, gallant, witty, and humane.

She felt safe with him because she couldn't imagine him ever touching her, though the thought of it occurred to her whenever she looked at him, and made her hope her cheeks didn't turn pink, the way they did whenever she indulged in shameful fantasy. Half her embarrassment was because she was also sure her fantasies were pathetic. Her experience of intimacy was limited and her knowledge of men who weren't too young or too old almost nil. She knew very well the man before her was everything she could never aspire to. He was titled, wealthy, and remote. That remoteness came from more than his upbringing; there was a part of him she was sure was inaccessible. It certainly was to her.

She never expected to hear from him again after he left. When he was gone he'd be gone forever. That was sad, but maybe not so bad, because that made confidences between them possible in a way they couldn't be if they were to see each other again. There couldn't be anything between them except, perhaps, a confidence?

It had to be done slowly, it had to be eased into, it wasn't a thing she could say straight out.

"Why is that?" she echoed his words softly, avoiding his eyes now, staring down into the growing violet shadows again. "Why don't I see more people? Because we live far from everyone else."

"There's a school nearby, surely there are schoolmasters' wives to befriend, and unattached young schoolmasters for you to beguile as well?"

He saw the edges of her lips curl. "My dear sir," she

said so quietly he had to hold his breath to hear, "I've had quite enough of living with a schoolmaster. Besides," she said a little more brightly, a little *too* brightly, "Mr. Gascoyne was not the most popular man, even among his peers. Those he was popular with are not those I'm comfortable with, and I've little in common with other men hereabouts who might be interested in me."

Her smile grew bitter and her voice became clipped as she repeated the words that had been flung at her that day she'd left for her ill-fated trip to Bath. "I'm educated far above my station, and that station is comprised wholly of that education, and my youth, which is fast disappearing."

"How old are you?" he asked as quietly as she'd spoken, so as not to break this strange moment of intimacy, because he believed she had something else to say that he had to hear.

"Four and twenty," she said. "On the shelf in our little community, and even in London, I'd think."

Her calm composure had always puzzled him. Now he saw it was a hard-won thing. She held herself straight, but seemed so vulnerable standing alone in the twilight he wished he had the use of his legs so he could go to her, put an arm around her and comfort her, even though he knew it would be the worst thing he could do.

"But surely you have more family, friends, people to introduce you to some society that would be more comfortable for you?" he asked, thinking of men who had some education and manners and enough money to live on, who could marry wherever they wished. Vicars, retired army men, merchants, farmers, and such.

"I don't think that's possible," she said.

"Why?" he asked without preamble, because he knew in that moment she'd tell him, and in another she might not.

She drew a breath, opened her lips—and suddenly stopped as she saw something below taking shape, something that came racing out of the violet twilight. "My goodness!" she exclaimed with a mixture of chagrin and relief, "you must be the most popular man in England! You've got another guest coming. He must be here to see you, he's a stranger to me." She peered down at the horseman emerging from the mists, galloping toward the house. "Either that," she said with a chuckle, "or we're being invaded by the Vikings again!"

"Vikings?"

"Well, his hair is fair, and he's very large, and he's riding at breakneck speed. He's a tall blond man on a very big white horse."

Drum gave a gruff laugh. "A Viking, indeed. He claims descent from them and fought like one when he was in the army. But don't worry, he doesn't need to fight anymore, he can charm any treasures he wants from his victims. It's Eric Ford," he said with exasperated humor. "Lady Dalton's brother. Yes, she's dark as a gypsy and he's fair as the sun, but they're half-siblings and wholly devoted to each other. She did say he'd be coming. I didn't know it would be so soon. I'm sorry, you must have had your fill of my friends today."

She absently touched a hand to her hair as she stared down at their new guest. "Uh, no," she said inattentively, "no trouble at all. I'll just go down and send him up."

Drum watched with a faint frown as she hurried from the room to welcome the tall blond stranger to her house.

"Miss Gascoyne," Eric Ford said, his big hand swallowing hers after she greeted him at the door and introduced herself. "I've missed my sister, haven't I? Yet I can't be sorry about anything now that I've met you."

Alexandria looked up at him—and up. She knew Drum was tall, though she'd never seen him standing upright. But this fellow was huge. He wasn't fat, but rather large in every dimension, and wide of bone and breadth. He was casually but correctly dressed in a snug jacket that showed a remarkable expanse of masculine shoulders, his long muscular legs were encased in tan breeches and shining half boots. Thick, honey-blond hair framed a classically handsome tanned face, and there was a warm look in his hazel eyes as he smiled down at her.

He positively took Alexandria's breath away, and so she immediately discounted every compliment he paid her. Men such as he didn't need to flirt with females such as she, she reasoned, so it must be his common way of communicating with women.

But the seriousness of his visit must have occurred to him, because his smile vanished and he immediately asked about Drum. "Is the earl all right? He's still here, isn't he?"

"He's fine. He had a rough fall, but he's mending. Please go right up, his room's at the top of the stairs. Have you come far? Are you hungry?" she asked belatedly, realizing it must take a lot to fill up such a big fellow.

"I'm always hungry," he said with a laugh, "but don't trouble yourself, I'll do."

"No trouble," she said, flushing, realizing he still hadn't released her hand. When she looked down, he saw the direction of her glance and let her hand go. She quickly took it back. "Go on up, I'll get refreshments," she told him. "Some chicken, perhaps? Or ham? Or a few slices of meat pie? Would you prefer ale, tea, or wine?"

"Yes, thank you," he said, grinning at her, before he went up the stair.

"Well, trust you to come out of disaster so sweetly," Eric said as he strolled into the room. "Fell into a pot of honey, did you? Faith, she is a little honey, isn't she? Gads! Your leg, is it?" he asked, circling Drum's chair, eyeing the splinted leg that was propped on a stool with the professional interest of an ex-soldier. "You've got a good excuse to stay here forever then."

"She's respectable," Drum said curtly, snapping his dressing gown over his leg like a spinster covering a hint of ankle, "and everyone's little to you. It's my leg and my head, and I'm lucky it wasn't more. It could easily have been. Someone shot at me, Eric," he said soberly. "They tell me it must have been some lad taking potshots at anything that moved. I've seen too much in my life to be entirely comfortable with that. I don't know. That's the point. I want to know, but I'm fastened here as though bolted to the floor." He pounded the arm of his chair in frustration.

Eric raised one tawny brow.

"My horse fell on me. Don't look so perturbed, he's fine," Drum added with a thin smile. "He broke my leg in two places, so it's taking an eternity to mend. My head's better, though the doctor acts as though it will fall off if I nod too hard. I'm glad you came, I need someone to cover the ground for me and look for a hint of what happened and who did it. You're an old trooper, with a nose as well as an eye. Speaking of which, leave her alone. Unless you're serious, and you never are."

"But I'm getting older," Eric said, propping one wide shoulder against the wall by the window. "Seriousness comes on a fellow like gray hair, nothing one morning—a full crop the next. I'll stay out of your way if you want, though."

Drum's face grew still, then his expression grew haughty. "My interest is that of a grateful patient. I just wanted to let you know she's a country girl and not up to snuff, and you're a consummate flirt. But do as you wish, you always do anyway. Still, I'd rather you did my work than court my hostess right now."

"Oh, I can do both," Eric said with a broad smile. "And I'm happy to. I've been at loose ends lately. Maybe it *is* time I settled down and raised a litter of my own. But until then I'll play Bow Street Runner for you. Have you anyone in mind? Anyone with a reason to put paid to your existence?"

"No more than most men." Drum shrugged.

"But you've got more money and power than most men," Eric argued. "Come, you must have thought of some possibilities. Even a saint can put someone's nose out of joint."

"*Especially* a saint, I'd think," Drum said with a laugh. "How do you think they got to be saints? Putting noses out of joint is a requirement for martyrdom. I don't aspire to sainthood, though, so I think we can put that to rest."

"Right, so who's harboring a grudge against you? Who has reason to? Someone who owes you so much they'd like to see the debt canceled—immediately? Anyone with a wandering wife he thinks wandered into your bed? Or a daughter he thinks you jilted? It might be someone beneath your notice too. Think back, have you dismissed any servants recently? There might be a disgruntled one brooding about some supposed injustice."

Drum gave a huff of a laugh. "Lovely to know what you think of me! No. I'm no one's banker and I don't go in for wild wagers. I don't entertain other men's wives because I believe in the old adage: Do unto others. I make it a point never to warm a married man's bed. I pay for all my pleasures and I don't play with innocents."

He thought of one particular innocent he was tempted to play with and went on quickly. "*And*, strange as it seems, I notice my servants. I pick them carefully and pension them off handsomely when they retire from my service. No. I think my attacker, if there was one, had to be someone who knew me from my days working against Napoleon. All my moral rules were suspended then. You know how it is, Eric; it's the same for a soldier as a spy. You do what you have to when you must. I made some richly deserved enemies. If it's one of them, he's also well trained. That's why I sent for you. You could do me much more good than Bow Street."

"I hope I can," Eric said. "At least, I'll try. Where do I stay? There's hardly room for me to stand in here.

This is a charming example of early English architecture, but I'll get a permanent crick in my neck if I don't fold double, though I'd be able to see your Miss Gascoyne better than way. So," he said, noting with interest Drum's sour expression at the mention of flirting with his hostess, "shall I pitch camp in the open, like I did in the old days?"

"No need," Drum said, "There's the barn. You don't have to sleep with the livestock, there are comfortable rooms in the loft."

"The barn?" Eric asked. "The one I couldn't help seeing as I rode up? The one with the strange new excrescence protruding from its side, fresh sawdust still seeping from it? Your handiwork, I heard in what passes for a town around here."

"Mine," Drum admitted glumly. "Well, I had to build it if only to provide conversation in this part of the world, didn't I? The truth is I needed constant care at first and I couldn't run Ally—Miss Gascoyne—off her feet, or let my men sleep in the damp. It just didn't turn out looking the way I thought it would. Yes, I'd like you to stay on. You'll be comfortable there."

"Hannibal's army would be," Eric commented, looking out the window. "Complete with elephants. Oh," he said, turning as Alexandria entered the room carrying a laden tray, "you shouldn't have brought that up, I'd be only too happy to come down."

She smiled. "But I thought you'd prefer keeping the earl company."

"So he would," Drum said abruptly. "I've things to talk over with him too. Thank you," he added belatedly.

"You're welcome," she said, shooting him a puzzled

look. He wasn't usually so curt. "Are you hungry? Thirsty? Would you like something too?"

"No thank you," Drum said.

"Then if you need anything, just let me know," Alexandria said, and turned. She spun right around again as she heard a great clatter and commotion in the yard. She and Eric went to the window and looked out. They covered it so completely Drum couldn't see a thing even when he levered himself up and craned his neck to try to get a glimpse of what was causing the hubbub.

"Oh, my," Alexandria breathed.

"Oh, yes," Eric said.

"If someone would care to tell me what's going on?" Drum asked in a pinched voice, seeing nothing but the two heads so close together as they stared out the window.

There was amusement and a note of sympathy in Eric's voice when he spoke. "Your father seems to have arrived. I thought it was the king at first, until I recognized the crest on the coach. It's much bigger than George's. He's got two other coaches following, and enough men to invade the entire coast. Ready to build another wing on the barn?"

"Oh, lord," Drum said wearily, sinking back in his chair. "I'm sorry," he told Alexandria.

"What for?" she asked, her thoughts racing. She wished Mrs. Tooke was back because she didn't know how she was going to feed such a horde by herself.

Drum fell silent. She didn't know yet, but she would, and he was even more sorry about that.

Eleven

ALEXANDRIA WOULD HAVE KNOWN THE MAN AT her door was Drum's father even if she hadn't been told who he was. He was tall and slender too, and wore that signature great narrow hawk's nose the way other men might wear a coronet. He carried his silver-haired head high so that he had to look down at all in his path, no matter how tall they were. His face was all crags and angles, the skin stretched tight except for lines at the mouth, as Drum's would be when he reached middle age. But those lips were thinner than Drum's, or at least, that mouth was held yardstick straight. And the eyes were as gray as flint. They lacked the startling beauty of his son's azure gaze, and had none of his humanity, either.

He was immaculately clad in black and white, the only notes of color the glow of the chased silver head on the walking stick he held and the gleam of the gold quizzing glass in his gloved hand. At least he didn't raise the glass to look at her, because that would have made Alexandria very angry indeed.

This was a hard, proud man, she thought, a man who considered those things a virtue. She recognized the breed. Mr. Gascoyne, a small, wiry commoner with a face more simian than human, would nonetheless have understood this nobleman perfectly.

"I've come to see my son," he said, slanting his head in a sketch of a bow—or ducking it so he could step under her low lintel. "I heard he was here."

He didn't even bother to ask her name, much less introduce himself as he stepped in. Alexandria felt her temper rise. She mightn't be in the habit of hobnobbing with dukes, but she'd observed the greatest snob in all England, and knew how to treat unruly boys *and* rude gentlemen.

"I am Miss Gascoyne," she said haughtily, blocking his way, so he couldn't march in to her house. "Since he couldn't be moved after his mishap, the earl's been staying on here with us."

He checked. One eyebrow rose. "I am Winterton," he said, inclining his head in what certainly was a bow. "May I come in? And may I see my son, please?"

There was only a shade of uncertainty in his voice when he said the word *son*. But it was enough to tell Alexandria that the man might be moved by more than he let on. She relented. She dipped her head and stepped aside. "Yes, of course, your grace. He's in the room at the top of the stair. His friend Eric Ford is with him at the moment, but I know he'll be glad to see you."

He hesitated. "Is he well?"

She smiled. "He's doing very well, your grace. He's broken a leg and injured his head, but all is mending, though not as fast as he'd like."

"Sounds very like him," he said. He stepped into the little hall, showing that his walking stick was for effect only, because his stride was sure-footed. A thickset, middle-aged man dressed in black began to follow him.

"I beg your pardon," Alexandria said huffily, because she hadn't invited this man in and was beginning to feel her little cottage had swinging doors. "I don't believe there's room for more than yourself upstairs, your grace. Eric Ford is a very large man."

"Major Ford is enormous, I grant," the duke said with a thin smile. "But there must be room for the doctor, my dear. He's come all the way from London to examine my son."

He made it sound as though Drum had been taken care of by a blacksmith until now, Alexandria thought angrily. "Dr. Pace set his leg immediately after the accident," she said, folding her hands in her apron to keep them from shaking. "If he hadn't, and done it perfectly, too, your son would be in much worse condition. As it is, the doctor says he's coming along beautifully. He visits your son every day. In fact, he's due back any moment now."

"Good," the duke said, and went up the stair. "Coming, Doctor?" he asked over his shoulder.

"I'll wait," the doctor said. "No sense crowding the patient or alienating his nurse."

Nurse! Alexandria thought in outrage. She wished she'd had on her best gown—she wished she had a best gown to have on. But she calmed herself, realizing a better gown would only have made them think she was a more highly paid nurse.

She sighed and asked the doctor into the kitchen, offering him something to drink, because she supposed she might have been called something much worse. Drum's guests had done that before, after all.

"Father!" Drum said. He tried to stand.

His father waved a hand. "Don't be absurd," he snapped. "Stay seated. If you could walk, why would you be here?" He peeled off a glove and nodded to Eric. "Major, I give you good day, sir. How odd," he continued as he paced to the window and glanced out. "I heard, when I stopped off the highway to rest the horses, that your cousin and his wife, and their friends the Ryders, *and* your firebrand of a soldier friend Dalton and his wife stopped here to see you today. And here's the major. But I had not a word of your injury from you, and had to prise it out of your staff."

"I told no one," Drum said, sitting back. "They discovered it for themselves."

"Perhaps because they are such excellent spies. I grant you that. But I am not so good at subterfuge," the duke said coldly. "Nor did I believe I'd have a reason. I would think my only son and heir would let his father know if he were on the brink of death."

Drum laughed. "Consider, Father, if I were on the brink of death, how could I tell you? But if I weren't, why trouble you? I'd thought to write a note when I was recovered. Why vex you unnecessarily?"

"Because you would expect the same from me," the duke said brusquely, turning to survey his son.

Drum nodded. "A very good point. I'll remember it in future."

"One hopes you'll not have to. Tell me what happened, if you please."

Drum told the bare details quickly. "Eric will be hot on the scent now, so we may have more answers soon," he concluded.

"Good," the duke said. "Now what about this Miss Gascoyne? She's very young, surely, to be mistress of this house. Where is the rest of her family?"

"Her parents are dead," Drum said simply. "It's only Alexandria and her brothers."

His father's thin brows went up at the way Drum called his hostess by her first name.

"Don't worry, sir," Drum said with a small smile. "We've covered all the decencies, with a respectable older female staying on here while I'm in residence."

The duke frowned. "She lives here by herself otherwise?"

"With her three younger brothers. But I assure you all the proprieties have been observed. In fact, that grotesque wing to the barn was put up by my men so that they could stay on and help with the chore of having me here."

"Had you known her before your accident?" the duke asked, too mildly.

"What?" Drum laughed. "You never cease to amaze me, Father. At least your estimation of my morals never does. No. I wasn't on my way to visit her when my accident occurred, either. In fact, I'd never clapped an eye or any other part of my immaculate person on her until she dragged me bleeding from the road where I'd landed myself. After that? I can promise you she has no designs on my virtue. She saved my life. That's all. I've discovered it's poor payment to suspect her of any ulterior motives."

"So you believe that barn you built her is just payment?" his father asked. "No, I'm not omniscient," he added to Drum's wary look. "I know you built it, in little more than a week, at that. It's all they're speaking of in the blacksmith's shop I paused at on the way here."

"If you'd stayed a moment longer you'd have realized that's all they had to talk about. That shop is almost the sum of the town, the boys say. Ally's brother's, I mean." Drum corrected himself. He smiled at his father's expression. "Your pardon. It's what the boys call her and I sometimes slip into that too."

"So long as that's the only thing you slip into."

Drum shook his head. "I'm flattered by your estimation of my abilities. I've a cracked head and a shattered leg, I'm staying with an utterly respectable woman in a crowded house where no sneeze can go unremarked, and you think I can slink out and seduce her? Thank you, I'm honored."

"I was merely wondering if she would slink in to accomplish the same thing," his father mused.

Drum sat up straight, his expression suddenly severe. "I think if you knew her you'd apologize for that, sir."

His father returned the look with a calm one. "Would I? Perhaps. Forgive me. My mind runs to matrimonial thoughts concerning you these days. Perhaps I attribute that idiosyncrasy to all others too."

"Precisely what got me here." Drum laughed, relaxing. "I was thinking about your lecture on marriage instead of watching where I was going, so the accident, or ambush, caught me off guard."

"Were you?" his father asked with sudden interest. "Any lady in particular, if I may inquire? The lady Annabelle, as I suggested? Or another?"

Eric, forgotten by the window, looked at Drum with sudden interest.

"Lady Annabelle? The toast of London Town?" Drum asked wryly. "How can I forget? You extolled everything from her toes to her eyelashes. The way you concentrate on her makes me wonder if I should be the one to consider her as wife—or you."

"Were I ten years younger, that question would be neither insulting or ridiculous, whichever you meant it to be." The duke waved away any protest Drum tried to make. "As it is, the lady is beautiful, accomplished, wealthy, titled, and charming. She'd suit me very well as daughter-in-law, and mother to my grandchildren."

"Don't sell yourself short," Drum said. "You're fitter than many men half your age, and richer than most of any age. You're eminently eligible yourself. Come to think of it, she'd be a very agreeable wife for you, and could certainly produce a better heir than me. She *is* beautiful, clever, and poised. But I know her and not just her reputation—which is also that of being a heart-breaker, by the way. They say she became a jilt and a flirt because her true love was thwarted when her ideal married another. As it happens, it was thwarted twice—by two of my friends. The two who were here today. First she was passed over by Damon Ryder, the idol of her youth, and then by the consolation prize she chose for herself, Rafe Dalton."

In a gesture eerily like that of his father, Drum put

up one hand to prevent any comment the duke might make. "Please don't think they were villains. It wasn't through any fault of theirs. They married elsewhere, where their hearts led them. She isn't a villainess either, just spoiled and self-involved. But since I know her through her failed campaigns for Dalton and Ryder and because I also interceded for them when I had to, there's no love lost—or to be gained—between us. The point is that a romance between us would be highly improbable. I see no reason why it wouldn't be fine for you, though."

Drum glanced over to Eric to see his reaction to his outrageous jest, and caught Eric's expression before he could conceal it. Was that a flicker of despair, or quickly throttled anger? Did his friend's interests lie with the lovely Annabelle? They'd met, after all, they did know each other. Annabelle was anxious to wed now, and probably eager to marry well to show the world that she could. If Eric had his intentions fixed there, a duke would be heavy competition. Drum suddenly realized it wasn't just a joke. His father *would* be a catch for a woman who wanted a title, an even better catch for one who had been crushed by the disappointments of young love.

"But times change and so do people, there's no reason I can't see if things have changed," Drum added quickly, to squelch any interest in the lady he might have aroused in his father's mind. "I'll call on her when I get back on my feet and back in London. Who knows what might happen?"

His father didn't answer immediately. He stood deep in thought. He cocked his head to one side. "Who knows, indeed?" he answered absently.

*   *   *

Twilight had given way to a soft blue evening by the
time Eric finished stowing his belongings in the barn
and came out to see how his friend was doing. Vin, Kit,
and Rob trailed after him like a string of ducklings,
gabbling at him as they did. The Duke of Winterton,
standing at Drum's window, could see the huge fair-
haired man and the three flaxen-headed boys in the
wash of golden lantern light that spilled down from the
barn's new windows. He watched the merry quartet for
something to do, his hands clasped behind his back as
the doctor finished his examination of Drum.

"Well, when can he leave?" the duke asked without
turning his head.

"In a month, at the earliest, perhaps," the doctor said
as he rose from kneeling beside Drum. "Sorry, my
lord," he told Drum, who was looking white-faced and
thin-lipped after the ordeal. "I had to be thorough and
that can't have been pleasant. But I'm satisfied. Whoever put you back together did a neat job of it. I
couldn't have done better. Now you must let your
bones knit, and there's no way even a superior physician like myself can help you with that."

The duke's expression didn't change. "So long?" he
mused. "Surely there must be a way we can transport
him before then?"

"How?" the doctor asked. "By having him fly? I
can't think of any other way to get him out safely. The
roads have ruts and potholes, hidden pitfalls everywhere that can cause even the best coaches to shake
and sway. We can't chance undoing all the good that's
been done. A bone moving from its proper place would
be undetected untii the earl tried to stand again. No,

here he stays, your grace, unless you want to chance permanent damage."

Now the duke turned. His expression was glacial. "You smile, sir?" he asked Drum icily, when he saw his reaction. "So happy to remain here then?"

"So unaccustomed to hearing anyone say no to you," Drum said. "I marvel. I don't think I've ever heard it before."

His father didn't have a chance to answer because the room was invaded.

"Oh, don't tell us Drum's going to have to leave!" Rob begged the doctor as he bounded in, followed by his brothers.

"Rob!" Vic shouted, his face growing ruddy at the look the tall, gray-haired man by the window gave them, his gaze going up and down them as though they'd come in without bothering to put on clothing. "Mind your manners, you haven't been introduced."

"Easily remedied," Drum said. "Father, Doctor— these are my hosts, in size order, Vic, Kit, and the hasty little fellow is Rob. Boys, this is my father, the Duke of Winterton, and Dr. Raines, who came all the way from London to see me. The doctor's impressed that I'm still alive. I'm impressed that I am too, after his examination." He shot the doctor a bright look. "If I've healed well it's because these fellows saw to it I never got depressed."

"A merry heart is the best medicine," the doctor agreed, as the boys bowed to their new guests.

"These three could have a dead man walking," Eric commented from behind them.

"It was Ally who did all the work," Rob protested.

"Which will be undone if someone doesn't leave

soon," Alexandria said from the hallway, where she stood on tiptoe trying to look in the room. "Mrs. Tooke's home and Dr. Pace is coming up. Boys, make your good-nights. I've brought a tray for our patient but there isn't even room to bring it in, much less put it down!"

The boys bowed again and began to leave. "I'll be back in the morning, Drum!" Rob called as his brothers pushed him out the door.

"Try to keep you out!" Drum laughed.

"They call you Drum?" his father asked incredulously, as though they were alone in the room.

Alexandria spoke before Drum could answer. "That's my fault, your grace. You see, it was the name the earl muttered when he was half-conscious, and the one the boys took to calling him. We're more casual here in the countryside, but I never should have allowed that to continue. I should have corrected them."

"You did," Drum reminded her. "I countermanded that order. Nonsense for them to call me 'my lord' when I was dependent on them for my very life."

"Nonetheless I should have stopped it." She bent to put the tray on the table beside him. Her voice was steady and calm, but Drum saw her hands shake as she set the tray down. "Is it true?" she asked him, looking up into his eyes. "You're leaving us?"

Her face bore a look of mild inquiry. But her eyes were on his as she straightened, and she held her breath until he answered. He gazed back at her, his own gaze as deep and melancholy blue as the new night. He shook his head, his expression sad.

She took in a sharp breath.

"No, poor lady," he said, with a small smile, "I'm

not allowed to leave yet. I'm so sorry, but it looks like they'll only let me go when I can waltz down the stairs with you."

She smiled back at him with relief she couldn't hide. "That's the new fad in London? Waltzing on stairs? Then I'm very glad to be in the countryside."

"As am I," Drum laughed.

The doctor grinned at them, Eric watched with interest, but the duke looked from one of them to the other, and frowned.

His frown was nothing to the scowl Dr. Pace wore as he marched into the room. He didn't waste a moment with Drum, he wasn't interested in the duke. All his attention was focused on the other physician. "Well, sir," he said without preamble after he was introduced, "what have you to say about our patient?"

"What I already said," the other doctor replied, "that I don't think I could have done better myself."

"Indeed?" Dr. Pace rocked back on his heels. "Well, well. Thank you, that's very good to hear."

"I'm pleased you two have done so well," Mrs. Tooke said from the doorway, "but it is late, Dr. Pace, and your wife, poor dear, is half asleep in the kitchen and begs to go home."

"Very well, Mrs. Tooke," Pace said. "I think you've had enough of doctors for one night, sir," he told Drum, eyeing his pallor. "You're doing well, but you won't continue to if we keep pulling at you. I'll see you in the morning. Good-night."

"Yes, good-night, Drummond," the duke said abruptly. "I have to get to my lodgings for the night too. Are you coming, Dr. Raines?" he asked as he strode to the door without waiting for an answer. But he halted abruptly when he saw Mrs. Tooke.

She looked back at him steadily, her eyes strangely sad and amused at the same time. He frowned, looking puzzled. He tilted his head to the side. "Mrs. Tooke?" he asked in a strange voice. "But surely I know you?"

"Surely you do," she said, dipping a curtsy. "I am— or was—Rosalind Usborne. But that was many years ago."

"Rosalind?" he asked, astonished. "But—*you* are *Mrs. Tooke*?"

She nodded, dropping her gaze. "Yes, my lord. I married Leon Tooke, remember? The young man who came to sell a horse to my father, and stayed to take me home with him? Possibly not," she said softly. "All most people remember was the scandal of it and not his name at all."

The duke's high cheekbones were ruddy. "I do remember now. The name didn't signify at first. I heard you were widowed, I'm sorry for your loss. My condolences. How have you been apart from that sad circumstance?" he asked, his usual bland expression back in place.

"I am well. And you, sir?"

"As you see." He waved one hand in a sweeping bow. "I flourish, the wicked always do. But thank you for your part in this, I see now that Drummond couldn't have had better luck and care."

"It was Alexandria who did it all," she said, meeting his eyes steadily now. "I merely volunteered to help her."

"Yes, well. You've done me a favor too and I'm grateful. If there's anything I can do for you in turn I hope you will let me know."

"My dear sir," she said, holding her head up higher, "I need no reward."

He nodded and sketched a bow. Now there was a distinct coolness in his attitude. "I must leave," he told Drum. "The doctor and I took lodgings at a fair distance from here, the closest available were an hour's drive away. I too think you need your rest, almost as much as I need my own. But I'll be back in the morning," he added with a note in his voice that was almost a threat, looking down his long nose at Mrs. Tooke, then pointedly at Alexandria, and then back to his son.

Twelve

"**M**UCH BETTER!" DRUM SAID WITH ENTHUSI-asm as Grimes carefully helped him lower himself to his chair again the next morning. "Why didn't I think of that?"

"If I can't heal you as well as Dr. Pace did, the least I can do is make you comfortable," Dr. Raines said with satisfaction.

"I should have thought of it," Dr. Pace said with chagrin.

"No, I should have," Grimes said sadly.

"Don't blame yourself, doctor, you did quite enough. And you're used to healthy men, Grimes," Drum told them. "But what a difference. Such a simple thing and such a relief," he marveled, then laughed. "God! I'll never mock the elderly again. Who'd have thought I'd ever get to the point when a few more cushions under my arse and a few beneath my leg could transform my day? Now I can look out the window without straining my neck, and it's opened my world. It's as good as a trip abroad."

He looked down at the yard, and could see it fully for the first time since he'd been brought to the cottage. He flinched. The barn was even worse now that he saw the whole property, but it was a pretty place, even so.

He finally got a look at the landscape surrounding the house. The garden in front was neatly tended, the lawn that sloped toward the lane was scythed, the drive neatly raked, the bordering hedges trimmed and showing the first peeks of pink blossoms. It was rural but tamed, and charming. The morning sunlight glinted off blue water in the distance, the pond the boys had mentioned.

Best of all, he could see everyone's comings and goings now. His men were exercising his horses. Alexandria was watering her garden. She wore her pink gown, but no bonnet, so he could see the sunlight spinning sparkling strands of gold in her glossy auburn hair. He smiled and raised a hand to wave, and slowly lowered it again. She wouldn't see his salute because Eric came striding out of the barn toward her.

Tall, broad, fit, his overlong honey hair wheaten in the bright light, Eric towered over Alexandria. Copper and gold looked very well together, Drum thought, his expression sharpening, seeing how she had to raise her hand to shade her eyes as she looked up at Eric and smiled—and smiled. Drum could see the radiance of it even from above.

"Yes, the barn was a mistake," his father commented, watching Drum's own smile fading. "Perhaps you can pull it down before you leave."

"No." Drum was glad his father had misunderstood his unease. "They need the extra room and have already found a dozen ways to use it. Maybe I'll redesign the place, though."

"I doubt she'll let you," his father said, his eyes on his son as Drum kept watching the couple beneath him. "She's a very determined young woman. The doctor and I woke early and left the inn at first light. I couldn't quit the place early enough! I only hope I didn't take more permanent reminders of it home with me," he added, brushing at his sleeve.

"So we arrived here earlier than we had said we would," the duke went on. "Your hostess made us cool our heels in her parlor until your man finished getting you dressed. Oh, she was polite and deferential, she gave us breakfast too, but she wouldn't let us come up until Grimes told her all was in readiness."

"Her sense of my dignity, I suppose. Not that I've much of it left anymore. It seems I've achieved instant old age and instant infancy," he muttered. "I'm helpless. It's not pleasant. No, and it's not your fault either, Grimes. I can bear pain, but this dependency is galling."

He kept watching the couple below. "I have to sit up here and stew, and wait, and rely on everyone else to bring me news and food, and company. I can't walk or ride, or even get downstairs to sit in the sunlight. Not to mention the indignity of bathing, and such . . ." He gave a cough of a laugh. "I never used to complain so much either. No wonder old men and babies get so cranky!"

"Doctors, Grimes, if you're done here now, could you give me some time alone with my son?" the duke asked. "I'm going to leave shortly and I'd like to give him some fatherly admonitions and advice. You can see him with your instructions when I've done, Doctors. If you'd be so kind?"

But the three men were already going out the door.

The duke waited until the door closed behind them. He passed the time watching Drum watching his friend and his hostess in the front yard. "She seems to like him," the duke commented, keeping his eye on his son. "She could do worse. Although I fear the major could do much better."

Drum's head spun around, he fixed his father with his bright blue stare.

"Don't call for a second to arrange the details of the duel," the duke said calmly. "Not only will I never duel with an invalid, I only speak the truth. She has no portion, family, or position. Ford isn't nobility, but he comes from an old family, has some money, and those remarkable looks of his, of course. He can aim higher."

"You've become a marriage broker," Drum said in a dispassionate voice to match his father's. "How very interesting. Most men in your position would try their hands at collecting butterflies or firearms, or ancient armor. But to each his own."

"I merely comment on what I see," his father said, unperturbed. "That was the point of my asking to be alone with you now. I'd best be brief, before we're interrupted again. This place may be remote but it's less private than a street corner in London. I wonder why you complain about being shut away. I'd think that actually being alone awhile would be a blessing around here."

"Alone and abandoned are two different things."

"You're the darling of the household," his father re-
torted. "Which is why I have some words of warning
for you." He paced a step or two, pausing when the
clear sound of melodious laughter floated up to the
window. Eric had said something to make Alexandria
laugh. Drum's attention wandered to the window
again.

"You complain about feeling alone and disenfran-
chised here," the duke said. "That's true and it's cause
for complaint. Being alone too much changes a man's
perceptions. I've read that prisoners of war have sometimes fancied themselves in league with their captors
after a while, even their torturers, developing a genuine
affection for them. Indeed, I've heard that men can become fond of certain rats if they're kept in a dark dun-
geon with them long enough. A great warrior became
fascinated by a spider in his cell, making a pet of it,
they say. All manner of strange infatuations can form
in a man's mind when he's helpless and alone."

Drum looked up at him at last.

"Familiarity breeds an aura of content," the duke
went on, "And it can become easy to mistake gratitude
for something more. You're vulnerable now, whether
you know it or not. The woman *is* kind-hearted and
lovely. But you know other such, you have the acquaintance of dozens of ladies who are more spectacularly lovely. In fact, I wonder if you'd even have started
up a conversation with Miss Gascoyne if you'd come
across her in London. Don't look so insulted; consider
it. Would you have?"

He took another turn around the room. "Then too,
there's the matter of celibacy, understandably difficult
for a young man. And one mustn't underestimate the

competitive spirit, which was always strong in you. It may even be an excess of charity since the poor chit has little and you, as a gentleman, would of course be impelled to gallantry. Whatever it is, it's obvious you've become involved with your hostess even if you've never touched her."

Drum sat very still.

"I credit your good sense enough to know you'd never consider marrying her," his father said, continuing to pace. "A misalliance is more than a social error. Look at poor Mrs. Tooke. As Rosalind Usborne she was a girl with the world at her feet. Now she's estranged from her family and works like a peasant for her daily bread. I shouldn't like to live with her regrets. It isn't just a matter of money. She's cut off from all she knew, forever. A man who married beneath himself would feel the same way once his infatuation passed, and marriage always puts an end to infatuation.

"Even if you're wise enough to avoid matrimony," the duke went on, "I wouldn't want to see you confusing the issue, and perhaps producing another sort of issue that might embarrass you one day. At least, Rosalind Tooke was honestly in love, I suppose that's some consolation to her now. This is very different. I very much doubt your heart is involved, but your sympathies and God knows what else is."

He paused, and raised a slim finger for silence. "You're a great prize, Drummond, even if you deny it. I just ask that you take care. I grant that the woman isn't angling for you, but she may have allies that are." Drum gazed at him with eyes so intense and cold that his father had to look away from that blistering stare. "I'm simply voicing my concerns," the duke added.

It was almost an apology, at least coming from his father.

"She isn't that sort of woman," Drum said softly. "I'm not that kind of man. I don't deny my attraction to her. I'm wounded, not dead. It's true we might not have met if I'd not been thrown literally at her feet, but we've more in common than my isolation. There is a certain fellow feeling too, our minds dovetail in matters of humor and taste. Still, I know my place, and hers. So does she. We're both adults, responsible ones. Hours or even weeks alone can't change that. She's got Eric Ford here now too. Unlike myself, he's a man with everything to offer her. His name and himself. There's something else."

Drum gave his father a sweet smile that emphasized the difference between them, because when he smiled they looked little alike. "You think I'm a prize, Father. Not everyone does. My name and money are my main attractions, and I never forget that. As for the rest? I'm clever. So what? I'm no Adonis, and women put great store in looks, even the sensible ones do. Well, but I absolve them for it, we men feel the same way about women, don't we? A woman with a beautiful heart is a lovely thing, but I've never known a man to lose his own head for one unless her face matched it, have you?

"No, my one real asset, aside from my title and fortune, is my charm, and well I know it. At the moment I don't even have much of that," Drum said with a wry grin. "Consider, I'm an invalid, confined to my bed and this chair, and cranky and tetchy to boot. Eric's a spectacularly handsome fellow, with the use of his legs and a very fine brain. But that's not the point. Even if Eric weren't here to divert her, even if she burned for me and I for her, you needn't worry about me forgetting myself, losing control, or doing something rash because I've fallen hopelessly in love. I've never been able to do that. It's why I'm still single. It is, I think, the great tragedy of my life."

His father's head came up. "I'm sorry to hear that," he said. "I'd consider it an asset."

"You never loved Mama to distraction?"

"Oh, I did. But I knew that I could, you see. I never let passion or whim steer my course in life, and I've never had cause to regret it. Neither should you. Some men come to love late. You've time to find a woman you can care for. No matter what you think, you've too much sympathy in your soul not to find yourself feeling affection for a woman you *can* take to wife."

Drum looked at his father in surprise. He'd never said anything half as kind to him.

"You have time, but you can't find a diamond unless you look for one. When you do return to London," the duke went on, "I urge you to reconsider Lady Annabelle. I believe she has a lot to offer. As a woman scorned, she'd certainly appreciate someone who cared for her now. If she's not to your taste, then consider Trelawney's daughter, or Maxwell's niece, or Lady Abbott's younger sister. I've been approached by the families and have investigated them. Any would suit."

"Like picking a race horse?" Drum asked, his eyebrows going up.

"Yes," his father said simply, "very like. I'm not being callous. Affection can come more easily once all other barriers have been hurdled. But it is a good comparison. Consider blood lines and temperament, appearance and cost. Then make an informed decision and see what happens. I can promise you they're all doing the same with you."

"Father," Drum said in exasperation, but didn't get a chance to say more because there was a tapping on the door. "Yes?" he called.

"I'm sorry to interrupt," Alexandria said from behind the door, "but it's time for your medicine."

"Are we done with paternal advice, Father?"

The duke nodded. "What more is there to say?"

"I can't imagine," Drum said, "and I'm very glad of it too. Come in, Alexandria," he called. "Our private conference is ended."

She opened the door and stepped in, bringing in a gust of fresh air scented with the wild perfume of the spring day with her. She wore her yellow gown and her smile was sunny too. "I've brought something for you to eat and drink to make you forget the taste of your medicine," Alexandria said. Her tray held a plate of iced cakes, biscuits, a dish of wild preserves and some wedges of cheese. A tiny vase holding stems of lily of the valley adorned the tray.

Drum watched with a bemused expression as she set the tray down beside him. She stepped back, surveyed her handiwork, and frowned. A few stems had rattled out of the vase because of the uneven weight of their creamy white bells. She bent to poke them back in the vase—just as he reached for a spoon. His hand brushed against the side of her breast.

They each jumped as though stung—only a fraction, only a centimeter. But she was usually so calm, and he so collected, that it seemed like they actually did leap. At least, Alexandria's heart did. And Drum recoiled as though he'd touched fire.

The duke's eyes narrowed.

"Give you good morning, your grace," Eric said as he strolled into the room. "What? Does a fellow have to break a limb to get some of those cakes? All I had was bacon, eggs, bread, kidneys, and ham for breakfast, nothing so rare and refined."

"But Mrs. Tooke just made them," Alexandria said with flustered haste.

"Those aren't the only savory things I see now that I didn't see at the breakfast table," Eric answered, smiling down at her with admiration. "What does a fellow have to do to get you to sit down to a meal with him?"

Drum sat up straighter. Eric glanced at him and their gazes locked.

The duke's head snapped higher. "I'll go down now," he said, "and have a word with the doctors."

By the time Drum's tray was cleared, with Eric's help, the duke was back in the room. He was followed by both doctors. Both were frowning. Drum was a little taken aback by their somber expressions.

"I've decided to take you home," the duke told Drum abruptly, raising a hand. "Yes, against the advice of both doctors. But with their consent. It's not advisable, but it is not impossible with the arrangements I will make. One seat will be taken out of the largest and best sprung carriage. That way you'll be able to lie flat. We'll install a makeshift bed for you and reinforce the splint on your leg with another splint strapped around it to support it. The whole will be wrapped in blankets and secured firmly so that if you're jolted, it will not affect your limb. It will be much like being borne home on a door, only more comfortable. We'll travel slowly

and carefully. Dr. Raines will accompany you. In this
way you will return home in one piece to recuperate
with your own full staff to assist you."

"This is very sudden," Drum said.

"It's very sensible," his father replied. "It's the only
sensible thing, in fact. Come, what's the point in vex-
ing Miss Gascoyne further? Crowding her house, dis-
rupting her life, upsetting her schedule, and putting
everyone here at sixes and sevens? Or in troubling
Mrs. Tooke any longer, displacing her from her family
and her life? You'll not lack for room or company or
diversion once you're in your own home again. I
thought of taking you to mine, but I think you'll do
better in London. Apart from the convenience of the
city, all the ton will be able visit you, all your friends. I
daresay it will be like recovering at your club. Much
more comfortable for everyone, all round. Don't you
think?"

Drum's glance flew to Alexandria. She looked as
shocked as he felt. It was wonderful to think of going
home, and yet at the same time it was strangely not. He
wasn't thrilled with the idea of being pushed along
London's streets like a babe in a pram. He wasn't anxious to go on exhibition, become the center of a group
of prattling poseurs and fribbles thinking they were
amusing him when they'd only give him a headache.
Or worse yet, becoming the unmoving target for a le-
gion of hopeful misses and their mamas.

He actually liked the quiet of the countryside, the
conversation of the boys. The boys would miss him;
he'd miss them and their nightly lessons, the long talks
with Alexandria. His mind scuttled away from that
thought as quickly as he'd recoiled from touching her

breast. How could he direct Eric in his search for who'd shot at him, he thought instead, and the barn, who'd see to the . . .

Drum was brought up short. His heart felt curiously leaden; he dreaded the thought of leaving here. That was proof enough. He was making excuses.

His father was right: He was enjoying this visit far too much. This little cottage had become his whole world and was blinding him to the real one. He had responsibilities and duties, and one of them, as a gentleman, was not enticing someone to whom he couldn't offer more than his company. There was no sense in such temptation for either of them.

Only one thing was certain. He belonged with his own kind. *If* it were possible.

"I think it would suit me fine," Drum said calmly, looking at his father. "If, that is, I don't end up walking on a tilt for the rest of my life because of this hasty remove."

"The doctors assure me that won't be the case. We need only travel slowly and with care. I intend to. I would never jeopardize your health. You know what I wish you to do, but in the end, it's your leg," the duke said, "and so it is your decision."

"So it is," Drum said slowly.

Alexandria looked at him, her eyes so wide he could see the sunlight glancing off them, making them wild with light.

The room was utterly silent as they all waited for his answer.

"Well," Drum said with a thin smile, "how can there be any question then? I believe it's decided, isn't it?"

Thirteen

*T*HE MOON RODE HIGH, THE NIGHT WAS ADVANCED, the world was sleeping, but Alexandria knew that Drum was awake. She stood outside his room and saw the soft glow from his bedside lamp through the chinks and edges of the old door, etching its margins, outlining it in rosy gold until it glowed in the dark stairwell like an entrance to heaven. He could have forgotten to turn down the lamp, he might have fallen asleep with it lit, but somehow Alexandria was certain he was awake and as restless and uneasy as she was. She held her candle steady, took in a breath, and softly tapped on the door.

"Come in," he said quietly, as though he'd been waiting.

He lay propped on pillows, a book in his slender hand. He wore a long silken robe with a lavish gold and red pattern. Reclining on his many pillows, his eyes heavy-lidded, he looked like an emperor ex-

hausted after a trying day of passing heavy judgment
on his many subjects.

"You're all right?" she asked at once.

"As right as I ever am," he answered with a little
smile. "My thoughts are the only things keeping me
awake. So. Our revels now are ended, are they?"

"That's what I came to talk to you about," she said
with determination, coming close to his bed so her
voice wouldn't carry. "I couldn't speak in front of your
father," she whispered, as though she were still afraid
the duke might hear her, "and Eric and Mr. Grimes
kept you busy after he left. Then I had dishes to do. But
now everyone's asleep and I knew you'd be too busy in
the morning for a private word, so I'm glad you're still
awake. My lord, don't ever feel you have to leave!
You're no burden, I told you that before. You don't inconvenience us. You can stay on here until you are able
to dance downstairs. Please believe that."

"Oh, I do. That's not why I'm leaving." He gazed at
her wearily. "Dear Ally," he said gently, "just look at
you! You're in your dressing gown."

Her hand flew to her neck and she gathered the old
gown close. "It covers me more than my day gowns
do," she protested.

It did. She was covered from neck to toes. Her
glossy hair was done in a night braid. A few stray
wisps fluttered around her face, and her face was
lightly flushed, showing how bright her eyes were. She
was dressed decently, but Drum's thoughts were far
from decent. Just the fact that he knew she was ready
for bed made her look infinitely wanton to him.

"It doesn't matter," he said, "because they are nightclothes. This is a cruel, censorious old world, Alexandria. You're here in your night wear—that would shock some people. That you're in those clothes while alone with me, coupled with the further fact I'm no longer in danger of my life, would shock others. When I was half dead it didn't matter. When no one else knew I was here, it mattered less. But now my whereabouts are public knowledge and everyone knows I'm fit—well, fit enough to ruin a reputation at least. I'm leaving for the sake of propriety, my dear. For your sake, believe that."

And mine, he thought, but didn't say. He couldn't see a hint of her shapely form now, but the lamplight etched her features clearly. He'd miss looking at that pretty, serious little oval face, that straight nose, the tilt of her upper lip. *Why speak of other people and what they'd imagine!* he thought in rueful despair. No question, he needed to see other women so he wouldn't concentrate so much on her. Charming as she was, still he didn't think she merited quite so much hopeless yearning. Yet she'd become the only woman in the world to him: nurse, friend, and object of desire. His father was right: time to move on, indeed!

"I will miss our conversations," he said, to change the subject. "I'll wonder if Rob will ever catch that grandfather of a carp he's after, and if Kit will actually move into the barn so he can study in peace. Will you write that letter to *Gentleman's Magazine*, giving them your opinion of the error they made in that quote from Molière, and will you remember to sign it only with your first initial so they'll publish it, because they won't print a letter from a woman? More important, will Mrs. Tooke teach you how to make that berry torte before she goes, as you had said you wanted her to?"

"You remembered," she said, pink with pleasure.

"I remember everything you've said, except when I was unconscious, and then you must acquit me. I'll even remember to send you a copy of Miss Austen's last book when I get home. You said you hadn't read it yet. I've enjoyed our conversations too much to forget them."

"I have too, and I'll miss them," she admitted. "But that's not the reason I said what I did. I hate the thought of you being harmed after all the good we did for you, and all for the sake of something as foolish as propriety. We're not mandarins in old China, to stand on such ceremony."

"We're very like them, though. Unfortunately, reputation is everything in our world, so we must consider the opinions of others if only because we are ruled by their perceptions of us."

"Oh, rubbish!" she said irritably, in her annoyance forgetting to stand on the very ceremony she usually did. "I'm talking about bodily harm. Why should you risk injury for the sake of *others*? I don't care, I really don't. Much it matters to me! By now you ought to know I'm not laying traps for you. As for myself? I'm ineligible and I know it, so I don't care what people say. I'd rather there were gossip about me than harm to you. Why not wait until there's no risk at all?"

He put the book down on his chest, his face grown somber. "Why are you ineligible, Ally? I've never understood that. Can you tell me? Will you? Don't worry about my gossiping, I'm a bottomless pit—throw a secret down and it will never surface again, I promise you. Your spinsterhood doesn't make sense to me.

You're lovely, you know. Well, if you don't, I'll tell you so. Another advantage of leaving—I can say things I couldn't if I knew you'd be seeing me every morning after, and maybe worrying about my ulterior motives.

"You're charming and generous, and monstrous clever too. You don't doubt that, do you? Don't look away, I might as well be speaking to you from the dead, because I'll be gone in a matter of hours and it can make no difference to you. But I'd like to know why you say you are ineligible. I'd think you could have any number of men at your feet. Are all the men around here blind and deaf?"

She laughed. "No, but they marry young, and have strange customs. They tend to marry girls they know, you see."

He didn't laugh. "Maybe so. But this isn't the whole world. Why do you insist on your ineligibility? Can you tell me, can you trust me?"

She looked at him for a long moment. He couldn't read the emotions in her eyes. They were brown in the sunlight, but now, in the night, they were infinitely deep and dark as the earth.

She stared at him, and hesitated. He was leaving, she thought, and she dreaded it because he'd come to mean so much to her. *But they'd never meet again, and so why not tell him now? Not all, but most, so he'd know who she was. That, at least.*

"Why am I ineligible? Apart from my lack of fortune, you mean?" she finally asked bitterly. "Aside from the fact that I was kept away from young men for most of my life and so haven't the slightest idea of how to deal with them? Those that dared look at me were met with scorn or savagery from Mr. Gascoyne. Yes, he's gone now. So why am I still unwed? Not counting my education, which separated me further from anyone in the vicinity? And disregarding the little matter of my being solely responsible for three young boys? Why else?"

He'd never seen her so agitated, though she was outwardly cold. But he could feel the emotion she contained emanating from her, she vibrated with it, the candle she held shivered though there wasn't a breeze in the room.

"Yes," he persisted, "Apart and aside and regardless of all that. Why else? There must be an 'else.' "

He saw tears start in her eyes, "No. Don't . . ." he said, cursing himself. Who was he to breech her defenses and make her cry because of his idle curiosity?

"No," she said, using a sleeve to scrub at her eyes like a girl. She tossed her head back, her face white and stricken. "It's all right. You might as well know. Why not?" She laughed. "He wasn't my father, you see. Like the boys, I'm also a foundling."

Drum's eyes widened and his lips tightened until he resembled his father almost exactly. It was only for a second, but it was an enormous lapse for him to show his shock and dismay. He'd been a masterful spy because he was watchful at all times. But he'd been relaxed, and so her announcement caught him off guard.

She was so immersed in her own loathing she didn't notice. Drum recovered quickly, as shocked and horrified by his unsought reaction as by the news that had caused it.

She kept on talking as though afraid to stop. "I came from the same foundling home the boys did," she explained, speaking to the candle she still held. "The other side of it, of course, because they kept the boys and girls strictly separated. Mr. Gascoyne always had an eye on finances, you see. And so when he adopted the boys he asked the matron which of the girls was tractable, good with a needle and her books, and with younger children too. She selected me. It was very clever of him, really. Four are as cheap to feed as three, and that way he got a nanny for the boys in the bargain."

Her hand trembled, causing the candle to cast uneasy shadows over his bed. "A fellow will overlook a girl's lack of dowry, sometimes," she said, pulling in a deep breath. "He might think her education was a bonus. He could even be bold enough to defy an old man's scorn and spite, I suppose. But even here, a man wants to know where his wife comes from. Apart and aside and regardless," she said with bitter precision, "of the fact that she comes from the Home for Orphan and Indigent Children.

"I was brought there when I was three or four, they say. The woman who brought me said she got me from the London Foundling Hospital years before, and could no longer afford to keep me. Her name was Sally and I helped her trim hats, that I do remember, but I was never her daughter. She had seven other orphan girls and had to get rid of all of us because her man was taking her to the Antipodes. She was going to set up shop there, and transport was expensive, and girls, after all, are easy to come by anywhere."

"I'm sorry," Drum said, because he didn't know what else to say, for the first time in his life. Because she was right and there was no denying it, even for her sake. He was shocked and disappointed, as much with himself as at her news. He hadn't realized how eagerly he'd embraced the notion that he could make her eligible. But a *foundling*? Drum felt his heart sink.

Orphans, like bastards, had no status at all, they weren't welcome anywhere. There were just too many of them. Their very existence was too dangerous to the tightly knit fabric of society. They were discards who very well might be bastards anyway. After all, if they had equal rights and equal opportunities, why should anyone honor and value legitimacy, marriage, and all the rest of society's difficult but necessary rules?

It might be unfair, but it was fundamental. Not just the upper classes cared about lineage. Everyone knew how hard it was to raise children, to feed, clothe, and care for them. If people were allowed to simply leave their whelps for others to raise, the institution of marriage would crumble. Morals were lofty things, but it was the stigma and punishments attached to not having them that enforced their rules. Remove the disgrace and shame, and the rules, rites and strictures of a well ordered world would eventually degenerate into chaos and anarchy.

So foundlings were fed enough to keep alive, and trained up in all the menial occupations legitimate persons wouldn't want. They could be indentured, or they could be hired on for a decent wage if they were of superior stock. If a foundling was adopted by a good family or made the ward of a wealthy man and then educated and well provided for, his lot would be easier. But it would never be the same as other men's. Orphans couldn't inherit the way natural sons and daughters could, even wards didn't have the same legal protection as a man's blood kin conceived in wedlock.

Drum felt sick. Alexandria's adoptive father had given her a fine education and possibly a share in his estate. But even so, she was an impossible match for a man like himself. It was more than his damnable pride, it was the way of his father, and the way of his world. Immutable.

Being attracted to a schoolmaster's daughter was difficult, to a foundling adopted by a schoolmaster, ridiculous. The rules were simple and known to every gentleman. The lower classes were fair game for frolics, nothing serious, everything salacious. The middle class was to avoid, they took things seriously or not at all. One's own class was for marriage, or sport, if one's partner were up to snuff and knew how to carry on a proper affair. He smiled thinly, thinking about "proper affairs." But Alexandria was too respectable for an affair and too beneath his touch for anything else. It wasn't a combination he could deal with.

He thought rapidly. She'd be a treasure for any man not concerned about marrying someone of equal rank. But where could she find one who would meet *her* needs?

He couldn't see her wedded to an ignorant farmer and being a happy peasant any more than he could see a nobleman marrying her. Of course, there was always the senile or idiotic nobleperson who married a barmaid or a footman or such, and was made infamous for it, the subject of gossip and scorn. Drum frowned. Mrs. Tooke hadn't married outrageously; she'd only married out of her station, and look what had become of her. She'd been cast out from her family and her class.

Alexandria had neither birth, fortune, nor connections to lose. She might find a man who didn't care—a man of some education and wealth who didn't need to gain money or property by marrying and didn't aspire to climb higher in society. Love might move mountains. It was her only chance, and she needed that chance.

"Neither fish nor fowl nor good red meat," she said harshly, reading his mind. "Now do you see?"

He didn't answer right away. He was too busy trying to find a solution he could offer, an answer that would ease her pain and his.

She saw his distress and misunderstood it. Her own eyes widened. "Right! Yes, how could I forget? I might ruin your reputation! So it's better that you're going, after all!"

"Only I can ruin my reputation," he said angrily. "And that's difficult for a wealthy well-born man to do, believe me. I'm leaving because it's better for everyone all around. I'm sorry, Alexandria. Have you no idea of your origins? Maybe I can investigate for you when I get back to London? I'm good at it."

She laughed. It wasn't the charming trill of laughter he associated with her. "Thank you. Mr. Gascoyne was thorough and knowledgeable. But the truth is that I could be a whore's daughter or a duchess's. Pray forgive my plain speaking, but that is what he told me. I am like Eve, sir. My father is God, my mother his consort, and I will not know either of them until the day I die."

"Could he have lied to you?" Drum asked desperately. "For his own purposes?"

She tilted her head. "He might have done. It would be his way. But he didn't. In the beginning he researched all our pasts in hopes that there might be some reward in it for him. He must have been influenced by the sort of thing written about in romances— gentleman's son recovered, lady's daughter found, kidnapped babies reunited with their noble families and such. His search came to naught. Kit has a vague memory of his origins, and they are humble. Vic and Rob have less, as do I. But the home knows. We're simply nobodies, with no way to know if we ever were important to anyone.

"I wrote to them after Mr. Gascoyne died, when there was no longer reason for secrecy, if there ever had been. I had read too many romances, I fear. But the answer was the same. I was abandoned at an early age, and have no family of my own. Even my first name isn't really mine. I was given it at the home," she went on, staring into the wavering flame. "They took me in on the day of the victory at Alexandria. Kit had his name, but Vin was named for the battle at Vincennes."

"And Rob for Robres?" Drum asked, doing quick calculations in his head, appalled at the thought of children so disregarded that they were simply named for the day they were found.

"Perhaps. There are only so many Marys and Elizabeths, Toms, Dicks and Harrys," she said, bringing up her head and looking him in the eye. "The names of flowers, rivers, and counties are used up quickly too. But there's no end of homeless children, so they had to be inventive. We're lucky the directors of the home were patriotic. It could be worse. They could have named us after animals, and called me Bossy, and Vin and Rob, Spot and Sport. At that it would have been an elevation in our states since we really weren't as useful or valuable as animals, you know."

"I'm sorry," he said softly. "I hope you know it doesn't change the way I feel toward you."

But it did. She could feel it. The easy camaraderie between them was gone. That wasn't the only thing that had changed. Any intimation of flirtation had vanished too. Though he hadn't moved a muscle, she felt him withdraw from her. He lay back and watched her through half-lidded eyes, his expression inscrutable.

"Well, then, past time for you to get to sleep," she said with a sad and knowing smile. "Tomorrow will be a busy day."

"Alexandria," he said again, "I'm sorry."

She nodded. "Thank you," she said, as she moved toward the door. "So am I."

"It isn't the way I wanted to leave," Drum said on a huff of a laugh as his footmen carried him down the stair the next morning. "Lord! This is embarrassing," he said while they arranged him in his bed in the coach. "Damn, damn, damn," everyone in the front yard heard him muttering as the doctors strapped him in and made last-minute inspections of the cushions, pillows, blankets, and straps that held him fast.

Finally, all was in readiness. Drum had made his good-byes to everyone at breakfast that morning. The boys wanted to linger to watch him go, but Drum instructed them to go to school. After breakfast, Mrs. Tooke took his hand and his thanks. Alexandria was formality itself as she bade him godspeed and farewell. He showed no partiality for her by word or gesture;

neither did she to him. He was immensely grateful, he said. It was nothing, she said, and stepped aside to let his men come into the bedroom to bear him out.

Now, his men were on their horses, his valet in the coach, and all the outriders ready to go. Eric ducked his head into the carriage for a few final words with his friend. "I'll investigate everything and let you know what I've discovered."

Drum, a little pale from all the activity, a little shaken from all the handling, held his friend's hand a moment more. "Don't write," he said softly. "If you've any news, come to me with it."

"Done."

"And Eric?" Drum said. "Be sure of the truth, and do what is right in everything here."

Eric paused. "Always," he said, smiled, and left.

Dr. Raines stepped in and the door closed. The duke signaled to his coachman, his own carriage leading the way. Slowly, the little procession left the front drive. Mrs. Tooke, Dr. Pace, Eric, and Alexandria stood in front of the cottage, waving good-bye.

Drum lay on his side, peering out the coach window. He saw Eric turn to Alexandria and say something to make her laugh. He saw her looking up at the big blond man. Drum watched until they were out of sight. He never stopped frowning, not then, and not for long miles afterward, remembering their laughter, remembering all he'd left, recalling all that he'd had to leave behind.

Alexandria went up to her bedchamber. It was truly hers again. The house was still. Dr. Pace had gone. Eric had left to see what he could discover in the neighborhood. For the sake of propriety, Mrs. Tooke was staying on until he left, but Alexandria knew she too would soon leave. The world was returning to normal, but Alexandria knew it would never be the same. The Earl of Drummond's visit had changed her. He'd brought her the wide world and shown her all she was missing. He'd shamed her too, without trying to. His reaction to her state bore it forcibly home to her. But that couldn't be helped, because that was just the way things were. She was a very practical woman; she had to be.

Still, she stripped the sheets from her bed with more energy than necessary. But Eric Ford had smiled at her, she remembered, and flirted, making her remember that the world hadn't ended, only turned one more time. Eric was charming and warm, but not for a minute did she believe he meant more than flirtation. Still, that helped. She'd survive this blow to her self-esteem. She'd had far worse.

At least she'd done Drum a service. At least he'd been genuinely grateful and she could believe that if things had been different, if she'd had any sort of birth at all, he might have lingered, he could have stayed on with her. She didn't blame him for going. No one knew better than she how disparate their stations were. But at least she felt it hadn't been easy for him to leave her. That was something. He'd remember her. That was another thing. He'd marry well, have children, and rush through the productive years of his life. But one day perhaps, when he was old, when he had time to think back on what might have been, maybe he'd think of this strange interlude in his life and regret her almost as much as she regretted him. That was not nothing.

He'd been drawn to her and it was hard for him to

leave her, of that she was certain. If fate had treated her more kindly . . . It was a good thing to think about and made her feel better. He would remember her one day. She would miss him for the rest of her life.

Alexandria pulled off the sheet and flung off the pillows—and stopped.

There, under his pillow, was a small fortune in gold coins. Ten of them lay in a heap.

He'd left her gold pieces as payment for her help. Of course. He was too discreet to simply hand them to her. He knew she'd refuse. This way, he'd paid her the way a traveler at an inn might leave a gratuity for a good servant when he left, where he was sure she'd find it.

She hesitated, then quickly picked them up with the tips of her fingers, as though they were dead mice, and dropped them into her apron. Then she went to the window and shook out her apron, and when that didn't make them fly she pitched them out as far as she could.

But she was practical and wise. And so after she'd stripped the bed she went outside and gathered up all the gold pieces again.

Then she wept.

Fourteen

"*I*F WE CHARGED ADMISSION, OUR FORTUNES WOULD be made," Drum said sourly, watching his father shuffle through the heap of visitor's cards that had been left with Drum's butler since he'd come back to London.

Drum sat in a great winged chair by a long window in his study, his injured leg stretched out in front of him. He could see the sunlight filtering through the trees in the back garden of his town house; he had his books and papers around him. He was dressed casually—a dressing gown substituted for a jacket, his shirt opened at the neck. A glass of wine sat at his right hand, along with a dish of comfits. He looked comfortable and at ease and in no way like an invalid, except for his immobilized leg. His expression was totally at odds with his state.

"I gather the thought of company repels you," his father said coolly, riffling through the visiting cards with interest. "I believe it's time you showed your face, though. Rumor has it you may not have one anymore. That's the mildest of the rumors about you, by the way."

Drum shrugged. "Much I care. Half London knows better. At least that many people were standing on the walk, gaping at me when you had me carried off the coach and into the house like a corpse being readied for a viewing. Night would have been a better time for my return. At the very least you might have used the servant's entrance instead of bearing me in on a litter like a warrior on his shield in front of the fascinated crowd. I submitted to it, if only because protesting all the way into the house would have made an even more delicious spectacle."

"So it would have done," the duke agreed. "And may I point out that even so, you complained too much to be mistaken for either a corpse or a warrior. Nevertheless, since we arrived in the morning I'd no intention of letting you lie in the coach all day until you decided it was dark enough to enter your own house. If we'd tried furtively to sneak you in by the back entrance, the rumors would have been worse. You should be flattered so many people want to see you."

"Yes. As flattered as the lions and the elephant at the Tower, I suppose," Drum said irritably. "Though my value as a diversion and curiosity must be greater than theirs since visiting me is by invitation only, and everyone is looking for an invitation."

"Because visiting you is impossible," his father corrected him.

"Not so!" Drum protested. "I've had company in."

"Yes. Four people. Your bosom friends the Daltons and Ryders. If the Sinclairs hadn't gone home to the country, you'd have had them too, I know. You need more diverse company. I should like to see it before I leave you."

"Oh, is that why you're still here?"

His father stopped looking at the cards and stared at his son.

Drum's lean cheeks grew ruddy. "Very well. I'm sorry for taking that tone with you, sir."

"So you should be," the duke said, dropping the cards back on their silver tray. "I've stayed to see you settled and on your way to recovery. But now I've a notion to see society again myself. The Season is almost over, yet there are still some persons of quality in town. I could go to balls and soirees, the gardens and such. But it would be easier to actually speak to people when they came here."

"You could go to your clubs if it's conversation you're after," Drum grumbled.

"So I could. But I wouldn't meet any ladies there, would I?"

Drum looked up sharply. "No," he said slowly. "That's true. Have you a notion to meet a particular lady, sir?"

His father nodded. "So I do. But that's not something I feel I must share with you."

Drum blinked. "Quite so. Well, then. Yes, that being the case, I'll have the horde in."

Because, Drum thought quickly, that way he'd see just who his father had his eye on, and if it was the Lady Annabelle, he'd do his damnedest to end any romance that might arise there. Not only because his friend Eric might already have fixed his interest with the vain and lovely lady, but because Drum could think of few things more distasteful than having her as a stepmama. He'd been sarcastic when he mentioned the possibility; he wished he'd kept his bitter humor to himself. Until now his greatest fear had been of finding himself permanently crippled. Now he could worry about finding himself lumbered with a stepmother younger than himself. Younger, clever, shallow, and vengeful as well.

"You're cold?" his father asked, seeing a slow shudder cross his son's shoulders.

"A goose walked over my grave," Drum said with a shrug, and smiled for the first time that day, contemplating what Annabelle would think of his saying that about her.

"You're entertaining us in style today," Damon Ryder commented, looking around the seldom used, beautifully appointed salon he'd just entered and seeing the trays of cakes and the number of glasses that had been set up on the sideboard.

"I have to. I'm entertaining more than you today," Drum said. "My father insists I make myself available to company. I think he won't go home until I do, so I agreed. He's been busy putting a word in every socially acceptable ear he could find, telling them it's all right to come visit me today."

"Well, what's wrong with that?" Rafe asked, picking up a lemon snap. "Lots of fellows have been asking after you."

"It's not the fellows he's inviting," Drum said. "Remember why he dragged me away from the Gascoynes' cottage? He wants to make me available to the fairer sex. He's looking for a wife—for me," he added hastily. There was no sense in telling anyone his deepest fears now. There was nothing anyone could do about them anyway, except possibly make matters worse if they tried to meddle. It was a delicate matter he'd have to handle himself.

"It's going to be like the ball the king gave for the prince so he could pick a wife!" Gilly cried, clapping her hands.

"Not quite so romantic," Damon Ryder said, exchanging a glance with Drum.

"He's going to be like a sitting duck," Rafe said around the lemon snap he'd popped in his mouth. "Can't even get up and walk away, can he?"

"Exactly," Drum said. "So I'd like it if you could stay here when the doors open to the public. You could save me if you see I need saving."

"Of course," Gilly said enthusiastically. "Who do you want us to protect you from?"

Drum winced. "I don't need protection. Just some . . . interception sometimes, perhaps."

"But Gilly's right," Brenna Dalton said seriously. "If you tell us who you think will annoy you I'm sure we'll do what we can to keep them away from you, but if you don't, how are we to know?"

"Who?" Drum asked, frowning. "Anyone who looks like they're giving me a headache, that's who. That's most of them. But not the Lady Annabelle, if you please."

There was a sudden shocked silence, broken by Rafe. "Sits the wind in that quarter then?" he blurted. "Well, I admit I'm surprised. But she's a good-looking female and there's every chance she's grown up since we last met, I suppose."

"Nicely put." Drum laughed. "You're saying she's not as self-centered and self-serving as she used to be? Maybe not. But it doesn't matter, I'm not interested in her for any of the reasons you might think. Still, I don't want you frightening her away from me."

"It's Eric, is it?" Rafe asked after a moment's thought. "You want to lure her away from him. I remember how he looked at her the last time they met. Why not? She's good enough to *look* at, if a fellow doesn't know what lies beneath," he added with a tender smile for his wife. "Makes sense, though I don't know if you should bother. I doubt she'll settle for a retired army man. Seems to me she'd want to hang out for a title to show everyone what she can do. So have a care. If she thinks you're the one who's interested you'll be shackled to her before you can take your first step. That mama's a dragon, and getting desperate."

"Don't worry. I'll be careful," Drum promised. "My legs are useless at the moment but in other ways I'm just as fast on my feet. The lady's suspicious of me anyhow, and rightfully so. Trust me, my motives run deep."

"So you're yourself again," Damon Ryder said, and they all laughed.

They chatted until the clock chimed three. Then Drum sighed. "I suppose I'm ready as I'll ever be." He picked up a bell from the table and shook it. Grimes entered the room immediately. "Tell Mr. Phineas I'm ready for company," Drum said. "If anyone comes by today, that is."

"There are a number of visitors already in the anteroom," Grimes said.

Drum grimaced.

It turned out he had a good reason to. It was a large salon, but not big enough for the number of guests who soon filed in. Even the ballroom might not have been large enough.

Drum didn't have a fear of crowds, but he soon felt he was suffocating. He'd never realized how mobility helped a man in social situations. Everyone else in the room could mill around, and every man there did, or else they stood in groups, chatting together. The only people sitting were himself and the mamas. They had brought every single young woman of quality in London to see him, it seemed. And he couldn't move an inch away from being seen.

It could have been a man's fondest dream come true. He was surrounded by women. The latest styles insisted women show most of what they had, and that it be ungirdled, untethered, and uncovered as much as could be, too. Spring was giving way to summer, and so fashionable gowns were not only cut low, they were made of zephyr-thin material. These woman were, if nothing else, fashionable. Drum hadn't seen so many nearly naked bouncing breasts and bobbling bottoms since he'd last visited a brothel. He felt no desire, only a vague sense of panic. There was, he discovered, too much of a good thing—especially when every one of those good things came with a price tag that could cost him his freedom.

He couldn't look at any women too pointedly or too often, or she'd descend on him to see if she'd scored a point over the other girls. Worse, her mother might. Worst of all, he was tacked to his chair, so he saw them all at stomach and buttock level. They had to bend to speak with him, and then he had to talk into their bosoms. His expression grew grim, and his conversation terse.

He couldn't have chatted reasonably with his nubile company even if they were dressed in suits of armor, he decided, because he'd seldom met a more trivial group of people. The only subject they brought up was his accident. When he said he was fine now, and refused to discuss it further, they had to fall back on the only other subjects they were expert in: the weather, and the gossip of the Season so far.

He knew he was being unkind and unfair. What should any strange woman talk to him about? It wasn't as if they could suddenly start discussing *The Odyssey*, or art, or literature, as Alexandria had, he thought. Even she might have had a hard time introducing a new topic under these conditions. But one thing he knew: She wouldn't have giggled incessantly, or shrieked with laughter over any trivial thing he said, the way so many of them were doing. He was sure she wouldn't have stared at him open-mouthed, seemingly rapt in ecstasy at every fatuous thing he muttered.

But she hadn't been on the catch for him, he reminded himself. Maybe she was behaving this way with Eric, he thought suddenly, and frowned at the thought because it seemed like a betrayal of her.

"Are you in pain, Drummond?" his father asked with a matching frown as he stood staring down at his son.

"Father!" Drum said. "Where did you come from? That is, I didn't see you come in."

"How could you, with such a bevy of lovely young women around you? I stopped by to deliver more company for you."

Drum belatedly noticed who was with his father—
Lady Annabelle, all in blue to match her magnificent
eyes. And her plump mother, all in gold to match her
ambitions. They both smiled down at him.

"But now I must apologize to the ladies," his father
went on, "because with this crowd of English womanhood in attendance, they must think I'm in the practice
of bringing coals to Newcastle."

"Never," Drum said with the most charming smile
he could muster, "How could you so malign them, sir?
They burn so brightly they cast all others in their
shadow."

Drum was being polite, but he hadn't lied about
Lady Annabelle. She was still beautiful, even though
she'd lingered too long on the marriage market, even
though he knew her too well to overlook the person
who lived inside that exquisite façade. She had raven
curls and alabaster skin, just as all her love-struck suitors said in their bad verse. A short upper lip over a full
lower one made her mouth seem to beg for kisses, her
long-lashed blue eyes were bright under their graceful
brows. Her form was sublime and further enhanced by
her gowns, because her taste was impeccable too.

Everyone said she'd become a jilt and a flirt after
her one true love had married another. What no one
knew, not even the lady herself, Drum believed, was
that was impossible. Because her one true love was
herself.

"And Duchess," Drum said to her mama, ducking
his head in a semblance of a bow, "forgive me for not
rising, will you?"

"My poor boy!" the duchess exclaimed, "just stay
where you are! What a disaster. How glad we are to see

you on the road to recovery. We wouldn't have missed seeing you for the world, but we heard you weren't receiving visitors. How pleased we are that his grace informed us otherwise and offered to bring us himself."

And how thrilled you are that he seems to be handing you my head and hand on a silver platter, Drum thought, and said, "I'm glad you came whatever the reason. But please remember my father still thinks of me as a boy even though I'm easily a decade older than your daughter. You know how it is with doting parents of your generation, always thinking your children remain children even when we're fully grown."

There, Drum thought, a not too subtle hint about disparity in ages to start things off, and stem other things, in case his father had been making sheep's eyes at the duchess's daughter.

His father looked down at him with a bemused smile. "How eager one's children are to put one into one's dotage," he commented to the duchess. "I only have a care for Drummond because he's so late to mature. I myself became his father when I was even younger than your lovely daughter is now."

Drum raised an eyebrow. "Your pardon, sir. In the last century things were different. We're not required to marry from the cradle anymore."

His father seemed genuinely amused. "Actually dear boy, you were born in the last century too. By the by, I hadn't realized. Are you still sleeping in a cradle?"

"No," Drum snapped. "I cut my eyeteeth a while ago."

"So I thought," his father said with a slight smile, glancing over at Lady Annabelle, who was raptly listening to their conversation.

Drum looked at her too. She stood next to his father and he couldn't help seeing they made a handsome pair; his father tall and straight, Annabelle so curvaceous and petite. She looked even better now because her eyes were sparkling, her lips curled in delight. *No wonder,* Drum thought with sinking heart. *We must seem like two rams locking horns over her. Just the sort of thing she'd adore. I've spurred her interest, damn it!*

His father had loved his wife deeply, Drum knew, and the temporary liaisons he'd indulged in since her death had never involved his heart. It would be good he found a lifemate. Drum loved and respected him even though they didn't always agree, because for all of the duke's coolness and irony he was a man of depth and honor. Drum might consider his father to be too proud and haughty, but he'd never known him to be cruel or dishonest.

It wasn't that Drum thought Annabelle would cheat and deceive an older husband by taking a younger man as a lover. It was that he was fairly sure she couldn't be anyone's lover in more than the physical sense. His father deserved more. He could be interested in having a new heir, and who could blame him? But his current heir thought he deserved more than that too.

Who was the lady set on charming now? Drum wondered. She stayed to chat and laugh, and he had to admit her conversation was light without being stupid, and her laughter appropriate and pleasant to hear. He saw the worried looks his friends shot at him from various parts of the room. He also noticed his father's considering glances as he gazed down, bemused, at the lovely Annabelle too. Even so, Drum felt a little let down when she left to give others a chance to talk with him. She could be good company when she set her mind to it, in spite of the fact that her quizzical smile hinted that she knew exactly how he felt about her.

By the time his father politely suggested to the company that his son was looking a bit peaked, Drum's mouth ached from the stiffness of his artificial smiles. When Drum's best friends moved toward the door with the rest of the company, he signaled them to stay. "I'd like a word with all of you," he told Rafe. "Wait a moment longer please."

"But if you'd give me a moment alone with my son first?" the duke asked.

Drum's friends retreated to the hall, Lady Annabelle and her mama told the duke they'd wait for him in his coach.

"You've done well," the duke told Drum when they were alone. "You'll have abundant company now. It would please me if you admitted them even when I wasn't here."

Drum groaned. "If it pleases you, I will, but I can't guarantee what will happen when I have the use of my legs again."

"I won't ask you to," the duke said. He hesitated, then abruptly asked, "What do you think of her?"

Drum's face went still. He couldn't mean any other woman. But why didn't he name her? And did he mean to ask what Drum thought of Annabelle for himself? Or for his son? More than that, this was very unlike his father—it was too blunt.

"I'm not sure yet," Drum said, carefully giving a vague answer for a nebulous question. "This needs time, don't you think?"

"Of course," the duke said in his usual cool tones. "We have that. I'll see you tomorrow," he said, clapping on his high beaver hat. "Give you good day," he told the Ryders and the Daltons as he strolled out of the house. "Thank you for watching over my son."

"*He* needs watching!" Gilly exclaimed when she came back into the salon. "Did you see the way he was eyeing her?" Belatedly, she realized she'd spoken out of turn. She looked stricken. "That wasn't for me to say," she added humbly.

"I don't see why not," Drum said with a smile. "You've always said anything you wanted to me, and always should. I value that and you know it, though I pity Damon for it," he added to make them laugh. "He did look upon Annabelle fondly. It may be no more than that. It may only be that he yearns for her for me. Whatever it is, there's nothing I can do about it yet. But I earnestly wish you would not say one word against her in front of him," he added, shaking a finger at her, "because that would do nothing but make him want to protect her. He has an incongruous streak of gallantry."

Drum fidgeted, and looked even more glum. "But what I wanted to talk to you all about was that seeing those eager young creatures here today set me to thinking. And not about what their mamas most wished I would." His long fingers tapped against the arm of his chair as he tried to frame his thoughts. He'd be pacing now if he could.

He was never at a loss for words. His friends knew he must be considering something momentous. They listened closely.

"There's no reason a charming, bright, good person like Alexandria Gascoyne shouldn't have an opportu-

nity to marry too," Drum finally said. He glowered
down at his splinted leg. "The fact that she has no title
or money might not matter so much here; London's
filled with all kinds of men, there must be some who'd
find her marriageable. She certainly has other assets.
Surely we can put our heads together and think of a
way to get her here, to repay her for her kindness to
me? That's the only way she'll find herself a husband
and a better life, because she'll find nothing but time
flying by in that backwater she lives in."

He looked up to see them gaping at him.

"*That's* what's got you upset?" Rafe laughed. "Your
father isn't the only one with a streak of gallantry!"

"I pay my debts," Drum said.

Then he sat back with a smile, and listened to them
fight for the right to take in a foundling. As to that, her
history was hers to tell them if she chose, he decided,
but her future was now his to sort out for her. He might
be immobilized, he might be powerless over anything
his father did, but this was something he could do.

It was the first time he'd felt good about himself in
days.

Fifteen

*I*T WAS A WARM EVENING AFTER A PARTICULARLY rare early summer's day. Eric Ford stood at the garden gate and watched the woman at his side lift her head to breathe in the fragrances of the garden and fields around them. He eyed Alexandria's lovely profile, from her fine little nose down to her shapely breasts. She'd drawn the masses of her hair up because of the warmth of day, and now he saw a few sunset-tinted slips had come loose to lay against her neck. She didn't notice his appraisal, expect perhaps in that tangential way in which people feel a prickling awareness of someone's eyes on them. She ran a hand along the back of her neck to smooth those tendrils as though she felt his eyes on them.

The work of the day was done, dinner had been eaten, the horses were in the barn, and the children were in the cottage. After the efforts of the day a sense of accomplishment and peace was falling over them, along with the night. It didn't take much of a leap of fancy for him to imagine this was his cottage, they were his children, and this woman, his wife. Or that after a moment, they'd exchange a secret smile, then an embrace. After that, they'd wait until they could go inside and close their bedroom door to exchange much more as the coming night darkened around them. It was how his parents behaved. He firmly believed it was what made sense of a man's life.

The lady he wanted would never be his. He didn't have a title and she wanted a husband of rank. He had too much pride to offer her less or to take less for himself. He did like Alexandria, though, and he was lonely. But he'd get no encouragement from her. He knew women so he knew that. His fantasy might match hers, but they both wanted another who didn't want them. It paired them, life wouldn't. That saddened him, not because he'd lost his heart to her, though he liked her very well, but because he was fairly sure she'd lost hers. And where his dream of love might have been possible, hers was not and never could be, and he didn't know how to tell her that.

He'd seen how she had looked at Drum, and how often she'd tried not to. It was clear she couldn't keep her eyes off him. He'd heard the note that changed in her voice when she spoke about Drum too.

"I wrote to Drum today," he said.

She turned to look at him and he saw the interest leap to her eyes.

"I've discovered some things he wanted to know and I hope soon to know more," he went on. "There's something I have to know from you too. I have to ask you if only because I promised to be Drum's ferret and I must be thorough, but also because I don't think he ever wanted to ask you himself. It may be important. Were you aware of Mr. Gascoyne's political leanings?"

She startled, her eyes flew wide and searched his. "Politics? Oh! Was someone really trying to kill Drum . . . the earl?"

"As I said, I don't know yet. But I did find out a few things about your father's opinions. He admired Napoleon?"

She turned her head and looked away. He had his answer, but waited patiently for her to speak.

"Mr. Gascoyne was—rather radical," she said, gazing at the ground. "An admirer of the French Revolution, actually. Silly, really, since revolutionaries preach sharing and he wouldn't share a cup of water, much less his money. They also teach the brotherhood of man and he thought no one was his equal. It was the theory that interested him."

She raised her eyes to him again. "But if you mean was he radical to the point of putting himself or anyone else in any danger? Oh no, *that* he was not. He lost his position at Eton for simply expressing such views, and that was the end of his expressing them. Someone overheard something he said and told someone else, so he was dismissed because he was considered a dangerous teacher for the sons of aristocrats. He made sure never to voice any political opinions again."

She cocked her head to the side, then laughed. "You ask because you think his ghost attacked the earl? I don't think even his departed spirit would dare. The only ghost hereabouts is the next town over and he's only a muddled old monk who seems to want to say vespers, they say, but his monastery is gone so he walks the road at twilight, muttering. He might frighten a horse, but he couldn't shoot at one."

"I mean that maybe your father had friends who were less fearful than he was. Friends with the same convictions."

Her smile vanished. She looked at the setting sun and nodded. "That's possible. He wrote to some. I met a few. I was very grateful he didn't encourage them to visit. In fact, their interest in me made him lose interest in them, I think. He had few illusions about friendship and those few he had were easy for him to shed."

"And his friends at the school where he last taught?"

She shook her head. "He had none. He kept to himself."

Now Eric nodded. "And he saw that you did too. Are you going to continue keeping to yourself even now that he's gone?" He asked because it was a warm and fragrant evening and she was lovely and he couldn't help himself. "It would be a shame," he said when she didn't answer right away.

He dared more. He trusted her intelligence and regretted her state of mind. His friend was a powerful man and a fascinating one, Eric had seen how women reacted to him before. He'd seen how Drum reacted to her too. Drum was luckier. He'd never be without company, left alone to agonize over what might have been, as this lovely woman was doing. But Drum *was* a friend as well as being a sensitive man, and so Eric felt sorry for them both—Alexandria for her obvious feelings and Drum for his obvious disregard of his own.

"Drum thought it would be a waste for you to remain alone," Eric said carefully.

He saw her nostrils pinch as she took in a sharp breath.

"He admires you tremendously," Eric went on. "He mentions you in his letters, always asking how you are, how you're doing now. He can't do more. You met his father, and his father means the world to him. With all his coldness the duke's a good man, and Drum's a good son."

"I don't expect more," she said woodenly.

"Then I repeat, it's a waste."

"Thank you for that."

He looked out at the fields. "Now's not a good time for me to try to win another thanks from you, I think, though I'd certainly like to. But times change, don't they?"

She turned a sad but smiling face to his. "Oh, Eric," she said on a gust of a laugh, "I certainly hope so."

She stood in silence a moment, wondering if she should stay and enjoy the evening with him now that difficult things had been said. But it was too lovely an evening, still and serene, with perfumes floating on a soft breeze, a fleeting time that held promises and threats and made people do impetuous things.

"Good-night," she said softly, and turned away from him, leaving him alone to stare into the growing night.

She forced herself to go into her house, though the stars were coming out in a sky so huge and brilliant it made the cottage seem even smaller and more confined than it was. She could have stayed at his side, but she knew what it might lead to, and she was confused and unhappy because she wasn't prepared for that.

Eric Ford actually seemed interested in her. She'd known few strangers, but he was so open and kind, she felt she knew him. He had so much to offer her, the most welcome right now that feeling of security she felt in his presence. He was so large, friendly, and sympathetic. He was also a staggeringly handsome man and anyone could see his heart was as big and warm as his personality, so he might not care that she had nothing to offer him but herself. Maybe he only wanted friendship, but his eyes told her more, and he wasn't the sort of man who trifled with a woman.

Alexandria stood in the kitchen and looked at the empty hearth. If she had a brain in her head she'd get on her knees and thank God for sending him her way, and then stand up, turn right around, and go back to him.

But she kept thinking about another man who was in no way handsome, and so she hardly understood why she thought he was twice as attractive. A man with a quick sense of humor and a fine sense of irony. A clever, learned, high-born man whose heart was generous too; but that heart was totally locked and bent to his purposes. And that purpose was to find a wife of his same class and condition. He made no excuses for it. Such was his pride in his name and his reverence for his haughty father that he probably felt he didn't have to. The truth was, Alexandria thought unhappily, he didn't, because the world utterly agreed with him.

More than all that, though Eric was a radiantly handsome man, and Drum was not, nevertheless, her *skin* reacted differently when she was in the room with Drum. It was the most peculiar thing. He had only to look at her and she'd feel the fine hairs on the back of her neck stand up and her heart begin to gallop. Such a thing had never happened to her before.

Eric was a good man and she knew she could trust him. She didn't trust the Earl of Drummond at all. How could she? She didn't know him. She didn't know if anyone ever could. He was a mass of contradictions, and she reacted to him the same way. He was too remote and yet the expression in his eyes was too warm for her comfort, and sent chills down her back. His presence in a room took all the air out of it too, making her both lightheaded and exhilarated. There was no understanding it, but no denying it. Even worse, now that he was gone the air didn't seem quite so important to breathe anymore. It was ridiculous, but she could no more help it than help breathing. Clearly, he'd bewitched her. She had to let time pass to see if she could escape his spell.

Alexandria went up the stair, moving as though her damp little cottage had already given her the rheumatics in her bones that it doubtless would one day. When she opened the door to her bedchamber, she almost expected to still see Drum there, sitting in a chair or lying on her bed, looking at her with that chilling, burning look in his knowing eyes. She'd said there were no ghosts in the neighborhood; now she knew she lied. She'd never seen the ghost of the cold man who'd owned this place, but she couldn't stop seeing the afterimage of the cool man who'd come to stay here, and had left with her heart.

Alexandria sank to the bed and bowed her head. There! She'd admitted it. That tall man with the absurdly long nose and beautiful azure eyes had come into her life and now she wondered if he'd ever leave it. She'd never been so smitten before. She smiled sadly, because she knew very well that the sum of her acquaintance of handsome, available gentlemen was now precisely two of them. So, she thought hopefully, it was possible this fixation might only be a passing thing.

She frowned. Even if this were a temporary madness, it would probably be long enough to ruin any chance she might have with Eric. If she really had a chance at all. He might not mind her lack of history and . . . But *might* was too big a word. And even if she could one day respond to him, by then he'd doubtless have already found a wiser woman, one eager to return his interest and engage his affections, because he was so very attractive and obviously ready to fix his interest with someone.

Alexandria lay back and closed her eyes. Drum was gone, but he'd ruined her chances for Eric, and maybe all men—how should she know?

She'd been visited by a comet. The Earl of Drummond was from another world, as remote from hers as the moon or stars. She had to get over the shock and grandeur of his sudden appearance and disappearance and then, and only then, could she get on with her life. Maybe if fate finally decided to be kinder to her, she could get on with another love as well. Maybe.

She sat up, pulled off her clothes, and lay back again, burrowing her face into the pillow. Her eyes opened again in shock. She hadn't put on her nightdress. She was naked, and she had never gone to bed like that! It was an outrageous, wanton thing. The foundling home sent children to bed dressed from neck to toes. When Mr. Gascoyne was here she'd dressed the same way. Even now that she finally was alone, she never dared sleep as God made her. The boys might wake, she might have to leave the room in a hurry . . .

But tonight was different. Tonight she fought with

herself to stay in her room. The sky glittered with stars, the leaves on the tree outside her window fluttered against it the way her heart was knocking against her chest, filling her soul with dares and options, making her yearn in heart and body. A strong handsome man stood at her gate, perhaps looking up at her window with desire and warm welcome in his eyes, waiting for her to come down to him again.

But tonight another man's spirit roved the room on the soft breeze too, running cool fingers over her heated skin, stirring the hair at the back of her neck with his breath, chuckling at her confusion, whispering impossible things into her ears. She turned, and turned again, shamed and excited by her own body and the possibilities the tingling sensations were hinting at.

She couldn't cover herself because she'd never been so conscious of her own body, so terrified and enticed by its power and potential. She'd never realized how smooth her skin was. She ran her hand over it, from where it stretched over her stomach, up the arch of her ribs, noting how soft and yet firm her breasts felt, how hard and pebbled their tips became under her palm, how her palm felt in response to that . . . She thought of hands, Drum's long, restless hands . . .

She dropped her hand and turned over with a muted groan.

She used all her control to settle her questing spirit. Her desires tugged at her like a kite trying to escape on the wind. She tried to anchor it with all her hard realities. She wanted to get up and fling on a long night-dress to conceal her expectant body even from herself. But she loved the breeze on her skin too much.

It was a long time before she slept.

*   *   *

The letter came the next morning. Alexandria's life was in chaos by that evening. Because that was when she showed to letter to everyone at the table.

"Can we come too?" Rob yipped after he'd had his chance to read it.

"Knothead," Kit said affectionately, ruffling his brother's hair, "absolutely not! It's Ally's treat, a vacation for her. She deserves some time without chores."

"I wouldn't be a chore," Rob said indignantly.

"Of course not," Kit said. "Your just being in her vicinity makes work for her. She'd worry about you every minute and would be watching over you instead of enjoying London."

"Besides, you've got a lifetime ahead to see it," Vic added. "This may be Ally's only chance."

"Thank you for remembering my advanced years," Alexandria said, snatching the letter from Rob and carefully folding it. "But I'm not going. I may be antiquated, but I think I've enough years left to go to London some other time. It's a lovely gesture and I appreciate the invitation. I will write to tell Mrs. Ryder so. But it's not for me."

"Why not?" Eric asked.

They were sitting around the table after dinner. The letter had passed from hand to hand after Alexandria mentioned it. She was proud of the invitation but embarrassed by whatever impulse had made her show it to them, and now wondered if she had because she really wanted them to try to persuade her to accept it. That made her even more embarrassed. She looked cornered as everyone studied her, waiting for her answer to Eric's question.

"Why not?" she asked in exasperation. "Because of so many things! I haven't the clothes, I haven't the money—yes, I know she'll be my hostess, but I can't go to London with no more than a fancy to see the sights and a tuppence in my shoe. I'm not Dick Whittington, you know." She didn't consider that small hoard of detested gold coins. She'd already squirreled them away and they wouldn't be touched unless there was a dire emergency.

"And," she added, holding up a hand in an unconscious mimicry of Drum, "besides that, who'll run the house if I go? Since Eric's going to London in a few days to report to the earl, you boys would all be alone if I left. Poor Mrs. Tooke's been an angel," she said, smiling at that lady, "but she must miss her family by now. And school's out, and so you'd need someone here all day. No," she said adamantly, "it's a lovely gesture. Maybe I'll accept it in a few years, but not now."

"I don't mind staying on," Mrs. Tooke said. "Don't hesitate a minute on that account. I love my family, but absence makes the heart grow fonder. I'm happy to stay on here with the boys."

"We won't be lazing about all day either," Vic said. "We have jobs this summer, remember? I'm being paid to help at the Montvilles' farm in the afternoons."

"I've promised Mr. Thatcher I'd give him a hand with his horses, and he's going to pay me too," Kit said proudly.

"And I'll help Mrs. Tooke, honestly I will!" Rob promised.

"Your clothes can be made to make do," Mrs. Tooke said. "Things are more relaxed in summer. The Season is ending so it's not necessary to be in the highest state of fashion, and light summer materials are less expensive than heavier ones. We can smarten up your gowns, I'm good at that. No one will expect you to go dressed like a girl about to make her bows at Court."

Alexandria's face flushed. "I can afford *some* new fabric for some new clothes. But there are so many other expenses."

"No, actually there are not," Eric said, sitting back and watching her. "A few coins for the Ryders' servants, and a few in case of accident or emergency are all you need. A guest isn't expected to pay for a thing, it's just not done in London. Besides," he added with a laugh, "the Quality seldom pays for anything in London."

"I'm not Quality," Alexandria protested.

His gaze softened. "You are in most ways. I know Gilly and Damon. They'd never let you put a hand in your purse, believe me."

The others at the table sat still, watching them argue the point, their eyes going from one to the other. Alexandria sensed their silent approval of Eric's argument and felt her own begin to falter.

"But they have a baby," she said weakly. "I'll be in the way."

"Gilly's a wonderfully devoted mama," Eric said, "but she is a lady, and has more than enough staff to take care of her darling when she's not there. I think she secretly looks forward to an excuse not to be such a devoted mama for a little while."

"I don't have a maid to accompany me," Alexandria said doggedly. "No respectable young woman goes on such a trip alone."

The heads at the table swiveled to Eric to see his riposte.

"You'll travel by public coach. I'll ride the same route. You won't be alone a moment, even without me. When you get to Gilly's house, she'll provide all the chaperone you'll need."

"She is a lady, I won't fit in," Alexandria protested, her eyes daring him to deny it.

"You won't have to, you're a visitor. As such you'll be able to see the sights, maybe take in a night at the opera or Vauxhall. You'll have a good time, believe me. It would be a chance to see something new. And something old, because your old patient will be there too. You'd be doing Drum a favor, at that, giving him a chance to pay his debt to you in some small way by letting him escort you to the theater or such. He's probably able to get around in an invalid chair by now. I think you deserve a treat, a vacation, a change of scene, and so does everyone here. It would be a once in a lifetime experience."

Their gazes locked. *He knows,* she realized in alarm. His eyes had held a world of resignation and understanding when he'd mentioned Drum, and he'd watched her closely when he did. And he'd said "once in a lifetime" with sorrow, but with finality.

That was just what it was. And so if she didn't go she knew she'd spend the rest of her lifetime regretting it. If she did, she'd probably spend the rest of her life regretting Drum.... Or maybe not. Was that what bothered her? Once she rid herself of the dream of the earl, would she be ready to accept another man? Did Eric sense that too? Was she using her fantasy of Drum to avoid reality, because she was afraid of how painful it might be? And when had she become such a coward?

"A once in a lifetime experience," she echoed thoughtfully, unconsciously raising her chin as she met his eyes. "Yes, it would be. Then perhaps I should."

Sixteen

*T*HE AIR THAT CAME THROUGH THE FRACTION OF
the open coach window was more than enough
for most of the passengers. The drizzle had stopped,
the sun was out, and now the breeze frankly stank of
warm ripe garbage, horse manure, rancid fish, stale
smoke, standing water, and things even more unpleasant to imagine. But Alexandria sat with her offended
nose almost on the window, eyes wide, breathing in the
stench of London in the summertime as if it were perfume, gazing at the crowded streets as though they
were heaven she was getting a glimpse of at last.

The racket made by carriage wheels, street criers,
and horsemen careening by over the cobbles was almost deafening, but still, she heard her fellow passenger's complaint.

"Would you mind closing that window?" the
woman on the opposite seat asked. "I suspect it's your
first look at London, but we're almost at the Bull and

Mouth and you'll soon have your fill of it. In the meanwhile, we should like to breathe, thank you."

The other passengers laughingly agreed.

Alexandria flushed and rose to pull the window down. The men in the carriage leapt to assist her. One was an old fellow coming home from a visit to a friend, another a weasel-faced man who said he dealt in watches, another a portly chap who slept through most of the journey. All had been amazingly polite to her since she'd stepped inside the carriage. The women she'd met on the journey had been charming too. She thought it was London manners, never realizing how fresh and lovely she looked.

A new straw bonnet framed Alexandria's face, and that face was aglow with expectation. She wore a pretty pink traveling gown stitched by Mrs. Tooke's clever needle, and a shawl with a floral pattern lay over her shoulders. Altogether she looked like a rose in bloom to the jaded Londoners who shared her coach.

She might look ablaze with anticipation, but the trip was as terrifying as it was exhilarating for her. She had as many alarming doubts as high expectations, but her fellow passengers' kindness made her spirits rise with every mile that took her closer to London.

The decision to accept the Ryders' invitation seemed to be the last one she had made for herself. Since then, she'd lost control of her life; it had been whirled away from her. The boys immediately took on her chores as though she'd already left. They said it was so they could learn them, but she knew it was so she could have time to make arrangements for her trip. She didn't need it. Eric made all the plans for traveling, Mrs. Tooke took over the making of her new gowns, saying, rightfully, that she could stitch up a garment faster.

All Alexandria had to do was worry about whether she'd made the right decision, and she did that a lot.

Her cohorts were too busy to sympathize. In their spare time the boys made up lists of things for Alexandria to do and see in London so she could report back to them about it. Mrs. Tooke went over pattern books with her every night until Alexandria's eyes were bleary and she'd agreed to leave the decisions to the older woman's excellent taste. Before she'd even received the Ryders' reply, urging her to come immediately, Alexandria had a new wardrobe and a sheaf of instructions from her busy family.

The night before the actual day of departure, Eric finished his investigations, packed up his kit, and readied his great white horse for the journey to London too.

"I'll be on the highway," he told her, "so if any problems come up, know I'll be near. I'll meet you at the coaching stops along the way, and when you get to the main stop in London, the Bull and Mouth, I'll be waiting to make sure you get to the Ryders' without mishap or delay."

He left the cottage for his quarters in the barn, the boys went to their beds, and Alexandria to her own. But she couldn't sleep. After tossing and turning one time too many, she crept downstairs and wandered through the familiar rooms, touching articles of furniture, wondering if she were doing the right thing.

The wavering light of a candle lit the stairs and Alexandria looked up to see Mrs. Tooke coming down, her wrapper pulled around her. "Still up?" she asked. "I thought so! A trip can make one nervous. There's no need to worry, you know. The new coaches are well sprung and the main roads have been macadamized, so the ride is very smooth these days. They don't tolerate as much drunkenness in the coachmen as they used to either—the coaching companies don't want accidents any more than their passengers do. Hundreds of people travel to London every day without mishap, so don't worry, it should be a swift and pleasant journey."

"Oh, it's not that, not so much as it is . . . Oh, Mrs. Tooke," Alexandria sighed. "Of course I'm excited, but the truth is I'm more afraid of London than I am of getting there! I don't want to make a fool of myself or be a burden to others. I wish I were already home, unpacking my souvenirs, with the trip to remember rather than to live now. Foolishness, I know," she said on a shaky laugh.

"You need a cup of tea," Mrs. Tooke said firmly. "Come, we'll go to the kitchen and put the kettle on."

"Yes, that's a good idea," Alexandria said. "If you could wait a moment? I wrote out some things to tell you, and if I wait I'm sure to forget them in the rush in the morning."

When Alexandria came back she handed Mrs. Tooke a packet of notes and instructions, her hands trembling as she did. "The truth is I did it for myself, not you. Because you already know how to run the house perfectly."

"I'm glad you did," Mrs. Tooke assured her, taking Alexandria's cold hands in her two warm ones. "This way I'll know I won't forget a thing. Don't worry, my dear. Everything will be taken care of here. You have only to enjoy yourself. Oh, and please give my regards to the earl, if you would."

That seemed to remind Mrs. Tooke of something else. She hesitated. "It would be wonderful if you could meet some likely young man there, because you certainly deserve to. But if you don't, remember it's not the end of the world. You're still young and very lovely. Maybe you'll meet some nice young women who will invite you to other places in the future too."

"Oh, this is adventure enough!" Alexandria protested.

"Perhaps. Perhaps not, you'll see," Mrs. Tooke said. Her expression grew far away. "You haven't traveled, but in my youth, I did. My parents took me to London, Brighton, and Dover, once to Scotland too." She hesitated, then focused on Alexandria and added, "Being in new places sometimes makes people forget who they are. It can broaden the mind, as they say, and that's all for the better. It's not so good if it makes you forget you always have to come home again."

"Don't worry," Alexandria said ruefully. "I know who I am—better than anyone else—and I'm not likely to forget. In fact, I wish I could."

"Mr. Gascoyne was a bitter man," Mrs. Tooke said suddenly. "You know that too well, poor girl. Everyone admired you for putting up with him so dutifully. No one listened to half the things he said either. You should forget the bitter things too. The past is done; your future is what you should concentrate on."

"Yes," Alexandria said briskly, skittering away from the subject of Mr. Gascoyne, who had never wanted her to leave the cottage except to work in the garden. "I'm going to London. I *will* have a good time. I'll be back within weeks to tell you all about it."

Mrs. Tooke's eyes studied her. "When I was young I

made what seemed to be the only decision that made sense to me then. Not that I was wrong, or that I regret my life. All I'm saying is that now I can see the world was very different than I thought it was or would be. This may be presumptuous of me, but I think it's important that you see the earl again. He was an invalid here, totally dependent on us, cut off from his normal world. In London you'll see him in that world and will see exactly how he's situated. You need that, I think you both do."

Alexandria dropped her gaze. She nodded. "I think so too. That's why I'm going there."

The kettle was boiling, but that wasn't why Mrs. Tooke went to brew the tea. "You're a very sensible young woman," she told Alexandria in a muted voice as she bent over the teapot. "You've had to be. Remember that too."

"Don't worry about us!" Vic had said as they'd waved good-bye at the coaching station.

"We'll see to everything!" Kit said.

"Bring back something for me, please," Rob called.

The boys and Mrs. Tooke stood talking to Alexandria through the coach window. Eric waited on his horse as the luggage and passengers were loaded in and on top of the carriage. The morning was gray and misty, but Alexandria wouldn't have noticed if it were raining fire. She caught her breath when the coachman cracked his whip and she felt the coach tremble and jerk forward. She waved as the guard raised his trumpet and blared a rousing tune to signal they were leaving. The lumbering coach pulled away, making Alexandria feel giddy and frightened, as if she were about to leave the earth itself instead of just the yard in front of the inn.

It took a half hour for her heart to stop pounding so hard it threatened to leap out of her breast. She finally sat back, folded her hands, looked out the window at the passing scenery, and began to get *really* excited. She became more so as the hours went by. Eric calmed her when he met her at the coaching houses they rested at. Other passengers chatted with her and made her feel that traveling like this was commonplace.

But now that she was almost at her destination her excitement was almost too large to contain. Now, at last, when she'd almost arrived, all her fears dropped away so completely she couldn't imagine she'd ever been frightened.

The streets outside her coach window teemed with people of all kinds and conditions. Surely one more insignificant female fresh from the countryside wouldn't matter or even be noticed. There were so many kinds of women everywhere. Ladies in fancy coaches, rag women pushing carts, maidservants, governesses, nannies, and women of fashion strolling or hurrying, often all to be seen on the same street the coach drove past. Surely, Alexandria thought in relief as her fascinated stare took it all in, if a woman looked well in her clothes and they were new and clean, it wouldn't matter if they were expensive dressmaker creations or homemade?

She counted her assets. She wasn't that old yet, or that young anymore. She had some money in her pocket, new clothes on her back, and hopes for new experiences percolating in her head. It could come to nothing, but she didn't see how it could hurt her. It was true that when going to a new place, all things seemed possible. *But they are,* she thought in growing delight, *they are!*

She sobered a moment, realizing she had to remember that some things were simply not possible, in spite of her wildest dreams. But as for the rest?

She was very lucky, Alexandria assured herself, gripping her purse in fisted hands. She hadn't felt remotely this way on the journey to Bath, those years ago. How could she? Then she'd been fleeing, curses echoing in her ears, alone, doggedly determined and filled with second thoughts. But she wasn't alone this time. Drum would be there. Eric was waiting for her. Her host and hostess, if not precisely friends, were people who would at least watch over her. And best of all, she wasn't fleeing now. In fact, lightheaded and dizzy as she was, she felt as though she were flying.

Alexandria sat back, took a sustaining breath, and willed her life to begin.

The Earl of Drummond sat back in a chair at his ease and watched a room filled with charming, beautiful, and wealthy young women vie for his attentions. He felt half like a rajah trying to decide who to pick for his harem, and half like a gentleman in the anteroom of a whorehouse trying to find the most pleasure for his money. The worst part of it was he knew both feelings were valid.

His circumstances weren't as wonderful as they seemed.

He sat because he couldn't stand. The women were competing for him because of what was in his pockets rather than what was in his trousers, his head, or his heart. He smiled to himself, wondering what they'd say if they knew what he was thinking. He sighed, knowing they probably did, and it didn't matter. They wanted him because of his wealth and title, and he wanted them because he was trying to do the right thing. There wasn't a word of love in it, and he realized there was never likely to be one.

He was very glad his father had gone home to his estates. When he returned, the duke had said, he expected his son to be walking, and soon after, doing that down the aisle beside the lady of his choice.

But that choice wasn't easy. Drum eyed the women surrounding him.

The beautiful Annabelle, in her signature blue, was there, of course, prattling, smiling, always with her lovely eyes on him. He was glad of it. At least she wasn't with his father. And she did make him laugh from time to time, almost as often as she annoyed him by how well she played this stupid courtship game in which he was forced to participate. He teased her, she twitted him, they flirted incessantly, eyeing each other with interest and distrust.

He felt sorry for her. Not enough to want to marry her or have his father marry her, though he realized he might have to offer, if for no other reason than to save his father from her. He supposed it would be better to take her to wife than watch his father be cheated for the rest of his life. At least Drum knew what he'd be getting. His father needed a woman he could love. He didn't, because it wasn't likely he ever would.

He'd have to see which way the wind was blowing when his father returned to town.

Still, it wouldn't be that bad if he did marry her himself, Drum mused. Their edgy relationship might make her exciting in his bed. And if he wanted an interesting wife who could bear him intelligent children, he might find one with a kinder heart, but probably none so beautiful and socially adept. But that decision could wait. She wasn't the only lively possibility; the room was stuffed with them. He sat back and watched his other visitors, dispassionately weighing their attractions and noting their faults.

Lady Mary McGregor was Scots, but had been sent to the best English schools. Her artificial laughter was wearying, but she had a magnificent face and form. Yet she talked almost exclusively about horses.

Little Miss Probisher was pretty and quaint, and almost on the shelf. That fact did wonders for her, giving her a vivid personality she hadn't had when she was younger. It also gave her jests a bitter taste and an acid edge. Margaret DeWitt was a rich man's daughter, and had the most sumptuous bosom Drum had seen in a long time, but he couldn't see much else about her that was half as fine. Violetta Vesey was dark and interesting, with flashing eyes. Olivia Carter was pale and interesting and wore a constant half smile. Drum suspected they were only interesting because of what they didn't say, and that was because they didn't *have* much to say. But they were good to look at.

Little Miss Meacham, youngest of an enormous brood, was the pick of that litter. She watched everything with fascinated eyes, making Drum realize she was doing the same thing he was. He wished he could talk to her and hear her impressions.

He couldn't, of course. If he made overtures to any of them, it would be noticed by all of them. He had to watch, then decide which to pursue when he was on his feet again. They knew that too, so they performed for him. It was amusing, it was annoying, and it was necessary, and he devoutly wished he could get up and run out of this perfumed bower his salon had become.

Drum felt a breath of fresh air as the door in the front hall opened again. "Major Eric Ford," his butler announced.

Drum smiled widely and honestly for the first time that day.

"You saved me," Drum said an hour later when he and Eric were finally alone in the salon. "They had someone else to preen for. Thank God for that face of yours."

"Saved you? You looked like a pig in clover."

"A nice description, but inaccurate," Drum said wryly. "A pig on a platter with an apple in his mouth, more like."

"Annabelle looks more tasty," Eric said with a sidewise glance at his friend.

"If your interest lies in that quarter, please tell me, and I'll kidnap her for you, or do whatever I can to see you two blissfully united. She's not so bad, but she's not for me. Or who can tell, she may be," Drum added hastily, because he still didn't know where fate would land him and it would be wrong to say cruel things, even to a friend, about a lady he might have to take to wife one day.

"How's the leg?" Eric asked, pouring himself a glass from the decanter on the sideboard.

"It itches madly. I'm tempted to rip off the splints and scratch myself to ecstasy. But it doesn't hurt or even ache as much as my poor bottom does now," Drum complained. "I'm exercising in my rooms so I don't turn to a pile of aspic, but I still can't walk." He closed his hand to a fist in frustration.

"I'm sorry the rain stopped," he went on. "I rejoice when I see storm clouds because I don't miss going out so much then. But I hate sitting here with the sun out while all the world walks by. It's even worse being pushed around London like a babe in a pram. I'm waiting for my crutches the way I watched for signs of a beard when I was a boy—as though they'll prove my manhood. God, I'm getting to be a whiner as well as a curmudgeon. Sunny days make me feel cheated and bitter, but then everything does lately."

Drum paused, thinking of all the things that made him feel that way lately, if they didn't bore him to oblivion first. Ever since he'd returned to London . . . His expression suddenly changed to one of avid interest. "At that, my leg's better than my head! How's Alexandria? And the boys?"

"The boys are fine. Alexandria's here in London."

"No!" Drum said, his eyes alive with light. "Tell me, when did she get here?"

"This very morning. I just left her with Gilly and Damon. She was excited about going there, but terrified when she arrived. They'll settle her down. She wanted to know when she could visit you."

"Now, an hour from now, any time she pleases!"

"I'll tell her. Now, would you like to know what I found out about your accident?"

"God! I think it *was* my head and not my leg that got the worst battering. Of course. Please, what did you discover?"

"Nothing specific. Everything suspicious. I couldn't find a hint of any boy with a borrowed gun. I did find a reason someone might be vexed with seeing you in the district, though. It seems Alexandria's charming father was a Bonapartist as well as a miser."

Drum nodded. "I'm not surprised. From what I heard, you could tell me he abused kittens for his Sunday sport. What of it? He's long dead."

"He had like-minded friends in the vicinity."

"Ah!" Drum said. "But they couldn't have known I'd be there any more than I did. And what would be the point? The war's done. Napoleon's dead. A disgruntled revolutionary might as well take a gun, stand in the middle of any village green, or London, for that matter, and start shooting at random. Improbable. I still favor the theory of that idiot boy and his stolen gun."

Eric stared at his friend. "I'm thinking of a more specific revenge. A madman who fixed on you for reasons only another madman would understand. Don't doubt it's possible. You worked for the War Office and everyone had guessed all your jaunts to the Continent in past years weren't pleasure trips."

"Half the men we knew fought that war," Drum scoffed.

"But uniforms make a man invisible. You went to Elba, and recently, before the little emperor died this year, you visited St. Helena too. Twice, I recall. Someone had to notice that, at least."

Drum shrugged. "I was a courier, merely."

"I believe you. But Bonaparte's English supporters are a strange bunch who followed him for philosophical reasons as well as their own motives. I've learned about them. Why would an Englishman work for a foreign leader? They were men who wanted to overthrow the world they knew in the hopes they'd do better in another one. But they wouldn't go so far as to show their faces or fight. They're bookish, ingrown men with no other lives, literally. Those who live through others have no life when their idol is gone. Linking themselves with their god by revenging themselves in his name would be just their meat."

"Meat, is it?" Drum laughed. "I see. Are you suggesting I hire someone to taste my food?"

"Maybe. There's even a mad rumor circulating these days that Napoleon was poisoned. I'm not going that far, though. I'm just suggesting you be cautious now."

"Oh, cautious." Drum's smile was rueful. "You don't have to worry. Be sure I am always and ever cautious in everything I say and do. I'm the most guarded man you'll ever meet—In everything, unfortunately for me."

Seventeen

AN EVEN LARGER COLLECTION OF NUBILE YOUNG women were gathered in the Earl of Drummond's salon the next day, posing, giggling, and in general trying anything to be noticed by their languid host. Drum was very grateful Eric was there, because in spite of what their mamas urged, many of the young women were willing to ignore a crippled, bony, sardonic fellow, even if he was an earl, to see if they could make a virile blond giant look their way instead.

Even Annabelle couldn't resist flirting with Eric, and they had a bitter history. Eric had once tried to lure her attention from Rafe solely to protect Rafe's new bride from her spite. Or had it been only that, after all? Drum wondered now, watching them as they stood together. They made a striking couple, each a picture of physical perfection. And certainly if any man could heal, or find, that beauty's heart, it would be Eric.

But it might not mean a thing. Eric was a kind man, the soul of civility, and Annabelle was socially adept enough to be the soul of artificiality. She flirted the way other women breathed. As she chatted with Eric she still found time to slide knowing glances at Drum, and frequently smiled at him as if to show she understood the nonsense of their set's mannered mating rituals too well to take them seriously. She looked especially fine today, in a celestial blue gown with a darker blue overskirt. She'd done her curls up high to give her petite figure height. The sapphire pendant she wore showed off her high and shapely breasts. Drum couldn't help admiring her.

Now that Eric had come to take the focus off him, Drum also couldn't help but be secretly flattered that he had some of the most sought-after females in Town here in his house, solely for the purpose of enticing him. He allowed himself to believe in that moment that it wasn't only because of his title and wealth. He wasn't in the habit of deceiving himself but it was such a comforting thought these days when nothing else seemed to be going right that he allowed himself to feel good about it.

So it was odd that when the butler announced two more guests he felt suffused in a sudden glow of warmth and delight that made his previous content seem feeble in comparison.

Gilly was lovely in white lace, but that was nothing new, she'd be exquisite in rags. Drum's gaze flew to the woman with her. Alexandria walked into his salon the way a woman might walk alone into a dark basement at three in the morning because she'd heard a noise she couldn't ignore. Her eyes had panic in them. Her face was pale. She looked as though she might bolt at any minute.

But those eyes were brilliant and her skin wasn't just pale, it glowed with health, especially in contrast to the wan indoor complexions of the fashionable women of London. He noted with pleasure that she was dressed as well as any of them now.

Someone had also styled her hair since he'd last seen her. She wore it back as usual but not so tightly drawn, so it was softer around her face. Her figure, in her new gown, was magnificent, sturdier than fashion dictated but in no way overblown. She looked like a warm armful of womanhood even though she was modestly dressed. Her gown was dark gold with a tiny pink flower pattern. It flattered, but the material was too thin to lie about what lay beneath it. Drum was expert about fashion but he was so busy noting that the gown suited her exactly, he didn't notice who had designed it.

Best of all, those brilliant eyes grew brighter when she saw him, and she smiled at last. He stretched out a hand to her. All chatter in the room ceased. He didn't notice. "Ally! My savior! Welcome. It's good to see you."

She came straight to him. "How are you?" she asked so anxiously he knew it wasn't just a social pleasantry.

"I'll be on crutches soon," he said with pride. "And I haven't had a headache in weeks. And you?"

"I'm amazed," she said. "London's more than I ever imagined, and you know I imagined a lot! It was my hobby, in fact."

"But now you'll have better things to do," Drum said with satisfaction. "Give you good morning, Gilly, my love. I see you've been busy."

Gilly preened. "Huh. I did nothing but give Ally a

good night's rest. The rest is just Ally herself. She's like a breath of country air in the city, isn't she?"

Drum nodded. He saw they were as private as actors on stage at the end of Act Three. So he decided to make a moment of drama out of Ally's introduction to society. "Yes. Let me introduce you to the company, Alexandria. Everyone," he said, taking her hand, raising his voice and addressing the room, "here is my friend Miss Alexandria Gascoyne. We met in a ditch in May. I'm very glad we did, and that she excused my rudeness at the time. The fact is I didn't even get up to make my bows to her or so much as tell her my name. She graciously pardoned me and had her brothers invite me into their home. I was rude enough not to scrape my boots before going in, and discourteous enough not to blot up my blood before immediately sprawling on her best bed. Then she called a doctor double quick and by so doing, saved my life."

The company responded just as he intended, bursting into laughter and applause.

Alexandria smiled. "I was too pleased that you still breathed to ask you to do more. Which was good, because you were so polite you might have tried and that would have been disastrous. At least you were the best houseguest anyone could want. You didn't ask for special food or drink or make demands, you didn't make any noise either, and never interfered with our household . . . at first."

He smiled back at her. "It's a wonder you let me wake up."

The company had been smiling too, but now they looked from their host to his new guest, and some of the young women's smiles faded, as most of the mamas' eyes narrowed. Drum held on to her hand. She gazed down at him.

Eric coughed. "But what did the fellow do when he finally came to his senses?" he asked. "Why, he built himself the barn of his dreams to house all the servants and friends he immediately summoned to help him. Poor Miss Gascoyne. Her horse was embarrassed and her chickens confounded, and that's nothing to what her neighbors said!"

The company laughed.

"Yes. A blunder, I admit," Drum said. "The barn became so inflated the chickens must have felt they had to lay golden eggs. I think I laid an egg myself designing it," he added with a puzzled frown to make them laugh again. "The truth is it fits Prinny's gilded palace at Brighton more than Miss Gascoyne's charming and historic house. Tell me, my dear Miss Gascoyne, have you torn down that atrocity I built yet?"

"The chickens would never speak to me again if I did," she said. "They've been giving themselves such airs they'd feel very no-account in just a plain barn now."

He laughed and pressed her hand in secret approval of her joke before he let it go, and Alexandria felt the tightness in her chest ease. When she'd entered the room and seen the glittering company she'd almost turned and run away. She knew Drum lived in splendor. But she hadn't seen enough splendor to actually know what it was before. Now she did.

His town house had impressed her from the outside, but that was nothing to how she felt when she stepped in. The checkered black and white marble entry was more splendid than the local squire's whole house. A

glance showed her that those were masterpieces of art
hanging on walls already covered with stretched silk.
The high ceilings had frescoes, their margins done in
gold, rose, green, and blue. She realized they might be
Robert Adam's work. A transom over the door let in
sunlight that picked out the huge black and white alabaster vases that stood in various niches.

There was a graceful staircase in the center of the
hall, carved to resemble flowing water caught in
stopped motion. Its gleaming mahogany was better
wood than any in her whole house, and his staff was
better dressed than anyone in her village. She'd seen
two footmen and a butler in uniforms that seemed to be
those of a very exalted army.

When she'd gone into the salon, her breathing had
literally stopped. The people there looked like they
stepped out of fashion plates. Mrs. Tooke had sewn a
beautiful gown for her, but Alexandria knew to the
penny what a bargain the material had been. These
women wore gowns from the hands of masters, light
silks and brushed satins embroidered by angels. The
fans they waved to cool their faces were more expensive than Alexandria's whole wardrobe. Their gowns,
hair, accents, those faces, everything about them was
diaphanous and cool, even the laughter she heard floating like their rare perfumes on the air. And apart from
Eric and Drum, there were only women here.

A tiny part of Alexandria's mind resented that. A
larger part was terrified by it. She'd been hoping to see
Drum. Instead, she saw the Earl of Drummond in a
high-backed chair, his eyes bored, half closed, a chilly
smile on his lean face. He was every inch a languid, elegant, rich, and powerful gentleman who could com-

mand the finest females in London to dance attention
on him—and didn't care if they did.

Then he'd looked up, and she'd seen life spring into
those lucent eyes. He'd smiled at her and spoken to her
and she'd seen Drum again. But Mrs. Tooke was right,
Alexandria thought; now she didn't think she'd ever
forget who he really was.

Well, good, she thought. And felt bad about it.

"This is the young woman who saved your life!"
Annabelle exclaimed with every evidence of delight.
"Well done, Miss Gascoyne! The ladies of London
salute you. How brave. Taking in an utter stranger!
And such a villainous looking one," she added with a
sparkling look at Drum. "How did you know he wasn't
a scoundrel who'd wake in the night, steal everything
in the house, and leave you all for dead?"

"My only worry was what we'd do if he didn't
wake," Alexandria said. "It's harder to be rid of a ghost
than a thief. I'd rather watch for a robber than a dead
man, wouldn't you?"

"What caused the accident?" another young woman
asked eagerly, pushing herself forward with a resentful
look at Annabelle, who, as usual, was dominating the
conversation.

"A rabbit, a squirrel, a bird whirring up to startle my
horse," Drum said with a shrug.

"Whatever it was, it must have been an extraordinary beast," Annabelle mused, "to have fired a gun."
She waited for the gasps to stop and added, "I asked
my father, you see, and he said the government was investigating. My lord Drummond was active for them
during the war as a foe of Napoleon, and still has many
enemies."

Drum stifled a groan. He supposed she said it to gild his reputation, because if she was after him she'd want him to look even better in everyone's eyes. Or, he thought gloomily, she might have hoped what she'd said would get back to his father and thought it would please him to hear her championing his son. It didn't please Drum.

"Or a boy taking potshots at birds, as everyone in the vicinity thought," Drum said in a bored voice that warned those who wanted to please him that he didn't want to pursue the subject. "Now. Since Miss Gascoyne is new to us and London, I have to ask you lovely ladies what sights you suggest she see. She was an excellent hostess to me, I want to return the compliment. Any ideas?"

The room was immediately filled with gabble as his guests competed for his attention, suggesting things that would make him think they were witty or wise.

Annabelle, of course, outdid them all again.

"I have the very thing!" she cried, cutting into all the mentions of the Opera, Astley's Amphitheater, Vauxhall Gardens, and visits to every cathedral, castle, gallery, civic building, and historical sight in town. "Why don't I have a ball? One that will introduce your rescuer to everyone? In a few weeks, say? Before everyone leaves town for the rest of the summer. By then, surely you'll be able to stand up for a dance with her. And with me, I hope," she added with a charming pout, "as a reward for my splendid idea?"

"Well, that is a good one," Gilly said grudgingly, speaking up before anyone else could, "but I'm the one to give it, thank you. I've known him longer, vexed him longer, and I know Ally too. My husband will be tickled. He wants to stay in London to finish up some business and this is a fine excuse. What do you say, Drum? I can do it up right—with your advice, of course."

"If Damon agrees, I think that's a fine idea," Drum said. "I'll ask him, though, if you don't mind."

"Huh," Gilly said gaily, "as if he'll mind! He likes a good party as well as anyone. What a time we'll have, Ally."

"But I don't need anything so grand," Alexandria protested, her complexion paler than it had been a minute before, her teeth worrying at her lower lip. "Truly, I don't need or expect such a thing. I'd be more than happy to see Astley's Amphitheater. The boys specifically asked me to go so I could tell them about it. I'd be content with that and a visit to Vauxhall Gardens, honestly I would."

"I believe you," Drum said. "But it would give me pleasure, so please allow it. You'll visit the other places too, I promise. I'll even accompany you." He held up a hand to silence the murmurs. "I've an invalid chair, so I can go anywhere, even without crutches. I've been yearning to get out of this house. Of course," he added sadly, "if Miss Gascoyne doesn't agree to Mrs. Ryder's ball, she'll also deprive me of my outings. Because if she can't go to a ball, I certainly can't ask her to accompany me around town. It would be terribly selfish of her, wouldn't it?"

He saw Alexandria's frown, and shrugged. "I'm used to getting my way, you know," he told the company. "And what else can I threaten her with? A fellow must use what he has at hand, and that is our friendship. At least, I thought she was a friend. I believed she'd want to see me out and about, and happy, but maybe I was wrong . . ."

"Nonsense," Alexandria said, flustered.

"No," he said airily, "blackmail. And you know I'll do it too. Your move."

"You're as bad as the boys when they want their way," she said. "Did you know they sulked and moped, making the house seem like a funeral? They said if I didn't go to London they'd stay that way all summer because they'd feel so guilty every time they looked at me, thinking that I had to watch over them instead of having fun."

"Of course," he said smugly. "That's what I told them to say."

He laughed at her expression. Eric joined in, as did Gilly. In a moment Alexandria did too. They were the only ones in the room that did, though.

"My God!" Eric said, pausing on the doorsill to Drum's bedchamber two weeks later. "What do you think you're doing?"

"Preventing myself from turning into a bowl of jelly," Drum grunted. "Close the door, please. I keep the servants away at this hour. But you never know when someone might look in. I don't want this getting back to my father."

Eric shut the door behind him, crossed his arms, and stared. His friend had transformed his elegant bed-chamber into something resembling a storage room in the attics. Six settees of different styles and shapes stood in a row, an equal number opposite, their backs facing, forming an alley that went from the huge canopied bed to the long window at the end of the room. The Earl of Drummond, clad only in his shirt and smallclothes, was inching through that weird path using only his hands, bearing his whole weight on them on the backs of the settees as he swung, suspended in air, between them. He went slowly, holding himself high enough so that his feet never touched the fine Aubusson carpets or polished wood floor. Grimes hovered nearby, obviously prepared to catch him if he fell.

Eric noted that his friend's lean body was deceptively strong. His hands were criss-crossed with veins that showed he used them for more than modeling riding gloves, his long arms were sturdy and well muscled, his good leg solidly built. Eric winced when he saw the heavy cage of wood Drum dragged along on his other leg. "Against doctor's orders?" Eric asked mildly.

"Not really," Drum huffed. "Doctor never said no."

"Because you never asked."

"Right," Drum said, on an explosion of breath as he reached the window. "Got here faster today, right?" he asked Grimes as he leaned against the sill, supporting himself on his good leg at last.

Grimes looked at the watch he held in his hand. "A full half minute faster, my lord."

"Good," Drum said. "Thank you, Grimes. I've a few things to discuss with Major Ford now. Don't worry, he'll help me back."

Grimes bowed and quickly left the men alone.

Drum grinned at his friend. "If I did nothing but sit and wait, my leg would be of no use to me by the time they decided to unlock the damned thing. I got to feeling weak as a kitten, Eric. Resting all day is as wearying as riding all day, in its way, but much worse in the long run. I never realized that a man had to use his muscles or lose the use of them. The world thinks the rich are lucky because they can lounge around and avoid laboring as common men must do. But rich men who do that have more gout, apoplexy, and liver complaints than other men.

"All right," he said to Eric's bland expression, "I can't prove it. But I know inactivity was driving me mad. I couldn't sleep at night, I couldn't do anything but twitch and moan all day. I can't use the leg yet, I accept that. I certainly don't want to lose it through my own stupidity, and if I move the bones before they're set, I might. But no one said I couldn't use my brain. I did, and learned how to exercise without troubling the leg. Grimes is too slight to bear my weight for walking. Certainly, I could hop, but that wouldn't be much exercise. I found this settles my nerves. Look at the ceiling above my bed."

Eric glanced up and saw two ropes hanging from a portion of a high beam that had been exposed.

"That's what I did when I first started, got my arms strong enough to do this," Drum said proudly. "I raised and lowered myself, until I knew I could do more."

"But you didn't want the duke to know. What if he sees that?"

"I'm hoping he won't. He seldom comes into my bedchamber. If he does? I'm not six anymore, I'm not afraid of him. I just didn't want him worrying and then worrying at me about it. He's very good at that. But this will ensure my being able to use the crutches the minute they give them to me. Then when I can actually walk, I won't—I'll run!"

"You've been getting around well enough in your invalid chair, I hear," Eric commented, strolling over to the window and looking out, to avoid his friend's penetrating gaze.

"To a tea?" Drum said bitterly. "To the Tower, to be wheeled around and shown the menagerie as a treat? To the Regent's Park to be set next to the other old gents in their invalid chairs, so we can gossip in the sunshine? To Astley's to watch the horse show from a chair on the aisle? Oh yes, I've been traveling, and I'm fed up with the way I've been doing it."

"And who you've been doing it with?"

Drum watched his friend with a measuring eye. "You want me to back away, Eric?" he finally said. "If so, just say it. She's been wonderful company. But if you've got a notion to court her in earnest I'll step back, even before I can do it on my own two legs. It didn't seem that way to me, though."

"It isn't," Eric said. "She enjoys my company as much as I do hers, I think. But she doesn't see me. Not as a man, at any rate. Not with you in the room, or the city, or the world, for that matter. I'm surprised, though. It isn't like you. I thought she was the last woman in the world whose expectations you'd raise. She's the kind of woman you always stayed away from, the kind you might desire, but never trifle with. Unless, of course, you mean to do more than that, and that would more than surprise me."

"Would it?" Drum mused. "As to my reasons for keeping her company—forget lust, I'm adult enough to control that. You can omit love too, I don't feel that, never have and doubt I ever will. But a great deal of real affection? Yes. It's a considerable surprise to me

too. I won't hurt her. I promise you I'd cut off my other
leg before I'd do that. I think I do have to promise you,
don't I? And not just because you're gallant."

Eric's expression grew guarded.

"I'm not the only man who's been seen around town
with her these days, am I?" Drum asked mildly. "There
are places I can't go even in my invalid chair, like row-
ing or riding in the park. You can, and I understand you
have. Again, I ask because I'll do as you wish. Do you
want me to step out of the picture?"

"No," Eric said stonily. "Again, as *I* said, there's no
point."

"So," Drum said, looking at his hands as though seeing the calluses on his palms for the first time, "this
isn't productive, is it? Let me tell you something that
is. I've got a list of names."

Eric's gaze sharpened.

Drum nodded. "My connections are still good.
There are four men who live in the countryside, two of
them relatively near the Gascoyne cottage. And more
who live in London. English Bonapartists who are
known to be deeply grieved about the passing of their
master. All on a list of men His Majesty watched all
through the war. Whether they still need watching is
the question."

"And you'd like me to find the answer?"

"If you'd be so kind. I can't yet. I hope to be on my
own two feet for the close. Mind you, it might be a
waste of time. We might get a letter from the boys any
time now saying they've found some poor chap and
have badgered him into confessing."

"I doubt it," Eric said. "Give me the list." He grimaced when Drum put his hand on a settee again,

preparing to wend his way back across the room to the desk he was looking at. "Here, I can't stand to watch you struggling—ah, exercising—anymore. Put your arm round my shoulder, lean all your weight on me, and hop on your good leg. I'm tall as a tree, and just as sturdy."

Drum grinned, even more when Eric half carried him swiftly to his desk. Once there, Drum touched a side panel and a tiny drawer slid out. He took out a folded paper and handed it to Eric.

Eric slipped it into his pocket. "Good. Might as well get to work right away. I've nothing better to do now anyway."

Drum hesitated. "I'm sorry about that. Women's minds are as devious and difficult as are men's. She can always change hers . . ." He stopped, his eyes widened. "Eric," he said on a gust of a laugh, "Do you know, we've been doing all this talking, and I'm not even sure which woman we're discussing! I've been out and about with Ally, of course, but also with Annabelle. Well, I engineered Ally's invitation and feel responsible for her now, and being seen only with her would cause talk she doesn't need, and Annabelle—the fact is I'm seeing her for many reasons now.

"Which of the two is it? Or could it be another? I also entertain a gaggle of females whenever I see Ally and Annabelle, to keep people's attention from being fixed on one woman. And to keep any one woman's from being fixed on me. So who is it?"

Now Eric grinned. "You don't know? Good. Just as well. No, better." He glanced at the improvised alley of settees, and then pointedly to the ropes on the ceiling. "You're a good friend, Drum. But you should know how a man needs his pride. See you soon, with better answers, I hope."

Drum chuckled as Eric saluted him and left with a bounce in his step. Then Drum's smile vanished.

Eric was right. He was playing with fire, or a woman's feelings, which was more dangerous. But he didn't plan on stopping yet, at least not until he understood why he was so fascinated with Ally. Now that he was in London he knew it wasn't the affection of a patient for his nurse that he felt, or the urge to please that a captive feels for his jailer. She had been both to him, and much more. How much more was what he had to discover.

He smelled honeysuckle, and his pulses raced. When he looked at her he felt soothed—until he looked again, and then he wanted the opposite of soothing. God, he longed to make love to her! He didn't know exactly why. She was lovely, but there were dozens of beautiful females in London. He could have his choice for a wife, or buy the others. He could send for a skilled courtesan whenever he wanted a lover. And he wanted one often enough. They'd be pleased to serve him even with the cumbersome contraption he had on his leg. But he didn't want any other now.

He knew as well as she did that there was no future in it. There was just now. He'd learned that was important. He'd had a close encounter with death, making him aware that now was the time a man should snatch at—even if he couldn't grasp it. Because later always came.

Still, there was no need to stop seeing Alexandria now. There were always ways a clever man could get around restrictions. They said he couldn't walk. He learned to walk using his hands. He knew he couldn't marry her, and she was only for marrying. But he was a civilized man of wonderful restraint. Why not see her? She'd be leaving town in a matter of weeks anyway. Why not keep his word and show her the best time he could? He owed her much more.

He might even find her a worthy husband. That would satisfy his conscience and do her a good turn. Too bad she didn't fancy Eric, he thought, but didn't feel badly about it. If she did care for Eric, then he'd have to see them together for the rest of his life. It would be uncomfortable seeing those two as a loving couple, to constantly remind him how he lacked the ability to feel love.

No matter, there were other men. He'd see she met them.

He went back to his exercising. It was a wonderful way to build his body back to health. And to stop thinking, too.

Eighteen

"*O*UT!" GILLY RYDER SHOUTED. "LEAVE MY HOUSE this minute or I'll have the servants come and drag you out! How could you? I invite you to stay in my home as my guest and you do this? Go behind my back? Deliberately deceive me? Huh! I'm ashamed of you, Alexandria Gascoyne. I thought you were as good as your word."

Alexandra hugged little Annalise one more time and then reluctantly gave her back to her beaming nursemaid. "I couldn't resist. I know you said I shouldn't feel I have to entertain the baby, and I don't. I was just going down to breakfast and I passed the nursery, and she enticed me, Gilly, she honestly did."

"Going upstairs is a funny way to go down to breakfast," Gilly said, taking her daughter from the maid's arms and nuzzling the baby's neck. "But you're right. Isn't she a temptress, though? Lud! I don't know how I find the willpower to leave her every day."

Alexandria's fond smile faded, her expression grew

severe. "Well, that's what I said, if you remember," she said briskly. "You're spending too much time with me. I'm having a wonderful time and you are the best hostess, I've seen every sight recommended to me and you have been there with me every minute to be sure of it. It's past time I went home. I can be ready to go in an hour."

"Give over," Gilly snapped. She gave the baby a last kiss and handed her back to her nursery maid. "Come along," she told Alexandria. "I'm hungry for breakfast and we've got some talking to do. It's rude to argue in front of the servants," she added after they left the nursery and went down the curving staircase. "If only because they don't know where to look when you do. They're not supposed to notice, and we're not supposed to notice they're there. For as long as I've lived with the Quality, I never understood that. People aren't furniture, even if they're paid to pretend to be."

She stopped on the stair. "It's not time for you to go home unless you're unhappy. Are you unhappy here?" she asked, glaring at Alexandria as though daring her to say yes. She went stumping down the stair again without giving her guest a chance to answer.

It wasn't the first time Alexandria had seen her hostess change from a dainty lady into a swaggering hellcat and then back again so quickly. She marveled such a tiny little nymph of a woman could so easily do that. But in the few short weeks Alexandria had been a guest here she'd learned that no matter how fragile her hostess looked, there were few women as strong in mind and heart. Or as honest and kind. "No, of course I'm not unhappy," Alexandria protested.

"Well, I didn't think so, because I'd have seen it.

Listen," Gilly said, swinging around again, "in a month Annalise and I will be in the countryside and we'll have yards of time together. Your visit's been as much fun for me as for you—only, is it that much fun for you? I know you're not unhappy, exactly. But the thing of it is . . . Oh, I'm bad with innuendo," she grumbled, "never got the hang of that either, though my benefactor, Viscount Sinclair, and Drum, *especially* Drum, are masters at it. I'll say it straight out," she said gruffly. "Thing is, I wonder if it's Drum who's making you want to go home."

Gilly's golden eyes warmed as she gazed at Alexandria, a world of compassion in them. "Seeing someone you love and want but can't have makes you want to stay and go at the same time," she said softly. "I know. If you don't see him, you dream about him. If you do, you wish you weren't near enough to feel so bad. Oh, I do know.

"When I was a girl I fancied myself in love with Drum," Gilly confessed. "Well, I did, I idolized him," she went on, seeing Alexandria's surprise. "Once I discovered that, it made everything all right. Because I realized I loved him best from afar. He was my ideal, my first male friend from the day the Sinclairs took me in, and my mentor after that. All I ever wanted to do was to please him. But as for him pleasing me? In *that* way? Oh, no. That wouldn't work at all. When I understood that, at last I was free to love another man."

She giggled like a girl. "I *adore* my husband, Ally. The best thing Drum ever did for me was to be that ideal, so I could feel calf love for him, then grow up to find another man to love the way a woman is supposed to—as an equal."

Alexandria's cheeks went pink. She raised her head in an unconsciously haughty way. "I do understand *equal*. That's it, isn't it? Don't worry. You don't have to give me a lecture, I have no designs on the earl. I'm sorry you think I do."

"Oh bother!" Gilly said, stamping her foot, "There's no talking to you! You're so full of pride—just like him. But you don't understand at all. That's his fatal flaw. Don't make it yours. Come along, this is getting silly. We can talk more privately downstairs."

Once in the morning room, Gilly closed the door, plopped in a chair and stared at Alexandria, who seated herself opposite, looking anxious. Gilly didn't see that so much as she saw a very different woman than the one she'd first met.

Alexandria had been, if not transformed, then brought out of the shadows by the changes a few weeks in London had wrought in her. New clothes, good French soap and a good French hairstylist, a few creams and lotions, and a dab of powder had burnished her. The best cosmetic might have been all the flattery she got from Eric and Damon's friends, and the other men who clustered round her whenever they went out in public. In the countryside she'd been a handsome woman in spite of her clothes and situation. Now she was a radiant one. She mightn't be beautiful, like Lady Annabelle and the other incomparables, but she did cut quite a figure. Not only her form, Gilly thought. Because Alexandria's face, too, was captivating. She had the sort of profile seen on a cameo, clean and aristocratic.

But she wasn't an aristocrat, and there was the problem. Gilly thought of what she and her husband had talked about the night before, and frowned.

"Drum's an easy fellow to admire," she said without preamble, getting on with what she'd promised Damon she'd try to say. "Easier for a woman to become smitten with. We've seen it happen before. He's charming, but so remote he frightens off some faint-hearted females. Others see him as a challenge. And some get all motherly and want to make him their lap dog. Huh! As if that were possible. He's not handsome but you can't forget his face—and those eyes! If he doesn't marry and produce children he should be hanged for it. Damon and I count him one of our best friends, and if he befriends anyone you can be sure that person's solid too.

"But Ally, he doesn't seem to be able to love, not like the Romeo-and-Juliet sort of thing, I mean. I've never seen it, at any rate, and I've known him a long time. It's not because of a broken heart, or a long-lost love neither," Gilly said, slipping into slang the way she did when she became agitated. "Ewen Sinclair's his cousin and he'd have known if it was that. We all talk about it among ourselves, you see. It's like he's got a missing part. He has women as friends, and has had more than his share for sport too, because though we're not supposed to know about all his ladybirds and such, of course we do. And he'll take up with only the best and most expensive. But he takes them as he finds them, leaves them, and never looks back. I don't think he's ever come close to real love!

"He's stiff-rumped, is what it is, in love with his name—aye, that's what he really loves! His name and all his fine ancestors. Like that cold fish of a father of his, I suppose. He can't forget them—well, he did once, when he proposed to me."

Alexandria's eyes widened.

Gilly waved a hand dismissively. "Not out of love. It was at a time when I didn't know my own mind. He did it to save me, and because I amuse him, because we're old friends, that sort of thing. He'd have been in the soup if I'd agreed! Truth is, much as I love him, the fact is Drum has a terrible flaw. He can't love a woman the way he does his heritage. Or won't let himself. He *is* attracted to you. Anyone with half an eye can see it. He likes to talk to you too, anyone can hear that. Well, who wouldn't? You're great fun, we've become such good friends I wish you could stay on here forever!"

Gilly looked gloomy. "But Ally, you're not a titled lady, and there's an end to it. He'll marry for prestige and pomp, to please his father, and soon, I think. That's why he's got his eye on horrible Annabelle these days, though he don't like her one bit, not really. Who can blame him? Still, she's got the right ancestors and his father's pushing her. Brr. That's going to be a cold match! But they both deserve it, though I wish he didn't.

"Anyway, there's no way he can do more than make you want more, which would be dreadful of him, and bad for you. Please know I'd do anything to help you if I could. That's why I'm being so rude now, I suppose," she said with a sigh.

Alexandria sat through Gilly's sermon, feeling her face growing hotter every second it went on. Now her stomach hurt and tears prickled in her eyes. But she didn't cry. She was deeply humiliated, too deeply to weep. Because Gilly was just trying to be kind, and that was even more embarrassing. "You're not being rude," Alexandria said. "I'm sorry I'm so transparent. I wish I weren't. I thought I wasn't."

"Huh. You have a heart. People who care are transparent, that's all it is."

"Do you suppose he knows?" Alexandria asked anxiously, wondering if she'd been a total fool.

"Maybe, he's a knowing one. What's the difference? All women fall in love with him one way or another eventually. Bizarre, isn't it?"

"No," Alexandria said sadly. "So," she said with a wavering smile, trying to speak without her voice breaking, "I was right. I should go home. Even if he doesn't guess, I'm embarrassed knowing other people do. Best I go home. The boys need me and I need them." She started to rise from her seat.

"No, wait," Gilly cried. "Don't fly away now. You can't go home yet. I'm giving that ball for you. It's important that you go and see how everyone takes to you. Besides, maybe you'll find someone else."

"Gilly," Alexandria said with determination, "listen to *me* now. I may have some feelings for the earl, and I'm sorry you saw them, but I swear I never took them seriously. Never! How could I?" She thought of all the hard reasonings she told herself in the night. She had to voice them now. It was painful but necessary.

"I have no birth, no fortune, no place in this world but my home and that's just a cottage in the countryside. I don't have much to offer any man, and nothing for such as he, and I know it."

"But you're lovely," Gill began to say.

Alexandria cut her off. "Oh yes," she said bitterly. "The London swell who tried to molest me that day at my house called me a 'fine strapping wench,' did you know that? That's not why I hit him. It's the truth. I'm not saying I'm hideous but the plain truth is I'm no great beauty."

She swallowed hard, remembering, not because of the fop who'd tried to kiss her, but because he'd touched on her greatest shame. She knew her attractions, they'd come with age. Bosom and hips were her only assets. She'd never been anything but a plain child, big for her age, competent and serious-looking, which was why Mr. Gascoyne chose her to mind the boys. The administrators never questioned his choice because it was clear she didn't invite the dangers a prettier little girl might have faced.

"I'm a big-boned countrywoman," Alexandria went on grimly. "The best anyone can say is I have a pleasant face and good hips for childbearing." Gilly started to protest, but Alexandria continued, "Think about it, I have. The Earl of Drummond's used to refined ladies of the ton—or exquisite ladybirds of the night, as you said. We met by accident, literally. That's the only reason he knows me. Why, if he'd seen me in the street, he'd have passed right on by. If his horse had thrown a shoe instead of a rider, Drum might have stopped at my cottage for directions to a blacksmith and stayed to chat a while because he's polite. Then he'd have gone on without a backward look, and you know it. But I'd never have forgotten him, even so. It's his having been helpless in my care that makes him fond of me at all, and only that."

Gilly looked anguished.

"Life's not a fairy tale," Alexandria said as Gilly struggled for words. Alexandria nodded in grim satisfaction, knowing there was no way her hostess could argue. "You're kindness itself, Gilly, but there are no fairy godmothers. Don't feel sorry for me, that's *not* why I said that. I came to London to look at an earl, if not a queen, so *I* could put myself in my place at last." She lowered her gaze. "I confess the thought of Drum made the thought of other men less bright to me. But that's all I hoped to do. I found more, in you and your husband, the sights I saw, and all the kind people I've met. I'll never forget you, but I'm *not* part of your world, and invitations to balls can't change that. My time here is up, more so now I know I risk being pitied or scorned if I stay."

"You won't be either!" Gilly protested. "I had less than nothing when I met the Sinclairs, and look at me now!"

Alexandria smiled. "Yes, look at you. You're the most beautiful woman I ever saw, I think, and more full of life and laughter than anyone I know. I'm only a woman who rescued a nobleman after an accident. I have my virtues. But I'm not extraordinary. I didn't even expect as much tribute as I've gotten. I'm content."

"That you are not!"

"In a way, I am. And I'd rather go home with my pride intact than go to a ball and feel as though everyone were looking into my soul and pitying me."

"I should have ripped my tongue out!" Gilly cried. "But I was only trying to give you good counsel."

"You did."

"Please stay for my party," Gilly pleaded, "or I'll never forgive myself. Don't worry about what people think. You're right when you say you aren't part of their world. Lucky you. Those people would gossip about a saint, it's what they live for. As to that, so what if anyone thinks you care for Drum? What a tiny scrap of gossip that would be. Half the females who meet him do, and what's new about that? Wouldn't interest them above an hour, I promise."

Gilly saw Alexandria's indecision and pressed on. "Now, the guessing about why Annabelle and Drum are spending so much time together lately is much more interesting. That tattle's the best to hit London since the rumors of a French invasion by balloon. Why, Damon says bets are being laid in all the gentlemen's clubs on when he's going to propose to her.

"Oh, Ally, the ball is my present to *you*. Please come, you can go home the next day, I promise! The best thing to come out of Drum's accident was my meeting you. I want to keep you as a friend. You're not high-born and neither am I, and you're bright as can be, honest and wise and good to boot. And handsome as you can stare, and that's no lie! I wish Drum would fall on his head again and let all that nonsense spill out so he could love you as he should," she said savagely, "because you'd be so good for him! But if he can't, I want you to have other chances at happiness. You're not common or ordinary. And you *do* deserve more."

Alexandria didn't want to disappoint Gilly, because she valued their friendship too. But she knew she'd already gotten what she deserved in coming to London, and her just deserts in other ways, exactly as Mr. Gascoyne had prophesied. She felt sick to her heart about it. She should have remembered her place. He'd educated her beyond it, but just as he'd said, teaching a pig to count didn't make it more than an educated pig. She sat quietly, her head averted. Gilly was afraid to speak again lest she muddle matters further.

Then Alexandria spoke again. "For you, then, I will. But then I *will* go home." She raised her head, sniffled, then eyed Gilly. "They're saying he's seriously courting Annabelle? Do you think he is?"

The little old man was hopping mad. He paced the study, his voice growing louder with every step he took. "And I'm here to tell you it's a vile lie," he roared, shaking his finger at the Earl of Drummond, sitting silently behind his desk. "Whoever's spreading it is my enemy because I'm as a loyal a subject as ye are, my lord, and I'll fight any man who says not! I come all the way from Sussex just to find the wretch who's ruining my reputation and the trail led straight to ye! They say yer incapacitated, so I'll wait, but if it's to be pistols at dawn to save my good name, then so be it!"

Drum's head was ringing. The fellow had been shouting for a long time and he hadn't been able to put in a word. Now at last the man stopped and glowered at him. "I never said you were an enemy," Drum said calmly.

This infuriated the little man again. His face grew redder. "Well, if ye didn't, then why's yer friend there asking all them questions about me in every lane and cottage near my home, eh?" Now he pointed at Eric, standing silent by the window.

"I never said you were an enemy either, Mr. Mac-Donald," Eric said.

"Nay, but ye *asked* if I were," MacDonald said with venom. "Ye asked everyone yer shadow fell across, and so then what's a body to think, eh? My neighbors are looking at me as though I had two heads, and me as loyal a subject as . . ."

"Mr. MacDonald," Drum said forcefully, "the plain truth of it is a fact few people know and I wouldn't tell you if I didn't feel it was only fair." He lowered his voice and the old man fell still, listening intently. "An attempt was made on my life by an enemy of our government. Your name came up in our inquiries," he added, raising a hand to prevent another outburst, "James MacDonald, of Ivy Close in Sussex. That is you? Well, then, sir, that's the only reason my friend pursued the matter."

" 'Tis that villain MacDougal!" the old fellow cried in fury. "I knowed it! Never forgiven me he hasn't, not from the day my James borrowed his best scythe and dropped it in the grass, forgetting it till the rust had taken over, and no amount of scrubbing . . ."

"It's the fact that you had an ongoing correspondence with Louis Gascoyne, a known apologist for Napoleon," Eric said.

MacDonald looked thunderstruck. "Me? I don't write letters to no one!" He grew still. The other men could see his fury fading and his horror rising. He put a hand to his forehead. "My dolt of a son," he said softly. "Och, Jamie, what a fool ye were."

He seemed suddenly much smaller and older. "My son James is likely the feller ye were seeking," he said on a weary sigh. "But if seeking were finding, I'd have him home where he belongs. He met yer Mr. Gascoyne in school, I take it? Well, he fell in with a lot of young hotheads there, so 'tis no wonder. He supported Napoleon?" He heaved another sigh. "So maybe that's why he went abroad. He left without a backward look and we haven't had a word of him for three years now. I made a bit of money and we sent him to a fine school

so he could take his place with gentlemen, but all he
picked up with was the riffraff. But that's our James all
over, ain't it?"

Since he'd said that last to himself, neither man
could answer.

"You haven't heard from him?" Drum asked quietly.

"Nary a word," MacDonald said, shaking his head.
"No, I lie! We heard a rumor that he'd took off to
America after the war, down to that New Orleans they
have. I suppose if he likes Frenchies that makes sense
now. But we couldn't credit it then."

"I'm sorry," Drum said.

"Nay," the old man said. "I don't blame ye. I blame
James, but there's nothing new in that, is there? Pardon
me for anything I said. If I hear from him, you'll
know." He bowed and left the room.

It was a moment before Drum spoke again. "That
makes three men who have marched in here threaten-
ing to blow off my head as result of our inquiries," he
commented blandly. "Two apologized, and one, I fear,
is still considering it. I don't blame them any more
than MacDonald blames his foolish son. Two of the
fellows corresponded with Gascoyne about his other
passion, butterflies. And one was merely a namesake
of a man who has passed on to the same place his
friend Napoleon has gone to."

"Leaving three here in London still not spoken for,"
Eric reminded him. "And those four in the countryside."

"Three, now," a familiar voice corrected him from
the door.

"Father!" Drum said. "You're back?"

"As you see," the duke said, stripping off his riding

gloves as he sauntered into the room. "I've been making inquiries of my own."

Drum frowned. "I'd rather you wouldn't, sir! It's dangerous."

"Oh? Dangerous for me, and not for you? Because you told me there was no danger to yourself. Don't worry. I'm well able to take care of myself, and I remind you, I look after my own. I went back to the scene of your accident and followed some lines of investigation. I believe you had the name of Mr. August Powell, Major? Cross it off your list. Powell's taken up with a higher cause than Napoleon's now, he's found a new idol to worship, literally. He's become profoundly religious, and can't stop praising God."

"It could be a ruse, sir," Drum said. "Madmen are clever."

"Clever enough to give away all their worldly goods and enter a monastery?" the duke asked sweetly. "Yes, that's precisely what the fellow's gone and done. A month *before* your accident."

"That leaves six on your list of highest suspects," Drum said. "Six men who are probably similarly converted since their revolutionary days. Give it up, gentlemen. There was a shot, it creased my horse and unseated me, I can't deny it. But the more time goes by the more I'm sure it was never aimed at me. Some things have to remain mysteries. I'm alive and getting well, and I'm content to leave it at that.

"So," he said, looking brighter, "I'm glad you're here, Father. I hope you plan to stay awhile. Seems Gilly's giving a ball to reward Miss Gascoyne and I think it would be a nice gesture if you were there to ask her for a dance too."

"*Too?*" the duke asked with interest.

"Yes," Drum said with a grin. "The hunt for an assassin may be a lost cause, but I've much better news. The doctor said I may have crutches soon, and since I'm healing so well and quickly, I hope to even be able to stump around without them by the time of the ball."

"To dance with Miss Gascoyne?" his father asked. "Charming gesture. But what about Lady Annabelle? I thought your good news might concern her, actually."

"Early days," Drum said evasively.

"But growing later," the duke said. "I'd ask that you remember that old adage: 'He who will not when he can, cannot when he will.' By which I mean, in less poetic terms, that someone may take the opportunity, and more, away from you if you hesitate too long to claim her. The lady is exquisite, and available. The first will remain so for some years. The second is a transient state. More than her hand in the dance will be sought by another if you don't act soon." He contemplated his son. "Still, if you don't mind that happening, all sorts of new possibilities arise."

Drum frowned, thinking about those new possibilities, wondering if he was finally being warned about his father's own matrimonial interests. Was he saying that if his son wouldn't have Lady Annabelle, he'd step in and take her for himself?

"Don't scowl," the duke said. "Your time's not run out yet. If this ball is such a grand affair, I think things can wait upon it. I'll return in time to attend. I wouldn't miss it for the world."

"Return?" Drum asked. "But you just got here."

"I came to report on my progress. I'm going back on

another trail that promises more. I'll be back again, never fear."

But Drum evidently did. Because as his father compared notes with Eric, Drum frowned. Whatever he'd said, he wasn't completely sure his accident had been just that. So his father might be putting himself in danger, one way or another. It might come from enemies of the state who might do something lethal to escape his investigating them. Or if he stayed in town, it could come from a lady who might have gentler, but equally devious and permanent plans for him.

Nineteen

*T*HE MUSICIANS WERE PLAYING A WALTZ, THOUGH IT was hard to be sure because the tune kept changing. Drum never got excited about such things, but now he couldn't wait to go in to the ball. It was a brilliant affair—literally. The ballroom was so brightly lit he had to squint and everything had a glistening aura around it. It was crowded too, but everyone made way for him as he entered. He was walking on both legs as though nothing had ever happened. His legs were strong and healthy; he could tell because he wore no breeches. He looked down to see two perfect limbs and that was enough for him, and everyone else, it seemed, because they all bowed or curtsied to him.

He looked for his partner. It was hard to find her because the other dancers kept turning into beggars and ducks, but then, in the way of dreams, they swirled back into people again. He saw Alexandria then too, standing before him, smiling, waiting for him to claim *her for the dance. He strode to her side, though he had to walk uphill and she kept moving away.*

She wore a pink gown. Sometimes it turned purple and then again salmon, but it always remained some-how pink, and he felt warmth in his heart and in his groin just looking at it. He finally reached her and bowed. She laughed up at him. Up? He'd never stood beside her before and the shock of it almost woke him to reality. But it was wonderful to look down into her eyes at last—even better to finally take her into his arms. He sighed with pleasure.

She was just the right height for him. She came to his chin and fit to his body, her breath against his neck and her breasts pressed and peaked against his chest. It was strange that she wore no clothing, but even bet-ter because of it. His hand went to her bottom to pull her closer, and the dream almost turned into another thing entirely.

He turned in his bed and the wood on his splint pressed into his leg, chasing erotic thoughts from his mind.

"We're dancing!" she said with a smile, reminding him his leg was fine, and they were at a ball.

He was very proud. "I said I would."

They danced, turning in slow circles, and Drum be-gan to leave the dream to drift into deep and dark and dreamless bliss.

"What are you doing?" his father asked.

"Dancing," Drum said, awakened to his dream again.

"Very good," his father said, and Drum looked down at his partner and into Annabelle's exquisite face.

She was very beautiful, all in icy blue, but he felt
suddenly as cold as ice and looked for Alexandria. He
saw her—dancing in his father's arms.

"Stop!" he shouted. "You can't do that. She's nothing but a commoner, let her go."

His father's arms fell from Alexandria, and since
she was twirling, she fell away from him and to the
floor.

There was a terrible look on her face in that moment, a look that touched Drum's heart because it was
one of guilt and fear intermixed. Drum paused. "I've
seen that look before," he said, "but when, and where?
Stop it please."

"You know when," she said, "and why."

He groaned, because he almost remembered. He
shook his head because he didn't. He ran to try to raise
her from the floor but had to look down because there
was a pain, a rat was gnawing at his leg. He was appalled and shook his leg hard . . .

"My lord?" a voice asked from his bedside.

Drum's eyes snapped open—then shut against the
blare of light from the lamp Grimes held high in the
darkened room.

"You cried out," Grimes said. "Are you in pain?
Your leg, is it hurting you?"

"Blast," Drum said. "I'd forgotten, I suppose it is."

Grimes pulled back the coverlet, brought the light
close and hissed in alarm. "A slat of your splint's been
splintered and it's digging into your skin. No wonder
you cried out!"

"Any blood?" Drum asked, wincing as he struggled
up to an elbow and tried to peer down at his leg.

"No, for a wonder. It's not too big a sliver but it

must have been painful. You likely bumped into a table or such today and chipped the wood. I said those exercises were getting too vigorous! We'll have to inspect the splint every night in future. It's getting old and the wood was never of the best quality."

"I didn't think to order mahogany," Drum muttered.

"Just lie still, my lord. We can break off the piece and smooth the slat down. I don't think it will affect the stability of the splint."

"A man shouldn't wear wood," Drum grumbled. "What's the hour?"

"Almost dawn. I'll take care of this and you can get back to sleep."

"No sense to it now," Drum said, yawning. "Light the lamps and pull back the curtains. If I were going riding as I like to do I'd be getting up now anyhow. Damn, damn, and blast. I can't wait to be free of this cage."

The lamps in the room bloomed around him. Curtains were pulled back to reveal the gray blush of dawn. Drum remembered his dream as it receded with the darkness. He let it go. He didn't know what it meant and didn't want to think about it. He'd dance at the ball in reality, Alexandria wouldn't fall, and his father . . . It was only a damned dream. He supposed he'd had it because he worried about how society would treat her. He didn't need the reminder. He would see to it that she wasn't insulted or hurt. He owed her that much, after all.

"Greer, Henderson, Copely, and Fitch?" Drum said gloomily a few hours later at breakfast. "They're all in London now?"

"And Norton," his guest added, moving to the side-board and helping himself to more eggs.

Drum shook his head. "Norton emigrated last year, my sources tell me. Creditors and an angry wife. Devil take it, Eric, we're chasing will-o'-the-wisps. The war is over, Napoleon's dead. And so is the whole issue. Was I attacked for any reason? Probably not. Will I be again? No, again. Our enemies have beaten their swords into plowshares. If they're still plotting, it's in the back rooms of banks. That's the only way to fight now. The armies on both sides are exhausted, men and munitions. The time for guns is over and even a madman knows it.

"In the remote possibility that an enemy of mine *did* fire that shot, it's because he happened to see and recognize me. If so, it was an act of the moment, as instantly regretted. He probably came to his senses and hared off, thinking himself lucky to be able to do so. Face it, there's no one after my life now except aspiring mamas looking for a wealthy son-in-law."

"Really?" Eric asked, raising a brow. "I suppose that's why you hired a Bow Street Runner to follow your father? He found out and told me before he left, he was very amused. Seems he'd already hired the same runner to watch over *you*."

"Greedy lout, he's collecting two salaries."

"No, he's collecting none. Your father dismissed him." Eric sat down at the table again. "Then he told the greedy fellow that he could work for you for all he cared, but that he himself fully intended to blow the head off anyone he saw skulking behind him, and ask for his credentials after."

"He would, too," Drum said with a small smile.

"Interesting way for you not to worry, though," Eric said.

"I can take risks with my own life—not that I think there is any," Drum added quickly. "But I don't gamble with my loved ones. Don't look so surprised. I may have a reputation as a cold fish but just because I never swooned over a fair lady doesn't mean I can't and don't love my father."

"I never said so," Eric said. "And I don't blame you. He's a remarkable man. He's a lot like you in that he seems cold until you come to know him, then you realize he's the opposite. I suppose he'd shudder to hear me say it, the way you're doing now. I'm glad I got to know him these past weeks.

"I admire my own father. No," Eric added, his fork in midair as he thought about it, "the truth is I love him too. That's important. A good mother teaches a man how to love other women because of his feelings for her. But a good father teaches him respect for women, and is the making of him. A boy needs a model to grow into. I know too many men who fear or despise or are even ashamed of their fathers. We're lucky, you and I."

"We are," Drum agreed. "What I remember of my mother is all good too. But since she unfortunately died young, that's only a sense of warmth and comfort . . . and beauty. She was very beautiful, I think. Her portrait agrees. You'd hardly guess it from looking at me. I'm my father's image. Just as well, I don't think a tiny nose and rosebud lips would suit me. I hear all little boys think their mamas are perfection. Do you suppose that's what they look for in their wives? If so, I'll never marry, because much as I like females I've never found a perfect one."

"No, and God forbid you did. How could any man live with perfection?"

"Well, the woman I wed will just have to learn how to do that, won't she?" Drum asked.

Eric grinned, then slanted a glance at Drum. "Have you found that lucky woman then?"

"Not yet, and I'm not likely to so long as I'm in this condition," Drum answered moodily. "The thought of being unable to hunt for a wife wouldn't have bothered me only weeks ago. Now it does because I'm finally aware of time passing. You said my father was wise, and he is. I don't want to be to old to dandle my children on my knee."

"Hunt?" Eric scoffed. "Hardly. You're the hunted one. This house is filled with your admirers every afternoon."

"As I sit like a stuffed owl, watching them. No. That's *not* how to find a wife. I need to walk and talk alone with a woman, maybe even lure her into a dark corner for a little test to see if we suit."

Eric stared.

Drum laughed. "I'm not a monster of depravity. And none of the ladies hanging after me are models of innocence, no matter what their mamas say. At least not any I'd be interested in. They're up to snuff—believe me, they know their way around. A fellow can expect a virgin bride, but not an unkissed one. Yes, there are women on the catch who try to snare a chap for stealing one, but everyone knows who they are—or should. But what's wrong with trying a kiss on for size?"

He snorted. "It's only fair for them too. We know that a woman who fits the bill in every other way might be stiff as a board in a man's arms. Well, a fellow who looks like Adonis might be clumsy as a ploughman at lovemaking. For that matter, a ploughman might have all the skills of Casanova! There are things only touch can discover. How do you know until you sample, if only a little? It's the only sane way to make such an important decision. I have to do that soon, but I'm not sure yet . . ."

Drum paused and fixed Eric with a grave blue stare. "I'll ask you again. Since I'm not in love or committed in any way, but will be looking for a mate, please tell me if I'm looking someplace where I'll tread on your toes—before it's too late. Not that I can compete with a Viking like you. But I wouldn't want to."

"I don't mind a one-legged man stepping on my toes," Eric said blandly. "Nor do I worry about where you tread. I'm a romantic, I believe in mutual attraction. The woman who wants me won't take another for profit *or* vanity's sake. If she wants you, I certainly don't want her settling for less. If she doesn't want you but is determined to have you anyway, then I certainly don't want her."

"And she is . . . ?"

"Without a name, as yet." Eric smiled. "I think. Maybe."

"Well, that's a help," Drum said. He put down his napkin. "So. On to more edifying topics. I'm off to Vauxhall this evening. Not only will a trip by water be good for me, but I said I'd meet Gilly and Ally there. Lady Annabelle and the usual clutch of other young ladies overheard the plans, applauded them, and said they'd meet us by the boat slip. Wonderful as I am, I can't please all of them by myself. Care to come along?" Drum saw the sudden light spring to Eric's eyes. "It might be interesting," he added, watching his friend even more closely.

But now Eric's defenses were in place. "Indeed?" he said as he went back to his breakfast.

"Yes," Drum said, grinning like a boy. "Because it will be my maiden flight on my crutches, at least in public."

Eric looked up, surprised.

"I can't wait to see their faces," Drum confessed. "I didn't tell anyone but I've been practicing alone so I wouldn't make high comedy of the moment by falling on *my* face. At first I thought I might need splints for my underarms. The damned crutches are agony on the underarms, would you believe it? The things one learns by being crippled. The doctor said I'd become accustomed. I did. But I can't wait for the day I can toss them away like a pilgrim at Lourdes. It will be soon, but not soon enough for tonight. Still, I won't complain—much. At least now I can be upright at last, which is a major step forward—forgive the pun. Coming?"

"Wouldn't miss it," Eric said, pulling apart a biscuit to mop up the last of his eggs. "The ladies are brave, and Grimes is bold, but whatever you say about how good you've gotten at walking with sticks, someone has to catch you in case you were only bragging."

Alexandria threw back her head in the joy of the moment. The boat wasn't going that fast—the boatman couldn't paddle as quickly as she wanted—but the breeze was strong, the Thames sparkled in the sunlight, and she hadn't felt as young and free in years.

"My father must have been a sailor," she said to Gilly's amused look at her obvious bliss.

She'd told Gilly the circumstances of her birth early in her visit, in case the Daltons didn't care for such a lowly guest. She'd wanted to be able to leave if it was a problem for them. But Gilly had endeared herself forever by only saying, "Pooh. Who cares? It's not who made you, it's what you make of yourself, is what I always say." Her husband had agreed, and Alexandria had been easy in their company ever since.

Now they sat in a long, low boat as the riverman rowed them toward Vauxhall. Usually Gilly went out on the town with a footman or a maid, but her husband accompanied them today. Damon Ryder took no chances with his lovely wife. Escorting her on a journey by water was a thing he didn't trust to anyone but himself.

"I'm so glad we came by water, like in the old days, instead of by Vauxhall Bridge!" Alexandria exclaimed, smiling as she breathed in the smell of the brackish waters of the Thames.

"Imagine!" she went on dreamily. "In the old days this is how everyone got around London. Only rich people owned coaches and even they didn't trust traveling in them. So for centuries if you needed to go anywhere you went by foot, on horseback, or by the riverways. The river was covered almost bank to bank with wherries and barges, skiffs and ferries, all kinds of boats. I've seen the pictures! I thought I'd see it too when I first came here, but though there are still so many boats it's nothing like I imagined. There are still river stairs everywhere too, but I was surprised to see people don't use them much anymore."

"You're right," Damon Ryder said. "They built over many of the stairs and are building over more. We've gotten used to our comforts. Coaches are a lot faster, less damp, and a more direct way to get where you're going."

Alexandria gazed at the old houses standing shoulder to shoulder on the riverbank. "Many of those houses had water entrances, just like in Venice. They're bricked up now too, I suppose," she said wistfully.

The Ryders exchanged amused smiles.

"Mind you," Alexandria added with an embarrassed laugh, "I haven't been to Venice any more than I visited the past, but I read about things and you can't know how exciting it is to see them for myself. And I do love water. It's a pity we don't have more than a pond near our cottage at home."

"Venice *is* astonishing," Damon said. "I have to take you there one day," he told his wife. "Perhaps you'd like to come with us then, Ally?"

"Of course I would!" Alexandria answered with enthusiasm. Then she felt foolish, realizing how inane she sounded leaping at a mere politeness, and how unlikely that invitation was to ever be issued again.

"One day, then," Gilly promised, "When we're done with all this breeding nonsense," she added. "Because I'm not very fashionable, and I won't leave my Annalise with a maidservant until she's at least seventeen!"

They joked about that and other things as their boatman sculled them over the water to the gardens. The boat picked up speed as it caught the current, and Alexandria felt her worries flowing away too as they left the buildings of London behind and ventured into the countryside. Only it wasn't the countryside as she knew it at all, she thought, wrapping her arms around herself as though she felt a chill, but really hugging the pleasure of it close. Because Vauxhall Gardens was only a short trip from the heart of London, and it was the premiere pleasure garden in all England, if not the whole Continent.

She'd read about it, seen illustrations of it in her bible, *The Gentleman's Magazine*. There'd be a rotunda, with an orchestra playing, there'd be artworks on display and more fashionable people than she'd ever seen on display, as they strolled the gardens to inspect the grottos and other carefully constructed sylvan retreats. Exhibitions and spectacles of all sorts were staged there too. There was a place to have dinner, and if they stayed on and the weather held, thousands of glittering lanterns would be lit so there could be dancing by torch and gas and moonlight.

"Here we are!" Damon said, pointing downriver.

Alexandria saw landing steps with many boats converging on a landing slip alongside an embankment, with steps leading to green lawns beyond. The dock was decorated with gaily colored banners and pennants. Their boat headed toward a slip marked by tall striped poles, like those she'd seen in illustrations of Venice. Alexandria caught her breath. This *was* a once in a lifetime experience. She'd hoard it up against the days ahead when there would be nothing new on her horizon, when she'd need to sit back and remember the joys of this visit in order to go on. She resolved to enjoy it, knowing that those joys were as fleeting as this moment on the swiftly flowing river.

As they approached shore, Alexandria straightened

and preened a little. She couldn't wait for Drum to see her. He might not remember her in the future, but if he did she hoped he'd remember her as she looked today.

Gilly had given her the new bonnet she wore. She'd protested she didn't need or want presents until an exasperated Gilly insisted the bonnet wasn't new or expensive, and would go to charity if she didn't take it. Alexandria half believed it, the other half being settled the moment she put on the sunbonnet. It was blond straw and the brim framed her face. She excused herself for accepting it by telling herself it protected her skin from the sun and wind, and not just because it set off her profile perfectly.

Gilly had hit upon the idea of pinning fresh red roses on the side of the brim. They matched Alexandria's new gown exactly. The gown was ready made, the only one she'd bought since she'd got to London. It wasn't expensive because it wasn't for formal wear, but was nevertheless the most beautiful thing she'd ever spent her money on, the most perfect thing she'd ever owned. It was rose-red, thin muslin with a gauzy overskirt. Her neckline was low, but not absurdly so, making her figure look lush, but still ladylike. She carried a blond silk parasol, lent by her hostess, and wore a locket on her breast and a smile on her lips to go with it. Alexandria felt she'd never looked finer.

Until she saw Lady Annabelle and the others milling on the grass watching them arrive.

Even from the boat, Alexandria could immediately see how splendid Annabelle looked, the way she stood out from the crowd. The woman rejoiced in wearing blue to match her eyes, Alexandria thought with sinking heart, so why the devil did she choose to wear dusky rose today? And such a gown! Silken, shimmering in the sunlight, magnificently styled to show its wearer's equally magnificent shape. A patterned shawl protected her white shoulders, but she wore it open enough to show the tops of those white breasts. Her charming pink bonnet had a stylish array of feathers that made Alexandria's brave roses look exactly like what they were: cheap and impromptu ornaments for a simple country woman. *A big, simple country woman,* Alexandria thought mournfully, eyeing Annabelle's perfect little figure.

There were at least a half dozen other young women in equally stylish gowns thronged on the lawn, all in radiant colors and looks, all waiting for the Earl of Drummond to come judge them, like Paris awarding the apple, Alexandria thought sourly. Still, she couldn't blame them. They fussed with their hair and fluffed out their skirts, but they were really trying to arrange their futures. The Earl of Drummond had a title and a fortune that each of the waiting ladies wanted to share with him, for life. Alexandria was only trying to collect another memory of him to brighten her life. Very different things, for very different people. She belonged here as much as they did, though.

Alexandria raised her chin, picked up the hem of her skirt, accepted Damon Ryder's hand, and stepped out of the boat to the shore, to wait with the rest.

She didn't feel that confident for long.

No one spoke to her but the Ryders. The other young women didn't even speak to each other, they were too busy posing as they scanned the river and waited. It was so painfully obvious that they were breathlessly awaiting Drum that Alexandria wished she'd never come. Then his boat slid into view, and she forgot wishing and looked forward to reality.

She saw Eric's tall form and bright hair first. But she sighed with relief when she saw Drum in the boat with him. She wondered how he was going to leave the boat. Had he brought his chair? They couldn't wheel it through water or up the steps. Would Eric have to carry him to it? How embarrassing. For one mean moment, she hoped he would. That might help her see Drum as only a man, after all. She glanced around and saw the sudden tension that gripped the welcoming party waiting for him. They didn't care if he crawled off. They were right. Nothing would diminish the Earl of Drummond. Not now, and never again. He could arrive on a door, the way he'd entered her house, and it wouldn't matter.

The boat docked. The little group on the lawn pressed forward to greet him. And then the Earl of Drummond rose to his feet! He rose to his full long lean height—with a crutch tucked under each arm. He wore casual clothing, a well-fitted dark blue jacket, white linen, tight-fitting buckskin breeches, and shining high top boots—*boot*. He wore only one. A thick bandage wrapped around the lower portion of one leg, covering his splint as well as his other foot. Otherwise, for the first time since she'd known him, Drum looked like any other tall, dark, wildly attractive gentleman.

She saw his teeth flash in a white smile when he saw their expressions of surprise. He looked like one of her boys might after performing a particularly difficult stunt. He took a step forward—and swayed on the two sticks of wood as the boat moved in a swell beneath him. The gasps around her were audible.

Drum turned to Eric. "Your arm, my friend," he said. "I can walk to shore, but I'd prefer not to swim there."

His title, his fortune—and his grace, Alexandria thought as she felt her own face relax into a silly smile. *His charm and effortless grace.* There was that. And *that* was the reason she stood there grinning like a fool, with all the rest of them, all the other hopelessly yearning females.

Twenty

$\mathcal{S}$HE DIDN'T KNOW HOW IT HAPPENED. ONE MINUTE, Alexandria was walking along the paths at Vauxhall with the Ryders, feeling as though she was in some royal procession, grudgingly trudging along behind Good King Drum and his consort, Queen Annabelle, with a long trail of ladies in waiting behind her. The next, she was at Drum's side—well, not too close to his side, because he had to have room to swing those crutches—and Annabelle had been maneuvered back a few steps and taken over by Eric. Alexandria's confusion must have showed on her face, because Drum grinned when he saw her expression.

But that was also because she had a moment of disorientation when she had to look up at Drum for the first time since they'd met. The world tilted. When it settled, she and the earl were in their proper places at last. He'd been imposing before; now he was imperial. She'd known he was tall, of course, but never realized just how lanky he was. Lanky was the wrong word. His form was sinuous and lithe. She couldn't think of a word to say to this tall, dark, and commanding stranger.

"Yes, very different, isn't it, now that I'm on my feet, or rather on my arms?" he asked with a grin as he swung along the path, "We've never been on an equal plane, have we? We still aren't because now I'm a head taller than you. It's very gratifying for me, but it must be a shock to you. After all, you've known me best in a horizontal position. You found me that way, but we really met in your bed and became friendlier the longer I lay on my back. Then when you came to visit me here I sat and stared into your . . . lap."

She suppose she should have been shocked by his sly use of words because that's what he probably wanted her to be. At the very least she could have turned her head aside and pretended she was blushing. Instead she laughed out loud. "Just what I was thinking," she said.

That pleased him. "Forgive me," he said, "but it's delightful to be able to joke without thinking of consequences. It's the privilege of old friends. Speaking of which . . ." His gaze took in every facet of her. "Let me presume further and tell you that you look lovely today. It's more than Town polish, it's Town gilding. New gown, new bonnet, new outlook on life, I hope? They all look good on you, you know."

"All three," she said happily, seeing how other visitors to the gardens were looking at them—at Drum because he was Drum, at her because she was with him and didn't look wildly out of place there. She held her head higher. "You're doing wonderfully on your crutches."

"I'm beginning to," he admitted, leaning on one for a moment, and pointing with the other to show her his skill before he moved down the walk again. "At first they were painful but I've got the hang of them now. Practice is everything. In fact, I'd bet I could go faster than anyone here if I wanted to, because I can swing out on them and cover more ground than I could on two feet. I'd love to show you, but you'd all have to trot—or sprint to keep up with me."

She had the instant image of all the ladies in his train picking up their skirts and dashing after him. She tried to repress a snicker. He must have read her mind. He smiled.

"Yes," he said, "it would be exactly like one of Mr. Rowlandson's cartoons, wouldn't it? Me flailing down the walk, crutches flying, all elbows and knees pumping away, the ladies in hot pursuit. Too bad I'm a gentleman or I'd test my theory."

"That's conceited of you," she said.

"Very," he agreed.

They laughed, but not for long. Soon Alexandria had to fall back to give another lady the chance to walk beside him. She was still so aglow from their little conversation she didn't mind. It wouldn't have done her any good if she did.

She noticed their procession was becoming a parade, picking up more people as it went along, like a snowball rolling downhill. Their party had set out with mostly women following in Drum and Eric's wake. Because of the assortment of fair young women, soon young and older gentlemen began to join their ranks too. By the time Drum sighted and hailed Lord Dalton and his bride, their company resembled a parading of the troops, or so Gilly murmured. Or a wedding party, as Alexandria overheard Annabelle's mama titter to a friend. Because somehow, her daughter had snagged the lead position alongside Drum again.

Well, and so what? Alexandria thought with a little hitch in her breathing that had nothing to do with the pace Drum was setting. She'd had her look at him. Still her heart sank as she trailed behind the elegant couple, because now she had to face the fact that she'd been fooling herself. Because with all she'd told herself, she *had* obviously hoped for more. Or else she wouldn't be feeling this low and cheated, and sorry for herself.

Facts were facts, but she conveniently kept forgetting them. Annabelle was a titled lady, and she herself was an anonymous foundling. Women like herself didn't marry men like Drum, except in fairy tales, and even then only if they turned out to be long lost princesses. *That* she was not. And if it wasn't to be a marriage, it couldn't be anything for them. There was really nothing else for them to do together, at least not in this world of theirs.

So she'd seen him. She'd have this day and then that ball. Then she'd go home and get on with it. What that "it" might be, she didn't know. But it would have to be enough. Alexandria stared at Drum's back and knew that was all she'd ever see of him in the future.

"I've seen cats let mice get farther away than Annabelle lets him stray," Gilly muttered darkly, seeing the direction of Alexandria's gaze. "But don't worry, Drum plays deep games."

"It doesn't matter, not really, at least to me," Alexandria murmured in reply. "It does to you because you're old friends and good ones, and will see each other often down through the years. So of course whom he marries is important to you. But it isn't to me, except theoretically. Please think about it. I have."

Gilly muttered something darker. Then she smiled, radiantly. "Huh. If I believed that, I'd still be in a wretched slum, lost and alone in the world except for my little sister and a future of hard work and harder times. But I always believed in impossibilities, or at least I was told to and taught to, and tried to, and look what happened! Nothing I planned and everything I'd have wished for if I'd known enough to wish for them. Life's surprising. No one ever knows what will happen in the next minute, do they?"

"No one," her husband, walking next to her, agreed. "Except me. We're going to the rotunda to see the art exhibition, so be prepared to exclaim with false enthusiasm, please. But then, if we're good, we get to sit down and eat."

"*She'll* snabble the seat next to him," Gilly told Alexandria, tilting one shoulder toward Annabelle. "But we'll have a fine old time. Just you see!"

To Alexandria's amazement, they did.

The weather held clear and mild. When they got to the rotunda Alexandria saw it was as grand as a palace, and as big as one too. She was overwhelmed by its cool majesty. After viewing the art, Drum's party sat down at tables at the side of the concourse, in the shade of towering trees. Waiters served punch, wafer-thin slices of ham, mutton, and cheese, followed by pastries, cakes, and ices they could nibble as they commented on the fashionable people strolling by. Those strollers seemed to step in time to the constant music they heard. An orchestra played, and when they tired, roving musicians and singers kept filling the air with song.

Drum's table was taken over by Annabelle, her mama, and a cluster of other fast-footed young women and their hopeful mamas. Eric sat next to Alexandria. The Ryders, another merry young couple, and two amusing young gentlemen friends of theirs completed their party. They laughed so much that other tables turned to look at them with wistful envy. And Drum looked their way more often than not.

That was something to remember, Alexandria thought as she laughed at a jest someone in her party made. She wished she could commission one of the artists she'd seen swanning about the rotunda gallery inhaling praise. She'd have him paint up this day in yellows and peach, for sunshine and mirth, so she could hang it on her wall and remember the warmth and joy of it forever. This day was hers, whatever the future brought.

And so what if half of that happiness was because Drum kept looking their way?

Drum couldn't dance, and so the entire party rose from their tables when the waltzes began, and strolled onward again. They bowed to old friends and introduced new ones. They exclaimed over each statue, arbor, and fishpond, and there were many. As the long summer afternoon stretched into twilight, one by one, little hidden lamps flickered on, like regiments of well-trained glow worms at work. Lanterns strung high in the trees blinked on as they were lit by teams of lamp lighters working quickly and silently. Skeins of tiny lamps on stands of rhododendrons looked like sparkling spiderwebs. Smaller ones glowed like stage

lamps to guide each foot along the wandering paths
that led from the grand concourse into darker retreats.

But Alexandria was getting used to the opulence and
spectacle. What had been magical increasingly seemed
only clever artifice. She began to see that the place was
entirely artificial, without a natural thing except for the
flowers and trees themselves, and she wasn't sure
about some of them. Everything had been cleverly engineered to please the eye. She admitted her jaded reaction might also be because she hadn't seen Drum
again, except from afar. It could also be because her
toes were pinching in her new slippers, or because
Gilly and Damon had fallen behind. They were
strolling together talking in whispers, lost in the wonder of the place and their own sweet murmurings. The
last time Alexandria had seen Eric, he'd been captured
by Miss Probisher. And Drum was likely still with
Annabelle.

It wasn't a good time for Alexandria to be left by
herself. It was twilight, a bad time for any woman to be
alone. Time for reflection, time for regrets. Now
Alexandria accepted the day was coming to an end and
that would soon mean the end to many more things.
Her visit to London was almost over. Her cottage
seemed a thousand miles away and yet she knew she
was closer to it now than she'd been scant hours before. Most of her journey was already a memory and
she knew the rest would soon be little more than that
too. When would there ever be another such time for
her again?

The day was done, the sun was gone, and so was the
man she had dared dream about. She suddenly found
herself as angry as she was sorrowful. Why should

some people get anything they wanted and others be left only to want things? Why should some be born with title, wealth, and the gender that gave them freedom to do what they wished, while others had to toil and do the best they could for themselves in a world that scorned those who hadn't been born luckier? She didn't hate Drum because of his good fortune, she only envied it, and grieved for the loss of the illusion of ever having him as the friend he'd called her. Friends were equals, after all. And where was her friend now?

Alexandria took off her bonnet and swung it by its strings as she walked along a narrow tree-lined path, deep in thought. She turned a corner and stopped short, her unhappy musings mercifully interrupted. She'd heard the burbling sound of running water above the far-off music, and had absently followed her ears. Now she stood gaping into a clearing that had suddenly opened in front of her. The water she heard came from a high waterfall, the water tumbling down over craggy rocks to fall in sheets into a pool. There was a cave just behind the cascade of water, visible only because it was outlined by hundreds of tiny wavering fairy lights.

"Your face," a voice said at her shoulder. There was laughter and affection in Drum's deep tones.

Startled, she swung around to stare at him.

He was gazing at the cascading water. "It's beautiful, isn't it?" he went on. "And entirely false, like so much in Town. They placed it here to amaze people and it never fails. The effect's achieved by dozens of tiny candles under glass, to protect them from the spray. They set them in the rocks behind and beside the waterfall, at the entrance to the cave. An old gent lives here. Yes. They actually pay him to live here, visitors are encouraged to think of him as the hermit of the grotto. He doesn't shave his beard, wears rags, and pokes his nose out now and then to give them a thrill. It's not much, but it's a livelihood. At night, he tends the candles, so it's not that he just gets to breathe for his pay. No one gets to do that."

"You do," she said automatically, and was shocked. Her hand flew to her mouth. She'd actually said what she'd just been thinking. Her eyes went wide, she was aghast. "I'm sorry, I didn't mean that."

"Didn't you?" he tilted his head and looked down at her.

He was as surprised as she was. She'd as much as told him he was unfairly privileged. But instead of making light of it or snubbing her as he would anyone else who dared say such a thing, he found himself needing to defend his entitlement. "You're not entirely wrong," he said. "I was fortunate in my birth. But I assure you I've not been content with that, I've added to my wealth. Damon got me investing, very profitably too. It's become an occupation of mine, along with meddling in politics. You're right, though, in that I was given the money to invest, have the time to meddle, and never had to go out and get a position the way the hermit did."

Alexandria wished she could take back her words when she heard the defensiveness in his voice. She'd been angry at him but that didn't give her the right to hurt his feelings. "You've been nothing but kind to me," she said honestly. "I had no right to say that. My mind was far away, you startled me."

"Almost as much as you did me," he said. He stood with his back to the lights so she couldn't read his ex-

pression. She could, however, see that they were alone
together.

She was alone with a man in a hidden grove in the
twilight, in a place infamous for its dark walks and se-
cluded places where couples went for trysts, and more.
But she felt entirely safe. He'd never take a liberty with
her. That made her smile. It was, she admitted to herself now, one of the reasons she was so sad and angry
with him tonight.

"I never should have said it," she said again, shaking
her head. "It's unfair as well as not true. Neither you or
I can help what we are, can we? Though of course,"
she added quickly, "you have no reason to regret your
birth."

"Nor do you," he said.

She laughed. It wasn't a merry sound.

He hesitated. He wanted to tell her that she was
unique, lovely and bright, so enchanting it would be
criminal for her ever to regret being on this earth, being
here with him tonight. But he held his tongue. Telling
her that might lead to telling her more, and the
damnable thing was that he wasn't free to do that.

When he'd seen her leave the company he'd made a
hasty excuse so he could slip away and follow her into
the darkness. He'd told himself it was to protect her
from possible harm. Now he realized he had only to
protect her from himself. His hands clenched hard as
he sought words to comfort her without committing
himself to anything but concern. He wasn't free to propose more. He had obligations and his father's expectations to consider and could never forget it. He could
offer her pleasure, nothing else, and his principles for-
bade that. He was blocked every way. He couldn't even

find a facile lie to speak now, when he most needed
one.

They stood in the deepening evening, the waterfall
plashing in the pool and the strains of faraway music
the only sound between them. He rested on his
crutches and still he towered over her, and the silence
grew. Now she felt vulnerable. Not because of his
height. But because she allowed herself to think of
possibilities. Now, in the growing darkness, they
seemed to be just a man and a woman in the darkness.
They both knew it. The sudden knowledge and the tension it caused between them was as much a part of the
moment as the sound of the rushing water.

He tilted his head to the side. *"If . . ."* he breathed
softly, considering her.

In that moment she wished he wouldn't be such a
gentleman. He looked a stranger to her now that he
was on his feet. She wished he'd act like one, one who
desired her. Because she'd wanted him for so long and
she wore the best gown she'd ever owned, and she'd
never have a night like this again. Of course he
couldn't marry her. She couldn't be his mistress either.
But the thought tormented her because though she
could never accept such a proposition, she wished she
could. She admired him for never bringing up the subject, and almost hated him because he might never
have thought of it. He sent her senses and her thoughts
in a whirl. Only one thing was sure, she wanted him to
want her too.

She silently urged him to. She couldn't do more.
However much she yearned to know what she'd be
missing for the rest of her life, she'd rather lose the use
of both *her* legs than reach out to him. He might recoil.

He might not. Either way, she could never face him again. But if he reached for her . . . ?

He couldn't hold her in his arms, of course, she thought quickly. He had to use his crutches. But he wouldn't need them if he held onto her. She could uphold him, she longed to. He could hold her, kiss her, this one time, just this once, because they were alone, and they'd never be again. And who would ever know except the two of them?

She'd been kissed a few times, on the sly, by trickery or force by local lads and trifling men. More, since Mr. Gascoyne had died. She was a stranger to the village and a woman alone, and she never forgot it after those times. She never walked by herself now except in her own garden. She'd never wanted to be kissed by any man but one of her dream lovers until Drum had appeared. All these months trying not to wonder what those firm lips would feel like on hers. Was she about to find out at last? Would they be warm? Or cool as he was? Would he make her feel in reality the way she imagined? She needed to know just once, so she'd know what to dream about in the future.

She swayed, leaned toward him, and closed her eyes. And waited. It was all she dared do, and yet she felt her heart pounding louder than the sound of the waterfall. She waited.

"Well!" he said abruptly, moving back one hop on a crutch. "What would people think if they found us like this? Vauxhall is as notorious for its dark walks and the mischief men and women get up to in them as it is for anything else. Neither of us needs that kind of talk. We'd better look for the others, don't you think?"

Her eyes opened. She felt as though he'd slapped

her. Her head went back as though he had. She didn't hear the regret in his voice because of his words. "Yes!" she exclaimed. "Do. Go! I mean, if I come with you it will make them think just what you said."

"But you won't be safe here alone. Let me take you back."

"I'm safe," she said, turning her head to stare at the waterfall she couldn't see through the veil of tears in her own eyes. Her face was hot, she wondered if a person could actually die of shame, and knew she'd be the first to find out. "I can't be far from the others, you found me easily enough."

"I saw your gown, it's such a distinctive color," he said softly. "You strayed down the path and were easy to follow, you glowed like a rose petal at last light. But now it's night, and not safe for a woman alone."

"I can't think it's that dangerous," she said, willing him to leave before he could see her face. "I'll wait a few minutes and then join the party again, at the back of the line. But you go first. You have much more to lose than I do, after all, don't you?"

"That's a terrible thing to say!" he said, shocked.

"Go, and send Eric after me then," she said, holding herself rigid.

"I'll send Gilly and Damon," he said. He swung his crutches and pivoted. He hesitated, then looked back over one shoulder. "I'm sorry, Ally. Sorrier than you know. But the problem is that I'm a gentleman, after all."

All her shame at her presumption and pain because of the lack of his boiled up and made her forget her place. "No," she said in a hard voice, "you are a nobleman, sir. *That* is the problem."

He went still. Then he nodded, and swung off into the dark.

There was no need for explanations when Alexandria rejoined the party a few minutes later. The fireworks display had begun.

"I told you not to wander off!" Gilly scolded.

"I was on my way back when I saw you and Damon, wasn't I?" Alexandria said. "Oh! Look! I've seen shooting stars, but I've never seen fireworks before. They're amazing!"

The musicians played in time to the pyrotechnics, orchestrating each explosion of color. Even though Alexandria was confused and angry, she couldn't help being overwhelmed and diverted. "Oh!" she finally said as what looked like a giant chrysanthemum exploded over them, dwarfing the vast night sky, making her clap her hands over her ears. "If I lived in London, I'd be here every night!"

"Then you'd have a long wait," Gilly said, laughing. "They're not shown every night."

"I've never seen the like, have you?" she said, so excited she held hands clasped as though in prayer.

"Too often, in battle," Drum said.

Alexandria's shoulders leapt. He'd made no noise when he approached, crutches made less noise on the grass than footfalls did, or she'd been too rapt in the display to hear him. He stood behind her now.

"That's why the men here tonight aren't as thrilled as you women are," he said. "The sounds, the smell of gunpowder, the air blue with it, it makes them remember too much."

"But they came here," Alexandria said.

"We're often drawn to that which is dangerous."

"I didn't know you were in battle," she said, wondering at the meaning of that oblique allusion.

"Oh, Drum served His Majesty everywhere," Gilly said. "Battlefields as well as boudoirs, though he'll deny it, of course."

"Of course," he said.

"Oh!" Lady Annabelle cried from Drum's right side. "Look, three stars in one!"

That made Alexandria feel better, in a terrible way, because he could be as oblique as he wanted. Reality stood at his side.

The fireworks went on until Alexandria's eyes were dazzled and her ears rang from the thunder and crash of the spectacular display. The air was thick with smoke when it was done, the candles and lamps seemed diminished. They were, not only by comparison to the pyrotechnics, but because they were burning down to their wicks. The night was ending. Harsh flares of torchlight lit the paths as lines of people began moving toward their carriages at the coaching stands, and others made their way toward the river again.

Now the night was filled with the sounds of people calling good-night to each other, their servants crying out for their coaches to come, and hired hackmen shouting their fares for those who hadn't brought private carriages. Further along, by the shore, a small navy of boatmen maneuvered for position, and gentlemen carefully handed their ladies into the swaying bobbing crafts.

Alexandria queued up with the rest of those in Drum's party who hadn't taken coaches. Gilly and Da-

mon were somewhere beside her, she couldn't see
much in the confusing press of people. They might be
members of the Quality, but they pushed and shoved
like commoners as they jockeyed for positions in line.
Alexandria stood bemused, watching long lines of people being taken up and carried off in boats.

A breeze had sprung up. The pennants on the gaily
striped poles snapped and fluttered. The boats rocked
in the water as it lapped at their hulls. Alexandria could
almost believe she *was* in some foreign land. Her excitement died as she remembered that for her this was
one, and it would soon be as distant and unreachable as
any nation across the sea for her. She'd removed her
bonnet and was glad the freshening wind whisked her
hair free from its bonds, grateful it blew in banners
across her eyes so no one could see the tears that
flowed down her cheeks, at last.

"Here's your boat, my Lord Drummond," someone
called.

"Go ahead," Drum's voice said at her ear, and she
felt his hand at her back, urging her forward.

She ducked her head to hide the evidence of her sad-
ness, and stepped forward. The boatman's hand
grasped hers and she stepped down. He abruptly released his grip as she reached the boat, so she almost
lost her footing.

"By God, man, have a care!" Drum said angrily. "I
can take care of myself until she is seated. Help the
lady now."

Lady? Alexandria's head whipped around, looking
for Lady Annabelle, shamed that she'd stepped into her
place. But Drum must have meant her, because she
didn't see the lady, and after a moment's hesitation the

boatman grasped her hand again and helped her to a seat in the swaying craft. Two men aided Drum. It wasn't long before he gathered his crutches in one hand and lowered himself to the seat beside her.

The little boat shoved off.

"Where are the Ryders?" Alexandria asked, looking around.

"Devil if I know," Drum said. "One minute they were there, the next, they weren't. I don't know where Eric got to either. We're alone. Don't worry," he added quickly, "no one will think worse of you for going back without a chaperone. Even the highest sticklers won't think I'd be able to get up to any nonsense in a boat, with three watermen at my side."

"*I'm* not worried," she said, as her initial spurt of joy at finding herself with him vanished.

He didn't answer. The boat slid into the dark. Two men rowed, another stood behind them, looking back at the velvet night. The river was ablaze with light. The sight thrilled Alexandria so much she forgot her situation. The pier they'd left was outlined by torchlight, the other boats had lanterns swaying fore and aft, the houses along the river showed lighted windows. It was like a convention of stars that blotted out the stars, all reflected on the raven surface of the swiftly flowing river.

As they went on and the other boats began to disperse to all directions, the night grew darker. That was when Alexandria noticed their boat didn't have a running light. She wondered how the boatmen could steer since she couldn't see much even though her eyes were becoming accustomed to the dark. Drum obviously saw more. After a few more minutes, he spoke again. But not to her.

"I'm Drummond, bound for the landing at Adam Street, near the Adelphi Wharves. That's Blackfriar's we just went under. Turn around, we're headed wrong. This isn't the way back," he said in annoyance. "Where the devil do you think you're going, man?"

The two men at the oars kept silent as they bent their backs. The man behind them swiftly knelt so his mouth was close to Drum's right ear and Alexandria's left one.

"Oh, I know who you are, my lord," the man said softly. "And I know where you're going. You don't. But that's how it should be. I have you now, my lord. That's how it should be too."

Twenty-one

*D*RUM SAT STILL AT ALEXANDRIA'S SIDE, BUT SHE could feel how he tensed at the strange man's words. She was afraid to even breathe in response to what he'd said. She hoped it was a joke, a bit of foolery on the part of some high-born, low-intellect acquaintance of Drum's. She waited to hear his answering jest. What he said didn't reassure her.

"You know who I am?" Drum said calmly. "Then you have the advantage of me, sir."

"Indeed I do," the man agreed. "In many ways tonight. Please take your pistol from your jacket pocket and fling it out in front of you." His arm snaked out and his fingers encircled Alexandria's neck. She couldn't swallow, much less cry out. "I have Miss Gascoyne in an awkward position, my lord," the man went on, his voice as tight as his grasp. "If you don't instantly obey me I can make it less awkward for her, rather permanently, I'm afraid. It doesn't matter to me, but it will to her. Come, I know you carry a pocket pis-

tol. I know many things about you. It will do no good
to lie or refuse."

"I wouldn't dream of it," Drum said. He reached
into his pocket. Alexandria gagged, because the hand
on her neck tightened. Drum's hand froze as his head
turned to her.

"Sorry," the man said, loosening his grip on her
throat a fraction, "but I don't altogether trust you,
Drummond, and I thought to make a point. I can snap
her neck in a second, or slowly cut off her air. Or let
her go. It's entirely up to you now."

Drum reached into his pocket again, pulled out a
small pistol, and threw it so far they could hear it
splash into the water. The rowers paused in their steady
rhythm, then took it up again.

"A bit overzealous, but good," the man said, letting
go of Alexandria's neck. Her hand flew to her throat.

"Now, be aware that there are three of us, all armed
and able," the man went on, "against only one of you,
and a crippled one, at that. Oh, excuse me, Miss Gascoyne, two of you, but only one capable of offering re-
sistance. You're lovely, but hardly a threat. I hope I've
made my point, my lord. Because I assure you letting
go of her neck does not necessarily mean letting her go
on with her life if you try any kind of stupid heroics
now."

Drum spread his hands in a gesture of defeat. "I'll
do nothing to harm her, but of course you know that.
Perhaps you can tell me how you came to be so knowledgeable, and why?"

"Certainly," the man said, rising to his feet. He
walked around to stand in front of them.

He was a heavyset, middle-aged man of medium

height, with gray hair, and he was properly dressed, if not like a gentleman of fashion. From what Alexandria could see of his face in the night, she'd swear she'd never seen him before. But she might have, because he was in no way remarkable. And he'd known her name.

"I'm Fitch," he said, his eyes on Drum. "Frederick G. Fitch, of Three Crown Court. I see you don't know me. Or perhaps you do. Your impassivity is another indication of your talent, isn't it? The trait of a bored nobleman, which you pretend to be. It's also the hallmark of a superior agent," he said, his voice becoming harsher, "and that, as we know, is what you are. And Miss Gascoyne," he said, with a mocking little bob of a bow. "How have you been?"

"You know me?" she asked.

"We've met, but of course you don't remember. You had little interest in Louis's friends, didn't you? I made inquiries after you, though. Did he tell you? No? I'm not surprised. I found you healthy and attractive, virtuous, obedient, and well brought up. I wasn't in the position of meeting many such women. I thought to take you off his hands. He was, however, always protective of his own interests. He rejected me out of hand. Much good it did him. You left as soon as he turned his back, and only returned when you were sure he was dying. If he'd have given you to me, he'd have profited. This way, only you did. But that's over now, isn't it? Because see what a poor choice you've made this time."

"Miss Gascoyne has made no choice," Drum said. "She found me after I'd been attacked and nursed me back to health. Now she's visiting London and I tried to repay her by taking her to see the sights. We have no other connection."

Fitch laughed. "Oh, indeed. And that's why you were on your way to see her before you were shot, is it?"

"I wasn't. I only detoured from the highway to take a rest from the road," Drum said. "You shot me, I take it?"

Alexandria saw the man's smile reflected in the moonlight—as well as the pistol he held in his gloved hand.

"Yes," Fitch answered proudly, "and Miss Gascoyne would have been unable to do anything but lament if only you hadn't turned in the saddle when you did."

"May I ask why you shot at me?" Drum asked, as though they were discussing politics at a gentleman's club, not being held at pistol point and rowed across inky waters to an unknown destination.

"Don't humor me!" Fitch growled.

"I assure you I have no intention of doing so," Drum said. "Obviously you feel I did you an injury, but for the life of me I can't imagine what it could have been. I believe you're in earnest and it *is* the life of me at question now. I simply don't know why."

"Now is not the time or place to discuss it," Fitch snapped, with a glance at the rowers.

Alexandria felt Drum let out a breath and she relaxed a little herself. Now she only trembled. So the man didn't mean to do anything to them just yet. Or maybe not at all. But he was one of Mr. Gascoyne's friends? She rapidly reviewed them in her mind. There weren't many. If she and the boys encountered any of his acquaintances by accident at the market or such, he'd had to introduce his family to them. But he'd done it hastily and with ill grace. Fewer still had come to their cottage. She didn't remember this man at all, but she could have met him years ago. The ones she remembered had been fusty old men with pale hands and shifting eyes, unused to children outside the schoolroom and less accustomed to young females. Mr. Gascoyne had encouraged her to avoid them and she'd been happy to obey.

She scanned the water to try to see where they were going. There were some lights on the opposite banks, but she didn't know London. Drum did. She'd have to put her faith in him.

Drum was obviously thinking that too. "My companions will immediately miss me," he said conversationally.

"So they will," Fitch agreed. "For what good that does them. They certainly weren't vigilant before; I don't worry about them now. By the time they know you're missing, then try to find out why, much less where you've gotten to, my work will be done. It was easier than I thought. I used the crowd to maneuver you into my hands. It was dark, there was confusion, I called your name and you stepped into my boat as nicely as you please. I hadn't meant to net Miss Gascoyne too, but now I think she'll have her uses. Now, I'll ask you to be silent, if you please. There'll be time for talk when we reach my destination."

Well, that was something, Alexandria thought. But she didn't like to think about her "uses" any more than she wanted to know what he meant about his work being "done."

Alexandria's spirits sank as they rowed deeper into a dark quiet area of warehouses and old houses and abandoned commercial buildings. Now the only light was the stars and moon. She didn't feel much better when their boat stopped in front of what looked like a blank wall thrown up against a riverbank. One of the rowers rose and groped along its front. She heard metal chink against metal as he finally found and grasped a heavy chain and padlock in one of his big hands. The boat rocked. The man dug in his pocket and fought for his balance as he fiddled with a key.

"Hurry," Fitch hissed.

The other rower held up a bullseye lamp and raised the shutter. A sudden shaft of yellow light showed a door set in what had appeared to be a bricked-up wall. The first man inserted the key and pulled. The door croaked, then swung open to emptiness, a vast blackness. They'd come to what was obviously a water entrance to a house or warehouse from the days when Londoners had navigated their city by boat—a door probably forgotten now except by Fitch, to be used for his strange purposes. Alexandria shuddered, remembering how she'd spoken of such things only hours before, how excited and light-hearted she'd been about them then.

Now she wondered if her tomb lay beyond that door, or what other indignities she might find there. If she could swim, she'd have thrown herself off the boat long before this. Now that they'd arrived, she wondered if she should, even though she couldn't swim. She felt Drum's hand cover over hers in a fleeting touch of reassurance, as though he'd heard her thoughts.

"In," Fitch ordered.

The rowers crouched, picked up the oars, and silently

maneuvered the boat through the door and into the darkness.

The air was dank and cold and close here. They were in some sort of room. The boat bumped against a landing and stopped. Someone secured it. It was dark and silent as the inside of a drum, the only sound the lapping of water at the bottom of the boat and against the strange dark shore they'd landed on. One of the rowers unshuttered another lantern. Now she could see, but Alexandria was no happier.

There was a flat landing space. The walls were black and so far back she couldn't see them. The ceiling seemed as high as the vault of the night sky outside. There wasn't much else she could see from the boat, and the place seemed as big as a playing field.

One of the men scrambled up a swaying mossy ladder to the landing. "Up," Fitch said to Drum, gesturing with his pistol.

Alexandria had been afraid of suffering indignities, but she forgot her fears because of the one Drum had to suffer now. He obviously couldn't get up the ladder to the landing with his crutches, he couldn't even rise to his feet in the boat because he didn't have room to get purchase. He tried, rose, staggered, then sat again.

"Try one trick, my lord," Fitch hissed, "and I'll treat myself to Miss Gascoyne before your eyes and then tend to you."

Drum shrugged. "You want me to crawl up the stairs, then?"

"I'm not a petty man," Fitch muttered. "Of course. Hake! Bring the gentleman up. Miss Gascoyne, may I assist you?"

Alexandria wanted to say she'd rather die, but she

discovered that wasn't true at all. So she watched Fitch go up the ladder, then raised her head and took his hand. Picking up the hem of her skirt in her other hand, she carefully made her way up the slippery rungs of the ladder. Then she stood on the landing and was glad it was dark so she didn't have to see Drum's face as one of the burly men picked him up, threw him over his shoulder and, cursing about his weight, clambered up the stair with him. By the time Fitch had another lantern lit, Drum was leaning on his crutches and looking around as she was.

The place was even bigger than she'd thought. The ceiling was as high as a cathedral's. They stood on a stone floor. There were crates stacked against the walls, but it would take stacks thick as a forest to fill up all the empty space. There were two staircases toward the back, on either side of the huge square room. They seemed to lead up to the next level, but thicker darkness lay at the top of them. Things had obviously been shipped to or from here, generations ago. Now, not even a sniff of what they had been remained because the stench of the place was only that of low tide.

"Good," Fitch said, "very good. Hake, take the boat and wait for me outside by the stairs to the right, where I showed you. Lock the door after you. Go now."

Hake nodded and went back to the boat. He pushed off and rowed to the door. When he got there Alexandria could barely make out his silhouette as he rose and drew the doors closed after him with a final thudding sound. Alexandria closed her eyes, wondering if she'd ever see the dark of night or light of day again.

"Now, Dubbin," Fitch said to the other man, "have you made sure of his lordship? One never knows what he has up his sleeves. You did inspect them?"

The man he'd called Dubbin grunted; it might have been laughter. "Aye, all. 'e's naught in 'is pockets, and naught up 'is sleeves but 'is arms."

"Good," Fitch said. "Get us some chairs then, and we'll see what his lordship has up his leg, shall we?"

Dubbin dragged two crates from the darkness and put them down near Fitch, close to the edge of the platform.

Fitch gestured toward the boxes. "Miss Gascoyne? Sorry I can't offer better facilities. Do have a seat, though. I've some things to discuss with the earl now. My lord? Take a seat, and be so kind as to hand me your crutches, after you do."

Alexandria sat gingerly on a box, her spine straight, her icy hands clasped in front of her. Drum swung over to a box, lowered himself to it, bent down, gathered his crutches, and handed them to Fitch . . . who took them in one hand and tossed them over the edge of the landing, into the water.

Alexandria gasped. Fitch couldn't have made his intentions clearer. Drum was completely helpless now, and his captor had shown him it didn't matter, because he'd never need to walk again.

"Now, Dubbin," Fitch said, "see what the earl has under that wrapping on his leg."

Dubbin knelt at Drum's feet. He took a knife from his coat. Alexandria shivered, not because of the threat of violence, but because Drum had been stripped of his crutches, and now would be of his bandages. She'd thought Fitch couldn't have made his intentions clearer a moment ago. Now he had.

Drum sat with his leg stretched out before him as

Dubbin made a cut in the bindings covering it. Dubbin unwound the cloth to expose a sturdy wooden splint, four stout slats of wood with wood screws holding them together, and a cord wrapped over them for more security. Dubbin ran his hands over and under it. "Naught," he reported. "Wood and leg, 'tis all."

Drum frowned, as though his leg pained him after Dubbin's rough inspection.

"But the other leg?" Fitch asked. "Hand Dubbin the knife you carry in the top of your boot, my lord, or he'll strip it from you."

Drum bent, withdrew a small knife from his boot, and tossed it to Dubbin, who pocketed it.

"Now," Fitch said with satisfaction, "Dubbin, pull the cords off his lordship's splint and unfasten the wood screws. He won't be needing it anymore."

Dubbin bent to his task. Within minutes Drum's cast fell away and lay like the peel of an orange in sections around his leg. Alexandria felt a lump rise in her throat and a cold knot in her stomach. Drum's face was impassive.

"Very good," Fitch said. "Now Dubbin, stand aside and be still. But watch them every moment, because snakes have been known to bite even after they've been crushed."

"Now you'll explain why we're here?" Drum asked, his voice cool and clear.

"I am happy to," Fitch said, turning to face him. "No, delighted. In fact, the only regret I've had about my last attempt was that you didn't know why I did it. I was flushed with success when I saw you fall—I thought it was done. But it wasn't. I felt cheated. It occurred to me later, on the road to London. I actually came back to find you and tell you before I finished you, in case I already hadn't, but Miss Gascoyne reached you before I could. I was glad you recovered, because my too hasty act rankled. I realized, too late, that revenge has less meaning if the one you're trying to pay back doesn't know why you did it, or how happy it makes him."

He paced a few steps, then turned to Drum again. "I'm bound for a new world tonight. Now I can leave knowing my act will be complete. It's a great consolation to me."

"So happy to oblige," Drum said dryly. "But can you bring yourself to tell me why? I accept your glee, but not the reason for it."

"No more games," Fitch said. "You know, it's time to admit it. You have no escape."

"Probably not," Drum said, "but no answers either. I made enemies during the war, but your name didn't signify when it was submitted to me by my sources. If I'd had dealings with you I wouldn't have forgotten. How have I offended you? I must have. Did I dispose of any relative or lover of yours? Ruin one or seduce another? It's possible. We did that to each other in those days, it was only another aspect of the war."

Fitch lost his air of civility. "Lies and more lies, you're a prince of lies!" he shouted, his voice ringing out in the vastness of the place. He heard his words echoing back and took a deep breath. When he spoke again his voice was pinched but calmer. "You know very well," he said. "It's the most important thing you ever did. You killed him—the greatest man who ever walked this earth! A man whose boots you were not fit to lick!"

"Did I?" Drum asked. "And who might that be?"

But now Fitch was pacing. "You visited him in January at Longwood House. You'd visited him before. You were a gentleman, a charming man, he said, who spoke French like a native and knew military history. Why shouldn't he trust you? There's supposed to be honor among gentlemen." Fitch tried to laugh, but it came out like a sob. "You didn't even have the courage to do it in a manly way by knife or gun, or even garrote. He was a soldier, a fighter, a man who deserved a clean kind of end, not what you dealt him."

Drum sat up. "January? I was at St. Helena then . . . Longwood House? You're accusing me of killing *Bonaparte*?"

Alexandria sat up so sharply that Dubbin took a step toward her. She sank back and stared at Drum. He shook his head. "Here's madness. He died of a disease of his liver, in May. I was in England then, you have to know that."

Fitch nodded vigorously. "But you delivered something to Lieutenant General Lowe, didn't you?"

"Messages from home," Drum said, sounding honestly perplexed.

"And poison," Fitch said. He held up a hand. "Don't deny it. The sweating, stomach pains, the nausea, pallor, and loss of appetite were unmistakable. The autopsy said it was his liver, but it was arsenic poisoning, we know that now."

"By God, man," Drum said, "That's nonsense. Who said such a stupid thing?"

"Marchand!" Fitch said triumphantly.

"The valet?" Drum asked, frowning. "He's mad or mad with grief. He was devoted to his master, but that's utter rot! Look, Fitch, there was no need to kill Bonaparte. His war was done, he was secured, it was over and he knew it. He did sicken; I think he let himself fail. He pined away because he knew the grand adventure was done. He was, in his way, a great mind, I grant you that. Perhaps he died for the same reasons a wild eagle can't thrive in a cage. We didn't kill him. *I* certainly didn't."

"He *would* have got free," Fitch said doggedly. "The Allies weren't safe while he breathed and they knew it. We'd have got him out again. I'm an Englishman and there are many more like me here, I'm going to New Orleans in the new world, where there are even more. Thousands of us. Where there's life there's hope; you were afraid of that. It would never be over until he was dead. So they sent someone to end it in a way that couldn't cast doubt. The Allies were judge and jury, his doctors mere instruments, but you were the assassin, Drummond. He began to fail from the moment you first arrived. Before I leave here I *will* see justice done."

"How much time and money did you put into him and his cause, I wonder," Drum mused, "that you're so mad with grief now?"

"What is money to honor?" Fitch asked. "What is time when you have a cause to believe in? I found a star and followed it. You extinguished it!" He gestured as he paced. Alexandria shrank in her chair as he passed. The man was mad.

"I was going to leave England," Fitch went on. "I couldn't bear being here anymore. The celebrations, the joy, the way my loss kept being pounded into my ears. I'd taught at that laughable facsimile of Eton, a

wretched school and a miserable life only made bear-
able by my dreams. When they were crushed I knew I
had to go. I'd just given notice at the school that day
and was on my way to London to clear up the rest of
my business before I left for good. I was riding toward
the turnpike—and I saw you! It was a stroke of fate.

"I recognized you!" he said, wheeling around and
staring at Drum. "Years ago I'd taken some lout on the
Grand Tour and persuaded him to stop at Elba. I spoke
to the emperor and knew my life's work then. But I
saw you there too, and asked about you. When I got
home I kept track of you, and your kind, your comings
and goings. We all did. We kept charts, in fact. Gascoyne too, did you never see them, Miss Gascoyne? Of
course not, Louis was a careful man," he answered
himself without turning his head to see her reaction.
All his attention was on Drum. "I never thought to see
you again, Drummond. When I did it all came clear in
an instant, like a lightning bolt slicing through my
head. I knew what I must do. Fate hadn't put you there
for no reason. One must seize the moment! I tried, I
failed. This time, I won't."

"I see," Drum said wearily. "Folly," he said with
sympathy. "Useless for me to deny it though, isn't it?
Longwood House was like a grand spa. We joked that
it was Napoleon's last resort, because we thought he'd
live out his life there in spectacular comfort. If it was a
prison it was a luxurious one. There were more doctors, French and English, than I could count, to attend
to his every sneeze. A steady stream of visitors from all
nations. Parties, routs, musicales, too. He was a greater
attraction than the pyramids, for God's sake! You've
seized on me as the villain because you need one. And

because I think, Fitch, if you could think about it reasonably, you'd see something has twisted in your mind now, you can't see straight anymore."

"You were there twice!" Fitch cried. "As well as on Elba. And you're a known agent of the government."

Drum sighed. "So are dozens of others. But you aren't interested in truth anymore, are you? Because if you don't blame me, who can you blame? How can you avenge yourself on the free nations? How can you avenge yourself on Fate, or God?"

"By putting an end to you," Fitch said with satisfaction.

"And Miss Gascoyne?" Drum asked softly. "Surely you can see she had no part in this."

"She did not," Fitch agreed. "But she does now."

Twenty-two

"MISS GASCOYNE WAS IN THE WRONG PLACE AT the wrong time the day I was shot at," Drum said patiently. "Coincidence made you both stumble upon me that day. There's more of the same going on now. That's all it is in her case. She helped a stranger, found me like a sick puppy in a ditch, and brought me home to mend. I met her at Vauxhall tonight because I wanted to show her a bit of London life before she went home. There's no reason to involve her in this."

Fitch laughed. "Now there is. My dear sir, I shall kill you today. How can I leave her now?"

"Then don't leave her," Drum said simply. "Take her with you. You said you wanted her once," he went on relentlessly, ignoring Alexandria's gasp. "Now you can have her, why not?"

"Because I won't have it!" Alexandria shouted. Drum gave her a warning look, but she was too angry to stop. He might be trying to save her life but she was appalled at his solution. She thought she had a better one, if only to buy time. She refused to believe in disaster; if she did, she'd have given up years ago. She didn't know what else she could do, but if she could delay what Fitch intended, something, anything might happen.

"Mr. Gascoyne *was* a clever man," she told Fitch quickly, "He trusted me, didn't he?"

Fitch turned to look at her.

"With good reason," she went on hurriedly. "I never breathed a word to anyone about his activities. Even when I got angry with him and left him, I didn't and I wouldn't. He died peacefully in his own bed, with no one the wiser. I'd never tell anyone about today, either. And truly, what has happened?" she asked with a sick smile. "Nothing. We simply came here with you. We can go back and say we got into the wrong boat and were lost, that's all. There's no need for violence. You can go to the new world and start a new life without worrying about what's following you.

"The earl said he's innocent," she went on desperately, because Fitch was still, his head to the side, watching her and listening closely. "I believe him," she said. "Not because I trust him. But because Mr. Gascoyne did have a chart. I've seen it," she lied. "Drummond's name wasn't on it, at least not more than once or twice. You should have seen how often some of the others are listed! I have. But Drummond was only mentioned a few times, I wouldn't have kept him in my house if it were otherwise, would I? I wasn't Mr. Gascoyne's daughter for nothing, you know," she added, with another travesty of a smile.

She didn't look at Drum; she didn't want to see his

reaction. She knew she was throwing away her reputation, branding herself a traitor, but she'd set herself on fire to change things if she had to.

"*Daughter,* is it?" Fitch laughed, showing all his teeth. "Is that what they're calling it now? Because you're no kin of his, legally or otherwise."

Alexandria went pale. Her eyes leapt to Drum and she saw his sudden absence of all expression.

"He never made a secret of it," Fitch said. "We always wondered what hold he had on you. He was old, as dry as dust, he certainly didn't have enough money to retain such a charming young creature once she came of age. As it turned out, he had no hold at all. You can't know how gratifying your flight from him was to me. And as for your seeing Louis's charts, I very much doubt it. He bragged that no one in his household guessed his mission. So you're a liar as well as a whore. I never doubted it."

He turned back to Drum. "Time's wasting. Now you know why. You took something wonderful from me and the world. I only return a bit of filth to the bottom of the Thames. Two bits of it, to be sure—I keep forgetting Miss Gascoyne. He let her call herself that so he could keep his teaching post, you know. Oh, you didn't?" he asked, seeing fire kindle in Drum's searing blue gaze. "Better still."

He turned from Drum. "Dubbin," he commanded, "keep close watch on his lordship. I have something to tell Hake before we go."

He stepped across the platform. He carried a lantern, otherwise Alexandria wouldn't have seen the door he went to. It was at the side of the wall where the landing met the water. He opened the door and stepped out into the night, closing the door behind him, leaving that end of the room in darkness again. They heard the slide of metal as he drew a bolt across the door from the outside.

The room was intensely silent. Alexandria was beyond embarrassment at what Fitch had said. Embarrassment was for the living, she realized as it dawned on her that she was almost dead. There was no time for shame or denial. She thought feverishly. She hadn't escaped so many dangers to die at the hands of a madman, but couldn't think how to turn this tide of events. The massive Dubbin stood between Drum and her, standing still as a stone, impassive. She looked at Drum. His head was turned to where Fitch had gone, he seemed to be listening closely. Then he nodded.

"Dubbin," he said conversationally, "I hate to be the one to tell you, but I believe your friend Hake is the one going to the bottom of the Thames now, and when Fitch returns, doubtless you'll join him."

" 'e said as to 'ow you'd try anything. Now pull the other, so's I don't 'ave to gimp, like you," Dubbin said with a sneer.

"Why else would he have to speak to him now?" Drum asked reasonably. "What could there be to talk about? Everything's been arranged, hasn't it? And why lock the door behind him?"

"Ain't mine to ask," Dubbin said with a satisfied grunt. " 'e pays, I does. Leave be."

"He means to leave here alone," Drum said. "He doesn't need anyone to row a boat, or tell a tale. Didn't you hear that splash? I did, even with the door closed. I doubt either Fitch or Hake is fishing. Hake just wants to earn a bit of gold, he's not the sort to turn on his master before he gets paid, is he? Fitch hasn't paid you fellows all yet. No man would before the deed is done, right?"

The calm reason in his voice made Dubbin stop smiling.

"Fitch wants to be away from here, free forever," Drum went on. "That's why he just sent your friend down to see how comfortable the riverbed is before he sends you and me there."

Dubbin frowned.

"Have a look when he opens the door again if you doubt me," Drum said with a shrug. "But be quick about it. And be careful, it could be your last look at anything. He doesn't want to leave witnesses. Would you?"

It was the last thing Drum said that made Dubbin hesitate. Alexandria saw it. He obviously thought slowly and his actions were just as sluggish and easy to read. He scowled and slowly turned toward the door.

That's when she acted. Alexandria sprang from her seat and rushed at him, head down, butting him with the full force of her body behind it. She was dizzied by the impact. But he was only thrown off balance and staggered a step. It was enough for her. She hooked her foot in back of his ankle and shoved. He staggered again and wheeled around, his hand in the air, aimed at her head. She grabbed that arm, hung on tight and bit down hard as she raised her knee and prayed she had the energy to use it as the boys had taught her. She did. He grunted and bent double. The pistol he held went skittering across the floor. She dropped down and followed it, scrabbling across the slippery floor on her knees as the slower-moving man turned and headed for her again, one hand on his offended groin, the other balled into a fist.

She was on her knees, his pistol in her two hands, as he approached. She raised the weapon, stared at his snarl, and used both hands to fire.

Then she closed her eyes.

The sound was deafening. Her hands felt searing heat and stung from the force of the firing. She dropped the weapon, and her gaze, and waited for his heavy hand to fall on her. It didn't, so she dared to look up. What there was left of his face looked surprised, before he stumbled back and off the platform. She heard the splash and was astonished. She was glad and horrified, sick to her stomach as she turned, unbelieving, to share the revelation with Drum.

He was half out of his chair. Dragged there, head back, with Fitch's elbow locked around his neck and his pistol to his ear.

"Nicely done," Fitch panted. He must have struggled with Drum, because he was still breathing hard. "I congratulate you, Miss Gascoyne. Good shot, and a lucky chance. The fool had his pistol primed; I doubt you could have fired it if he had not. Now throw Dubbin's weapon after him or I'll return the compliment to his lordship, and then come for you. The pistol can only fire once. But I saw you fighting like the alley cat you are and don't want you holding anything that can be used as any kind of weapon. My pistol's a splendid over and under, by the way. I have two shots, more than enough to deal with the two of you if you disobey. Throw it away."

"Don't listen to him," Drum told her carefully. "Take it and leave, Ally. He'll kill me anyway. You have no chance at all if you obey him. Try for the door he just left. He didn't have time to lock it again. You might get away now, if you go. Go!" he said before Fitch tightened his arm, cutting off his breath.

"Throw it now!" Fitch panted. "I won't wait."

"Don't," Drum gasped, his eyes on her.

She looked into the steady gaze of those strangely beautiful azure eyes of his and realized she couldn't live with herself if she was the reason their brilliance had been extinguished. And since she doubted she'd live much longer than that anyway, because a discharged pistol was a paltry weapon, and life was a paltry thing without Drum, there really was no decision to make. She said that. Or at least she might have. She really didn't know what she was thinking or saying anymore.

But she threw the pistol after Dubbin and heard it splash.

"Very good," Fitch said, releasing his hold on Drum's neck, letting him drop to his seat again, where he sat laboring for breath. "In many ways. You saved me the trouble of paying Dubbin, my dear. But you paid him in the same coin. The earl was right. I was returning from seeing to Hake when I heard what was said to Dubbin. I covered Hake's lantern and slipped in slyly. I never trusted the earl. Clever of me. What fools they were. The one, for trusting me, the other for underestimating you. How hard it is to hire good help these days! But then, I wasn't after good help, precisely. Only muscle and bone, and greed. There's plenty of that about! Now, which of you first, I wonder?" he asked thoughtfully.

"I'm sorry, Miss Gascoyne," he said after a pause. "I

believe it must be you, because I do want his lordship to know what it feels like to be helpless as something he admires perishes. That's the whole point of this exercise, you see."

"A schoolmaster to the end," Drum said, nodding.

"I will live on to teach the greatness of the emperor," Fitch said through tight lips. "You'll teach the fish how to dine on your lying tongue. No," he said, obviously thinking deeply, "I must deny them that pleasure. No water for you. The river door doesn't go all the way down, the riverbed is uneven, so the tide cleanses this place every day. Dubbin will join Hake soon—but don't leap into the water thinking you can find your way out through it," he cautioned Alexandria, "because you'd have to go all the way to the riverbed to find that exit, and when and if you did, you'll doubtless be in Dubbin's position too.

"I'll have to leave you two here on the platform, where no one will ever find you." Fitch spoke as though to himself now. "You'll remain here until you fall to bones. The staircases are sealed, as is the water door. I'll seal the door I leave by too. That's it. That's perfect. There are dozens of abandoned warehouses and old homes along this row, all decaying and covered with moss. You two will simply disappear."

He paused. Then smiled. "No, I lie. Perhaps they'll find you in a generation, when the district is rebuilt. They're always rebuilding London. But as for now? When you don't turn up, I think they'll assume you eloped with Miss Gascoyne and fled for the Continent, my lord. Yes. It makes sense, if they believe her fiction of respectability. After all, if you lust for her—and you do, I've seen your eyes—you can't take her under your protection. Not while she pretends to be virtuous. No, you'd have to marry her, and where else could you live with such an inferior being? It will break your father's heart, of course, but that's only fair too. You broke mine."

Useless to protest, Alexandria thought dully. Her only hope was that Drum, hearing the madman say he obviously lusted for her, would know the lie for what it was and discount the rest too.

"Now then," Fitch said briskly, "time's run out. I believe you're first after all, my lord. I've changed my mind. I need you and your trickery out of the way. And perhaps thinking of how I might revenge myself on Miss Gascoyne after you're gone will be just as painful to you as seeing her die. That's a thought too, there's many interesting things I can do before I dispose of her. So, now, say a prayer, my lord, and bow your head. Quickly, because it will be quick. Which is far more humane than the way you served our emperor."

Drum bowed his head. Fitch took a few steps back. Alexandria tensed, preparing herself to run at him and to her death if need be.

Before she could move, Drum did. He leapt up and swung around, his elbow crashing into Fitch's face, his other hand grasping Fitch's wrist and forcing it up high. He was much taller than Fitch, because he was on both feet—without his cast. Alexandria was as taken by surprise and shocked as Fitch was. But Fitch recovered faster.

Drum was younger and taller, but Fitch was heavier, and empowered by insanity. They grappled. Drum kept forcing the hand with the pistol toward the ceiling as he struggled with the maddened man. Fitch grimaced and kicked out again and again, trying for Drum's leg. Drum kept his grip on Fitch's arm, forcing it back, trying to dance out of reach of Fitch's flailing legs. They fought in deadly earnest, the ragged sounds of their breathing the only sounds they made. Alexandria moved forward and back again, seeing an opportunity to leap in, losing it a second later. The pistol kept rising and falling and wavering.

Fitch grimaced, angled his lower body back, and swung out with his leg. His boot connected squarely with Drum's leg. Drum loosed his grip on Fitch's arm and staggered back a step. Fitch wore a rictus grin as he brought his pistol forward. Drum's fist smashed into his face, sending him reeling back into the shadows. Drum followed him.

Alexandria snatched up the lantern and ran forward to see the two men rolling over and over on the floor. And the pistol—lying on the ground near them. She ran to get it—and the men saw her. Fitch let go of Drum and clambered on his hands and knees toward it. A second later, he'd kicked it from her grasp and sent it spinning. She ran for it, but the mossy floor was slick, and the weapon spun across the landing into the water.

The men heard it. Fitch rose, his eyes rolling, and ran for the far door. Drum rose and, limping, followed. They met as Fitch swung the door wide. Alexandria saw them silhouetted against the night. They grappled, they grunted, someone cried out.

Then one of the figures broke away with another wild cry, as the other fell to a knee.

Alexandria raised her lantern in a shaking hand, and saw Drum rise and stagger to the door—which slammed in his face. He clawed at the handle, but the sound of metal grating on metal told him what he discovered when he tried the latch. In frustration, he threw his shoulder against the door. It held. They were locked in. Fitch had got out.

Alexandria ran to Drum. He took her in his arms. She held him tight. "You're all right? You're all right?" was all she could say over and over again. His chest rose and fell like a bellows, she felt tremors coursing over his long frame, but he was warm, and he breathed, and he lived.

His hand stroked her hair. "Yes," he said. "Yes, don't cry."

Amazed, she realized she was weeping. She took a shuddering breath, then her eyes flew wide. She tugged at him, trying to drag him back into the darkness. "He'll be back, he'll be back," she cried frantically. "Come, hide, he'll be back for us!"

"No," he said, exhaustion clear in his deep voice. "No, he won't be. I dealt him a killing blow. He'll never be back. Hush, hush," he said, cupping her face in his hands. "Believe me, it's so. I know the work I do. Here, see?" He took his hand from her and held up a long, wicked-looking stiletto blade. It wasn't clean.

"It was hidden in my splint," he said. "We put a groove in a slat for it, because I *was* an agent, and a man who did that kind of work never goes unprepared, out of habit and necessity. I *did* work against Napoleon—though I never poisoned him, if he even was poisoned. But there's always a chance of last vengeful enemies out there, so we keep up our defenses. I lost my pistol and my small knife, as well as the swordstick I kept in one of my crutches, but I still had this, thank God. I slid it out and up my sleeve before Dubbin examined my splint. It was gone, thank God, before he disassembled it. And it did its work.

"A man can move and run, even speak after such a blow," he told her. "But not for long. Fitch is dead now. I'd bet my life on it. What's that worth?" he said wearily. "Better, and more important, I'd bet yours too. A heart can't beat when it's been punctured, Ally. Trust me. He won't be back, ever again. By dawn they'll find him floating in the Thames with Dubbin and Hake. Or lying in the bottom of his boat. He's gone."

She let out her breath and rested her face against his shoulder. He stroked her hair as her pulse and breathing slowed. He felt her stiffen a moment later, and knew why.

Because she'd obviously realized what he had known when he'd tried to get to the door before Fitch locked it against him.

Now there was no one who knew where they were—not their friends, not even their enemy.

Twenty-three

ALEXANDRIA KNEW SHE SHOULD BE WORRIED. NO, she ought to be in despair. They were locked in a place without food or water and no one knew they were there. But she couldn't summon panic. Not when she was in Drum's arms.

She rested on his chest. His neckcloth had unwound during the scuffle, his jacket was open. His shirt was of the finest linen so it was thin, and the warmth of his skin felt so good against her icy cheek. She could hear his steady heartbeat and feel the utterly alien shape of him against her own body. She marveled at the differences, the hard strength of his long frame, the long corded muscles beneath the living flesh of him. His scent was that of a gentleman, clean, with top notes of soap and starched linen and a touch of sandalwood. The other scent, of honest male sweat, made him and their situation very real.

It was bliss to actually rest against him and feel his hand stroking her back, the other on her hair—until

she realized it. Then it became disturbing. This was the
Earl of Drummond, the lofty man she could never aspire to. This was Drum, the man she laughed with and
fantasized about in spite of all her efforts not to. This
long, lean man was her ideal, and she was as close to
him as his eyelashes now.

She had to leave his arms. She didn't. She decided
to steal this last moment because it was a pleasure he
would never guess, and whatever became of them,
she'd never have it again.

She burrowed closer. But that nearness and her way-
ward thoughts of him suddenly made her nipples draw
up, puckering as though with chill. They tingled, and
she stiffened, shocked into reality. She prayed that if he
noticed her reaction he'd think it was only because of
the cold, and quickly drew away from him.

"What do we do now?" she asked him abruptly,
looking down, looking away, trying to hide her embarrassment.

He didn't seem to have noticed. He dropped his
hands and looked around the room. "We take the
lanterns before they burn down and try to see if there's
any other way out. I doubt it. Fitch was too thorough
and too pleased with himself. But we must try. You take
a lantern and go left. Go up that stair as well. He said
the door was sealed at the top, but one never knows. I'll
go right, we'll meet back here and compare notes when
we're done. Don't be too long," he cautioned her. "If
anything frightens you, shout and run right back here."

"No," she said. "*I'll* go in one direction, then the
other. You stay here. Your leg," she said when he
frowned. "I don't know how you stayed up on it so
long, but we mustn't try it further."

He smiled. "Don't worry. I think it's all mended. At least, it feels sound and worked when I needed it. It only aches from lack of use. I've been practicing putting weight on it for days now so that I could surprise the doctor when the splint came off. And because I hate to feel helpless," he admitted. "Don't frown at me as though I was one of your boys. I didn't risk anything. He was going to remove it in a week or so anyway."

"But Fitch kicked you! I saw it."

He winced at the memory. "Yes, I felt it too. But he kicked the wrong leg. Never mind, I can do this. Now go, we can't waste lantern light."

He turned and stepped off to the right. She bit her lip because he was limping badly. She couldn't see which leg he was favoring but his pace was halting and uneven. He stopped, then turned back to show her he was smiling. He sat on a crate and tugged at his boot. "It's hard to stand straight when you've one shoe on and one shoe off," he said, then grunted. "Grimes earns his pay, they're deucedly hard to pry off. No, I can do it . . . there!"

He shucked off the boot and tossed it to the side as though it were not fine Spanish leather. "Now I'm on an even keel again," he said, rising and standing with one bare and one stocking foot. The absurdity of it occurred to him and he looked up to share it with Alexandria. Then he saw her expression.

"Ally, don't worry," he said softly. "Yes, this is a bad spot. We can get out of it. Let's find the best way, shall we?"

He rose and jauntily walked off into the shadows, his lantern throwing a bouncing light before him. He came to the stair, and paused. The steps were high and narrow, made of cold, unforgiving stone. But he took them easily enough. Alexandria let out her breath, picked up her lantern, and went in the opposite direction.

After climbing five stairs, he glanced back over his shoulder. She'd left. He stopped, bent double and grimaced, damning his aching legs, the mad Fitch, and fate.

His legs did ache. The one, deep inside, because the muscles hadn't been used in months and every step reminded him of that. The other, with a searing pain because Fitch had been wearing heavy boots, and had got him in the shin. He'd be lucky if that wasn't broken now too. But he was still alive. His other leg had mended. And Ally was still alive. He had to keep it that way.

He worried about her more than himself. Ally was clever; she knew they were in a perilous position, but he doubted she knew the extent of it. It was his job to keep it from her because the truth was that he didn't know if they *could* get out in time. Fitch and his hired help were dead. Drum doubted if they'd told anyone else their plans, so there was actually no one who knew they were here. They were in an abandoned district with many empty buildings. There were other such districts. London was huge.

Certainly his friends and family would search, but how long would that search go on until they were found? And what condition would they be in by then? How long could he and Ally survive without food or water? The Thames was London's lifeline, but Drum didn't think any sane man drank from this part of it.

He was astonished they'd survived. He wouldn't have

without Alexandria's help. He'd been waiting for his chance, suppressing his anger, allowing indignities, keeping his patience only by hoarding the fact to himself that he could walk again, watching for the best moment to act at last, the moment when he could surprise them to maximum effect. Then she'd gone and courageously tried to disarm Dubbin. She'd done it. It had happened so quickly it overset his own plans. He hadn't expected her to fire when Dubbin went for her; he'd only known he had to protect her. So he'd leapt to his feet without looking or thinking—and Fitch had garroted him in the crook of his arm before he got a step away.

Then he'd had to wait again, because it wasn't the right time to let Fitch know he was able to fight back like a man.

Thank God for his stiletto. Damn Fitch for his intricate plans.

He straightened, wincing, and went up the stair again. She'd be back soon and he didn't want her to be alone. He'd admired her before, even more so now. But he'd been shocked to learn she was not only not Gascoyne's daughter, but his mistress.

The knowledge sat like a weight on his heart. He knew her well enough to know that whatever she was to Gascoyne, it hadn't been a thing of her choice. But foundlings had few choices. She was lucky not to have been impressed into a brothel, forced to serve ranks of men. Being one man's mistress was a treat compared to that. The thought made him shudder. Bright and lovely Alexandria forced to accommodate strange men day after day . . . He refused to imagine it, or what she'd had to do to keep a roof over her head when she lived with Gascoyne.

It was a hard world, and she at least had gotten an education, he told himself, but his heart hurt for her. Too bad, he thought again, as he had since the day he'd met her. If only time and fate had aligned themselves differently . . .

But in a selfish sense, a sense that made him angry with himself, at least it was better for him. He'd been willing to think of her as a scholar's daughter in order to make her acceptable, then anxious to bring her to London to have her meet possible suitors . . . No. He'd been too near to death for any more self-deception. It was time to admit more. He'd brought her to London because he'd wanted her near. Now this revelation?

He didn't blame her for not telling him. But it only proved once more that she wasn't for him, no matter how he ached for her. And he did. He couldn't deny it any longer. When he'd held her in his arms just now and felt her shivering against him, he'd had the surging desire to set her shivering in expectation of his lovemaking.

She'd been cold, but as she'd warmed he smelled the sweet summertime scent of honeysuckle rising from her body. It took the chill from this dank place, but it warmed more than his heart. It was an agony to feel her so close, those firm breasts, those smooth arms, that supple body. He was relieved she'd pulled away when she had or she'd have realized how much he wanted her.

That shocked him. He'd been astonished by how his body rose to her, unbidden. He'd lost control.

The nearness of death was what had fueled his desire for her, he told himself now. He'd been in enough dangerous situations to know that. Sex was the best way a man could prove he was alive, his body made demands when his mind feared extinction was close. He had to overcome that. She deserved more than his attentions; she needed life. If he won it for her, he wanted her to leave here as free as she'd been before she came in but he had to remain free of obligation to her too.

He was a gentleman, but it was more than that. He wasn't the man for her—he'd known it when he'd thought she'd had only a dull life, not a degraded one, before they'd met. And if the vagrant thought occurred to him that here was a solution, for such women made excellent mistresses, he strangled it at birth. He refused to add to her sad history. It wasn't just that. He wasn't so noble, he thought bitterly. Because in all honesty he also wondered if once having had her, he could ever let her go, or go himself to any other woman. Their situation was impossible and had been from the beginning, though he'd twisted and turned to try to deny it.

He still could do something for her, though. He could keep her alive. It was the only thing he could do for her—the best thing he could ever do for her. But he had to discover how, and fast, before their luck and his control ran out, because the door at the top of the stairs was locked.

She was sitting on a crate again when he got back to where he'd left her. The glow of her pretty rose-colored gown was extinguished by the gloom. Her lantern had sputtered out. She shook her head. "I tugged and tugged, but the door didn't even move. It must have been sealed over, there's no other way out," she said in a breathy voice he realized was on the edge of panic.

"There will be," he said with a confidence he didn't feel. "I've an idea or two. Let me try one now."

He took the lantern and went to the door Fitch had left by. He knelt and ran his hands along the sides of the door. It was solid, but old, and the place was damp, so it didn't fit precisely anymore. He took out his stiletto. He could just slide the tip of it in between the door and the frame, and slowly forced it upward. It was hard going, even though the door didn't fit. The space between it and the frame only admitted the tip of his knife. He gritted his teeth and slid the blade up—until he felt it hit an obstacle. He was sure it was the bolt on the other side.

"Do you think you can raise it?" she asked from behind him.

He shook his head without turning it. "I can try. If I can't, maybe I can see how much room there is, maybe we can insert something stronger, perhaps we . . ." He cursed beneath his breath.

"What?" she asked excitedly, kneeling beside him.

He let out his breath, and drew the knife back so she could see. The end had snapped off. "Well," he said, "it was a thought. I've others. We can try hacking away at the door until we can reach the bolt."

They both were still. They had only the one knife. The door was a thick slab of weather-hardened oak. It would take hours, maybe days. They each silently wondered if they had those days.

"I've other ideas," he said quickly, "but the best one is not one I'd try now."

He reached into a pocket and pulled out his watch. "No doubt Dubbin had his eye on this," he murmured. "I'm glad he didn't lift it with Fitch's eye on him, though he probably planned to take it later. But my father gave it to me and it's seen me through much . . . Oh God! It's way past midnight. No wonder I'm not thinking clearly. We'll do better in the morning, especially if some light enters here in the daytime. If so, we can certainly see and do more then. We should save lantern light too. I think we should try to sleep and try again in the morning."

"Sleep?" she asked, looking at him as though he were mad.

He chuckled. "Yes. It's possible. I've slept in worse places, at worse times, believe it or not. The mind needs rest as much as the body does in times of crisis. There's nothing else we can do now but wait until dawn. Would you prefer we sat up and talked about our problem all night?"

"Yes," she breathed, her eyes wide.

"No," he laughed, rising to his feet. He offered his hand to help her up. "That would only make us more weary and much more anxious. We need our wits about us to get out of here."

"But sleep?" she asked, confused. "Where? On the *floor?"*

"Not quite," he said, his hands on his hips as he gazed around the vast room.

In the end, he found a huge crate in a corner and dragged it to a spot not far from the door, but to the side, so anyone coming in wouldn't see them right anyway. He tipped it over on its side so it made a sort of impromptu cave. He bent double to step in, and crouching, took off his jacket and laid it over the wood. Then he backed out, turned down the lantern, and left it at the entrance to the crate. He bowed.

"Your room, m'lady," he said. "I wish I had a coverlet but at least you won't have to lie on the floor. And you're protected from the breezes and . . . anything else," he added vaguely.

He didn't want her to know he thought the place was likely home to other sorts of vermin than the ones they'd met today. People might have deserted the district but he doubted the river rats had. Nor did he tell her he wouldn't close an eye. He'd rest his body but not his vigilance. Fitch was dead; he'd suffered a wound no mortal could survive. But who knew who else might frequent this place? River rats came in all sizes, shapes, and species. The banks of the Thames were home to mudlarks, scavengers and foragers who earned their livings picking what they could from the river. It was also a hunting ground for other vagrants, thieves, and riffraff of every stripe.

"You expect me to sleep in there?" she asked.

"More easily than you would out here," he answered. "The enclosure will keep you warmer."

"And you?"

"I'll stay just outside the crate." He saw her expression. "Do you want me to sleep on the stair? Look, Ally, you'll be safer this way. And so far as compromising positions go, I doubt ours can be more so."

"I didn't mean that," she said, flustered.

"Well, I did. When the world hears we were kidnapped and held here at risk of our lives, they'll consider the proprieties. I'd never presume, you know that. But I want to be where I can watch over you. When we're free we'll face whatever's said, if we have to pretend we were tied up or in a swoon the whole time, we will. You won't be harmed by gossip, I promise. The thing is to get free, the rest will be simple compared to that. Now, please go to bed. Tomorrow will be a busy day."

He saw her indecision and added in what he hoped were prosaic tones, "If you have to use the necessary, you can go to a dark corner before bed."

"Oh no!" she cried. "I can hold it—I mean I don't have to—oh, lord!" she said. "You know what I mean. I will if I must, but it's not that terrible yet."

He chuckled. "It will be, and you don't want to go out in the darkness later, do you? Go now, you'll have privacy. I'll escort you, then come back when you call me to escort you back. Look, Ally, you're a practical woman, and a human one. Will you lie awake wriggling all night?"

She laughed. She protested. But in the end she let him walk her to the furthest wall, waited for him to leave, then hurriedly attended to things so she'd be able to get through the night. Because it was more vital than she'd let on. It had been hours since she'd visited the ladies' convenience at the Gardens. The process now was awkward and embarrassing. She was glad she had a handkerchief and had no hesitation sacrificing it for her cause. It was a good thing it wasn't her time of the month as well, she thought; *that* would have put the icing on it.

Women had the worst of it in every way, she thought gloomily. No doubt he was glad she'd gone so he could find relief as well. But he had the whole Thames for his purposes, and she had this musty corner . . . where she heard something small make a scribbling sound as it scurried over the stones. She bolted as soon as she decently could, and called for Drum's escort back.

"Do you think I dare wash my hands and face before

I lie down?" she asked, to make conversation as they walked back to her improvised boudoir. It was such an awkward situation she had to say something. Of course men knew women used the convenience; it just wasn't something decent females discussed with them. Life was absurd, she suddenly realized, at least hers was, because it was so hemmed round with the petty and inconsequential. Here they were facing death, and she worried because he knew she'd just relieved herself!

"I wouldn't drink that water," he told her, "but if you want to wet your handkerchief and wash, I think you could."

"I haven't one," she said with embarrassment.

Well-bred women always carried one, he thought—and thought again, remembering basic biology. "Here's mine. Go, I'll rinse it out and use it when you're done." He grinned as she snatched his handkerchief and went to kneel at the brink of the platform so she could wet it down.

He watched to be sure she didn't tumble into the water, then used the handkerchief himself when she handed it back to him. When he rose, he saw she'd settled herself and was sitting on the floor at the entrance to the crate.

"I don't feel like going to sleep yet," she said softly.

"Frightened?" he asked as he sat beside her, stretching his aching leg out in front of him. "Don't be. I'm here, on my feet again, or at least I can be, so there's nothing to fear now. The morning will bring us light as well as insight."

"Well, I hope so. But I feel too on edge right now to sleep." She waited a second then said, "It's hard to believe, isn't it? I mean, there we were having a lovely time at a pleasure garden, and the next thing we knew someone was out to kill us! Who would've guessed such ugliness could come out of nowhere in the midst of such loveliness?"

"It's the way of things." He shrugged. "Ugliness is the other side of beauty, the way death is the opposite of life. Both can happen when you least expect it."

"What would you know of ugliness?" she murmured almost to herself.

His head swung round, so she saw his expression of hurt surprise. She was aghast at her rash comment. "I didn't mean that," she said. "I only meant that since you're a gentleman you . . ."

He took her hand. "Don't apologize. You're right. I've found ugliness, but I had to go out to find it. Even so, it has never touched me personally—at least, not as personally as this has. I've seen war, privation, and pain, and have been in danger before. But I always felt at a remove, even when I was in the thick of it and my life was at risk. In fact, I've lived this long—and you know? Now I realize ugliness hasn't touched me very much until now."

"Because you feel responsible for me."

He gazed at her a long moment. "I suppose so," he said. "Tired enough to go to sleep?"

She shook her head. He hadn't released her hand, and she clung to it. The room was growing cooler, the darkness seemed to press in on them from every side. Their lantern was the only sign of warmth and hope, she was reluctant to leave its glow, and his side. She could feel the warmth rise from him and, perversely, she shivered.

He put an arm around her. "Chilly? It's damp as a

ditch in here. I wish I'd worn a cape, that would be the thing. Come, sit closer."

They sat in silence. The sound of water lapping was soothing, but the occasional small squeaks and stirrings made Alexandria crowd closer to him. He blessed the mice, and drew her closer still.

"Drum," she said after a moment. "I wasn't, you know."

He turned to look at her.

Her face was solemn. "I wasn't his adopted daughter, he never made my presence in his household in any way legal. I never told you or anyone because it shamed me. Nothing else did, I promise you. Because I wasn't his mistress either, or anything like that. But I might have been. That's why I left. I thought you should know. Well," she said, but her voice broke. She cleared her throat and went on more firmly. "Who knows what tomorrow will bring? I was ashamed so I didn't tell you before, but there's no sense lying when things are so . . . there's no sense to so much when I think about it now. Anyway, that's another reason I was so ineligible at home. But I want you to know I never lay with him."

He wanted to tell her it didn't matter, but it did, so he stayed silent.

"He only kissed me—well, not exactly even that," she went on with dogged determination. "He never touched me, or said anything to make me think he even saw me as more than a nanny for the boys and a housekeeper for himself. But in the last few years I could see he was watching me. We never talked about my future, but once, when a local boy began hanging about the kitchen after he delivered produce to us, Mr. Gascoyne told me that I wasn't to encourage him, oh, for a number of reasons, all valid, I suppose. But then he said he had great plans for me, if I continued to be a good girl.

"I believed him," she said quietly. "Then, a few days after the birthday the Foundling Hospital assigned to me, when I thought I was eighteen years old, I was doing the dishes one night after the boys had gone to bed." She paused, swallowed, and went on.

"It was such a little gesture," she said sadly. "But lord! It changed everything. I felt something on my neck, and I couldn't believe it. He put his mouth on my neck! I froze, it felt terrible. My skin crawled, my stomach felt cold as his lips did. I thought of him as a father, no, not even that. But close to that, you understand? I turned around, astonished. He laughed. 'It's time,' he said. He was actually being playful! It was such a rare and terrible thing to see. 'Alexandria,' he said, and bowed. 'You've been a good girl, and a hard worker. So. It's time, I think. Will you do me the honor of becoming my wife?'

"He must have seen my face, because his smile vanished, and he said, in very businesslike tones, 'I've decided I might as well make you Mrs. Gascoyne now, so that you can stay on here. After all, you are of an age when people will start talking.'

"Well," she said, looking down at her folded hands. "You can imagine. I said no. He was appalled. And very angry. He told me he wouldn't keep me on if I didn't agree. He told me not to be stupid, not to throw away the only chance at respectability I'd ever have. He said everyone knew I'd been living with him with no chaperone, and they'd all believe the worst of me when he told them he'd never even made me his ward, and he would.

When I asked what they'd think of *him*, he said they'd congratulate him on making me an honest woman, and would shun me if I didn't, because then what would that make me? He said I had nothing without him. He finally called me . . . a great many names. And told me he hoped I'd see things differently in the morning.

"I did," she said simply. "By then, I'd packed and left. I went to Bath, hoping to stay with a girl I'd kept a correspondence up with from the old days at the foundling home. She'd married a haberdasher who set up a shop there. I told Kit and Vincent my direction and they promised not to tell him. But I only was there for a few days when a messenger came to tell me Mr. Gascoyne had gone out looking for me and got a chill. It led to his lungs. By the time I got back he was already gone. So I killed him, I think."

Tears were streaming down her face. "But I *couldn't* have married him. He gave me so much, but I couldn't, I just could not!"

"Ah, Ally," he said, drawing her close, "don't weep. Of course you couldn't. And you didn't kill him, of course you didn't."

She turned and blindly sought to hide her face against him. He held her close and cradled her head to his chest. It was a cruel, dark world, and he'd always known it, but as he said, he'd never really felt it before. Now he felt her sorrow and his sympathy for her actually hurt. He held her close, rocking her, trying to comfort her.

That was his first mistake.

Twenty-four

SHE WAS WARM, SHE WAS FRAGRANT, SHE WAS DOCILE in his arms. She was braver than he'd ever imagined, and he'd known she was courageous. But even so, Drum could feel Alexandria's breath hitch every so often as she struggled for control. It reminded him of when he'd once held his friend Ewen's boy Max after a storm of the child's weeping, though it was nothing like it. Alexandria's body reminded him of other things, and he never forgot who it was he held. Or why.

The night was deep and dark and he knew too well it might soon become deeper and permanent for both of them. He felt as though they were the last two humans on a bare and bleak planet. It was inconceivable to him that death might come to this brave, bright, vibrant woman, in spite of all his efforts. But lack of food and nothing but foul water . . . His hands tightened involuntarily, as though he could hold her to life. She grew quieter, as though she knew just what he was thinking. Then she raised her head and looked at him. Her cheeks were pink, her lips were parted, her breath was stilled.

He told himself he was a gentleman, he reminded himself of his control, he remembered the next day might very well bring their freedom, while he accepted that it could bring his death.

Then he lowered his head and kissed her as he'd wanted to do for so very long, because if this first time was the last time, he would, at least, have that.

It was far more than he'd imagined.

She exulted. He could feel it on her lips. Where he led, she gladly followed, lending a sweetness that with all his wide experience, he'd never known. He expected desperation. He received ecstasy. Her soft lips parted against his, she let him taste the dark sweetness of her mouth, then tentatively tasted his. The touch of her tongue triggered his own response. There was such excitement and pleasure that it was a while before he came up for breath, smiled down at her—and then kissed her again.

Of course he knew he had to stop soon. This could never be. Still, for all he always thought he was in control of himself and his body, he'd never had to stop the act of love once he'd begun it. But then he'd never felt this way before. He'd never begun the act of sex with any woman he wasn't sure he would complete it with.

This was *Alexandria*, he told himself as he cupped one of her firm breasts and felt her shiver, then press closer to him. If only she would draw back, he could stop. If her small capable hands weren't feathered against the back of his neck, if she weren't urging him on, as eager as he was. Whatever she said, she couldn't be inexperienced, Drum thought as he struggled with himself against the insistent joy of her, against the overwhelming desire he felt for her now. An innocent wouldn't press herself so close, or throw her head back when his lips moved to her neck, or make such small sounds in the back of her throat as she did, urging him on, making *him* shiver with anticipation.

Her lovely rose-colored gown was only a whisper of material. An exhalation moved it from her shoulders as he lowered his mouth to taste the cool honeysuckle nectar of her skin. A small tug dragged her gown from those smooth fragrant white shoulders as he sought the firm breasts that were lifting to his lips. But the taste of one of those small puckered peaks was like an electric shock that went through his entire body, waking his mind to what his body was doing.

With difficulty he broke from his attentions to her, fighting for his famous control. He drew back a fraction, though he couldn't drop his hands from her. She watched him, her eyes half closed, breathing rapidly. He regained some power over his emotions by reminding himself that this was a woman who was depending on him. Moreover she was a social inferior, a woman he was honor-bound to protect from himself. But he couldn't protect himself from her. Because he saw her smile at him with sad fellow feeling.

He lowered his mouth to her again, and he was lost.

This was for now, and he didn't know if there'd ever be a then. They could be dying even as they simulated life. This was too much pleasure, much too much. And she burned like a fever in his arms.

"Ally," he murmured helplessly against her breast, "I can't seem to stop. Tell me to. Tell me to leave you if you want me to. Because I will. In a moment I won't be able to, I think." He waited for her answer, because though he was driven, at the last, he had too much training even for passion to overcome.

She knew it. He'd moved away, and she realized that somehow they were lying on the cold stone floor. She hadn't known it until then. He was propped on his elbows as he looked down at her. His lean face was intent, his eyes blazing blue even in the dimming lantern light. She saw a fine tremor in those arms and realized it wasn't from the effort of holding himself up. He'd given his passion as well as his honor entirely over to her. She was so moved by his lovemaking she could scarcely think. He'd made love to her! And swamped her senses enough to make her forget her fear, her terror of the night and what would come after it.

But her mind was clear. No passion was enough to make her forget what she was doing. This was too new, she'd been virtuous too long, it was too important for a single woman to be virtuous for her not to think of consequences even as she gave way to his passion.

If she lay with him she'd be ruined. But she didn't know if she had a life after this day anyway.

He'd think worse of her after his passion was spent, everyone said men reacted that way. But this was Drum.

If they escaped this place, she'd never see him again or feel this way again unless she became his mistress, which was a destiny she'd fought against all her life. If they didn't escape this place at least she'd know love.

And what of pregnancy? And what of it? If she lived she'd never regret a memory of him or a child of his. If she didn't, it didn't matter.

She'd never even have contemplated such an act if

they hadn't just seen death and didn't wonder if they'd be next. But then it felt as if she'd contemplated it from the moment she'd met him. Mr. Gascoyne said she was the daughter of a whore and would become one too. She'd denied that all her life. Her life wouldn't be very long, it seemed.

The look in his eyes as he gazed at her now! She wished she had the time and courage to really look at him too.

Her body clamored, her mind resisted. Obviously his did too. She knew if she said no, he'd rise and go, and come back to her after a while as a friend, and forgive her this. She didn't know if she would forgive herself, though.

"Ally?" he asked.

But there was really no decision to make. They were victims of fate and desire. For the first time the inequality between them didn't matter. Neither did the matter of her virtue. Only life mattered. Affirmation of it was everything. He wanted her. That was everything else.

"Please don't stop," she said. And swallowed the "I love you," because she was afraid that was the only thing that might have made him stop.

He smiled. A smile of such charm and relief and congratulation for her cleverness that she thought it made her decision worth everything. Then he lowered his body to her again and she realized she hadn't known the half of it.

He stripped off his shirt and waistcoat and bundled them behind her head. She shivered at what she saw, more at what she felt. This was so bold of her, so strange, so impossible, so incredibly sweet. His chest was lean and muscled and felt hard as wood under her fingers, warm as his breath in her ear. He used one arm to cradle her head further from the cold stone floor, the other hand to kindle her desire, and his mouth to send her up in flame. His lips and tongue on her breasts made her gasp. His hand roving over her body made her shiver. His hand on her stomach, then lower, circling, pressing, then slowly entering her *there*, made her squirm against him. His mouth following his hand made her tremble, and then when he put it *there* she was so shocked that she tried to sit up. But he brought his head up and chuckled in her ear, until she relaxed so he could shock her again.

He stripped her gown away, he stripped off his breeches, assuring her his leg was fine and not to worry because it didn't hurt half as much as his impatience did. Then he showed her how patient he could be as he bore her back and toyed with her again.

It was all thrilling and tender, and then less so and more so. She stopped thinking so she could feel it all more.

He thought she was marvelous: willing and giving, robust enough for all his passions, lady enough for his sensibility, and female enough to make him feel potent and in control again. He'd been duped and imprisoned. He didn't know if he could save them. But this, this lovemaking, was a thing he knew how to do, and her every reaction proved it to him. This was Alexandria, and her every movement showed she wanted him as desperately as he needed her now. He could rejoice over that now that he'd ruthlessly banished all the warning voices in his head.

He trifled with her and let her need drive his higher.

He couldn't remember the last time he'd been so consumed by lust. But still he restrained himself. Brute passion was good in its time and place, but this was neither. They lay locked in the dark on a stony bed, if he couldn't give her other comforts he'd give her this sweet wooing instead.

When his desire became so close to pain he couldn't tell one from the other, and when her body was damp with desire and she moved fretfully beneath him, he knew it was time to stop and begin the glorious end to their play. He rose over her and positioned her, parted her, raised her bottom in both his hands and brought himself to her, to the very core of her.

She tensed. He paused. One last second of his famous control was left to him. Her eyes were wide. "Ally?" he said.

And she gave him a tremulous smile. He entered her in one long swift fluid movement that he couldn't have stopped if the world had stopped around them. Then he knew, of course. But it didn't matter anymore. He went on because there was no control now. He moved rapidly to a harsh rhythm far beyond any man's control as he sought the ecstasy that shimmered at the edges of his last consciousness.

He found it, with a gasp and a cry, and found it again and again as he heaved against her. He went on without her.

There was no way she could follow him now. Suddenly there was nothing for Alexandria to do but stiffen in shocked surprise. The stretching ache of it made her pause in her anticipation, the sharp pain of his thrusts hurt enough to stop all her pleasure. But not her joy. She'd never been this close to anyone, and this was *Drum*. And she was giving him such enormous pleasure that he'd moved beyond himself. She felt pride mingling with her alarm and pain and disappointment. And fascination. As he went on, somewhere in the completion of their joining she felt the tingling seductive promise of what might have been for her if she'd known more.

He shuddered one last time and dropped beside her, breathing hard. His body was damp with perspiration, his voice hoarse. He cupped her cheek in one hand. "I didn't know," he said. "I'm sorry."

"I'm not," she said, touching his forehead, his cheek, his lips.

He gathered her close, and buried his face in her neck.

She lay looking up into the darkness of the ceiling somewhere high above them. His heart beating next to her was the loudest thing she could hear in their prison. His arms held her safe from the night. She felt at peace, angry only because she knew that when he moved away from her, she'd be afraid again. As her body cooled, the room grew darker as the dying flame in the lantern spluttered, going into a wild fluttering dance.

"I hurt you!" he said suddenly, sounding appalled, raising himself on one elbow.

"No, no, it's inconsiderable."

"But you're weeping."

She realized she had tears on her cheeks and dashed them away. "No, it's only that I was thinking. After *that*—what we just did?—it will be even worse to die."

"Oh," he said, relaxing, considering her words. He was silent for a long time, then he raised himself over her again. "Then let me show you how very much worse it will be."

"What?" She looked up at him, her surprise and hesitation visible in the flickering light.

"No, we won't do *that*," he said gently. "There can be too much of a good thing for a beginner, you know, and I'm only human. But you didn't find what I did in what we shared. I'd like to show you a glimpse of what can be."

"Here and now?" she asked a little fearfully.

"Yes. It won't hurt, I promise. If we could do that, we can do this," he said, his mouth at her ear, his hand drifting over her again. "We can do anything we please until morning. And I think you need something to help you sleep."

He kissed her again and caressed her, doing everything only for her this time, while he kept whispering, "No, don't be afraid. Don't be ashamed. Yes, this is what men and women do too."

She was embarrassed, she was shocked. She hoped he'd never stop, she knew she wouldn't sleep if he didn't put out the fires he started in her body. Then he did, and she shivered and shook, and closed her eyes in ecstasy.

"There, let it go, Ally, yes," he breathed. "Isn't it good?"

She could only nod, exhausted by the deepest content she'd ever known. Then, as confused as she was sated, she gave up trying to understand and drifted off into deep and dreamless sleep in his sheltering arms.

He was gone from her side when she woke in the morning.

She knew it was morning because sunlight showed at the edges of the door and slithered through the long cracks in it. Light infiltrated from other tiny chinks and crannies in the walls, suffusing the place with dim dawn. It wasn't bright. Only less dark.

She rose and clambered into her gown, looking for him as she did. He was standing at the water's edge, frowning down at it. He heard her stirring. "I think I know what to do," he said without turning his head. "I believe we have a chance. A good one," he added as he turned and saw her.

She ran a hand through her hair and looked down at herself. "I look terrible," she said sadly.

He smiled. "What have I done? To think the redoubtable Miss Gascoyne is more worried about her appearance than her life now."

She grinned. "Well, no. If you can bear looking at me, I can. And come to think of it . . ." She tilted her head to the side. "What is the world coming to? The immaculate Earl of Drummond has a beard!"

He ran a hand over his chin and grimaced as he heard the rasp of his newly grown stubble. "Nothing you haven't seen before, my dear. I lay in your bed for a very long time when we first met, remember?"

They smiled at each other.

Then he grew serious. "Morning's the best time to try my scheme. A man's energy is at its highest then."

He didn't mention the fact that as they had neither food or water, that energy wouldn't be at its height very long. Which was why he'd decided on this desperate act. He'd coursed the room for an hour, looking for a way out. He'd found only two. He'd leave her his broken stiletto so she could try the other if he failed.

But his was the best chance to succeed. If he didn't? He hated leaving her, even in death, but he couldn't see any other way around their problem.

"I'm going to find that passage under the river door we came in through. Look," he said before she could speak. "The tide runs swiftly now, see? It's going out. I can let myself go with it, and seek an underwater exit. Dubbin's body is gone. He was swept away sometime yesterday, as Fitch said he'd be. I intend to find that same route out—alive, you'll see."

"You can't! He also said you'd never find it, remember?"

"He would say that, wouldn't he? I'm a very strong swimmer, Ally. I have excellent breath control. I drove the other lads mad with envy when we were young. It was a game with me, I've held it for so long as three minutes, I can go down and look for an opening. If that fails, I can feel for one. But find it I will. It's our surest way out."

"But the others will be looking for us," she argued. "There's no need to court more danger. You could get trapped or caught on something down there. Don't go now! They'll find us, I know they will. Eric's clever, and Gilly's smart as she can stare. Damon is thoughtful and thorough, and Rafe's brave and resourceful. Why, I'm sure your father will send out a huge search party when he hears. They'll have half London looking for us soon. There's no reason to take such a risk now."

He put his hands on her shoulders, his expression sober. "Ally, by the time they search half London it will be too late for me to try. My strength will be gone."

"We can chip away at the door," she said stubbornly.

"And so you will, if I don't succeed. But I will. We can't wait. We haven't the luxury. London's a huge city, with a thousand places a man can hide or be hidden. I know, I've searched other cities for wanted men. I must try this, it's our best chance. I have to take it."

"And I have nothing to say about it?" she asked angrily.

"I brought this down on you," he said reasonably, "all of it, from the first. It's mine to mend. Even if I hadn't caused this, I'm not the type to sit and accept my fate."

She shook her head vehemently, seeking the right words to make him stay. The thought of him diving into that black water, perhaps never to leave it, made her cold to her bones. She had no claim on him and wouldn't presume to make any, even now. They'd made love, he'd changed her life, but she knew very well that if they got out he'd go his own way. That wasn't her real objection. It was because he was unique, a man of grace, charm, and wisdom. If she couldn't have him, at least the world should, he was such a valuable man. He shouldn't gamble with his life. She couldn't allow it. She didn't know how to prevent it—until she remembered his essential nature. If he didn't care for himself, she knew he'd care about her.

"What's to become of me if you don't come back?" she demanded, her hands on her hips.

He touched her rumpled, tumbled hair. Such disorder was so unlike his fastidious Miss Gascoyne, his nurse, his friend, his lover. He remembered how she'd gotten so tumbled and wished with all his heart he didn't have to face the cold embrace of the Thames now. But he knew what he had to do.

"If I don't come back, you still have a chance," he told her honestly. "I'd like to be here with you, no matter what happens. I don't want the worst to happen, which is why I'm trying this. Maybe I'm being a coward, not wanting to face that eventuality. Perhaps I'm being selfish, because it would surely kill me to see you helpless and be helpless to do anything about it. But I have faith in you, as you must have in me. If you're left alone, you'll face it bravely. I'm going to try to see that you don't have to. I think this is our only rational hope right now, and as hope is all we have, I have to try it."

"You'll leave me here alone in the dark to face death by myself?" she asked, hating her own insincerity because it wasn't the thought of her death that terrified her now, but she was willing to say anything to keep him safe.

"Good try, Ally. But it won't work. You know I have to try, so don't make it harder, please."

She did know that, but she hated it, and tears of anger and frustration sprang to her eyes.

He took her in his arms. "Now won't you feel silly when I succeed?" he asked, tipping her downcast face up to his. He kissed her forehead, and set her aside. "Now, I'll try to get back in by the door Fitch slammed shut as he tried to escape. He didn't have time to lock it so it should be easy enough to lift the bolt from that side. Wait for me there. I'll be at the door as soon as I can."

He kissed her with all the fire of the night before. He kissed her again, with all the tender love of a friend. Then he stepped away. He went to the overturned crate that she'd never used for her bed last night and bent to the waistcoat he'd folded and laid there for her pillow. He tenderly took his watch from a fob pocket. He looked at it a moment, then quickly rose, went out, and laid it on top of the neat little pile of his clothing that they'd slept on. It was that extra care, that little farewell gesture to a treasured piece of his history as much as anything that frightened Alexandria.

He misunderstood her look of dismay. "I don't want anything to weigh me down," he told her. "I'm leaving my breeches on only so I don't shock anyone out for a boat ride on a fine morning when I come bubbling up under their craft, naked as Adam, asking for directions."

He knelt, picked up the broken stiletto and handed it to her. "For any eventuality," he said. "Now, I'm going to dive and look. If that doesn't work, I'll dive and feel for the door. Don't worry if I don't come up again, it won't necessarily mean I'm drowned. It may mean I'm out for a swim on the Thames at last, and I'll be back for you."

She stood very still. "And if you're not?"

"Ah, Ally, let's not think of that."

"I must," she said, fighting back tears.

"Then know that I died trying to free you. And that's the best way any man can go, trying to help a friend."

She went very still. She nodded. He gazed at her steadily, kissed her again, then turned from her and lowered himself into the water. She watched him swim out toward the great river door. Then she saw him bow his head and submerge. His narrow high arched feet appeared where his head had been, then the water closed over them. She waited breathlessly. He bobbed up again, waved to her, and went down again. She stood waiting.

He submerged and reappeared a half dozen times. Soon, she was able to hear his rasping breathing even from where she stood. She didn't think she breathed at all as she waited for him to return each time. She simply stood and watched.

Then he dived, and she waited. And he didn't appear again.

She stood waiting for a very long time. She watched the dark water for the smallest ripple. She counted to sixty, and sixty, and sixty. The fifth time, she sank to her knees. The tenth time, she put her head in her hands. Time crawled by. She counted to sixty ten times again in case she'd been too frantic to count correctly the first time.

He didn't reappear. She didn't hear a sound from the other door, not a scraping of the bolt, not a knock on its surface, not a shadow to fill any of its slivered slits of morning light.

She was too filled with horror to weep.

She remembered he'd said the best way a man could die was in an attempt to help a friend. Those simple words broke her spirit at last. She slumped to her knees, lowering her head into her hands, and wept bitterly. Because he might be dead. Because the thought of it almost killed her too. And because whatever she'd been for him, he'd said a man should be prepared to die for a friend. Even then, even at the last, he hadn't said "love." He never had.

Twenty-five

*A*LEXANDRIA SAT IN THE DARK IN A HUDDLE FOR what seemed like hours. She couldn't bear to look at Drum's watch, because that would be admitting he never would look at it again. When she finally raised her head she saw that time had passed, the sunlight moving on to illuminate different slits and crannies in the door. She knew she should get up and try to find a way out of her prison, but she didn't have the heart to. If she did succeed in getting free, then she'd have to live with the knowledge that Drum had died for nothing.

She tried not to think of what the end had been like for him. The darkness, the murky water . . . there were eels in the Thames. She tried not to think of them, either. Instead she saw Drum's face in her mind's eye as it looked in laughter and in seriousness, and remembered how it had been when he was in the throes of passion too. He'd felt that for her. She'd given him that much, at least. It was too painful to cry. She found it hard enough to breathe. The silence was immense. She was the last woman alive in the world now that the only man she wanted to share it with was gone.

She heard a new sound, a rasping sound. She froze, and looked up. Someone was moving around outside the door! She leapt to her feet and ran to it, then stood with her hands clenched around the hilt of the broken stiletto, and prayed. It could be Fitch. Drum said he was dead, but Drum had said he'd get out, hadn't he? It could be Dubbin or his friend, the unlucky man in the boat. It could be anyone. She waited, clutching the stiletto like a talisman, wondering who it might be, afraid even to hope it could be Drum.

The bolt was drawn back. The door swung open.

"What are you doing standing here in the dark?" Drum asked. River water ran down his naked chest onto his sodden dripping breeches. His hair was plastered to his head, and his face was pale as any drowned man's. He smiled at her.

"You look terrible," he said.

She cast herself into his open arms. It was a long time before she could speak. When she did she was as wet as he was, but reveling in the warmth of the flesh that glowed beneath his skin and slowly took the chill from them both. He stroked her hair and held her close. All he could say was, "Hush, you'll get sick crying like that. I'm here, aren't I?"

"Why did it take so long?" she wailed.

"I had to find the opening under the gate. I did, but when I came up I found myself in a tight spot between two pilings. There was just room for my nose to poke up and get some air." He chuckled. "It's the first time it's been of use to me. I don't think I'd have been able

to breathe if I was one of your short-nosed chaps. So I
had to dive again and again looking for a way to get the
rest of my body out. But I'm here, please stop crying.
I'm wet enough as it is."

That made her smile. She took a steadying breath.

"And I've got a boat," he said. "I dispossessed the
previous owner. Well, he'd no use for it anyway, the
only river he has to cross now is the Styx." He felt her
shiver. "Yes, the unlucky Mr. Hake. But we have a
boat, it has oars, and I think we should go home now.
All right?"

"Please," she said.

Gilly greeted them ecstatically. She refused to let
Drum go home to change his sopping clothes, ordering
him to Damon's room, telling Damon's valet to find
him something that fit. She sent Alexandria right up to
her room with a maid, and then sent the footman to
scour the city to find Damon, Eric, Rafe, and everyone
else searching for them and tell them the lost couple
was found.

They all met again in the afternoon after Drum and
Alexandria had been washed, dried, dressed, coddled,
and fed by an army of servants. Only then, with their
friends sitting around them, and the door to the salon
closed, did Drum tell them the whole story. Or, as
Alexandria noted with relief, *almost* the whole story.

She felt comfortable, drowsy, and safe, with all her
newfound friends close by. She hardly believed what
had happened now. All of it seemed fantastic, except
for the way Drum had loved her. That was fantastic
too, but it was something she'd never forget that
warmed her to her heart. She tried not to look at him

now because she didn't want the whole world to know it. She couldn't take her eyes from him, even so.

"We had some scares too," Rafe said when Drum was through telling of their adventure. "The river brought up three corpses this morning. An old woman and two men. The river patrol said that was a light night's haul, the Thames is the last resting place of many poor souls. The woman probably chose her own watery grave. We were afraid to look, but of course neither man was you. The one with the . . . ah . . ." He paused. Sliding a look at the women, he went on, ". . . indistinguishable face must have been your Dubbin, the other Fitch. He was a well-dressed older fellow with a neat dagger wound piercing his heart."

Drum nodded. "I suspect it's Fitch all right, but I'll inspect him too, to be sure. When did you say they found them?"

"This morning," Eric said, "washed onto the bank by the incoming tide."

Drum nodded. "The next tide will probably give up Hake. I should have been on my guard. Let it be a lesson to all of you fellows. Peace is too new and fragile to take lightly. Be prepared at all times. Thank God for Ally's bravery. I'm only sorry she had to share my misadventure to exhibit it. About that . . ." He paused and lowered his voice. "I'd like it to be put about that we made our escape at dawn. And that we couldn't have done it sooner because I was literally tied up all night, and so was Ally.

"Our lives were at risk, but you know very well it doesn't matter how dire our situation was, the old cats of both sexes are obsessed by the carnal, scandal, and gossip. No matter what else happened, they'll start whispering about the fact that we were gone together overnight unless we make it clear that nothing could have happened between us but murder. That way it will become a tale of terror, and nothing more. Agreed?"

"Of course," Eric said, as the others murmured their assent.

Drum looked at them each in turn, and nodded with satisfaction. Then he looked at Alexandria.

She sat very still, suddenly ashen. He'd told them nothing happened. Of course. She understood why. It was what she wanted. It made perfect sense. But she felt as though he'd struck her. She managed a tiny smile. "Good," she murmured.

Gilly glanced at her, then looked again. "Now I think we should let Ally get to sleep!" she said firmly. "Poor girl, she was brave as brass, but now the shock is probably setting in. That's the way of it after a good fight. Even the winner starts to shake."

The others grinned at the way Gilly expressed it, but agreed.

"Excellent idea," Drum said, his gaze on Alexandria, "I could use some too, but I'm going home to have it. I'll be back in the morning—after I make sure it *is* Fitch on that mortuary slab. I may make mistakes, but I don't make the same one twice."

He said good-bye to the others, waiting until they started walking to the door before he spoke to Alexandria privately. "Everything will be all right, you'll see," he told her as he took her hand. "You'll forget the bad things, people always do. It's the way we survive. Now, sleep. I'll see you in the morning."

She nodded, hoping he'd think she was too exhausted to speak. His eyes searched her face. He finally seemed satisfied with what he saw, said, "Get some sleep," again, and hesitated. Gilly was returning to the room, though, so he only held Alexandria's hand another moment, then bowed, and left.

"Gilly?" Alexandria said when the men had gone to the door, "may I speak with you a moment?"

Gilly frowned. She knew more about pain than most people, and there was something in Alexandria's voice and more in her expression that alarmed her. "Of course," she said. "Come, we'll go upstairs and get you to bed, you can tell me there."

But Alexandria told her the moment they got to the bedchamber. "I'm going home," she announced. "I'd like to pack my things now. I know the ball you're holding was supposed to be for me, but with all the best intentions in the world, I can't stay. It would be wrong, and more wrong still if you made me. It's time for me to return my life to normal."

"Oh, bother!" her hostess said, stamping her foot. "Don't be so poor-spirited! That's not like you. So you had a scare, so what? It'll fade, you'll see. Running away will only make it worse. I've found that if a thing worries you, you must face it out and stare it down and only then will it go away. See, *it* has to go—not you."

"No," Alexandria said sadly, "in this case, *I* must. Trust me."

Gilly looked at Alexandria solemnly for a long moment, her face sober. Alexandria felt her color rise, and looked away, unwilling to face that steady golden gaze.

Gilly's eyes widened. "Oh. I see. I don't know what happened, do I? If you want to tell me . . . ? No? You can, you know, I keep secrets better than the deepest well. Well, you know I'd never do a thing to make you unhappy. You're certain?" She sighed. "But you will say good-bye to him first? I mean, leaving a note is craven. That's not like you either."

Alexandria was shaken by Gilly's intuition. But how could she know the truth of it? She might think Drum had rejected her, then again, maybe not. The lady was quick and she'd a hard life in her youth, so she knew the best as well as the worst of men.

"Of course, I'll speak to him," Alexandria said, though she'd meant to leave a note. "I'm not a coward, at least not a very big one. I'll say good-bye and explain it to him. But I really don't have to, because I'm sure he already knows."

"Oh, *damn* and blast!" Gilly said sadly. "He's a good man, really he is. But he thinks too much of the proprieties and he cares too much for his father's opinions, the stiff-rumped fool!" she concluded angrily. "He'd break rather than bend, and be sure, if he keeps this up, he will break one day. And that's a shame, because he could be . . . Well, what does it matter? We all could be better than we are. That's no help to you. I'm sorry, you can't know how sorry, but I understand. *We* will stay friends though, right?" she asked anxiously.

"Of course." Alexandria turned to her packing, because she couldn't face Gilly's perceptive stare. She knew what she'd said was only a polite fiction. Once she left London she'd be leaving all her connections to it forever. She had to, in order to save her sanity. Because she was also leaving the man she loved to save her self-respect and his pride.

He'd dressed with care, even for such a fashionable fellow. In fact, Drum looked so elegant and cool and devil-may-care when he appeared the next morning that Alexandria almost hated him for it. Her whole world had been turned upside down. He'd changed her mind and body; she was a stranger to herself now.

But he stood on his own two feet and smiled down at her, the perfect picture of the perfect gentleman. Immaculate, unapproachable, entirely himself again. He wore a fitted blue jacket and half boots. Buff trousers covered his long legs, his neckcloth was high, his linen white. His waistcoat was a work of art in blue and green, making his eyes seem brilliantly blue. Only happiness could account for their sparkle, though. They grew grave when he looked at her.

Alexandria supposed he was worried about what she might say. So was she. She had to say it fast and get it over with. She wished she could look as fine as he did now, this was the last time he'd see her. Her hair was tidy, her face was clean, and she'd put on one of her old gowns to travel in. It was the one Mrs. Tooke had made that she'd been so proud of, but her sojourn in London had showed her there was nothing spectacular about it. She looked rested, she supposed, because she'd slept through the night after she'd packed her things, though *fainted* might be a better description for what had happened when she put her head down on her pillow at last.

But she was nervous and frightened and sick at heart, and could only hope she was a good enough actress to hide it.

"That's one of the gowns you wore before you came to London," he said before she could speak.

"Yes, it is. And that's fitting because I'm going home. It's time. Don't blame yourself," she said quickly. "I have to get away from the scene of the crime Fitch almost committed. I miss the boys too. When I thought I might die, I thought of what I'd leave behind," she said and flushed, because although it was true, the part about the boys was a black lie. She hadn't thought of them at all, she'd only been thinking of Drum. And that was reprehensible too. That would change now, she'd devote the rest of her life to the boys.

"Because of what happened?" he asked. "Because I made love to you?"

She glanced nervously around the salon even though she knew no one else was there. "Yes. No—I mean, I understand." She lifted her head high. "You don't have to feel guilty, you'd never have done it if I hadn't asked you to. I know that as well as you do. We were lost and alone and in need of comfort. But that was then. As for now? Things have changed, of course. It's better that I go, you see."

"I don't," he said sternly. "Ally. I came here this morning to ask you to be my wife."

That shattered her composure. "Oh, no, you don't!" she cried.

He stared at her, surprised.

"I mean, no thank you." She looked at her hands, all hope of acting gone. She was upset and unhappy, but it didn't matter if he knew it now. She had to free him.

"You don't care for me?" he asked quietly.

"Too much to marry you," she admitted. "You want to do the right thing. So do I. No, my lord, I will not marry you, but thank you for asking. Don't worry, I'll be fine."

"*I* won't be!" he said angrily. "And I'm not doing

the right thing. I never do anything that doesn't please me. I came to ask you to marry me because I love you. Nothing more, nothing less. I assumed you felt the same way about me." He frowned. "I shouldn't be yelling at you, forgive me," he muttered. "I'm new to this sort of thing.

"Do you know what *I* thought about when I thought we might die?" he asked, his eyes searching hers. "You, just you. You've tangled my thoughts and emotions since I met you. If I'd been alone yesterday, I might have got free sooner. I was a superior agent, I won commendations. Now I see a man can be brave when he has nothing to lose. But I couldn't act with you there. I quaked at the thought of losing you. I almost went mad at the idea of harm coming to you."

He took her hands in his and held them as he looked down at her. Something in her face made him go grim around the mouth. His voice grew harsh. "Look what you've done! You brought me to life, you can't leave me now. I woke up this morning and almost frightened poor Grimes to death! I *sang* as I washed. Sang? The truth is I felt like dancing. I dreamed of you and woke to the thought of you, and dressed and came right to you, and now you say you're leaving? Oh no *you* don't! If I have to truss you up the way I told the others to say you'd been tied by Fitch, I'll keep you here until I can get you to the altar."

Her lips trembled with sorrow and laughter. "Don't let your gallantry ruin your life. You don't have to repay me any more than you did when you left my house. In neither case is it necessary, and this is so much more than a handful of gold."

He frowned in incomprehension.

"The gold coins you left under your pillow," she said, and looked down, because she was shamed she hadn't brought them to London to return to him.

"Gold coins?" he murmured. Then comprehension lit his eyes and his face grew tight. "So that's what he was doing! My father kept me waiting in the coach because he said he'd left something in my room. I'm sorry, did that upset you? He had no right."

"But he did," she said, glad of something to pounce on for her argument. "That's just the point! Think of the reality. I have, believe me. I'm a foundling. I'm no one, with no rank or fortune or even a real name! I'm not the goose girl whose nobility shone through her rags so the prince knew she was a princess. I'm just a woman you found yourself entangled with. I did you a favor, you felt grateful. You like me, I'm glad of it. You feel responsible for me, I grant that. You desired me, but you'd never have made love to me under any other circumstances, I know that too. You don't have to marry me. You'll hate me one day if you do, and you'll bless me if you don't, you'll see."

He held her with his blue unblinking stare. "Think of your father," she went on, almost pleading. "You can't do it to him. He has Lady Annabelle in his eye for you, or one of those other fine London ladies. Your offer honors me. I respectfully decline. But I'll remember and I'm grateful for it."

"I love my father, but I don't want to marry him," Drum said through gritted teeth. "I don't want to have children with him, or share his bed. I love him, but he's just going to have to learn to love me if I don't always obey him. I'm no longer a boy. He deserves no less than a man for his son. As for Annabelle? He can keep her in his eye, or his ear, or his a—wherever he chooses," he said wildly. "I am *not* a human sacrifice," he added, as much to her as to himself.

"I know who you are," he said, concentrating on her. "Goose girl be damned! We're not talking about fairy stories. You're the right woman for me. Never doubt it. Why do you think I never married any of those 'fine London ladies'? Or Lisbon ladies, Roman ladies, or women of any class or kind? Because I never met you. I was willing to sail through life without even feeling a breeze, that's no way to live. I admit I thought my name and my father's desires were paramount. But they aren't now. They haven't been since I met you. By God, Ally, I built you a damned *barn!*"

In the midst of all her doubt and turmoil, that made her grin. Reluctantly, he did too.

"I didn't know why then," he went on. "I only knew I wanted to do something splendid for you. I still do. I asked Gilly to invite you here because I couldn't stop thinking of you. And if yesterday hadn't happened, something else would have, believe me. Yesterday just hurried things along, thank God. As for rank and position in society? This is 1821, my dear. We're marching into the thick of a new century. The world's changing. We must too. What's in a name, Ally? Only what we make of it. I remember thinking, before I was shot off my horse, *Why do men say they* fall *in love?* I never understood. Until I did, literally."

He grinned. "True, I was a hardened case and so I had to fall harder and more often than most men—off my horse, on my head, into your bed and your care and then your good graces. But once there I knew that's where I belonged. I don't pretend to understand it. I've always tried too hard, I think. Now I see love's a thing you feel but may never understand. It defies reason. Gloriously."

"It's just because of . . . it's because of what we did," she said. "That doesn't matter."

"To hell it doesn't!" he shouted. "It was astonishing, don't deny it. Unless . . ." He paused, his face still. "Do you regret it? Was it bad for you, after all?"

"It was wonderful!" she cried.

"Then listen!" he said grimly. He gripped her shoulders hard, as though he longed to shake her. She blinked. He dropped his hands as though her skin were oven hot, took a deep breath and gazed in surprise at his two hands. "I'm a man of utmost control," he marveled. "And look—you're making me lose it again. That's just it. My control was a mark of pride with me. I was cool and collected, but in fact, I was numb as an amputated thumb. I only know it now because of you."

He looked at her tenderly. "Ally, I didn't have a shred of control when it came to you. I meant to kiss you and let you sleep. I meant to cuddle with you, then say goodnight. I made the most remarkable love to you because I couldn't help myself. It never happened before, and will never again with any woman but you. Marry me. Unless, of course," he said, unconsciously lifting his head so he looked almost disdainful, "the thought of spending your life with me repels you?"

"You asked for Gilly's hand once," she said softly, "when you thought she needed you and it was the right thing to do. You will always act out of kindness for those in need."

"Yes," he said impatiently. "And that's why I've married so many times, which is what I'd have to do if

I were so kind. England's stuffed with foundlings, orphans, and widows. And though I might have offered for Gilly, I never told her I loved her. I never told *anyone* that but you. I can't believe I actually said it. By God, don't you remember I said it? If you don't, I'll do it again. It's such a pleasure to say," he added, grinning like a boy. "I love you, Ally."

"But you told everyone to say we had no chance to do anything . . . together last night," she said, the hurt she'd felt clear in her voice and eyes.

"You wanted me to brag about it?" he asked incredulously. "I shouldn't have lost my head, I shouldn't have compromised you, I'm not proud of that. And I didn't want any more talk about us than there will be. There'll be some, you know. Are you afraid of that?"

"Aren't you?" she asked.

He smiled. "I quite look forward to dealing with whomever dares."

She had to protest. She couldn't accept so much joy, it seemed wrong, it seemed fantastical.

He misunderstood her silence. "Ally," he said a little desperately, "I need you."

That she could deny. "Oh, do you?" she asked angrily. "Why would you need me? Look at what you have. Everything."

"Everything but a heart," he agreed. "When I volunteered to spy and fight for my country, it was the only time I felt alive—until now. I'm a glib fellow, and know I should tell you it's because you're beautiful. I ought to praise your grace and charm, and so on and on. That's all true too, but it doesn't matter. I only know that from the moment I met you, I was yours. Any other reservations?" he asked, seeing her wavering. "Because I tell you, my title be damned. I begin to think it mattered so much to me because it was the only thing I had that I was sure would lure the ladies."

She grinned at that great lie. But he shook his head. "The truth is I'm not the most handsome fellow. No, don't try to spare my feelings. The nose is a proud family emblem only because since there's no way we can cut it off we might as well say we like it. I'm aware of the fact that it gives my face all the appeal of an affronted camel. Nor am I nearly the wisest or the best-tempered man—almost, but not quite." He saw her reluctant grin, and added very seriously, "But one thing I do know: I'm the right one for you. Your answer, please."

But he knew it. Her expression told him before she could. He smiled, took her in his arms, and kissed her until she wanted to agree with anything he said. Still, the minute he released her she held on to his shoulders for balance and gasped, "Oh, but your father! You can't do it."

"I can," he said, his own eyes blazing. "What I can't do is debate it endlessly. Say yes. Believe in me. We'll have such a good time. The boys will live with us. We'll have children, we'll take in more, we'll enrich our lives and others. Ally, we came so close to losing it all, let's win it back again."

There was really nothing she could say. So she said yes. Then he didn't let her say anything else for a long time.

Twenty-six

*T*HE DUKE OF WINTERTON STROLLED INTO THE
room in the midst of a celebration. He stripped
off his gloves and gazed at his son. Drum had his arm
around Alexandria. They were in the center of a crowd
of his friends, the Ryders, Lord Raphael Dalton and his
lady, and his old friend Eric. They were holding
glasses of champagne. The duke was sure of that, he
couldn't mistake the sight and scent of a good champagne. He paused in the doorway of the Ryders' salon,
and cleared his throat. Then again, more loudly. They
finally turned to look at him, and appalled silence fell
over them all.

Drum knew his father was intensely interested as he
walked into the room to join them. He could tell by his
father's casual look. Drum could feel Alexandria's
body grow still, and his own throat grew dry. "Sir," he
said, "give you good day."

"You're celebrating?" the duke asked mildly. "You
found and finished off the man who tried to kill you, I

understand. Or so everyone in London is saying. I heard it three times just on the way here from my town house. I was given to understand that he tried again here in London, and you annihilated him. Congratulations."

Color came into Drum's face, he took his arm from around Alexandria, clasping her hand instead to steady her—and himself. He'd wanted to tell his father the news of his engagement in private. He'd meant to take the brunt of whatever storm would break over his own head. But if he didn't tell him here and now, Alexandria would be terribly hurt, and he couldn't have that. He braced himself. He'd slain his dragons and won his lady, but now he had to win the approval of the man he most respected. Or not. He'd cast his dice and he would go on. He loved his father, but he loved Alexandria, and though he didn't want to choose between them he realized he already had.

"Congratulations of another sort are in order, Father," he said. "Alexandria has pledged to marry me, sir. Wish me happy."

The room went still. The duke's expression didn't change, but Drum could see some of the rigidity go out of his posture, and he was stricken. There was no way around it, but it hurt him to hurt his father. He didn't know how vulnerable he himself looked at that moment, not at all like the urbane Earl of Drummond. Nor did he know how well that vulnerability became him in Alexandria's eyes.

Some of those watching him bit back satisfied smiles, some sighed. All worried. Drum held Alexandria's hand tight and waited for his father's next words. They all did.

"I wish you happy," the duke said mildly. He took Alexandria's other hand. "I have wanted a daughter for some time now, my dear. Welcome to the family."

She stared at him, incapable of words. She'd dreaded this moment. Of all the things she'd rehearsed to say, nothing was appropriate. Of all the reactions she might have guessed he'd have, this was never one of them. She was prepared for scorn or sarcasm, even outright anger. Never this charming smile. She didn't know what to say.

For once, neither did Drum. His friends were mute, astonished.

The duke didn't seem to notice. He smiled at Alexandria. "Mrs. Tooke has never left off singing your praises. I began to think that if this slowtop wouldn't have you, he was a fool. But we do not have fools in our family. Well done, Drum."

"You've spoken to Mrs. Tooke again?" Drum asked pointlessly, because it was the only thing he could think to say.

"Yes. While continuing my inquiries I had to return to the scene of the original crime several times, of course. Mrs. Tooke was most hospitable to me, and as she dotes on Miss Gascoyne, I know she'll be more than merely happy to hear this news. Don't look so shocked because I am happy as well," he said with a thin smile, noting everyone's expressions.

"My dear," he told Alexandria sympathetically, "please never fear me. I know all. Mrs. Tooke told me everything about that ghastly Gascoyne, and I congratulate you on your courage and resourcefulness. Nobility of purpose and person is all important, more so than titles. It is how those titles were attained in the first place, you see. Drummond's own ancestry, which I've never been able to get him sufficiently interested in, by the way, holds many surprises, if he'd but care to look. As a countrywoman you must know that the best breeding is not always inbreeding along strict bloodlines, but rather a careful choosing for the right traits and abilities. Which you have, my dear, in plenty.

"I wish to see my grandchildren. I should like to be an influence on them, if you don't object. Time's flying, no one is more aware of that than I am. Perhaps your episode yesterday made you aware of it too. It's past time my son was wed. I'm relieved he's ending his bachelorhood and am well pleased with his decision, though I'm old and wise enough to know it doesn't matter, because I raised him to stand behind his decisions, and he has made his choice."

He raised his head higher and looked at Drum, seeming for once to be slightly uneasy. "Speaking of which, I've some news for you myself. I suppose this is the best time and place to tell you, because it's also of a matrimonial nature. I don't wish to steal your thunder, my dear," he told Alexandria, "but at my age, matrimony isn't a thing to be delayed, don't you agree?"

She could only nod.

He did too. His cool blue gaze locked with Drum's. "I don't know how you feel about acquiring a new mother as well as a new bride, but that is the case. I've chosen a bride myself. I tried to push you into marriage. That was a mistake. But it was a fortunate one, because I learned from it. A man must find what's in his own heart. I did. The quest for a wife for you made me see the advantages of such a union, even for such an ancient fellow as myself. You may believe I'm being hasty, perhaps at my age even foolish, but a man in love must follow his heart, and be damned to all else, don't you agree?"

Drum hid his dismay. If his father wanted Annabelle, if it made him happy, so be it. He rued it, but accepted it. "Indeed, sir. Congratulations. When may I wish the lady happy?"

"Almost at once. I've asked her to follow me to London. Oh, and don't worry, my dear," he told Alexandria. "She's bringing the boys with her."

"The boys?" Alexandria asked, confused.

"Indeed, she'd hardly leave them alone, would she?" the duke said. "In fact, it's Rosalind's devotion to her loved ones, her warm and giving nature, that made me see I'd found a gem in her, one I couldn't leave behind. We two have a history in common. We shared many memories and found we could build more from them. She genuinely loved her husband, as I did your mama," he added, to Drum, "but there is time yet, we think, for more love in our lives."

"You're marrying *Mrs. Tooke*?" Drum asked, amazed.

"Why, of course. You disapprove?"

"God! Never!" Drum said, laughing. "Only I thought it was . . . Never mind who I thought it was, you've delighted me."

"I'm not such a fool as to marry a woman young enough to be my daughter," the duke said haughtily. "I want a wife, not another child. Though, if that does happen, because there still exists the possibility that it might, I'd be very pleased and can only hope you would be too."

"Of course," Drum said, smiling. "I always wanted a brother."

The duke's high cheekbones turned ruddy. "I'll admit," he said quickly, "at one time I believed it would serve my purposes if you thought I might be courting the Lady Annabelle. She's young and lovely, that's undeniable," he added, with a sidewise glance at Eric, who was listening closely. "But I believe she needs to learn what we already have, that marriage is not a means of advancement or a matter of expediency. There is somewhere a man for her. If she never finds him, I pity her. But I'd pity her more had she married you without her heart or yours being involved. You have a great one, Drum. I'm grateful to your lady for discovering it for you."

Drum drew Alexandria closer to his side. "I'm eternally grateful to her. Such an easy lesson it was, after all. I only needed the right teacher." His eyes were on Alexandria. "She protested she had no rank or name. But her rank is above all women for me, and her name is mine to call 'wife' and that's all I want. Wish me more than happy, Father."

"I don't have to," the duke said. "You are and will be. I wish you joy and good fortune."

"He has it!" Gilly cried. "As do you too, Your Grace! What fun! Two marriages. Shall they be held together? A double wedding?"

"Gilly!" Drum said with loathing.

"Mrs. Ryder!" his father said in exactly matching tones.

Alexandria laughed, and shed a tear, and laughed again.

"Weeping?' Drum whispered as the others began to talk together. "What a watering pot you've become."

"It's because I can't remember ever being happier."

She laughed, then grew serious. "But you know? Even so, unimaginable as it is, I begin to see that someday I might be. *We* might be."

He brought her hand to his lips. "Depend on it," he said.

A man of decision and resolve, he kept his promise, of course.

Wondrous Worlds of Romance from
Edith Layton

"Layton writes pure enchantment."
Mary Jo Putney

"One of romance's most gifted authors."
Publishers Weekly

THE CONQUEST
0-380-81863-9/$6.99 US/$9.99 Can
A heart must be won . . . and cherished

THE CHANCE
0-06-101434-6/$6.99 US/$9.99 Can
To find true love, you have to take the chance.

THE CHALLENGE
0-06-101433-8/$5.99 US/$7.99 Can
Which was right—her head or her heart?

America Loves Lindsey!
The Timeless Romances
of #1 Bestselling Author

KEEPER OF THE HEART   0-380-77493-3/$6.99 US/$9.99 Can

THE MAGIC OF YOU   0-380-75629-3/$7.50 US/$9.99 Can

ANGEL   0-380-75628-5/$7.50 US/$9.99 Can

PRISONER OF MY DESIRE   0-380-75627-7/$6.99 US/$8.99 Can

ONCE A PRINCESS   0-380-75625-0/$6.99 US/$9.99 Can

WARRIOR'S WOMAN   0-380-75301-4/$6.99 US/$8.99 Can

MAN OF MY DREAMS   0-380-75626-9/$6.99 US/$8.99 Can

SURRENDER MY LOVE   0-380-76256-0/$7.50 US/$9.99 Can

YOU BELONG TO ME   0-380-76258-7/$7.50 US/$9.99 Can

UNTIL FOREVER   0-380-76259-5/$6.99 US/$9.99 Can

LOVE ME FOREVER   0-380-72570-3/$6.99 US/$8.99 Can

SAY YOU LOVE ME   0-380-72571-1/$6.99 US/$8.99 Can

ALL I NEED IS YOU   0-380-76260-9/$6.99 US/$8.99 Can

THE PRESENT   0-380-80438-7/$6.99 US/$9.99 Can

JOINING   0-380-79333-4/$7.50 US/$9.99 Can

And in hardcover
THE HEIR
0-380-97536-X/$24.00 US/$36.50 Can

HOME FOR THE HOLIDAYS
0-380-97856-3/$18.00 US/$27.50 Can

Available wherever books are sold or please call 1-800-331-3761
to order.   JLA 0301